Another Stu
by Bill Ricardi

Book 3 of Another Stupid Trilogy

Version 1.2: 'Revamp' - Copyright Bill Ricardi - 2019 - All Rights Reserved.

Reminder: Members of the **Bill Ricardi fan club** and mailing list get access to *'Another Stupid Spell'* (and many other cool Panos resources) for **FREE**. Full details on the benefits and how to join are at the back of the book.

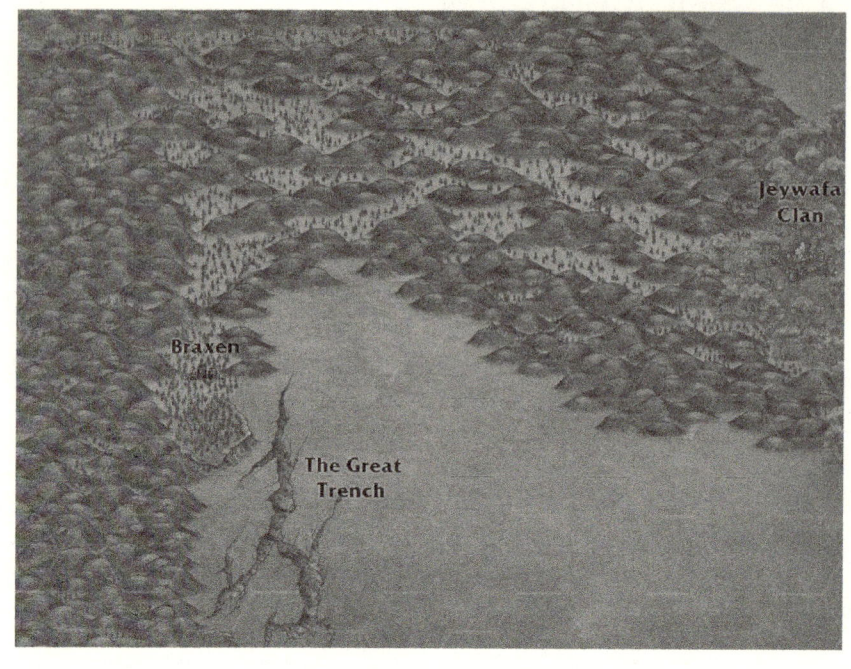

Foreword

"...and I— I took the one less traveled by, and that has made all the difference."

- Robert Frost, *'The Road Not Taken'*

It has been a crazy, wonderful year.

I need to thank my friends and my family. Particularly my loyal Beta Readers: Tim Vecchiarelli and Ian Lee.

And of course, Hugor and Hugorky Rodriguez have created a cover that I am proud of, once again bringing Sorch to life.

To Stephen and Terry and Daniel, the three authors who continue to inspire the series even to this very moment.

To Loki and Rick, one who scampers and one who supports.

But the new kids on the block are the audiobook team at Podium Publishing: Greg Lawrence, who took a look at the series and saw a brave, smart orc who needed a home. Victoria Gerken, who took my hand and led me through the darkness while whispering, 'It's your turn now.' James Patrick Cronin, unparallelled voice actor for Another Stupid Trilogy and the new soul of Sorch. And Emily, Alexandre, Tamara, and Jessica, and the entire Podium team. Thank you.

Chapter 1

"I am Captain Sorch Stonebender, breaker of the Voodoo Engine, hero of Royal Moffit... and the second smartest orc on Panos."

I realized that I had been caught mid-soliloquy when I heard my mate and my son howling with laughter somewhere behind me.

Rather than acknowledge the mirth of my family, I feigned stoicism and stared out upon the ocean. I reminded myself that I was the suave, striking orc captain of this 15 ton caravel. I bought it with gold that had been earned through blood and through trials. I was the master of all I surveyed, the leader of-

Benno's voice cut through my musings like a flaming sword through snow. "Do you think he imagines himself in some kind of uniform when he does this?"

Ames was quick to pile on. "Well he's getting old kiddo, his memory isn't everything that it used to be. In that poor addled head, he's probably concocted a full and glorious naval career."

I heaved a long suffering sigh and looked over my left shoulder. A pair of wicked, toothy grins were waiting for me.

On the left, my mate. The white furred were-cat regarded me with narrowed, emerald green eyes. I knew the difference between Ames' upset glare and their amused peering; gods know we had been together long enough. The jovial little tail flicks were a dead giveaway as well. My feline's chest was shaking just a bit, likely trying to avoid laughing directly in my face.

On the right, my son. He was pretending to be innocent. The younger orc was looking slightly above my head, bare green arms folded across his chest. It was amazing how many of our mannerisms that the lad had picked up in just the last two years. Sometimes it was like I was looking into a mirror, only to find a pair of green, hazel-flecked eyes staring back at me. Eyes that were filled with intelligence. When I qualified my initial statement, it was because of Benno. I had once been the smartest orc on all of Panos. Now that mantle was laid firmly upon his shoulders.

I asked, "Don't the two of you have something better to do? Tying a rope or making lunch or something?"

Ames reminded me, "I'm taking the wheel because **you're** supposed to be making lunch. Captain Stonebender."

Benno murmured, "...breaker of the Voodoo Engine, hero of Royal Moffit. Lunch lady."

I stalked past the two of them, but not before grabbing Benno by the ear. He yelped and swatted at my arm. When I let go, he dutifully followed his old man down to the galley. Sandwiches were on the menu today, as we had to finish the bread before it went stale. We would have none for the return journey. To be fair, no leavened loaf would survive this salty sea air for long.

Even though I was the one who paid for her, the R. M. N. 'Taboo' was technically part of the Royal Moffit Navy. The designation was a gift from the King and Queen for 'services above and beyond the heroic standard'. It meant that technically she could be pressed into service in times of war, but I still had sole authority to assign crew to her. The important part of the R. M. N. designation was: I didn't have to pay docking fees or duty in any port on the South coast. They say it's good to be king, but sometimes it's even better to be the king's favorite orc.

The Taboo had made good time so far. We were two days out of Limt and sailing East-Southeast towards the open ocean. We'd reach our destination within an hour. According to ancient maps, this area once hosted a family of twenty small islands. All of them reclaimed by the sea within the last couple of centuries.

In the galley, Benno and I formed our usual assembly line. I used my dagger, an instrument that had not seen action outside of a kitchen for half a dozen seasons, to slice up our bounty. Bread, smoked fish, and cheese were passed to my left. My son artfully assembled the pieces and added the appropriate garnishings and condiments. He had a knack for food. If he wasn't such a damned fine mage, we would have put him to work in the Spastic Vole as a chef.

I watched those nimble fingers, just as comfortable making a tuna sandwich as they were conjuring a stream of Acid Bolts. Benno was about 14 now, which was considered adulthood within the Southern Tribes. He had gone from scrawny young whelp to strapping young man in no time at all. But his fingers would never be like mine. He wouldn't grow up with the abuse, the manual labor, and the exposure to the elements that I had to endure. He would earn his first calluses when he started to adventure, or when he began crafting at the Arcane University, or perhaps when he took up a musical instrument. Images of my past and a myriad of his potential futures washed through my mind. I tried to sort through them in an orderly way, but something was distracting me.

"Dad? Hey, Dad?"

My eyes quickly found my son's. "Sorry." I murmured.

Benno smiled at me, gently. He said, "You were far away."

I quickly took up two of the wooden plates. "Yeah."

The younger orc picked up his own meal. "It's happening more and more. Do you think we should talk to Max, or maybe Hemitath?"

I shook my head and said, "Not right now kiddo. Please."

He bit his lower lip a little bit. Then Benno shrugged and let the matter drop. He walked up the narrow stairway leading to the forecastle deck, and I followed in silence.

I had made a couple of modifications to the Taboo. Some of them involved adjustments to the rigging and sails so that they were easier for Invisible Servants to handle. Given how many mages would likely be using the small ship, that seemed like a wise investment. But another change was the installation of benches on either side of the ship's wheel. They provided the captain with a little more shelter from sea spray, as well as additional cover in battle. But most importantly, the benches meant that our little family could eat together without abandoning our posts.

Family meals were important to the three of us. Despite having mostly given up adventuring, the last couple of years were anything but routine. I spent much of my time learning complex magic, oftentimes directly from Master Gideon and Headmaster Max. Benno had to contend with formal training, puberty, love, and lessons on psychic communication from Assistant Donnelly. Ames juggled responsibilities at the Spastic Vole with envoy tasks for Max and Hemitath. The feline was one of the key figures that encouraged and coordinated trade and tourism between Ice House and the Southern Tribes, after the new Circle of Transport had been opened up in the middle of the Jeywafa Tribe's village.

Even with all of these demands on our time, the three of us ate together as often as possible. This policy often annoyed the 'powers that be', but they understood that they could either agree to this small concession or they could lose the considerable combined talents of our little clan. It was over the dinner table that I got to know my son. It was in the kitchen that Ames and Benno bonded. It was while doing dishes that we shared our deepest secrets and forged a strong family dynamic.

I ate my sandwich quietly as my mate and my son sat on the bench opposite and chatted away. For some reason my mind was drawn back to a weekend outing some months ago. Rather than the smiling, voracious creatures of the present, I was seeing my family's past. My son in tears, his food untouched. I was remembering how he sobbed into Ames' fuzzy shoulder after confessing that he had just broken up with his first lover. My boy's unnatural intelligence, natural magical talents, and potent psychic abilities made him the most formidable young student at the Arcane University. But he had been laid low by a stupid wager between teenagers regarding who could romance and bed him first.

I forced my awareness back into the present before I started to drift again. I cleared my throat and then mentioned, "I think we should go over the mission parameters one more time."

Twin groans arose from the opposite bench.

Ames asked, "For the third time, really?"

Benno took a different tack. "Yes Father, let us review these parameters that you speak of, for they are important both to the mission and to me personally."

That healthy dose of sarcasm set Ames off, and I was forced to wait until my mate finished laughing before I could continue.

I said, "He gets that from you, you know."

Ames' only reply was a sweet smile.

I sighed, then launched into the mission plan.

"We're here on a charter from the greater Elven Council, supported by the Arcane University. The weather situation on Panos has continued to deteriorate, to such a level that sponsored magical exploration of the skies, the oceans, and deep underground caverns has been undertaken. The goal: To find the source or sources of the radical changes that have been happening to our world over the last decade."

Benno and Ames were both somber now, quietly listening as they finished their fish sandwiches.

I mentioned, "Because this is Benno's midterm break, I accepted this mission on behalf of the entire family. You wanted to do some field work and see exactly what your parents do on an adventure... here's your chance kiddo."

The younger orc nodded. "I won't let you down."

"I know. Anyway, there are a couple of reasons why we've been told to investigate this particular sunken island. First of all, it is clear evidence of rising sea levels. So if the former inhabitants had any idea what was happening at the time, they may have left clues that apply to the more rapid and dramatic shifts that we're seeing in recent times. Secondly, the leyline nearest to our old village branches off and terminates somewhere close to this area. Nobody in modern times has studied that phenomenon, so it makes sense to send a couple of mages."

Ames said, dryly, "And a cat."

I said, "A cat who loves water, for some strange reason. But we hardly have time to explore all of your faults right now."

Ames made a particularly rude gesture towards me. I took it in stride.

"But perhaps most importantly, we've had dealings with both of the gods of magic. The area we're going to explore is supposedly an early temple of magic, though the god or goddess isn't named in any of the texts that we have access to. It might be pagan and powerless, a misguided effort. Or it could be a dedication to Omi-Suteth before these people had a name for her. We'll know more when we get there. Questions?"

There were none. That was fair, given that it was our third overview of the subject.

We finished our meals and Benno collected the wooden plates. Ames quickly banished me to washing-up duty, wanting to experience that feeling of captaincy in peace for a while. I headed back down to the kitchen, where dishes from our last three meals awaited our attention.

As I tapped water from one of the casks into my trusty magical cooking pot, Benno absently shuffled dishes around in the sink. I murmured, "Blaze." Then I turned to regard my son as the water was heating up.

"Are you okay, kiddo?"

Benno forced an insincere smile. "I'm fine Dad."

He wasn't.

I squeezed his shoulder gently. "Come on, spill it."

The young orc sighed. "It's nothing." A pause. Then he murmured, "As long as you're okay."

I snorted. "What, the daydreaming? I'm getting old, losing my mind. What's your name again?"

My son leveled a scowl at me, making it clear that he didn't find my flippant attitude amusing. "With your history of visions and mental invasion, I don't think that any of this trivial."

"I'm not trying to trivialize things. Honestly. If you want to have a discussion about it, take a minute to organize your thoughts and we'll get into it."

Benno absently tapped his digits against the edge of the sink. For a minute, that steady cadence was the only sound in the small galley. Then my son said, "The most dire conclusion is that someone is intentionally messing with your head. It's happened before after all." He reached over to empty the warm water into the sink before it got too hot to handle.

I took the pot back so that I could tap more water into it. After considering the best way to address Benno's concerns, I said, "Well we know it isn't Koroth. Kiddo, these kinds of... internal retreats. They aren't happening at critical times. But I think that we can both agree that they're happening for a reason, right?"

Benno nodded as he halfheartedly shifted the dishes around in the warm water.

I slid the pot away from the water keg, allowing the magical cooking implement to heat up once more. "Then let's find out what the reason is. Have I ever told you the difference between 'wonder' and 'why'?"

The younger orc frowned a little bit. "No, I don't think so."

I dipped a sponge into the water, and then rubbed a fragment of soap against it until it started to lather. "Wonder is about imagination and contemplation. But it's only the first stage. Wonder is the tool of the artist, the philosopher. You can wonder about the daydreaming all you like, but the more constructive thing to do is to find out why. Because why is-"

Benno leapt on the word. "Science. Why is science."

I grinned toothily at my boy, before passing him the soapy sponge. "And experimentation, and reasoning. We do magic and science to improve ourselves. To improve the world. Every problem can be pondered, but pondering alone rarely presents you with a solution. Move beyond the wonder and seek the why. When we find out the 'why', we can take the next step."

Then my boy surprised me. "So we start a journal."

I frowned a little bit. Honestly, I hoped to distract him with my lesson rather than come up with an immediate course of action. "Okay."

Benno's mind was working, and he was gaining steam now. While he vigorously scrubbed the dishes and handed them over to me for a rinse in the hot, clean water, my son outlined the gathering of evidence. He said, "We record the details of each daydream and then categorize them. Was the dream about something personal, professional, or something of a regional or global scope?"

I poured the water out into a basin before it reached the point where it would scald my hands. "Kiddo..."

But there was no stopping or distracting my boy now. "We put the events in chronological order. Then we find the common threads between the things that you were remembering, and see if they correspond to whatever you were doing or talking about at the time."

"Benno? I think..."

"Once we have a good sample size, we take it to the people who know you best and ask if they see patterns. We'll take notes on that, and then present the whole case to Max and Hemitath to get help with the final analysis!"

I sighed. "Benno."

The younger orc said, "Yeah Dad?"

I was about to shut down his plan, but in the silence that hung between us, I changed my mind. If it would make Benno feel better, it was worthwhile. "That sounds like a great idea."

He beamed at me. My son's smile never failed to trigger an internal surge of pride.

Once we finished cleaning and securing the dishes, I told Benno to go get ready. We would be at our destination within half an hour.

In short order, the three of us were standing on the quarterdeck. We commanded the Invisible Servants to furl the sails and drop the anchor. There would be a little drift, but the ship should remain fairly stationary while we went about our business.

Upon seeing our diving outfits, Ames commented, "The two of you are going to be useless, aren't you."

My son and I frowned and looked at each other.

I could see how we might look ridiculous to a non-mage. Both of us wore our Amulets of Enhanced Enchanting, of course. Other than that, we were stripped down to just our breeches, which meant that everything we needed for magic had to be toted around in pouches. Seven pouches in Benno's case, more in mine. This was because everything would be floating around underwater, so the component for every spell had to be kept separate.

We also slathered ourselves in grease. It was an insulator after all, should temperatures get cold down there. The two of us did smell like bacon as a result.

I cleared my throat, "In our defense, this is what we're taught at the Arcane University."

The feline refrained from further comment. Ames had stripped down to shorts, held up by a sword belt. Their short sword was peace-knotted so that it didn't drift away on the descent. The cat left the vast majority of their gear in the cabin, taking only one pouch of lockpicks on this undersea venture.

We prepared a couple of copper chains with Light cantrips so that we would have wearable illumination when we needed it. Once that was done, I asked, "Is everyone ready?" My mate and my son murmured affirmatives.

One of the tricks that both Benno and I learned from our friend and classmate Titan was the 'Minor Polymorph' spell. It allowed us to temporarily gain aspects of other species. We would have to sacrifice one of our more potent combat spells in order to facilitate the shifting, but that hardly mattered; a Fireball was useless underwater, and Lightning Bolts were suicidal of course. Given the environment, our spells were mainly focused on obfuscation, physical manipulation, and pure force.

My son retrieved a sticky cocoon from one of his pouches, and I followed suit. The incantation took quite some time. Nearly a minute of chanting and concentration preceded the disappearance of our material components. Twin sensations washed over me. The gut wrenching drain of Glogur's curse scratched at the fortress of my mind, clawing away at my hard-earned intellect. But at the same time, the flesh of my neck blossomed with heat and energy. A fully functional set of gills was my reward. I was assured that this version of the spell would allow us to handle the pressure of the deep ocean as well. We didn't expect to go down very far, but better safe than sorry.

After glancing over to make sure that Benno's spell had worked properly, I dug a small vial from one of my many pouches. The University had provided the spell in potion form so that Ames could join us. The process was much more rapid for the feline. In seconds, the white fur on either side of Ames' neck had receded. Parallel slits appeared as the breathing filaments formed.

We tossed a pair of rope ladders over the rail to facilitate boarding once we were finished. Then the entire family made the plunge.

The water was warm enough this time of year, at least at the surface of the ocean. The real shock came as I took my first breath underwater. In order to use my gills, I had to suck in a large quantity of water and then close my mouth. The sensation of my throat constricting to force the fluid out of the sides of my neck was... unique. I thought that something had gone horribly wrong. But sure enough, my body seemed satisfied with this absurd breathing process.

Once everyone got used to their gills, we dove. Normally underwater communication would be restricted to hand gestures. But we had a secret weapon. We swam in close formation so that Benno could reach out and touch Ames and I as needed. The three of us had practiced using his mind-to-mind communication in both mock-combat and real social situations. This was the payoff. We were able to converse normally, despite being surrounded by tons of water and rapidly plunging into the ocean's cool embrace.

We found the sea floor after just a couple of minutes. That was reassuring. It meant that we were in close proximity to the sunken island. Panos' sun still provided a little illumination at these depths. Even so, it took several minutes of orientation before we figured out where we should be going. Detecting the gentle upslope that would get us closer to our goal would have been the ideal job for a minotaur. Instead, two orcs and a feline painstakingly measured shadows and lengths of string. Eventually we figured it out.

We swam along the ocean floor, heading in the direction of the incline. Other than some rather beautiful angelfish, we were alone. Every once in a while, a distant but sizable silhouette played at the very edge of our vision. Possibly a shark or large tuna. Whatever it was, it didn't approach.

Eventually the undersea landscape rose sharply before us. Ames reached out to touch Benno's shoulder, and he in turn put a green hand on my back.

The feline's voice spoke directly into my mind, *"Did you say that the temple was built into a cliffside? I see a cave of some sort."*

I strained my eyes upwards, but saw nothing. I trusted my mate's vision far more than my own, however. Using Benno as a conduit, I replied, *"That could be it. We'll follow your lead."*

My muscles were burning a bit from all of the activity. I consider myself a good swimmer, but this was a longer and more intense outing than I was used to. Benno was grimacing as well. His younger body didn't suffer the same kind of muscular strain as mine did, but he still hadn't developed his full adult muscle mass or typical orcish endurance. Ames, who seemed to be more fish than cat at the moment, had to slow the pace significantly in order to allow us to keep up.

A rock overhang left the cave's entrance in shadow. I fumbled with one of my pouches, but eventually managed to loop the Light enchanted necklace around my neck. My son followed suit once he realized what I was doing. Ames gave me a pat on the head, which I assumed was approval. With the mouth of the cave illuminated, we swam inside.

The rough, algae covered stone gave way to smooth, lovingly hewn hallways. The soft blue-white glow of our Light spells revealed the work of artisans from the last millennium. Bas-relief portraits of benevolent goddesses lined the walls, seemingly unphased by over a century of watery isolation. They watched us with infinite kindness and patience as we approached the shrine's grand stairway.

Apparently the internal cavity of the temple was intact, as the ocean was unable to push out the trapped air. By the tenth granite step, we breached the surface of the water. Ames touched Benno's shoulder, who in turn touched mine.

My feline's voice sounded in our minds, *"The air could be stale or poisonous. Grab my ankle and tug me back under the water if I start to choke."*

Benno and I were thinking the same thing, but he stated it first, *"You mean continue to choke. You're going to have to cough up all of that water before you try to breathe the air again."*

Ames looked at me, clearly alarmed. I was already nodding, confirming my son's statement.

The were-cat's thoughts were tinged with disgust that we hadn't shared that piece of information earlier. *"I hate you both so much right now."*

Benno and I each grabbed one of Ames' ankles. Once the feline's gills were clear of the water, the reaction was immediate. Ames' body went rigid. The next breath that the were-cat attempted to draw caused a primal reaction within my mate. Seawater spewed from the cat's maw, gills, and nostrils. This was followed by a horrific gasping sound. The coughing went on for half a minute as the remainder of the fluid was expelled from Ames' lungs. As terrible as this looked, Benno and I saw and experienced it in training. Thus we didn't confuse the reaction with poor air quality.

Once Ames assured us that the air was breathable, Benno and I went through the same process. By the time I was able to use my lungs again, my ribs were sore and my head pounded. But I was in for a pleasant surprise. Not only was the air breathable, it was pristine. I inhaled deeply. The crisp, clean sensation that followed was a balm to my aching chest.

The three of us climbed up the remaining half a dozen steps. The vista that awaited was nothing short of beatific. The domed worshiping chamber was massive, cavernous. It was easily thirty paces in every direction. Hovering directly in the center of this sacred space was a crystalline orb. Pure golden illumination poured from the levitating quartz, as in if a Noon Sunlight spell had achieved some kind of permanence within its flawless depths. The natural light gave rise to patches of moss and flowers in every corner of the temple. Ivy rose along the walls and coiled around the eight stone pillars that supported the void within the cliffside. Colonies of bees had built impressive hives behind ancient statues whose details were eventually worn smooth by the traversal of hundreds of millions of tiny legs.

At the center of it all was a white marble altar. It bore no symbol and supported no objects. The perfectly rectangular slab of stone simply bathed in that inexplicable sunlight for all eternity.

We spanned the distance between the stairs and the altar in what seemed like both an eon and the briefest instant. I couldn't seem to recall the steps taken, as if time itself was meaningless here. Intention was everything. And my intent was to reach out and touch this perfect altar.

Benno's hand suddenly clamped onto my wrist, the motion so quick and powerful that I was sure he would end up leaving a bruise. He said, "Wait." The word was filled with wonder and a little horror.

Ames asked, "What is it kiddo? A trap?"

I couldn't tear my gaze away from the holy stone. I listened for Benno's reply however. No matter how much I wanted to feel the essence of the altar, to be one with it... I trusted my son.

After a pregnant pause, the younger orc murmured, "The aura. It is one of dimensional magic. It's more powerful than any aura I've ever been exposed to. It feels like it could swallow us all effortlessly."

The words poured from my lips before I even knew I was articulating them. "Take us there."

Ames murmured, "Inside it, hon? That Astral thing?"

I felt Benno shaking through the powerful grip he had on my arm. He was scared. "Are you sure?"

I murmured, "Trust me. We're going to see an old friend." It was my voice, and I knew that I was speaking the truth. But I had no idea where the knowledge or intent of the words was coming from.

My son's grip upon my wrist loosened, just as Ames laid a fuzzy paw on the lad's opposite shoulder. We all closed our eyes and waited for Benno to use his rarified talent.

"Well. I didn't expect you to dress up for the occasion, but I'm not certain that undressing for the occasion was all that appropriate either."

The voice was one that I had heard before. When I opened my Astral eyes, I already knew who I would see. The woman in the blizzard. An old friend.

I cleared my throat, and then mentioned, "I'm afraid your temple is under the ocean now, Omi-Suteth. It was quite a swim."

The old goddess of magic took a form that I would understand. She was a vortex of snow encased in a feminine outline. The white cyclone was beautiful when seen in contrast to the perfect darkness of the Astral horizon.

The goddess nodded. "Fine. Well, are you going to introduce me to your family?"

I had to smile. It was such an absurd situation to be adhering to formalities. Nevertheless, I said, "Ames, Benno. This is Omi-Suteth. We have history."

I glanced over to see why the two hadn't made a polite greeting of some kind. Were-cat and young orc were standing there with their jaws hanging open.

Omi-Suteth said, "It's alright mortals. I assure you, there will be no smiting or cursing as a result of any perceived breach in protocol."

Ames finally managed, "I-it's a pleasure."

While Benno only got out a simple, "Hi there."

I said, "They're normally far more talkative than this."

The goddess explained, "A mortal's perception of deities changes based on experience and expectations. Did you not notice that this encounter is far more…"

I considered an appropriate word. "Conversational?"

"Yes, that's the word. Less intimidating. Dare I say, less one sided. That's because you are not a novice when it comes to communing with the gods, are you Sorch Stonebreaker?"

I took the moniker in stride. Omi-Suteth taking liberties with my name was nothing new. "I suppose not. I'm an old hand."

The vortex of snow drifted close. Spectral 'hands' hovered over my forehead. "The latest spell that the Headmaster created for you. It shields you from Glogur's legacy in a fairly impressive fashion."

I murmured, "It does indeed. We call it Max's Expanded Intelligence. Normally a single casting shelters me from a reasonable amount of drain."

"But at great cost."

I agreed with the goddess. "At great cost. One of my most powerful spells for the day, and a sacrifice of gold."

Benno's voice cut through whatever reply Omi-Suteth might have had, "The cost is far too high. Why must we pay it? When is enough enough?"

Ames' paw clamped down firmly on my son's shoulder, in silent warning.

Omi-Suteth wasn't angry, however. If anything, the goddess' tone was sad. "Young magus. Sometimes we do things that we wish we could take back. In the heat of the moment or in the cold fury of the aftermath, hurtful things get said. Unwise challenges are issued. And... and though a remnant of love might remain, all else is lost."

Benno grit his teeth. He didn't reply.

Ames spoke up instead. "Goddess. We've come seeking your wisdom. There is a blight upon our world. Rains do not fall in some places, but drown others. The sea rises, taking not only your temple, but the homes and livelihoods of mortals. The sun bakes down in other places, stunting the growth of plant and animal alike. Can you tell us why?"

Omi-Suteth asided to me, "You've chosen well."

I had to smile at the divine complement.

The goddess turned to address Ames, the miniature tornado of ice and snow approaching the wary-looking were-cat.

"Panos bleeds. The fault lies both in the behaviour of her people and in the manner of her creation. The gods are not faultless in this matter. And yet our agreement, sealed by Koroth the Broker, prohibits us from providing any kind of direct solution I'm afraid."

Ames frowned. In other situations, I might expect my mate to resort to less political language. "So you know what's wrong, but you can't help us?"

The goddess said, "I cannot. But another among us can. Sorch has shaped, and broken, but now he must mend."

Benno looked at me, "Dad? You can fix this?"

I held my arms up, helplessly. "If I can do something, I'm willing. Please tell me how I can help."

Omi-Suteth said, "You must be open to new opportunity."

The silence, even in the Astral plane, was deafening.

I said, "Okay, could you expand on that?"

"You must be open to new opportunity."

It was Benno who expressed frustration first, "I think we might be in the wrong place. I thought we were speaking to Omi-Suteth, not a two-copper medium at the harvest fair."

Omi-Suteth was taken aback. "My child, I-"

But Ames joined right in, "We travelled half way across Panos for 'open to new opportunity'? Are we going to meet any tall dark strangers on the way?"

The goddess sensed the tide turning against her. She said, "That's all I can tell you, I'm afraid."

My own frustration boiled over, "I stopped a demonic invasion, had my body completely obliterated, and blew up the Voodoo Engine to reach this point. And you're giving me the same advice that I could have gotten from a tipsy carnival trollop with a bunch of tarot cards?!"

"...goodbye my children."

And with that, we were banished from the Astral plane.

Knowing that we had less than an hour before our transformation wore off, Benno suggested that we head back to the ship immediately. We didn't discuss the fortune-teller level 'wisdom' that we received until after the three of us were safely back on the Taboo. There was a lot of whisky imbibed with our evening meal. In our heightened state of agitation, some rather impolite things may have been said about Omi-Suteth and her breeding habits.

And yet, I had a feeling that we were on the right path. Or to be more precise, if Omi-Suteth really was correct, we would cross paths with the right people soon enough.

Chapter 2

The night watch was when it was worst. I shouldn't actually say 'worst' though. The memories were rarely painful. Perhaps 'intense' is a better word.

We were on our way back to Limt to meet some old friends and take the Circle of Transport back to the Arcane University. The Taboo was cutting effortlessly through the gentle waves. All I needed to do was keep my hands on the wheel. But with nothing to focus on, it was quite easy for my mind to drift. When we started this trip, it was Early Fall of the year 2720.

But in my head it was the Spring of 2719, and I was keeping the company of were-wolves.

Master Gideon was a gentle man, a loving father to his daughter Jess and his soon-to-be step son Leeson. He was patient with the younger students, respectful of the faculty, and generous with the rest of the staff.

Most of them had no idea what a truly frightening son of a bitch he was.

Gideon's combat prowess was more than just theoretical. He had seen combat, and a lot of it. The burly brown furred were-wolf never talked about specific battles that he participated in; but when he spoke of combat tactics and magical destruction, it was clear that he was relating first hand experience.

"Wrap it around your forearms when you pull, or your fingers will snap like twigs!"

Perhaps unwisely, I was bound to Master Gideon by a seven pace length of pulsing black chains, thick enough for naval use. The Ebon Chains of Binding were wrapped around both my waist and his, twin strands of the eldritch metal stretching across the breadth of the Advanced Summoning chamber.

I don't recall who cast the spell this time around, but I found myself hoping that it was the were-wolf. This memory was from before my mastery of Max's Expanded Intelligence, and a single casting of the Ebon Chains wiped out most of my intellect enhancement for the day. This was one of the elite combat spells that I had chosen to learn in order to accomplish my graduation tests at the end of the year. I had no issues with the theoretical aspects of the casting. However, Gideon made it clear that he expected a more practical demonstration of my prowess when the day came.

The were-wolf was showing me his technique for reeling in the hapless victim of this highly personal combat spell. "Wrap the arm, then step forward and pull at the same time. The spell will take up the slack for you automatically. You've seen Hemitath's snake strangle her prey. Would you rather be the boa, or the rabbit?"

It didn't surprise me that Master Gideon watched Dutch hunt. For all I knew, he may have even been an active participant. I grunted and shouted across to the combat mage, "The boa, but rabbits generally don't have massive claws and dripping fangs!" Nevertheless, I reeled in the were-wolf as per his instruction.

He did the same, closing the distance while keeping maximum tension on the binding chains. "Keep that fact in mind. This is an incantation generally reserved for were-wolf arcanists or other naturally beweaponed combat mages. Never had an orc student, of course. But things get gritty really fast once you're in range, so pick your targets carefully."

Sweat beaded from my brow as we reeled each other in. Finally, the two of us were in melee range. Master Gideon nodded approvingly. "Good. If you have another mage or a cleric on the other end, don't make the process smooth. Yank the chains as you pull, keep them off balance and unable to cast. Then when you get here, open up at your best range. Kick the knee. Launch a haymaker. Leap in and grapple. When you have the advantage, draw your dagger and get in there. You only have a minute or two to convert the spell into a kill. The Ebon Chains of Binding disappear when the duration runs out or when one of you is dead. Got it?"

I shivered at the causal descriptive language that my Master used to illustrate the scenario.

I said, "Got it."

The big were-wolf tilted his head, situated just inches away from my own. "You're doing very well. Have I mentioned that?"

I shook my head. I said, "No, but I'm glad to hear you say that."

He surprised me by putting his feedback into precise scope. "You would dominate nine out of ten graduate combat mages. With judicious use of Silence and the Ebon Chains of Binding, that goes up to nineteen out of twenty."

My eyes widened at the quantified praise. Sadly the mystical chains chose that moment to expire. Unprepared for the sudden lack of tension, I tumbled backwards onto my ass.

Master Gideon sighed. He said, "But you still have a lot to learn. Go, bathe and get some rest. I'll see you in a couple of days."

Time became vague in my memories. I knew that what I was seeing took place at least a few weeks after that training session. Spring was starting to fade into summer. I knew that because the sun was doing a decent job of staving off the cold, even as I was being kissed by a pair of delicate, talented lips.

Pulling back from the intimate touch allowed me to see the face of my admirer: Parsnip. The ginger half elf lass was modeling her purple robes today. Her lips tasted like honey and wheat, and I found myself straining to remember which of us had drunk the mead, and which had drunk the barleywine. She wore this odd little smile on her face, reflecting something between joy and mischief.

Then she shoved me off the cliff.

The terrifying sensation of falling was only magnified when I saw Patricia leap after me. My mind shifted from thoughts of my own death to finding some way to save her, despite her betrayal. But the mentality of present-me gave way to the mood of past-Sorch. He... I was exhilarated. I was confident.

As the two of us plunged from the edge of that sheer mountainside, I managed to twist in the air so that I could spot the rapidly approaching ground. I remember that my only regret was that I wouldn't see my friend's face when she witnessed the success of her efforts.

I timed the Soft Fall spell a little early, just in case something went wrong and Parsnip needed time to save me, and then herself. But just as I had in practice sessions, I completed the cantrip without any issues. I was suddenly light as a feather, and watched the half elf plummet past. Her laughter drifted back up on the wind. A moment later and Patricia was floating effortlessly. She drifted down to the muddy ground below. I knew that when I joined her, another kiss awaited.

"This is amazing. Come on Max, give us a kiss!"

The tone of the aged archmagus was as dry as charcoal in the desert, "Under. No. Circumstances."

I laughed and collapsed in the chair opposite the Headmaster's desk. It was months later, after midterms came and went. I was experiencing the effects of Max's Expanded Intelligence for the first time: The euphoria. The incredible rush of potential. The moment that the gold coin slipped from my fingers and into the ether, the doors of perception and inspiration were opened wide.

Max examined me, his most important test subject. "How bad is the physical exhaustion? I needed several hours of bed rest, and even Gideon was winded and needed to lie down."

I couldn't seem to stop grinning. I said, "You and Master Gideon worked on something together? Is the world ending?"

Headmaster Max snapped, "It isn't the first time we've collaborated. Now answer the question."

I considered the sensation. It was like a hard trek through the snow, but at the end of it all there was a mug of heavily sugared betel nut tea.

"Exhausting, but it's worth it. And I feel light headed. Did you feel light headed? Almost like you were drugged?"

The old mage seemed genuinely confused. "No. What kind of drug does it feel like?"

"**Good** drugs."

Max snapped his fingers right in front of my eyes. "Sorch. Focus."

I asked, "Why are you calling it Expanded Intelligence? I thought it was going to be Max's Mental Magnification?"

Max sighed. "I lost a bet with Hemitath and I'm not allowed to use alliteration any more. Now. Tell me how you feel?"

I launched into an explanation of what was happening in my mind and body. I hardly remember any of the specifics, but Max took copious notes on the side effects. After about fifteen minutes, I felt like I could stand up without falling over.

The old human paced behind his desk. "Alright, I'll allow you to use the new enhancement for a trial period. Clearly it has species-specific side effects, and we'll need to document them. Given the status of the other orc students, you're the only suitable subject. For the moment."

I tilted my head, curiously. I asked, "For the moment?"

Max smirked at me. "Yes. Your offspring is rapidly catching up, you know. Give him a year and he'll be burning through your gold as well."

Again, time seemed to become meaningless. Until it didn't.

I stared absently at a small stack of gold coins on the kitchen table. "Toby? Why are you piling money all over the house?"

My friend's big bovine head popped out of his bedroom. "We're teaching Janet how to count." The minotaur's calm baritone timbre made everything sound reasonable. If anything, becoming a father enhanced his already seemingly-infinite patience.

I shook my head a little bit. "You can use copper for that you know." I paused, then asked, "Toby, you do know how to change a diaper, right?"

He laughed and then admitted, "No." The minotaur's head disappeared back into his room.

I called out in the direction of the foyer, "Tara, surely Melflavin has invented some sort of amazing diaper-changing contraption? Your husband is hopeless, I fear."

Tara walked back into her kitchen, a set of merchant's scales in her big hand. "If we had invented that, my temple would be an economic powerhouse. Toby is just going to have to learn the same way I did."

I looked up at the cleric as she set the scales down in the middle of the table. The minotaur priestess physically recovered from last year's close encounter with a Disintegration spell, but there were some clear cosmetic after-effects. Her dark brown fur was soft, velvety, like that of a newborn calf. Her horns, once long and sharp, were now rounded stubs that measured barely a finger's length. But in my eyes she was as beautiful as ever.

I had been caught looking. My friend smiled at me and asked, "What do you see?"

"Nothing. I mean, I was just thinking that you look great. Nobody can wear an autumn floral dress quite like you."

It was pretty clear to me that she caught my evasion. The six months after the battle with the Necromancer had been about managing pain, and just when she recovered fully, Janet was born. There were long periods of malaise and mild depression. But Tara came out the other side stronger than ever, happier than she had been in decades.

She allowed me to avoid the subject, instead saying, "Yes, breastfeeding does help a girl to fill out a dress."

My cheeks turned a nice forest green as I assured her that wasn't what I meant. Though she wasn't wrong. Motherhood suited her well.

Toby saved the day by stomping out of his room with a freshly diapered bundle of golden-brown fluff cradled in his arms. "Victory!" said the paladin. He brought little Janet over to see me, "Uncle Sorch is here. He wants to hold you."

And I did. The small minotaur was always well behaved for me, minus the occasional nose grabbing or hair tugging. She liked the way I bounced her in my arms, making these adorable little cooing noises designed to turn fully grown orcs into helpless baby-servants.

Not that I was strictly needed here. My friends were excellent parents. Although they hadn't given up travel all together, Toby and Tara stopped doing anything dangerous so that they could properly raise their child. When they did leave Ice House, the minotaurs split their time between helping Hemitath with the tribe, and rebuilding the Eastern Hook temple that we liberated for Tara's church. At home, there was always the training of new paladins and clerics for the Order of the Snow to accomplish. And of course, being part owners, the minotaurs were the unlikely caretakers of the Spastic Vole when Ames wasn't around and when the druid investors had other affairs.

I stared into little Janet's brown eyes, filled with curiosity and wonder. I heard a voice asking, "What do you see?" But it wasn't Tara or Toby.

I murmured, "I see the future."

That's when a firm smack on the rump snapped me out of my daydreaming. "Hey. What do you see when you're in your own head like that?"

I grumbled a bit at the rude awakening from Ames. Back in the here and now I said, "A lot of things. Just then I was remembering a trip up to Ice House to visit the minotaurs and the baby."

Fuzzy arms wrapped around my chest and belly from behind. I leaned back into Ames' warm figure. The feline said, "So good things, then?"

I looked out on the ocean's horizon. The faintest bands of yellow and gold started to appear off to the right, heralding the rising sun as we tacked North towards the main continent. "Yeah. Very good things."

Ames tucked that warm, whiskered muzzle into the side of my neck and watched dawn arrive over my shoulder.

I thought about our own family's recent history, though I didn't leave the here-and-now to do so. Six seasons. That's how long it took me to graduate from the Arcane University after destroying the Voodoo Engine. I was told by Gideon that there were several post-graduate roles available and all I needed to do was put in a request.

But I missed this. Despite Rick and Will's retirement, despite Tara and Toby's parenthood, I knew that I wasn't done with travel and adventure. Ames had waited for me long enough. I could tell that the non-stop political and intelligence work was wearing on the feline. The truth was, both of us were yearning for some action.

Besides, Benno was in good hands over at the University. In fact, he was on pace to be the most advanced student under 16 years of age. I wanted him to have a normal University experience without worrying whether or not his dad would approve of his grades, or his social activities, or his course selection. So two seasons ago, I went back on the active roster for the Adventurer's Guild. I made it known that I was only interested in missions alongside my were-cat. There were no objections.

I made a slight course adjustment, putting the rising sun somewhat behind us. We were close to our destination now, and would need to tack a bit to get far enough West. It wasn't a difficult task until one factored in amorous were-cats. A steady grip on the wheel and enough concentration to command Invisible Servants did not go hand in hand with sharp teeth nibbling at one's ear or soft, warm paws creeping below the captain's belt.

The heartfelt groan that carried across the forecastle deck made both Ames and I jump a little. Our son asked, "Again? Aren't you two going to get too old for that eventually?"

We murmured insincere apologies for Benno's benefit.

The younger orc walked over and gently shouldered me aside. "Go, take your lewdness below decks. My watch was starting in a few minutes anyway. Remember, no breakfast, we're eating with the guys in a couple of hours."

We headed down to our little cabin, where I cuddled my white furred feline until Ames fell asleep. I was completely fine with that outcome; teasing didn't always have to lead to something more. Besides, it wasn't like physical intimacy was lacking from our relationship. Something about these recent episodes and visions from the past reminded me of my passionate attraction to Ames. Every time we made love was like the first time. I joined my mate in peaceful slumber as our sturdy hammock rocked and swayed from the motion of the ocean's waves.

I woke to the kind of loud and rhythmic door knocking that could only be accomplished by a mindless Invisible Servant. I cursed under my breath and shook the were-cat awake. I suggested, "Let's get decent and pack quickly. We need to help Benno dock this thing, and then I don't want to be late for breakfast with Will and Rick. You know how busy they are these days."

The R. M. N. Taboo was provided military berth, and there were plenty of hands available to help our small crew secure the mooring. The three of us thanked the naval personnel for their assistance, and then hurried North to Limt's Merchant's Quarter.

One of the unexpected side effects of becoming a more well known figure was creating a small amount of social equality. I no longer navigated Limt with my head under the hood of a cloak. Not that everyone approved. But I stopped caring so much about that approval, and the city guard made it clear that the mere sighting of an orc was not a valid complaint. Other orcs had also started to brave the city streets, particularly the bazaar area. It was a slow process, but observable.

The Magic Shop was difficult to miss these days. In two years, it transformed from a medium sized and somewhat financially unstable establishment to one of the largest stores in the city. The old polished oak plaque still hung at the site of the original shop, but the word 'Warehouse' had been tacked on at the bottom. The old store was converted into storage space for the new establishment.

Rick and Will took over the large corner property next door to their old shop. They purchased the property upon the retirement of the former owner Mr. Banas, a locally lauded instrument maker. Gone were three full showroom floors of pianos and violas, replaced instead by weapons, wands, and wonders. The catalyst for their success was consignment contracts. The partners simply intended to use those agreements to keep them afloat. Instead the arrangements became wildly popular with multiple caravan and auction companies South of Ice House. Although my friends still maintained some of their own stock, two thirds of what they sold was on behalf of other parties. Even the Adventurer's Guild and the Arcane University got in on the act, each endorsing lines of magical supplies and products.

As soon as the three of us crossed the threshold, we were inundated with the sounds of people talking and haggling. Benno led the way, being quite familiar with the layout from his extracurricular work placement activities. I counted no less than four staff members helping the dozen or so customers buying, selling, or consigning mystical goods and services. I marveled that my friends' shop attracted this kind of crowd on a mid-morning early in the week.

"Sorch, over here!"

I craned my head around to find the speaker. I soon spotted Will, practically jumping up and down to get my attention. I felt a little pang of guilt when I noticed that he was waving his right arm in the air... the only one that he had left after sacrificing the other for me.

But my small human bore no animosity towards me for his lost limb, and demonstrated his unconditional friendship with a warm bearhug as soon as I was in range. Real and artificial arm met behind my back as the little mage tried in vain to lift me off my feet. I laughed and returned the embrace, resting my chin atop his head. My friend's dirty blonde hair was cropped very short these days. He looked quite professional.

Ames and Benno also got hugged, though Will's efforts were more sane and reserved in their cases. He flashed us a winning smile and said, "Come on, Rick got Benno's message, he's already cooking back at the apartment."

Mentally I kicked myself for not thinking of preparing a Max's Message spell to give the humans advanced notice as to our exact arrival time. Luckily, my son covered for me. Picking up the slack that I had left behind was something that Ames and Benno were doing more frequently these days.

The warehouse, formerly the shop floor of The Magic Shop, was packed with crates, barrels, and bags. Will explained, "Everything that we receive is given a category and a priority. As soon as space opens up on the shop floor, we replace it with a similar item from stock. Perishables, as well as the University and Guild products, are kept downstairs. We still have an apartment upstairs, though most of the time we sleep at the Arcane University these days."

We mounted the stairs just in time to hear Rick comment, "And we still have an orc sleeping in the cot downstairs sometimes. But we went with the newer, smaller model."

Benno laughed at the taller human's comment, and went over to squeeze the older mage's shoulder as he slaved away in front of the stove. Rick flicked his green eyes down and to his left, then reached out to ruffle Benno's hair even as his other hand deftly flipped fried eggs.

I shared a surprised glance with Ames. I knew that my son was part of the work experience group that frequented The Magic Shop, but I had no idea that he was so close to Rick. Those little demonstrative gestures were something that I had never seen from the tall human.

Our chef said, "Go ahead and set the table. We have rashers, eggs, toast, and fried tomatoes."

After several days at sea with little more than fish and preserved food, the fresh fry-up was a gift from the gods themselves. We devoured every greasy and buttery scrap.

We talked about our recent outing, and the awful advice that Omi-Suteth had dispensed. The guys were in disbelief. Eventually they agreed with my assessment: Just go about our normal routine and keep our eyes open.

As we were digesting, Will talked about the possibility of opening up a second location for The Magic Shop. Of the cities discussed, United Diben was the top candidate. Benno explained that he did some analysis with Rick as to the best location. The tall human nodded and absently patted my son's shoulder.

I was once again struck by that level of familiarity between my friend and my offspring. Benno was an adult, technically, and it was his life to live. But I was worried about some kind of fallout with Will if my suspicions proved to be correct.

So as Ames started to talk about the Spastic Vole, I leaned over to murmur in my son's ear. "Listen kiddo. I'm not saying what's right or wrong here. But just so that I don't say anything dumb and I'm prepared for whatever comes, I have to ask. Is something going on between you and Rick?"

His reaction was a little less subtle than I had hoped.

"Ew, Dad, no! He's three times my age."

It took a moment to register what Benno might have been talking about, but the copper dropped for Will. The younger human started howling with laughter. When Rick figured it out, he dropped his head into a splayed hand, as in if rapidly developing a headache.

Ames slapped the side of my head, prompting me to say something to redeem myself.

I cleared my throat and said, "Sorry. I wasn't making a judgment. I was, um… just curious."

Benno explained, a little more calmly, "You remember I had a rough time after my breakup. I just needed someone to talk to who wasn't family. That's all."

Will vouched for his mate's caliber in these matters. "Rick is an excellent listener. Not always a great talker. But an excellent listener. And don't worry, now that we have a permanent staff on board, he's not lacking for any attention in the bedro-"

Rick raised his head and his voice, cutting Will off mid sentence. "Yes, well. Now that I'm saddled with that particular line of thought, your penance is to do the dishes. I need to pack an overnight bag before we go."

We were quiet as Rick made his way into the other room, slow by necessity due to his artificial leg. When the door closed, Ames looked angrily between Benno and myself.

The were-cat hissed, "Why in the deepest hells didn't the two of you keep that in your minds? You're one of the few psychics in all of Panos. We even practiced social situations."

Benno looked a little ashamed. "I didn't even consider that."

I admitted, "Neither did I."

Ames turned to Will and said, "Will Flemming, I'd like to introduce you to the two smartest orcs on all of Panos."

The small mage smiled disarmingly. "It's fine you guys, really. I'm sure that secretly Rick is flattered that you think he has that kind of charisma. Come on, let's get the dishes done and then we'll head over to the Temple."

Silently, I wondered why I hadn't thought to use mental communication. Were these visions messing with my reasoning? I dismissed that somewhat, as Benno also missed the opportunity to be more subtle. It might have simply been an area that deserved more privacy, rather than exposing my son's intimate life to potential psychic leakage. Sometimes in mind to mind communication thoughts flowed so rapidly and freely that one could share too much information unintentionally.

Not another word was said about our domestic outburst. After making our way over to the Temple of Vinara, the five of us climbed up the steps of the oversized white gazebo located in the back garden. We stood upon the inlaid copper circle for less than a minute.

And then we were elsewhere.

Chapter 3

The family was sitting around the granite dinner table in Max's private dining area. We had agreed that four bodies inside of the Headmaster's small office would have been rather cramped. Instead we took coffee and tea seated in those elegant redwood chairs.

"I would rate your mission an unmitigated success."

Those weren't the words that I would use, but I didn't express my irritation aloud.

Benno, deciding that it was his turn to be the political one, asked, "What makes you come to that conclusion, Headmaster Max?"

The old mage shrugged. "I don't know, that's just what we're supposed to say when a bunch of idiot adventurers come back from a mission."

Ames sighed. "Max."

The Headmaster explained, "We didn't know if the source of the changes came from the gods or from mortals. Now we know that it is both. We also know that there was some kind of flaw early in Panos' creation. Honestly, nobody else has come close to retrieving this amount of information on the subject. Why did you think that I would be unhappy with the result?"

I said, "Because of the fortune teller wisdom at the very end."

Max shrugged. "Sounds like her hands are tied in that regard. Besides, it seems like she believes that you'll be approached with the next step soon enough. In the meantime, the rest of us will continue our research. You three go about your business, and report any strange offers or opportunities that you might get."

We were forced to agree, as much as the entire family hated such a passive plan.

"Now on to the next matter. It sounds like there's a functional, if inaccessible, temple sitting in the middle of the ocean. Useful?"

Benno and I both said "No." at the same time.

Ames hesitated and then said, "Perhaps."

All eyes turned towards the were-cat.

"There's one magical community on Panos that might be able to make use of that temple. The lizardmen."

Headmaster Max snapped his fingers. "Now that's thinking globally. A very good point Ames." He turned to Benno and myself. "Where are your heads at? You're supposed to be the intellectuals in the room."

Benno said, "I'm afraid that's been pointed out to us a few times in the last week, sir."

I nodded my agreement. "It has. But I'll attempt to make up for our lapses. Professor Sevritz, the elementals teacher. He would have ties to the lizardman magical community. Before he gets too busy with the new term, it might be wise to ask him to reach out."

Max nodded, slowly. He said, "There's hope for you yet, mister Stonebender. I'll talk to him this afternoon. Your compensation has been deposited into your Guild accounts. Now. As young Benno needs to resume classes and the two of you need to stay open to whatever comes along, I have no use for any of you."

With that statement, Max picked up his mug of coffee and simply walked out of the room.

After expenses, we had earned around 200 gold pieces each. It wasn't as much as we made in the past, but at least there was no combat involved. Benno could now apply for provisional membership in the Adventurer's Guild. Ames had gotten some time away from the daily grind, and not lost money in the process. Importantly, the bounty would cover the price of intellect enhancement spells for Benno and myself. At least for a while.

We finished our beverages without the Headmaster's supervision, and then let ourselves out. We passed through the South Wing's checkpoint and climbed the stairs. Benno headed back to his room, which he shared with Titan. The reports that I received from the halfling, clandestinely, noted that my son was a highly considerate lad. Whatever issues that the halfling once had with his former roommate were solved by pairing him up with my son. I was happy for the diminutive mage. I was also glad that Benno had someone with him who I trusted implicitly.

Ames and I continued spiraling upwards after dropping off Benno. The two of us stopped on our usual floor, where the guest and teachers' quarters were. As I turned left out of the stairwell, I nearly collided with Parsnip.

The half elf stopped short and laughed a little bit. "Be careful, I have live cargo."

Parsnip managed to give both Ames and I gentle kisses on the cheek without squishing her 'cargo'. The infant in her arms was swaddled in a blue wool blanket, protecting the child from the somewhat chilly air that circulated through the halls of the Arcane University.

"How is he?" asked Ames in a low rumble.

Patricia's smile said it all. "He's great. Walk with me, I'll catch you up."

I remained quiet as my mate and my dear friend gossiped. They were shoulder to shoulder, while I remained a step behind. I was never quite sure what to say to Parsnip these days. I suppose at some point that I decided to err on the side of tact and caution when dealing with a new mother. It seemed like a wise move, but I felt like I was distancing myself from Patricia at the same time.

I had good reason.

As the four of us, if one included the bundle tucked into Patricia's chest, slowly meandered up the hall, I recalled the conversation that heralded the beginning of my uncertainty. It happened last year. I was swamped with studies, it being the start of my final season at the Arcane University.

Parsnip and Celestial were a couple at that point, and I was extraordinarily happy for them. They lived together in staff quarters, which meant that Patricia's issues with dodgy roommates were at an end. I'd never seen Celestial so satisfied with life. His constant quest for the new, for the obscure and fascinating, came to a sudden halt. Instead he poured quite a bit of effort into the examination and understanding of his new love.

One would think that an engagement announcement would spell the end of my trysts with Parsnip. But as it turned out, Ames and I were a fairly normal and subdued couple in comparison to Celestial and Patricia. When my were-cat and I were invited over for dinner that first night, we thought it was a social occasion. No. It was a carnal occasion. I may have led a relatively vanilla, sheltered life compared to Ames, but even the feline seemed taken aback by the open and adventurous nature of our friends.

Two moons before my final exams, I was invited to Celestial's quarters just after lunch. As busy as I was at the time, I planned to just stop by and be friendly. I would let them know that I was flattered but quite focused on my studies. Perhaps I could suggest getting together after dinner on the next weekend and including Ames in that little outing.

When I entered the new professor's chambers however, I knew that I wouldn't need to give them any excuses. They were both sitting at their tiny dinner table, looking somber. This wasn't one of 'those' visits.

Patricia said, "Hi dear. Why don't you have a seat?"

As I did so, several things raced through my mind. Were they about to tell me that they've decided to have a monogamous relationship? Were they planning to leave the school at year's end? I already knew that if either of these things were the issue: Whatever they decided, I would support them of course.

Celestial shared a glance with Parsnip, then said, "Sorch, do you remember that night a few weeks back? We finished off that lovely bottle of ouzo that you brought, and then you and Ames spent the night?"

Parsnip added, dryly, "All night."

I felt heat rise to my cheeks. Maybe this **was** one of 'those' visits.

I said, "Of course I remember. Well, most of it. We chased the ouzo with a nice dessert wine, so maybe some of it gets a bit… fuzzy."

The dark skinned, azure haired human stared at me for a moment. "You recall enough to agree that in the early morning, the four of us did just about everything one can imagine together. Yes?"

I cleared my throat and nodded. "Accurate." I murmured.

Again, the couple traded looks. It was Patricia who broke the news, "I haven't had my period since then, Sorch."

Seeing the shocked look on my face, Celestial quickly added, "That wasn't the only time that Patricia and I were together around that time, Sorch. Odds are that this is just a precautionary thing."

However, my half elf friend was being a bit more blunt. "You could be the father, Sorch. Half elves and orcs are a viable combination. Normally I'm more careful with herbal supplements and the like, but Celestial and I are trying to start a family."

The human mage added, "And we were pretty tipsy to be fair."

I looked between the two of them. I examined each of their faces to see if this was a joke told in very bad taste. The looks that I got back were ones of concern.

My chest felt tight. The words that I was saying didn't sound right at the time; too rushed, too high pitched to be me. "If it turns out that I'm the father I'll do whatever you think is right. I don't know what… I mean, how does this normally work? What happens now?"

Patricia reached across the little table and stroked my hair. The effect was immediate. I let out a held breath and relaxed at this gesture of kindness. She said, "We'll keep you posted, but I assure you that either way, your involvement with the future of the child is entirely voluntary. We've discussed it."

Celestial was nodding. He said, "Exactly Sorch. On the off chance that the baby is a half orc, you can be like a second father figure. Or you can be more of an uncle. Or you can forget that it ever happened. Don't feel trapped by any of this. We consider it a blessing, no matter who the father is."

I leaned into Parsnip's touch and absorbed their words. My mind was chaos. But their openness and acceptance went a long way towards suppressing the panic that I was feeling.

"Okay."

Back in the here and now, Ames glanced over their shoulder at me. "Okay? I asked if you wanted to go back to the Vole for dinner or eat here. 'Okay' isn't an answer."

Parsnip giggled. She said, "Well it's an answer, just not to the question asked."

Hesitantly, I stepped right up to my half elven friend. "Can I see him?"

Patricia tilted her head, ginger locks falling off to one side. Then she reached down and opened the blue wool blanket. The tiny boy stared back up at me with his aquamarine eyes. His light green skin was so delicate in contrast to the fingertip that I used to stroke his forehead.

I said, "I want to eat here. With my whole family."

Ames and Patricia shared a smile. The feline said, "I'll wrangle Benno, you tell Celestial. We'll meet you down there."

As my mate disappeared back the way we came, I continued to stroke my new son's brow.

Patricia watched me, an oddly satisfied smile on her delicate lips. "Come on little Granite. Let's tell Daddy that second-Daddy is joining us for dinner."

We walked towards Celestial's room in silence until we were just outside. Then Parsnip reminded me, "No expectations. You be you."

"I'll try."

My human friend soon joined us, and did his best to catch me up on current events in their lives.

Celestial mentioned, "Max agreed to a lighter class-load for me in my first year as a full Professor. And Patricia is going to take classes part time, aiming to graduate mid 2722."

I chuckled a little bit and asked the half elf, "That long? You're going to milk this motherhood thing for all it's worth, aren't you?"

Parsnip smirked up at me. "There's a lot to get done. We have a wedding to plan. And the two of us are going to give Granite a little brother or sister."

I heard Celestial murmur to himself, "Just the two of us this time around."

Patricia hadn't heard that. I stifled a laugh that would have given my blue haired human friend away. Instead, I said, "I'm happy for the two of you. If you need catering, the Spastic Vole is at your command. Just let Ames and I know the date when you decide."

Celestial said, "I didn't know you could get catering for the conception of a child, but that's very generous of you Sorch!"

Patricia asided to me, tone long-suffering, "He's been a father for two moons, and already the jokes are unbearable."

We made our way down to the dining hall. Benno and Ames had saved a table for the six of us. For the very first time, I got to enjoy dinner with my entire extended family. It was wonderful. And the evening wasn't destined to end there, as it turned out.

A passing Invisible Servant handed Celestial a crumpled up note, just as we were debating over which of the two desserts to order. He raised a brow, and then started to read. This was followed by laughter.

Seeing our curiosity, Celestial read aloud, "Oh ye who doth consort with orcs. Who seek those after dinner snacks. Please rise and stand; put down your forks. And bring your sweet tooth to the stacks."

We debated whether or not the last line should have been 'sweet tooth' or 'sweet teeth' for a little while, but the general consensus was that this was a more than passable attempt at iambic tetrameter. Clearly this was a message from Green, whose interests had taken a sharp turn towards bardic magic over the last couple of years. Upon finding his calling, the once-awkward man grew in confidence and ability. He quietly filled Celestial's shoes when the rest of the gang found some housing stability outside of the Apprentice Library. Now it was the young human leading the midnight study sessions.

We sauntered over to the East Wing, passing Granite around so that no single nose or chin received too much abuse from those grabby little fingers. The six of us spiraled down to the bottom of the Apprentice Library, encountering fewer and fewer students as the subject matter of the texts became more obscure.

The rich smell of chocolate greeted us, rather than the more familiar scent of cornbread. Glass pitchers, normally filled with water, instead contained a thicker, amber-brown liquid.

I said, "Please tell me that I'm looking at Moria's fudge and Titan's honey mead, and not vice versa."

The halfling said, "Hey. I make pretty good fudge."

The wererat had to laugh. "You absolutely do not."

Sitting at the head of the table was Green. He was grinning at the exchange between Titan and Moria, while continuing to tune his four stringed lute. The human said, "Welcome. I see that you deciphered my message."

Celestial replied, dryly, "You know we would have gotten here much faster if you had just said: 'I have beer and chocolate.' Hells, Patricia might have taken out a couple of guards in the process."

Parsnip nodded. "I would have taken hostages if necessary."

There was a series of handshakes and hugs and kisses by way of greeting, depending on the nature of any given pairing. My favourite one was somewhat of a ritual at this point: I offered Moria a solemn handshake, and the wererat grumbled, instead straining up on tippy-toes to deliver a kiss to my green skinned cheek.

Seats were taken, and generous amounts of fudge and mead were distributed. I demanded life-updates from our hosts, not seeing nearly enough of them in recent months. Pointing at Titan, I said, "You won an award."

I don't recall having ever seen the halfling blush. He blurted, "How in all the hells did you find out about that?"

I said, smugly, "I have spies everywhere." The reality was, I stumbled onto the story in a fringe publication called 'Lesser Races'. It was a sort of newsletter published in Ice House, dedicated to non-human, non-orc, and non-elf stories. I liked to keep up on were-cat news.

Soon the whole table was admonishing Titan for keeping secrets. Benno's cajoling was particularly spirited, as the halfling even kept the news from his own roommate.

Titan held up his hands in surrender. He said, "Okay, okay. It isn't too big of a deal. Some recent seismic activity ruined a bunch of hillside homes in one of the big halfling communities up North. I knew that my particular magical specialty could help out. So I went up there and dug out a bunch of new homes."

I peered at the halfling. "Wait. So you're telling me that the award was for you turning into some kind of giant mole?"

Titan mumbled something incomprehensible.

Ames prompted the halfling, "What was that?"

Louder this time, Titan said, "Giant gopher."

There was a lot of unrestrained laughter from all around the table.

It was Benno who rose to his roommate's defense. He said, "But seriously, you single handedly created dozens of homes for these people?"

The flushed halfling nodded.

My son said, "Well. That's the real magic, isn't it?" He raised his glass of mead. "To Titan."

We all echoed, "To Titan!"

When the toast was over, we found a new target for our inquisitiveness. It was Celestial who got the ball rolling.

"So Moria, have you decided whether or not this is going to be your last year at the University?"

All eyes turned to the now-squirming wererat. Well almost all eyes. Little Granite was focused on trying to grab a fragment of that forbidden fudge.

Moria murmured, "I haven't made the final decision yet. This whole potion thing really took off in ways that I didn't expect."

Green commented, "Quasi-elementalists aren't supposed to have any kind of commercial value. You're ruining a perfectly good stereotype."

My were-cat was having a hard time following this line of thought. Seeing Ames' confusion, the wererat explained, "I'm using new techniques to create more concentrated potions. It still takes the same amount of time, but the potency means that every batch has more applications."

Benno chimed in, "Rick and Will have already trialled a small batch of her potions. They flew off the shelves. Less volume, more impact, same price. Hard to argue against."

Moria was self-deprecating. "It's just a little trick. Anyone could have come up with it, I just got lucky."

Patricia pressed, as she restrained Granite's little hands to keep them fudge free, "Didn't you do your entire dissertation on it last year? Wasn't it something like a 250 page volume?"

"Yes."

I snorted and said, "Oh one of those simple little 250 page alchemy tricks. That's all."

The wererat sighed, "I honestly don't know what to do. My father is over the moon. He's telling all of his friends. The next family get together is going to be unbearable. I could go off and do this full time, or I could stay on here and become a magical research fellow. I have no idea which path is best. But I guess it's nice to have options."

Benno raised his glass for another toast. "To options."

"To options!" we all echoed.

It was Ames' turn to prod one of our hosts. The feline said, "So, Green. I couldn't help but notice that your real name was in the most recently published rolls from the Adventurer's Guild. How did that happen?"

The dirty blond human's expression became somber. He murmured, "That was my first time, I'm still a provisional member. We thought that we were going on a research mission. Nobody could have predicted the peril that we were going to face."

The bottom floor of the Apprentice Library went quiet, except for the cooing and babbling of my youngest son. I asked, "Do you want to talk about it, buddy?"

Green pushed away from the table, the legs of his chair scraping across the floor. He stood and started to pace, slowly. "I-I'm not sure I can talk about it yet. I'm still too close to the whole matter." He paused, and then asked us, "Can I use some presentation magic? It would make things, you know. Easier."

We all gave the young man our consent, wanting to be supportive. Green adjusted his spectacles before reaching out to pick up his lute. He started to strum out a short, flowing tune.

Bardic magic was a mystery to me. How one could replace hand gestures with instrumental manipulations and vocal components with musical chords was beyond my expertise. It took a lot of talent and an unwavering commitment to the craft. But practitioners of the bardic arts were able to do some amazing things. They traded raw spell power for a much broader scope. Their illusions were meant to entertain an entire audience; their inspirational battle magic, an entire battalion.

Soon the tabletop became a grassy valley. Our glasses and plates morphed into trees and ponds. The illusion was vast, sweeping past the edges of the table and putting us right into the middle of Green's retelling of the tale.

When the transformation was complete, Green allowed his lute playing to slow. The chords became more of a background sound, allowing the young man's voice to take center stage.

"It was a month before midterms, and we had a long weekend for the elven holiday. Headmaster Max approached me, probably because there were no other bards available. He said that this would be the perfect mission to get my feet wet. Strictly research. No real danger. If only I had known then what I know now."

Four figures appeared at the edge of the illusionary field, features vague and obscured save for one individual. The one well-defined figure was Green himself, or at least an exaggerated caricature of the young man.

"They needed a bard to soothe any savage beasts that they might happen across. We didn't expect much wildlife, to be honest. It was the grasslands Northeast of Limt, butting up to the foothills. I was just there in case we needed to gently coax a bear out of its lair or something. I wasn't prepared for what we encountered. None of us were."

The tone of Green's strumming changed. The chords became deeper, more urgent and rhythmic. Suddenly the entire illusion shifted and zoomed in. We were surrounded by tall grass in all directions.

The bard said, "Out of nowhere, a pair of glowing eyes peered at us from the grass. Then a second. Then, dozens more."

Undeniably feline eyes surrounded us on all sides; a large hunting pack. Cougars were common in these foothills, where prey was plentiful and man was scarce. There was a single low growl from somewhere behind me.

"We had no time to prepare. The trap was set perfectly. There would be no soothing music, no time for prayers or incantations. Because just as our minds were registering the danger, they leapt."

There was a sensation of vertigo as a dozen felines broke cover and flew right at our faces. At the same time, Green strummed a couple of quick chords and our perspective rose up and tilted.

The bard announced, dramatically, "Kittens!"

There was a chorus of groans. Green manipulated the perspective. The tall elephant grass was just normal sized grass. We watched as the pack of farm kittens, being observed by their mother with a hint of disapproval, attacked the boots and ankles of the four adventurers.

Green said solemnly, "Nary a sock or cloak was left intact that day, I'm afraid."

Ames nodded, "Cats are dangerous creatures."

Celestial rolled his eyes. He said, "Please don't encourage him."

Parsnip noted, "At least one of us was more than a little impressed."

In the half elf's lap, Granite was absolutely spellbound. He watched the illusionary kittens frolic and 'attack' the four adventurers. The baby boy's jaw refused to close.

Manipulating the four stringed lute deftly, Green shrunk the entire illusion down to just a few handspans. Then he focused in on the leaping kittens, and placed the feline diorama just above the head of mother and child.

We made small talk and finished our fudge. All the while, Patricia rocked the half orc in her arms as the boy stared upwards in wide-eyed wonder. Inevitably, Granite fell asleep a few minutes later.

I murmured, "To the bard."

My friends joined me in raising a glass to Green. He smiled and stilled the strings of his lute.

I drained the remainder of my drink in a single pull. When the music had faded, I felt a were-cat elbow poking me in the ribs. I glanced over and nodded, indicating that I thought this would be a good time to make an exit. Ames and I said our goodbyes, leaving the younger folks to battle over the remaining honey mead. As we made our way back to the South

Wing and our plush guest room, the two of us shared a comfortable silence.

That night, I slept better than I had in a year.

Chapter 4

...of course even the deepest of sleeps can be ruined by a freezing cold paw on one's nipple.

I shouted and nearly fell out of bed. I heard Ames wince at my violent reaction.

"Sorry, sorry. I rushed up here right away, haven't had time to thaw. You need to hear this."

I sat up in bed and grumbled. My Light cantrip was centered on the closest thing I could grab: Rock. I tended to keep Rock handy when I slept, just in case. Wrapping myself in a bathrobe, I headed over to our small dining table and sat. I placed Rock in the center of the table, illuminating most of the room.

I grumbled, "You have my undivided attention."

The were-cat sat opposite me. "I got a message at some ungodly hour in the morning. They said it was Guild business and they could really use my help. So I arranged transport and went to an early meeting to get the details. With me so far?"

Still half asleep, I said, "Mmm hmm."

"So these people, who I've never met before by the by, have sweets and warm cocoa waiting for me. They tell me that they have a quest and that I've come highly recommended. All the while they're plying me with all these delectable little treats. It was bizarre."

I nodded. "Mmm hmm."

Ames continued, "As they're going over the details, I start putting it all together. They never said Adventurer's Guild. They're constantly giving me these amazing hors d'oeuvres. Their quest is about crop failures near Tatertown. I had been summoned to a meeting with the Culinary Guild!"

My mate's words rattled around my head for a while. I was trying to rate the quality of Ames' joke. It was somewhat funny. Just not at this hour.

"I'm going back to bed."

Ames stood up so quickly, their chair fell over. Cold paws pushed down on my shoulders, encouraging me to keep my seat. The cat said, "No, no. Sorch, I'm being serious. We've got a quest from the Culinary Guild, and I think we should do it."

I stared up at the were-cat. "The Culinary Guild. The one you had to join because you used their name to con that poor kid at the asylum? The one that you've been part of for two **years** and the most interesting thing they've done is a charity bake sale? The Guild you called a 'glorified club' and, I quote, 'a complete waste of time and space'?"

The feline said, in a somewhat defeated tone, "Yeah, that's the one."

"They. Have a quest. For us."

"To investigate crop failures near Tatertown, yes."

I was fully woken up at this point. Something in my head clicked. I said, "Oh gods. And we have to do it, don't we?"

Ames looked puzzled. "I haven't made any commitment yet, if that's what you're asking."

I groaned aloud. Then I reminded Ames, "You must be open to new opportunity."

The feline blinked those lovely emerald green eyes at me. Ames said, "You're right."

I mumbled, "This is such lizard crap."

Ames decided to rub it in by being overly enthusiastic. "We're on a quest for the Culinary Guild! Hooray!"

I scowled at my mate. Wanting to burst the feline's bubble, I started to list all of the obstacles in our way. I said, "The minotaurs aren't available, which means we need to find a healer or a medic."

Ames took a paw from my shoulder and extended a single claw, signifying the first objection had been dealt with, "A fellow Culinary

Guild member, and powerful healer, has already agreed to help. Do you remember Hierophant Petrinoth from the greenhouses in Ice House?"

I must have looked suitably impressed, because my reaction made Ames nod. "Okay, more than acceptable. But with the human lads retired, we need more firepower."

More hesitant this time, the cat said, "Max will give us Benno and allow him to start late by a week. We said we'd let him adventure with us, and more than just deep sea diving. But if you don't think he's ready I can keep looking."

I threw my hands in the air. There was no valid objection, even if I didn't like it. I said, "He's apparently one of the most promising students here. He's got to sacrifice his most powerful spells for Max's version of the enhancement, but there's no doubting his prowess. Let's show him the family business."

Ames ticked up a second claw, but saw that I wasn't happy. The paw that was still on my shoulder drifted up to stroke my cheek. "Okay. Anything else?"

I said, "We're still down a front line fighter. I don't want you isolated up there without Toby or someone else to watch your back."

Ames nodded, as in if expecting this objection. A third claw extended to join the other two. The feline said, "That would be our local guide. I met him at the meeting, and apparently you know him. It's Bruce."

I stared at my mate for a moment. "I have no idea who that is."

"Bruce? He said he knew you from a number of years back."

I snorted and said, "Dear, I was in a swamp a number of years back. Is this person trying to snow blind you with some story abo-"

The were-cat cut me off, "He said you saved his life? On a caravan trip. You dragged him into the passenger's seat when he was wounded fighting some undead?"

My jaw dropped. "The hells you say. The kid with the... was he wearing some kind of coppery scale mail armor, real shiny like?"

"That's him."

I muttered, "Of all the damnedable things." Then louder, for Ames' benefit, "He was green back then, but if he's still alive after three years on caravans, I imagine he's capable."

Ames smiled at me, sweetly. "Then I'm afraid, my dear, we have a party. We can all be in Tatertown by noon, getting briefed and making plans. Shall I make the arrangements?"

I nodded. It seemed that fate had decided.

As Ames ran around making things happen, I prepared my morning spells. Knowing that we'd have time to study at least once more before encountering serious danger, preparation included Max's Expanded Intelligence. When the casting was done, a gold piece evaporated, going off to join the dozens that had been sacrificed before. My Amulet of Enhanced Enchanting flared briefly, as if barely able to contain the power being channeled through it. The rush of raw intellect and an almost spiritual euphoria completely overshadowed any sensation of drain caused by the orcish curse. I collapsed in my bed as the physical strain hit, panting like I had just run two thousand paces. But at the same time, I basked in the almost addictive afterglow of the powerful enhancement spell. Oftentimes, this was the best fifteen minutes of my day outside of the time I spent with Ames.

After I recovered, retrieved Rock, and bathed, I went down to the cafeteria and grabbed a cold breakfast. The sandwich had four herb cheese, tomato, and fresh dandelions. I was particularly proud of the dandelions. My friendship with the cooking staff allowed me to introduce a couple of aspects of orcish cuisine to key decision makers. Upon experiencing the crunch and taste of what they once considered useless weeds, dandelions started making a regular appearance on the menu.

I ate my sandwich on the jog. We agreed to meet in the reception hall to register a destination and then take a place in line. As this wasn't a mission for either the Arcane University or the Adventurer's Guild, and we were going to benefit from the excursion, my family would have to wait in line for the Circle of Transport like everyone else. Students who were used to seeing us cut to the front gave us a good natured ribbing. We allowed Benno to defend the family honor. Although some of his jibes and retorts were more crude than what I would have chosen, I still gave him high marks.

When our names were called for the use of the Circle, there was a chorus of booing and laughter. We stepped up onto the runed copper plate, Ames waving to the crowd as if emulating some kind of feline royalty. I thought of a great final jibe that I could shout out to the gathered students...

...but suddenly, we were elsewhere.

The teleportation site for the Temple of Vinara in Tatertown was in the centre of a vine garden. Towering walls of wisteria, trumpet vines, and clematis surrounded us. Intricate frames had been built so that the plants grew in the shapes of horses, or towers, or lions. It was amazing.

After exchanging polite greetings with the keeper at the back gate, we looked down upon the sprawling city of Tatertown from our hillside vantage. Miles of wood and brick suburbs surrounded a core city center. Towering factories and mills dominated the middle of the landscape, before giving way to the docks and the naval yard in the distance. Tatertown mixed the old and the very new, sometimes without much grace. But nobody could fault their dedication to progress and commerce.

The reason we were able to see all of this was simple: No temples were allowed inside of the city limits. Tatertown was the only major city on Panos to have an ordinance enforcing a strict separation of religious and government services and activities. Anyone could worship as they liked, but religious organizations were not afforded the rights of businesses or private landowners. That meant no place of worship could benefit from the city watch, from the fire brigade, from the city-built sewers, or from the roadworks. Every temple had to be located outside of the city limits and provide for themselves.

What this meant for us was a long walk into town. Or so we thought.

A sharp whistle interrupted our hillside sightseeing. Sitting in the back of a straw-lined cart was a young, well muscled man. He was dressed casually at the moment, but I remember him being fitted for the scale mail once worn by a certain undead warchief. His black hair had been hidden under a helmet at the time, but his distinctive nose and ready smile were enough identification in my book.

As we approached the hay cart I said, "Benno, this is Bruce. Bruce, my son Benno."

The warrior offered a tanned hand for my son to shake, and when the greeting was done, used the same grip to easily haul the young orc into the back. "Hey there Benno, good to meet ya. Get comfortable, we're headed to the far side o' town. Hia Ames, good ta see you again." The were-cat received a similar boost into the straw-lined cart.

Bruce's smile broadened when he took my hand. He said, "Well look at that, we're both still alive." This handshake was more firm and enthusiastic, probably because he knew that my adult orcish build could handle more raw power.

I laughed as I was catapulted into the cart with the rest of my family. I replied, "We are, at least for the moment. Thank you for coming to get us, that would have been a long trek."

Bruce shrugged. "Ain't hardly nothin'. Cid and the ladies are doing most of the work. We're headed to my dad's cabin, our druid friend is already there." He raised his voice and shouted, "We're ready Cid!"

I noticed the peace-knotted tulwar on the warrior's hip when he adjusted the lay of it before sitting down in the hay. "New sword?" I asked. I seemed to recall that when last I saw him, the young man was fighting with an old broadsword of questionable pedigree.

The human laughed a little. He said, "New everything. I'll catch ya up. Oh, I'd let you handle the sword but it's meteorite steel. Anti magic. Dun want any accidents, since yer a mage-type."

I eyed the slightly curved military sabre with a healthy amount of respect now. "It sounds like you've been doing a lot more than caravan trips there, Bruce."

"And how." he said in agreement.

Bruce explained that he finished out the year with Advanced Scouting and Commerce before joining up with Anderson's Light Brigade, a mounted mercenary company operating in the northlands. He said, "I wasn't makin' use of my full potential. I can ride good, I can fight from horseback. I'm tough. The fancy new armor wasn't perfect fer riding, but it did th' job."

During his stint as a mercenary, the young human saw action all over the North and Northeast of Panos. He served with distinction during the undead uprising, and was credited with saving several men during a night raid. He did his year and a half tour with Anderson's Light Brigade and was discharged with high honors.

Bruce said, "I woulda stayed with 'em too, they're a bunch of good folks. My commanding officer was… uhhh… she was great. Very hands on." He cleared his throat, and then continued. "But my dad told me 'bout more and more incidents happening close ta home. So I joined up with the Adventurer's Guild, an' here we are."

As the trip was going to take the better part of an hour, I caught Bruce up on my progress. He heard about the more public events, but seemed genuinely interested in the rest of the story.

When I finished, the black haired human said, "Oh I had heard about the salt mine thing. Congrats on finally opening up shop by the way. Bunch o' the farmers 'round here have stake in the first shipment."

I blinked at Bruce. "Excuse me?"

He said again, "The salt company. They just recently started ta offer bulk shipments. Good prices too. More local sources are scramblin' to compete."

Ames said, "There has to be some kind of mix up. Provenance on the mine was so murky, they said it would be years before we got a reply."

Bruce snorted. He said, "It's called 'Sorch's Salt Company', I dun think it could be noone else. Them nice minotaurs came 'round a few months back and started gettin' contracts signed."

The rest of us traded glances. Toby and Tara had been holding out on us.

The human started laughing. "What kind of life must y'all lead to not know somethin' like that was happening? Crazy. But anyway, congrats on that."

Benno assured the man, "My parents are, indeed, crazy."

We skirted the eastern edge of the suburbs before arriving at a long, single story log cabin. It was adjacent to a huge wheat field, which seemed healthy enough considering recent climate issues. There was light coming from one of the windows, indicating an occupant.

At Bruce's urging, we stepped inside. Hierophant Petrinoth was there, already hard at work. The short, blonde elf was arranging a series of parchments, the purpose of which was unclear at a glance.

The elf was pleased to see us, and particularly pleased to see Ames. "My dear." was his greeting, before kissing the were-cat with an amount of ardour that I wasn't necessarily comfortable with. I had to remind myself that Petrinoth was one of Ames' oldest 'clients', and they enjoyed that level of familiarity on a semi-regular basis. I schooled my emotions when it became my turn to be greeted by the druid, offering a handshake and a tight smile.

After Benno was introduced to the elf, we all took seats around the table.

Petrinoth had been designated as the Culinary Guild's chief representative, and thus the party leader. After we were all comfortable, the elf launched into an explanation of the circumstances. The druid said, "There is a zone of decay that is causing crops of all sorts to wither and die on the vine. Last we checked from the air, it was of a vaguely circular shape, butting up against the eastern foothills."

Benno asked, "How did you check from the air, sir?"

Petrinoth chuckled and said, "I became a bird. And you can call me Peter, young man."

The younger orc blinked. "Oh."

Peter continued, "In fact, the grass in the lower foothills was also being withered. So we can be fairly sure that this is not a targeted attack, or if it is, badly so. These parchments represent the flow of water under the ground. I was trying to find some kind of pattern that would explain this, you see. But none of these tributaries or groundwater flows match up with the impacted area. So I'm at a loss, really."

Bruce added, "If it keeps spreading, it'll be devastating. Farms 'round here are already getting screwed by the weather and heat. This could be the nail in the coffin fer a bunch of farmers if it continues. Local food scarcity will go crazy. Poor will starve, businesses will go down, people will lose their jobs and homes. Disaster."

I said, "We can go through some of the possible causes, if it will help us prepare."

Fresh parchment was grabbed and the table cleared. After discussing and eliminating several possibilities, the group ended up with a short list: A new virulent plant based disease. Sabotage carried out under the cloak of night. Mystical or divine rituals.

Hierophant Petrinoth considered. "If it's the first, then the Guild's continued examination and experimentation will eventually discover it. If it is either of the latter two reasons, we should be able to physically observe it. Assuming we go out there under, as you say, the cloak of night. True?"

We all agreed with that assessment. Thus, we had our course of action.

Bruce offered to pick up some supplies from town. After getting a list from Peter and myself, the human mentioned that he would light a signal fire to summon Cid. As I had seen Cid's face and knew his name, I offered to let him know that he should stop by via Max's Message. When I contacted the farmhand, the return message was 'Gods above and below! Uhh, okay, I'm on the way.' Bruce laughed when I related Cid's startled reply.

The bedrolls provided were warm and well padded. Probably elven make, courtesy of our druid friend. Everyone got some rest so as to refresh their arcane and divine favour. Ames slept as well, mostly because the day started quite early for the feline. And cats aren't exactly known for refusing naps.

We prepared spells that would help us if we were correct about the sabotage, namely things that would allow us to combat, chase, or disrupt the perpetrators. In our discussions about synergy, Petrinoth promised to bring some interesting tools to bear, but urged us to avoid heat or fire based magic.

Peter reminded us, "The area has been suffering from drought. Not every field would be susceptible, but a spark in the wrong place could start a wildfire that would bring devastation. In fact, if we're dealing with saboteurs, that could be their back up plan. So please be aware."

Just after sundown, Bruce returned with the supplies and material components that we requested. He was now wearing that stunning set of coppery scale mail armor. It had been enchanted centuries ago, thus its longevity. But it wasn't until our people started to repair the armor that they discovered the details. The scales were tougher than normal, and they also made the wearer completely immune to electricity. Between the young warrior's anti-magic blade and his anti-lightning armor, he would be difficult for many mages to deal with. Including myself. I was glad that Bruce was on our side.

After double checking our kit, the five of us left the cabin. Cid and his wagon were waiting for us. Benno added a Light spell to the end of the lantern-pole, greatly increasing Cid's visibility. Then the party piled into the back. The plan was to ride the horse drawn cart until we reached a reasonable parallel with the blighted area, and walk the rest of the way.

The human talked about what he knew, and we let him go on because it was an amusing way to pass the time. First we learned about the names of the horses drawing our cart. Then the breeds. Then their sires and dams. We listened politely as Bruce espoused the positive attributes of various horse breeds. Peter, of course, commented now and again. The druid's experience was mainly with cold and mountainous creatures, but he knew his way around an equine.

The young warrior glanced over at us, realizing how quiet we had been for most of the trip. "Not much for horses, are you?"

I said, "Oh they're fine. We just prefer riding giant wolves."

Ames and Benno nodded agreement.

Bruce looked at us incredulously. He turned to Hierophant Petrinoth for confirmation.

Petrinoth said, "Hmm? Oh yes, I prefer giant wolves as well."

The human started to shake his head. He said, "Crazy. The lot of you, certifiable."

We related our dealings with the southern elves over the last few years, and how for a long stretch, wolf riding was the fastest way to get to my homeland. Bruce listened with rapt attention. Ultimately the story led to a request to arrange a wolf ride for the human, and we said we'd see what we could do.

Soon after that conversation Cid stopped the horses and called back, "Here. No closer."

Our driver pointed us in the right direction, making sure that we noted the relative position of two big hills to the East. Once we were oriented, Cid took the wagon home. I thought that he might be more interested in the horses' safety than our own, but then again, that **was** his job.

Peter murmured, "I'd like to use an alternative to your Light spells if I could. My way will give us more of an element of surprise. If we find ourselves being blinded by a large source of fire, I'll cancel the enhancement and we can rely on your Light. Is everyone alright with that?"

We each murmured our agreement. Hierophant Petrinoth was in charge after all, and he was quite an accomplished channeler of divine power.

The druid called us all together, and we gathered in a tight circle. His incantation didn't take very long, only a bit longer than a Blessing from Shaman. But the effect was immediate. And amazing.

The Heat Vision prayer enhanced my night vision in a manner that I never would have thought possible. I could see the outline of everyone in crystal clarity. As we exhaled, our hot breath faded from red, to fragmented orange wisps, until it finally dissipated in a light blue mist. I could even see the passage of cool night air through the tall corn stalks. This in no way interfered with my natural orcish affinity for darkness. I could only imagine how much of an enhancement Ames' keen eyes were experiencing.

Bruce summed it up best when he said, "Wow."

Peter chuckled softly. "I'm glad you like it. Let's get a move on."

Navigation under the effects of Heat Vision was trivial. It might as well have been broad daylight instead of slightly overcast moonlight. The enchantment also made it plainly obvious that the crops were thinning as we approached our destination.

Ames held up a paw, clenched into a tight fist. My mate sniffed the air, then hissed, "Something rotten ahead. Not just plants."

Peter wasn't ready for that report. The elf whispered, "What is it, undead?"

Ames' reply was terse. "Unknown."

Swords slid from sheaths, and our druid drew his sickle from where it hung upon his hip. Benno lined up behind Bruce, and I behind Ames. We crept forward, using caution.

What we discovered was out of the ordinary, to say the least. Peter could take comfort in the fact that we weren't wrong about any of our three theories, not really. But nobody could have predicted this.

Standing at the edge of a diseased clearing of their own making were abominations that seemed to be part man, part mushroom. I would later be told that the proper name for these beings was 'fungus walkers'.

They were taller than any of us, though none of them reached the height of a grown minotaur. The 'body' types of these deformed men ranged from thick and rugged, to thin and wiry. Growths of fungus distorted their features so as to leave their faces indiscernible under layers of moldy material.

The half dozen creatures had formed a circle and were moaning, creating a low harmonic that shook the ground slightly. Spores were shaken from their skin, drifting like embers on the night wind. Their ritual seemed to be aimed at increasing the spread of this stuff, and thus making the area of devastation grow. I watched as the unholy yeast blanketed the plants in front of me, immediately causing them to droop and decay.

"Stop!"

The horrified command fell from Hierophant Petrinoth's lips. When he moved forward into the clearing, the rest of us quickly followed suit.

The six creatures did, indeed, stop. They raised their heads towards Peter, each of them slowly orientating the front of their bodies in our general direction. The druid launched into a brief, but exasperated plea in Elvish.

What really surprised me was my son, translating for us as Petrinoth spoke. "Brothers. You are children of Del-Nekbenth. You normally live in peace under the earth. How… why do you attack us, or attack our things."

Ames hissed, "When did you learn Elvish?"

Benno murmured, "Hemitath. Still learning."

The reply was guttural, tone low enough to make my guts feel queasy.

Benno struggled with this strange dialect. "You attacked. Attacked the ground. Del-Nekbenth did not help. Forced it up, or forced us up. We came but… it comes. We prepare for it. Prepare. Plant ourselves in your meat?"

As a unit, the fungus walkers started to shamble forward.

I grunted and said, "Close enough, kiddo."

Ames and Bruce backpedaled a little bit, which was understandable. Not only were these creatures large, but their method of attack was unorthodox to say the least. As they closed on our front line, they started to windmill their arms, almost chaotically. There was a method to their madness however, as hardened minerals lined the outer edge of the fungus walkers' 'hands', giving them an improvised bludgeoning surface to utilize.

I picked on the smallest of the creatures, knocking it out of line with a quick Force Bolt. I wasn't sure how much damage I had done, but at least our front line would be less swamped. Benno had a similar notion, his Web entangling the two creatures to our far right. As the fungus walkers attempted to get free of one another I saw Benno grit his teeth and narrow his eyes against the drain. By contrast, I hardly felt the curse's effect given how minor my spell was in comparison to the rest of my repertoire.

Peter took a less cautious approach than the rest of us. He charged at the closest foe with a cry of rage. Clearly he felt betrayed by these creatures of nature purposely destroying crops. The small elf rolled under the flailing arms of the ponderous fungus walker, and mercilessly hacked away at its hip and side with that keen sickle. The druid scored three deep blows, hobbling the creature before he was forced to back out.

Ames fared better once the were-cat understood the creature's attack pattern. The rogue went right for the ankles, dipping low for a quick stab, and then weaving back out before one of those massive arms could do more than dig a furrough into the ground. It was a tiring method, but safer than what the human was attempting.

Bruce was using his armor to full effect. Despite the stinging and the bruising, the warrior realized that he needed to step in to land telling blows. He took several glancing shots across his armored arms and chest, none of which penetrated the armor, but all of which caused pain. However, his return attacks were far more telling. The first slash opened up the fungus walker's shoulder. The next stab took it through the gut, the tip of his tulwar briefly poking through the back of the creature. Though their registration of 'pain' was clearly different to ours, Bruce's foe slowed, its attacks weakening by the second.

Seeing that the webbed walkers had broken free, I started to cast a more involved spell. Benno took the opposite route. He squeezed a small waterskin as he incanted, spraying both of his foes with a Fan of Frost. I was worried about how close my son was getting, but that was replaced by a different worry when the Force Bolt caught him square in the chest and knocked him back five paces, decimating a row of corn in the process. My Acid Bolts took form, the guts in my hand melting away. I launched them at one of the partially frozen creatures, burning through its deformed face. It fell without a sound. I felt the drain more keenly this time, but my adrenaline was flowing. I needed to check on Benno.

Knowing that the thinner creature was a spellcaster, Peter disengaged from his maimed foe, who was limping hard and would be unable to follow. He chanted a prayer that sounded familiar to me. Soon the dying stalks had their revenge. The druid's Tangling Plants surged from the soil, no longer limp and helpless. They coiled about the thin fungus walker, immobilizing it.

Ames took their foe's leg, while at the same time Bruce sacrificed a blow to his left forearm in order to cleanly behead his opponent. But neither could rest. The wounded human charged towards the wounded fungus walker before it could hobble too close to our concentrating druid. Ames, seeing me retreating to check on our son, triggered the Ring of Leaping. The feline landed on the partially frozen creature's back, hacking away with claws and short sword. It flailed, elbow swinging back to catch the were-cat in the ribs. Ames continued the assault despite, or perhaps because of, the pain.

I lost track of what was happening, having to turn my back on the battle. I fell to my knees when I found Benno. Blood was streaming from his mouth, and he was coughing. I immediately came to the conclusion that he was suffering from a punctured lung, having seen it before when Ames had been run through. But when I reached down, the younger orc just looked annoyed and slapped my hands away.

"Mah vit nye vun."

Hearing Benno able to talk sent a surge of relief through my body. I stood quickly and offered him a hand. "What was that boy?"

He spat more blood and tried again as I hauled him back to his feet, "Ah bit mah tongue."

We rushed back towards the clearing, but the battle was all-but over. Ames had cut the frozen creature's throat from ear to ear, and was limping over to deliver the coup de grace to the one legged fungus walker that they stranded earlier. Bruce, quite viciously, maimed the opposite hip of the foe that our druid has slashed up earlier. Even with one arm wounded and bleeding, it was no match. The human split open the creature's mushroom laden skull, and then grimly stalked over to the spellcaster, who was helpless to break free of Peter's actively channeled Tangling Plants incantation.

After all of the creatures were dispatched, we took stock of our own condition. Hierophant Petrinoth's assessment was: "That could have gone better."

Ames had broken at least one rib on the right side, and bruised a shoulder on the left. Bruce's left forearm was mangled in a nasty looking blunt cut, where the skin was both split and bruised. Benno's breastbone was sore, and he bit his tongue hard enough in the fall that his spellcasting wasn't assured.

The first thing Benno wanted to be sure of is that his Amulet of Enhanced Enchanting hadn't been damaged. I assured him that it was in better condition than his face. A Minor Healing incantation from Peter was all that it took to get my son speaking properly again. His chest was still sore, but he would live.

Human and were-cat also received Minor Healing in order to stop the most intense pain and bleeding. They seemed disappointed when Petrinoth told them to bandage the afflicted areas using the poultice that he provided. Without more healing, the two would be fairly limited in future engagements.

What we didn't know was that the druid was just getting started. Peter called the human over first. He laid a palm on the medicated bandage and started to chant. The expression on Bruce's face when the incantation ended was somewhere between amazement and disgust. The fidgeting began almost immediately.

"Don't take it off." said the druid, dryly, when the human's hand crept towards his bandage.

Ames got the same treatment, Hierophant Petrinoth's small hand pressed over my were-cat's ribs while the leathers were still off. The feline started to squirm, paws clenching in order to muster enough self control. I could tell that my mate wanted to tear that bandage right off.

Peter explained, "Your flesh and bones are knitting themselves back together. The odd sensations shall pass. It's a side effect of the Regeneration, but within minutes the area will be numb. Within ten you'll forget you were wounded at all. Within an hour, it will be like your injury never happened, no matter how ugly it might have seemed."

While we waited for the Regeneration to take a deeper hold, Peter and I scouted ahead. On the Northeast side of the scarred clearing, we discovered furrows in the earth, getting deeper as they led into the partially withered corn field.

When we returned, I let the others know what was happening. "Trenches. Stretching out into the field, bordering on the foothills. Hierophant Petrinoth and I think that if we follow them, we'll have our source of… strange fungus people."

I reached down to help Ames out of a low crouch, but the feline brushed my hand aside gently. I watched in wonder as the were-cat stood, free of pain. Similarly, Bruce was flexing his once-horribly-injured arm, clenching and unclenching his fist. My esteem for advanced druidic healing increased sevenfold.

I checked in on Benno, asking, "Can you talk?"

He responded, primly, "If I so choose."

The five of us walked through the clearing, Peter's Heat Vision prayer giving us the confidence to move through the dead, trampled vegetation without fear of falling prey to an ambush. At the Northeast edge of the zone of death, we walked into the gully that was once obfuscated by the cornfield. As more healthy plants started to rise around us, the trench deepened. Soon the raw earth was surrounding us. The trench was three paces wide and two deep.

Hierophant Petrinoth sounded upset as he murmured, "The fungus walkers simply don't do this sort of thing. They normally don't come anywhere near the surface world, nevermind act out in a malicious manner against surface races."

None of us could come up with an explanation for Peter. Somehow, I doubted the truth would give him much solace given the death toll that had already been charged.

The trench made a sharp right turn, heading directly towards the foothills. We saw two hulking figures about a dozen paces out. Hip to hip, the large fungus walkers virtually blocked the entire width of the trench. There was frantic activity going on behind them. But all we could see was that pair of mushroom-headed behemoths, easily taller than any minotaur I'd ever seen.

Ames led with a shot from their hand crossbow. The little projectile didn't do a lot of damage, but it did force the huge fungus walker to step up or get slowly picked apart.

Bruce and Ames didn't shy away from the confrontation. Our recently injured front line waded in, each hugging the opposite side of the trench, using the earthen wall as partial cover as they approached the outside range of the giant fungus walkers' reach.

Seeing that Benno was having an issue getting a clean line of sight, Peter reached out and grasped my son's shoulder. He took some webbing from his pouch, similar to what the two of us used to cast our Spider's Web spell. But when the druid's prayer was over, Benno's eyes went wide. I'm sure there was some psychic communication between the two that I wasn't privy to. All I know is that my son was soon scaling the side of the trench like an arachnid. His green hands and booted feet seemed to be able to stick to the walls at will. Upside down, but with a higher perspective, my son took out a patch of fur and an amber wand before starting to chant.

I was a bit annoyed, as a badly aimed Lightning Bolt could have started a wildfire up above. But I trusted that my boy had a plan that would have prevented that eventuality. Perhaps I was just frustrated because the limitation of 'no fire' forced me into a rather different repertoire. And since I wasn't about to use Ebon Chains of Binding on one of those things, I started to cast my last effective combat spell.

The creatures held their ground. They seemed less interested in our demise, and more interested in being an effective barrier. The leftmost fungal foe lashed out with the back of their fist, attempting to make Bruce become one with the earthen wall. The human hopped back, narrowly avoiding the tremendous blow. He retaliated with a strong riposte, digging a small hole in the knuckle of his foe's hand. It hardly noticed. Ames' giant reached out to grab and crush the cat. The feline deftly dodged away from the edge of the trench, hacking at the fungus walker's wrist with that wicked little short sword. The creature quickly withdrew its hand, reassessing the wisdom of that approach.

The guts in my hand melted into green ichor, which formed the bolts of acid that leapt towards the fungal giant that Ames was fighting. They burned into the creature's left shoulder, melting through mushrooms and flesh and scarring bone. It didn't scream, though the injured arm hung uselessly by its side. I allowed the drain to peck away at my mind, before shoring up my mental reserves. Shortly after, Benno's Lightning Bolt struck the chest of Bruce's opponent. The big creature jerked and shuddered in place. Now it moved more slowly, swinging with less power and conviction.

I was about to scold my son for firing off a Lightning Bolt so close to our ally. But then I remembered Bruce's enchanted armor. My boy could have fired directly **through** the human and Bruce would have remained unharmed. Tactically, Benno seemed to be one step ahead of me.

Our elf decided to be nimble. Having waited until Benno finished casting, Peter used my son as a ladder of sorts, grabbing the well-anchored orc and pulling himself up. He scrambled up to the lip of the trench and raced past the area that was clogged by our two giants. It looked like he wanted to see what we were about to walk into.

Even though it seemed like our front line had matters well in hand, my son scrambled forward like a spider along the trench wall. When he was just above and behind Bruce, the younger orc squeezed a small waterskin and performed his brief incantation. His second Fan of Frost caught the fungus walker in the face, blinding it.

That was all the opening Bruce needed. He pounced forward and lashed out with his wicked looking tulwar, cutting clean through the creature's ankle. It tumbled over silently. The next dismemberment involved head from shoulders, normally the final word in such a conflict.

Ames was dancing around at the very edge of the fungus walker's range. Having only one arm left to swipe or grab with, the only thing it could do effectively was hold the were-cat back, suffering minor stabs and cuts all the while. But when Bruce joined in, the battle was over swiftly. The two skilled combatants picked apart their wounded foe in seconds. Ames' short sword found the base of its skull, and it stopped moving.

There was a horrific clattering and rumbling from up ahead that shook the ground beneath our feet. It felt like an earthquake. For a moment I feared that the walls of our trench would collapse upon the four of us. But as suddenly as it started, the noise and the shaking stopped. We rushed forward to see what happened around the next bend.

We saw Petrinoth standing in front of a pile of dirt and stones at the side of the foothill. It looked like half the hillside had slid down, exposing raw earth to the night air where once there was grass.

Peter cursed roundly in Elvish, or at least that was my guess from the general tone. He said, "The rest retreated into a cave and took out the entrance. Look for a gap, we need to find out why... why all of this has come about."

Ames did find a gap, but it was only about the size of a cannonball. Still, the druid was pleased.

"I can turn into a ferret and get in there."

The rest of us traded glances. It was Ames who spoke up, "You don't know what's down there. It might be suicidal."

The elf held up both hands, in a gesture intended to stop further objections. He said, "I won't be doing anything brave, I assure you. I want to slip in, see if I can find any signs of why these normally peaceful folks would turn to violence, and slip back out. If I see anything dangerous in there, I'll scamper back right away. If something goes wrong, if there's a further collapse, I'll wait on the other side. As I've heard told, Sorch has used the Stone Shape spell to heroic ends in the past. He can make a ferret-sized hole if need be."

I considered the plan. He would be alone. But as a druid, he was best equipped to handle the situation. "I can at that. We'll rest here. If you're not back in an hour, we'll assume that we need to camp and prepare the right spells for a rescue. I'll send you a Max's Message before we bed down, to make sure we have assessed things correctly."

Peter nodded. He said, "Your enhanced vision will be wearing out soon enough. Assuming you'll need your Light spells to read, stay in the trench and you should be well enough concealed."

With that, the druid started to shrink in place. Unlike the were creatures that I've seen transform, this was far less 'messy'. There was no crackling of bone or slide of sinew and muscle. There wasn't any fear of ripped or lost clothing. Hierophant Petrinoth and everything he owned simply melted away, until only a ferret remained. The little creature chittered and dook-dooked at us before scampering up to the narrow gap in the caved-in rocks. Then he was gone.

Bruce said, "Druids ain't right in th' head, are they?"

I thought back to my experiences with Shaman. I replied, "Nope. Not even close."

We made our camp inside of the trench, just in front of the collapsed area. Even though I wasn't as effective in combat as I had hoped to be, I could still provide aid and comfort to my party. The cast iron pot made an appearance, giving us heat and a healthy meal after our exertions. Potato, turnip, and salted mackerel stew was on the menu. When we were done, I made coffee for Ames and Bruce, just in case the were-cat and human had to watch over Benno and I, should we need to memorize a suite of spells and mount a rescue.

As the warrior and my mate were drinking and chatting, I noticed my son sitting on his own, staring off into the distance. Our enhanced vision chose that moment to fail. I murmured a Light cantrip, centering the radius on my cooling Pot of Heating. That left my son just on the edge of the field of light. I ambled over to sit by his side.

"Copper for your thoughts?"

He grumbled and looked away.

I tilted my head and asked, "Are you still sore about the thing with Rick? I said i was sorry."

The younger orc turned towards me so he could snarl, "Go 'way. Me no talk like dis."

In that moment, I saw everything that was present in my own mind contained within my son. The pride. The anger. The passion. The inner strength. Everything that tribal life followed by unexpected opportunity could forge in a young man.

I reached out and stroked my boy's hair. I assured him, "I'm not going anywhere."

Frustrated tears rolled down his cheeks. He hated this level of drain, and I could tell that the boy had pushed himself right to the limit. My hatred for Glogur's curse paled in comparison to Benno's. And in times like these, the unfairness sat in my son's guts and festered. We talked about it before, and I said the same thing then that I did this time:

"Talk to me. Tell me a story."

I noticed Ames glancing over. Those emerald green eyes showed recognition of the situation before looking away. My mate knew that this was an orc thing.

Benno growled and ducked away from my head petting. "No."

I took off my gloves and reached out again, this time to rub away the wet, salty trail of tears with a calloused thumb. "Yeah. Tell me about your new boyfriend."

That shocked him out of his self pity. After a speechless moment, he asked, "How you know?"

"A father knows."

Benno hesitated, then he said, "Can't say lots. Promise not to. His family and job not know."

I nodded, wiping my boy's cheeks dry with my hands.

He continued, "He older. Real smart human. Gots good job. Kinda shy. But real cuddly."

Just to avoid any misunderstanding I asked, "And not currently mated or married to anyone else, right?"

The younger orc snorted and punched my shoulder lightly. "Not Rick, Dad! And no, not mated."

Trusting that he would understand that I didn't want to hear about bedroom antics, I asked, "What do you do together?"

Benno's eyes got distant. "Long walk. Study. He like art, we go see art. Stuff and things."

I smiled, making sure that my son knew that I approved of his happiness. I asked, "When do I get to meet him?"

The younger orc hesitated. His hesitation was rewarded.

Bruce called out, "He's back."

A ferret entered our camp. I slipped the Silk Gloves of Secrecy back on, before we all stood and walked over.

We watched the creature. And waited.

Ames said, "Maybe this isn't him. Maybe this is just a normal ferret. Staring at us. Like we're idiots."

There was another moment of uncomfortable silence, and within that moment we contemplated the possibility that Ames was right.

But soon after, the little creature grew and took the shape of a small, but intact, elven druid.

Peter took a deep breath, then he said, "Sorry, I was just catching my breath. There was a lot of scurrying. Go ahead and sit down, I'll try to define exactly what I saw."

The druid described the winding caverns deep underneath the foothills of Tatertown. When he descended significantly, he started to see signs.

"The caverns that the fungus walkers likely called 'home' had been devastated. Some kind of earth elemental had been at work, deep underground. It stirred up the trouble, forcing the fungal creatures out of their traditional territory. For some reason they blamed us, and took to the surface so that they could retaliate."

I said, "They might not be entirely incorrect. If Omi-Suteth was right, the recent environmental disturbances are partly the fault of the gods, and partly our fault. Though who knows, perhaps the fungus people also have some blame in the matter. They're part of the mortal realm too."

Bruce mumbled, "As much as a mushroom can be, I s'pose."

Peter shrugged. He said, "They're long gone now, and I saw no signs of the elemental lurking about. We can have the Tatertown militia keep an eye on this area. Some of the local engineers can help repair the trenches and stabilize the hillside for reseeding."

After everyone agreed that we were done here, I took out a thin strand of copper and cast Max's Message. Cid wasn't as startled this time, more sleepy. He promised to have someone at the meeting point within a couple of hours.

Back at the cabin, we rested until dawn. After morning intellect enhancements, we said our farewells to both Bruce and Peter. The two of them promised to come visit us, and to put our names on the Guild rosters as preferred partners.

Hierophant Petrinoth said, "I'm glad to report that everything I've heard about your family ended up being true. The Culinary Guild will likely need to consult with the northern Elves. However. I'm positive that they'll see this as a success. Each of you should expect the 500 gold bounty shortly. As a member of both guilds, I'll make sure that it's deposited directly into your Adventurer's Guild account, which you should be able to access back at the University. Del-Nekbenth's blessing upon the three of you!"

Bruce's goodbye was much more low key. Each of us got a hand shake. The young man's easy smile was infectious. He didn't need to say much. "T'was fun. Let's do it again soon."

Cid gave us a ride back to the Temple of Vinara outside of town. With classes already started up again, Benno needed to get back to the Arcane University right away. Ames and I had a different destination. My dealings with druids had not come to an end as of yet.

We were going to see Shaman.

Chapter 5

There was one thing that changed both my tribe and my village more than anyone could have imagined: Access to large amounts of quality lumber.

A few months ago, I had learned the story from the man himself: Kronz. When the first tradesman appeared on the Jeywafa clan's newly operational Circle of Transport, it was assumed that the huge box of lightly charred wood was fuel for the upcoming celebrations. It took two translators and a lengthy demonstration for the merchant to get his message across: The wood was for barter, and it was charred to preserve it against the moist swamp air.

The merchant happily walked away with a large stack of reconditioned mundane weapons, one of the more common local commodities after the army of the undead had been defeated. Kronz, the orc craftsman who bought not just one but three of those lumber shipments, was called an idiot by most of his peers. When the rest of his wood appeared the next day, along with a box of iron spikes called 'nails', Kronz got to work.

You see Kronz once travelled with an infamous orc captain by the name of Blue Briar. He had seen human cities, and he had worshiped in the temple of Melflavin the Tinker, He Who Wept and Made Swamps Grow. He studied the construction of both shelters and seafaring vessels. Most importantly, he knew how to put hammer to nail. It was a noisy few days.

So when Kronz traded in his tent for a small wooden house, there were vague murmurs of disapproval. When smoke started to rise from the stone-lined fireplace, tribemates thought that surely his blackened wood home was going to burn to the ground. But when people stepped inside, their jaws dropped. There were no insects. Inside this prison of wood, the air was cooler in the hot seasons and warmer in the cold. The entire place was more dry than any tent the orcs could construct. And it offered unparalleled privacy and security.

Soon after that first wooden home went up, Kronz had a visitor. Hemitath, the Skua of Chief Shaman, commissioned a larger house to replace the royal tent. Demand immediately became far too much for poor Kronz to handle on his own. He enlisted his entire extended family on both his mother and father's side, as well as the full time assistance of his three daughters. The company's first foreman was his uncle Kronz. The second was his younger cousin, Kronz. Soon the company of Kronz, Kronz, Kronz and Daughters was the busiest and richest crafting organization in the Southern Orc Tribes.

So when Ames and I stepped out of the copper teleportation circle, passing under the wooden sign that read 'Magic, Peace, and Multiculturalism', there was hardly a tent to be seen. Indeed, the only temporary structures were ones intended to be mobile, festive, or otherwise traditional for the sake of tourism. My homeland was now a city of wood and of stone. And of multitudinous people.

In two years, the Jeywafa clan doubled in size. Not just in terms of the amount of ground in use by the village, but in terms of permanent residents. Representatives and merchants from the major races had moved in. Orcish men and women from other tribes, particularly the nearby Fistuntuls, married into the clan. Even a smattering of humans got caught up in the recent wave of partnerships. Every once in a while, interracial couples could be seen walking around town, and a few of the women were gravid with half orc bundles of joy.

With new families came new construction. The public baths, one of the star attractions of Jeywafa village as well as the conception site of many of our newest little clanspeople, were located beneath the Circle of Transport and the newly constructed Temple of Kenvunk. But even as large as these central features were, the supporting infrastructure put them to shame. Entertainment consisted of traditional (and traditionally rowdy despite being in a building rather than a tent) orcish ale houses, a few select brothels, and a small but hugely popular playhouse owned by a minotaur acting troupe. There was a large open market to the East near the retaining walls, and permanent trade and craft stores surrounding it. The western part of town butting up to the hills was where everything was made, from weapons to weaving, from arsenals to art. Everything was either new or rapidly evolving.

The end result being: I was lost in my own village.

Ames peered around with keen were-cat eyes. "I think we're to the East? Where's the sun?"

Even in my own ears, my voice sounded defeated. I said, "Directly above us. It's noon."

We wandered around for a little while, looking like tourists.

Then my mate spotted a town watch patrol. "Oh thank the gods." Ames waved both paws in the air, flagging them down.

Perhaps a fraction too late, I pulled up the hood of my cloak to hide my face in the vague hopes that I wouldn't be recognised. The young, pike carrying guardsmen were already pointing at me and murmuring to each other, however.

The taller of the two asked, in Orcish, "Hey, 'scuse me. You'se that guy yes?"

I cleared my throat and asked, "What guy?"

"Guy from side of crates of salt?"

Ames choked back a guffaw. The blow to my ego was incalculable. This was my life now.

I sighed and said, "Yeah, probably."

The tall orc nudged his shorter brethren. "Told ya."

Ames managed to remain composed. The feline asked, in Common, "Which way to the royal chambers, please?"

It was the shorter one who understood and answered. "You go North. Few minute. Pass bread place. You no miss." He pointed the tip of his weapon in the correct direction.

After thanking them and receiving a thump on the back for being the best salt mascot on all of Panos, we proceeded North. The smell of baked bread did indeed come just as we caught sight of the Chieftains' Hall. It was a large building made of the same charred wood as the rest of the nearby structures. However, it was one of the few buildings in town that was two stories high. The banners of every tribe, both inside and outside of Shaman's mutual defense coalition, flew above the gates.

As much as the other advances had helped the Southern Orc Tribes, the political gains of becoming a major transportation hub helped most of all. For the first time since the Second Great War, elvish and human embassies flanked the orcish seat of government. Not only was Chieftains' Hall a place for every tribe to conduct official business with each other, any tribe could take meetings with foreign powers here. It was neutral territory.

And of course behind all of this, in both a literal and figurative way, were Hemitath and Shaman. We passed through Chieftains' Hall on our way to the private residences in the back. At least one of the minor chieftains was holding court in a side chamber. I didn't recall his name, but I believed he was from a small clan to the Southeast. He was talking about trading peat and coal for masonry tools and training. On the other side of the table, some humans were nodding in agreement. When I paused to listen to the details, Ames grabbed me by the belt and tugged me away.

"What's your rule?" asked the were-cat.

I sighed. "Don't get involved in the politics." was my reply.

The reason was evident when we arrived at entryway to Shaman's private wing. Immediately upon seeing us, and very unlike the younger and less experience guards in the city center, the three orcish veterans bowed.

The eldest among them said, "Sorch of the Engine. Great Cat of the North."

The truth was, the level of fame and influence that Ames, Tara, Toby, and myself wielded in these parts was frightening. Even the most innocent political interaction might be at odds with Shaman and Hemitath's intentions, and that could cause strife. The minotaurs and the were-cat only got involved under Hemitath's direct instruction, and I had vowed never to get involved at all.

We returned the bows of the house guards. "Are they in and taking visitors?"

The old warrior bobbed his head. "Yes. Take lunch in library. Go ahead, me let steward know."

Truth be told, the private residence was quite modest. There was a simple kitchen, two bedrooms, a living room, and the library. Everything was made of wood save for the shale flooring. The library was just a quiet place to eat, and a secure location for Hemitath's spellbooks and magical studies. It was a far cry from the residences in Hemitath's home city of Arbitros or her quarters at the Arcane University. At the same time, it was sheer luxury compared to the drafty, leaky, bug infested tents that Shaman grew up with.

Shaman was sitting in a padded rocking chair, slowly shifting his weight back and forth to promote that soothing motion. He was dressed in a clean white cotton shirt and short tan pants. His green-gray skinned face broke into a broad smile upon spying us. "Look who here."

Hemitath, who had been reading through today's foreign missives, was leaning over the dinner table. As she sat up her long hair, which went silvery-white in the past couple of years, floated into her face. After sweeping it back, the ancient elf mirrored her husband's smile. She said, "Look who, indeed. It's the kids."

I chuckled a bit. In recent years, Hemitath and Shaman took to calling us their 'kids' and Benno was the 'kids' kid'. Neither of us had any objection. Shaman was more of a father to me than any man had ever been.

The older orc gestured. "Sit, sit. Wants food?"

Hemitath added, "We just finished, but there's more fresh bread, and we have some sugared boysenberry jam."

Ames and I politely declined. We knew that these two would stuff our bellies full if we allowed them.

I said, "We're just checking in after a mission for the Culinary Guild, of all things." I awaited the inevitable questions that would come on the tail of such a statement.

Instead, Hemitath said, "Oh yes dear, we heard."

Shaman said, "Yeah, yeah."

Ames and I must have seemed disappointed, because the old elf started laughing. "But why don't you give us the details, we've only had an overview from what our people at the Transportation Guild were able to pick up."

Ames launched into a full recollection of the mission. I related how it might have tied in with Omi-Suteth's advice on researching the weather and crop issues. Shaman rocked away in his chair as he listened. The older orc wore a look of vague satisfaction, but not one of understanding. I was glad that he was proud of his 'kids', but I wanted so much more from my friend, afflicted by Glogur's curse when he was forced to cast an arcane spell without any intellect enhancement.

At the end of our tale Hemitath said, "I think I agree with your druid. Tatertown isn't the first victim of this upheaval, simply the latest. You'll remember that two years ago, there was coastal flooding in communities on The Shore. That was traced back to water elemental activity. And of course we've had crop issues since well before that. Something is causing the elements to turn, in a very real and literal way."

Shaman said, "Lizards no answer call now, too far away. Is strange time. You fix."

I sighed. "I'll try, chief. Two guilds and a university, not to mention every major government, are trying to figure it out. My family will do their part."

Shaman snorted. "Don't disappoint. Not dis time."

That tone wasn't very much like the Shaman I knew. It hurt that he seemed to want to belittle our current and past efforts. Hemitath caught my eye and just shook her head a little bit. I knew what she was trying to convey: 'It's not him talking when he says things like that'. She had said that to me privately so many times over the last couple of years. You would think that the sting of Shaman's brief cruel streaks would have faded away. No. It doesn't fade away.

Changing the subject quickly, Ames asked, "So how are things here? Has the economy sorted itself out?"

The elder elf had to laugh at the question. She said, "In a year and a half we went from being a wood importer and weapon exporter, to being a copper exporter hiring a massive amount of outside labourers, to being a coal exporter and tool importer. All the while developing a tourist trade."

The feline joked, "I hear you started importing salt as well."

Hemitath said, "Oh yes, we saw that Sorch. Congratulations. How did that particular business endeavour come about?"

I held up both hands, helplessly, "We honestly have no idea. We need to talk to Toby and Tara."

The elf said, "Well this is an example of what I was talking about. Your salt may be the next big thing. We just don't know. The economy, if anything, has become more surreal."

That worried me. I asked, "By now things should have settled down, right? Last I heard, most of the surrounding tribes came together to share in the prosperity of the Circle of Transport and share the knowledge of new trades among all of the orcs. We stopped a war, the humans and the elves have embassies. What's the problem?"

Hemitath said, "We're the problem, Sorch. At least partly. We're succeeding on the tourism front. But knick knacks and tribal eroticism, even if they've made the Southern Tribes a popular destination, aren't exactly a set of stable industries. We're starting to offer more tangible services; eventually a combination of traditional mining, mercenary work, and the peat harvest are going to become significant contributors to the economy. But right now, everyone is rushing towards whatever the latest craze might be. There's no stability."

A light snoring sound punctuated Hemitath's last statement. Shaman had fallen asleep in his rocking chair. The three of us took the opportunity to move out into the living room. I sat on the wooden bench with Ames, while Hemitath's lighter frame took advantage of the comfortable wicker chair.

I asked the same question that I always asked, "Any improvement?"

The elf slowly shook her head. "He still can't read scrolls. Not even in the Astral with Benno's help. Research on spells that improve the intelligence of others has failed. No druid, no cleric, nobody has a solution. Not yet."

Ames murmured, "The outbursts are getting more harsh."

The archmage looked down and away for a few moments. She said, "He's angry. He's trapped in there and he's angry. Shaman is still the sweet, genuine man that we knew. But irrational expressions of his frustration are going to happen."

I said, "Are you holding up?"

Hemitath wiped away the beginnings of a tear, then straightened her shoulders. "Yes. Lizzy has been irreplaceable. She's learned to take cues, make prompts, and otherwise help to guide her master. Dutch picks up the slack when Lizzy is resting. They've been an amazing help."

The were-cat looked around. "Where are they?"

"Oh, they're sitting in on that meeting in the hall."

I was incredulous. I asked, "You have your familiars sitting in on political negotiations?!"

My tone made Hemitath laugh. She explained, "Not as spies, not really. Everybody knows who owns those two silly creatures. They enjoy being around people. Probably because of the snacks that they get. But if there are raised voices or if tempers flare, Dutch lets me know right away. If one of our people needs to get us a message, Lizzy delivers it. Like I said: Amazing help, those two."

As if on cue, the amazing and yet occasionally infuriating Lizzy came in on the wing. There was a little note strapped to her leg, as in if the flying lizard was some kind of messenger pigeon. As soon as Hemitath untied the little scrap of parchment from Shaman's familiar, Lizzy flew over to perch on Ames' shoulder. I, in contrast, received a protracted and heartfelt hiss from the temperamental creature.

I said, dryly, "Good to see you too."

Ames scritched under the flying lizard's neck, making the little beast croon happily. The were-cat said, "Oh, she misses you dear. That's her way of saying you don't visit often enough."

I wasn't convinced.

Hemitath called over, "Thank you Lizzy, you can get back to the meeting."

Ames allowed the lizard to break the scritching-based trance. She nearly fell off of my were-cat's shoulder, straining for that last moment of contact. Then Lizzy launched herself into the air. A couple of lazy spirals later, and she was gone.

I asked, "Something go wrong at the meeting?"

The former Headmaster of the Arcane University considered the contents of the note. "No, this is from Shaman's right hand man. They need more people working on the retaining walls. Making them thicker and higher. It's a constant battle. We've had to hire full time teams to build up the earth around the village. Otherwise the rising water will keep encroaching."

Ames and I shared a look. The feline said, "So you're starting to see issues here as well. Sorch mentioned that the water was rising when we rode in to deal with the Necromancer."

Hemitath said, "And it hasn't stopped rising. In ten years some of these houses will be on posts. In twenty, the Circle of Transport may stop working."

The last bit of news alarmed me. "Why would that happen?"

"It needs to be connected to the element of earth. The copper plates interact with Panos in a very specific manner. They can't be floating or submerged."

That grim news cloaked the room in silence for a while.

Hemitath decided that we needed some encouragement. She said, "I'm glad that you're helping out on the environmental missions. I'm going to have my contacts within the elven clergy contact you directly with any news or developments."

I said, "That's kind of you, Skua. Thank you."

"I'm simply emulating your own kindness. These issues are unlikely to directly impact Ice House or the University in the short term, and yet you're in the thick of things. It's a great example for little Benno."

Ames said, "He's not so little these days."

The elf laughed. She admitted, "No, no he isn't. But he'll always be little in my mind, even if he outgrows his daddy."

I sighed. "He's already outgrown me in one way. He's not just the brightest new student at the Arcane University, he's smarter than I am. I'm finding it hard to keep up."

Hemitath offered, "A little advice?"

I nodded.

"He may be smarter. But you're more experienced. He still looks up to you, and you're still his father. Everything he has accomplished is on the tail end of your efforts, Sorch. And of your efforts, Ames. He owes you two everything… don't let him forget it."

We both laughed at the wise elf's advice.

Ames elbowed my ribs, "She's right. We helped save entire cities, arguably an entire continent."

I noted, "We couldn't have done the last bit without him though."

The feline said, "Sure but don't tell **him** that!"

Hemitath smiled. She said, "That's the spirit. I have a meeting of my own to attend shortly, and I need to be properly dressed. Message me if there are any breakthroughs?"

Ames and I promised to do so as we stood.

As the elf showed us out, I mentioned, "Between Tatertown and here, we've gotten used to the climates far away from the equator. Going back to the Arcane University and Ice House is going to be hellish."

Hemitath's delicate elven features folded into a tiny frown. "Certainly, but you aren't going back just yet."

We paused at the threshold. I asked, "Umm, why not?"

I received a little slap on the shoulder from Hemitath. She asked, "What have you been promising for the last, oh I don't know, fifteen visits?"

Ames caught on to what the elf was talking about. The were-cat slapped my other shoulder. "Yeah Sorch, what have you been promising?"

I groaned and said, "Oh that. But is today really a good day?" I frantically searched for an excuse within my mind, but nothing was coming.

The former Headmaster said, "Today is the **perfect** day, dear one. The children are in the classroom, the teachers are available to take notes I'm sure."

Ames said, mock-proudly, "My mate, the professor."

I said, "Oh gods and demons. Fine. Let's get this over with."

Hemitath's little frown transformed into a brilliant smile. "That's the spirit, dear. I'll have one of the guards escort you over to the schoolhouse. So you don't lose your way."

And with the 'I got lost' excuse eliminated, that was that. I was going back to school.

Chapter 6

We were escorted to a large wooden structure on the West end of the village. Soon after Shaman and Hemitath endorsed the use of wooden buildings, a number of public projects were commissioned. One of the first to be built was a proper schoolhouse. It was intended to replace the traditional activity of wives and mothers gathering together between hunts to teach the children survival lessons.

The women of Jeywafa clan embraced this new, more organised and regular schooling rota. The wisest and, frankly, the sternest among them took on roles as full time schoolmarms. I knew many of the older women from my own youth, and I knew that they were not to be trifled with.

So it was with trepidation that I stepped into the simple, rather clean schoolhouse. It had four classrooms and a meeting hall that doubled as a staff area. Seeing nobody in the main hallway, our escort pointed his spear to the door on the far western wall. "Try dere." he said, before taking up a position by the exit. Thus preventing my escape.

With a far too happy Ames leading the way, we trekked into the meeting hall. There we found a stern looking orcish woman standing at a workbench. Her gray hair was neatly combed, her black dress perfectly ironed, and her boots were polished to a mirror shine. She seemed to be sorting brightly colored stones into piles. Upon seeing me, her haggard countenance transformed into one of deep suspicion.

"You." was the greeting that the elder schoolmarm had for me.

My reply was immediate and instinctive. "Good morning Mrs. Tasslewick."

The woman scowled at me for a moment. But then Mrs. Tasslewick underwent an amazing transformation. Upon turning to face Ames, the old orc was all kindness and smiles. "Great Cat of North. Is honor to have you."

That's when I knew that today was going to be filled with unfairness.

Ames' Orcish wasn't perfect, but the were-cat managed to say, "Honor is mine. Mate here to teach kids about past."

The effort wasn't perfect, but hearing Ames speaking the native tongue was enough to make the schoolmarm absolutely radiant. She said, "He go to first class on right. Older students. If dey get it, we try younger ones next time. We have tea and talk."

Ames did their best to hide a lizard-eating grin. The were-cat said, "You heard her dear. You may go now."

Mrs. Tasslewick knew Common well enough to take up her cue. She gave me a brief scowl and waved me off dismissively with the back of her gnarled hand.

I sighed and marched out of the meeting hall. The first classroom on the right was called 'Python', apparently. Glancing at the sign across the hall, I saw that it was called 'Boa'. The two rooms down the hall were called 'Asp' and 'Noodle'. I assumed the size of the snake corresponded to the age of the children that the room hosted. With some trepidation, I stepped into the python pit.

I was greeted by three dozen sets of beady little eyes staring right at me. Briefly I wondered if our escort would really stab me if I decided to make a break for it.

Each orc child was around 9 or 10 years old. To be fair, they seemed more intrigued than malicious in any way. I heard murmurs of 'salt guy' ripple from desk to desk. The words were spoken with curiosity and amazement.

At the front of the class, the half-orc schoolmarm rapped her pointing stick against the slate board. I didn't know her. She was dressed similarly to Mrs. Tasslewick, but looked to be about two decades younger. "Dis not just salt guy. Dis Sorch of the Engine. He blew big hole in village. You misbehave, he blow you all up."

The class was suddenly quiet and attentive. I wondered if it was the best idea to leave the threat of Fireballing a bunch of ten year olds hanging in the air like that. I didn't even **know** the Fireball spell. But I skipped past the clarifications, opting for a greeting instead. "Hi kids. Hope you study hard."

The schoolmarm rapped her pointing stick on the front slate again, this time to get my attention. She asked, "You gonna teach history, yeah?"

I quickly nodded.

That stick was leveled right at my forehead as instructions were conveyed. "Keep word simple, no fancy magic school talk. Keep in Orcish, we no use Common til afternoon. Have question, ask me. Got it?"

My reply was immediate and humble, "Yes ma'am."

I turned to address the classroom, in Orcish of course. I said, "Hi. Name is Sorch Stonebender."

"GOOD MORNING MISTER STONEBENDER!"

I was unprepared for this unified assault upon my ears. I cast a quick glance back at the schoolmarm, but she seemed to be looking upon the class with approval. I tried to address the subject at hand, since history was less likely to produce loud and unexpected social niceties.

"Here to talk about Panos. Panos where we live. Clerics of Melflavin use big tube to look at sky. Dey say we just one of many rocks that spin around sun. Dunno much about other rocks. Do know about small rock dat spin 'round Panos. Dat's the moon. Some say dere's smaller moon hidden behind first, but no proof. So we just say one moon for now."

I could tell that I already lost about half of them. They were sitting up straight so that I wouldn't Fireball them, but a lot of those beady eyes were starting to glass over. It was time to impress them.

I said, "Panos cold at tips, hot at edges, and cold again towards middle. Middle gots ice and mountains and snow. Who here seen snow?"

Every single little green hand in the class shot up, much to my chagrin.

I asked, "What, really?"

One of the little monsters said, "We have field trip to Ice House!"

Another said, "We got to eat turnips!"

"I saw man pee on dead rat!"

The schoolmarm said, dryly, "It was interesting field trip."

I cleared my throat. "Okay, good. So you know how cold it get. We way, way South of dat. So super warm compared to Ice House. But dey say if keep going South, so far that sea start to spin, it get cold again. Big block of ice in ocean dere. Then warm again when get to other side."

Again, I was losing them. They saw a man pee on a rat, and I was coming in a distant second.

"Panos use ta be full of demons."

Suddenly those little eyes got wide. Got 'em.

"Demons and angels, all use ta live here. But old gods use them to fight, and all lose power. So they agree to put angels high in clouds, and demons way underground. They make rules for game, rules we dunno. Then they make orc, and human, and elf. They used in big game, but no tell them rules. We know different god have different way to win big game. We know war not only way for any of 'em to win. And we know new gods join in game too when they get here."

A little hand went up.

"Yeah?"

The orc girl asked, innocently, "Why we have war if no need to?"

That's when I realized that I wasn't prepared for these questions.

Before I could answer, another little voice said, "If orc and human make half orc, what do orc and elf make?"

"Why you blow up middle of village?"

"Do we get test on all dis?"

Luckily, the schoolmarm stepped in. She said, "Hey, he not smart 'nuff for dese questions. He jus' talk about Panos."

I had just been put in the position of accepting being called an idiot, but at the same time I could avoid a lot of difficult questions. I was okay with that.

I continued, "Human mostly stay in plains, elf in forests, and orc in hills and swamps. Elf good at stealth and magic. Human at build stuff and talk to gods. Orc good at hunt and fight. Other race like wererat and halfling and stuff are magic or holy creations from old gods. Dey good at lotsa things."

I paused. I did decide to tackle one of the tougher questions. "You ask about war. People fight war for lotsa reason, not just gods. First huge war 900 years ago. Human fight elf for using too many trees to make stuff. Second war about 130 years ago. Orc fight elf over big holy war and someone kill wrong big important guy. Lotsa people die, real sad. Then new gods come along, and a little fight over dat. But since then, no real big wars between races."

Another little green hand went up. Just one.

Warily, I asked, "Yeah?"

"If war bad, why you kill Necromancer?"

The rest of the class was quiet this time. Dozens of young orcs looked at me for an answer.

I took a deep breath and said, "He was bad guy. He use dead people to try kill living people. All he want was do bad things for another dead guy named Harrington. Had to stop him to save village. Save you all."

Another voice piped up, "My daddy is a necromancer. You no hurt him, right?"

I stared at the small creature. "Your daddy not necromancer."

"Yeah-huh!"

I rolled my eyes a little and said, "Only smart orc can be necromancer."

I regretted the words as soon as they left my mouth. I had heard about theoretical research into time travel magic, and in that moment I wished that they were successful. Because I really needed to go back about three seconds and shut myself up.

The boy started crying. He said, "Mean Mister Stonebender call my daddy dumb!"

I felt the room turning against me. I quickly said, "No, no, your daddy can be smart without being smart orc! Uh, smart orc just mean… orc who use magic."

They weren't buying it.

"So we all dumb cuz we no use magic?"

"Well, Glorm's dad **is** kinda dumb…"

"He not necromancer either, he make fences."

"My daddy can beat up Mister Stonebender. Me go get him right now!"

"Me do magic too. Pull finger."

"I gotta pee!"

The half orc schoolmarm reached her limit. She shouted, "ALL YOU'S SHUT IT!"

The screaming, crying, and sniffling all came to a sudden halt.

The woman was clearly fuming at me, but there was a certain protocol that had to be followed apparently. "We go on break now. All thank Mister Stonebender before he leave."

"THANK YOU MISTER STONEBENDER!"

Despite the fact that around half of them hated me at this point, their unified and deafening gratitude shook the walls of the schoolroom. I beat a hasty retreat.

Ames and Mrs. Tasslewick were just outside the classroom, waiting for my exit. They grabbed me and quickly ushered me into the staff area before the mob of kids could isolate me in the hallway.

Once we were in the relative safety of the meeting hall, I breathed a sigh of relief. I was about to apologise for my performance when Mrs. Tasslewick made her assessment.

"That go real good. You come back in few weeks, talk to next class down. Use smaller word."

Ames' eyes were brimming with mischief. My mate said, "Oh, he'd be happy to."

I stared at the old schoolmarm in disbelief. I said, "But dey all wanna kill me!"

Mrs. Tasslewick snorted. She said, "Not all. And they no throw rocks or nothin'. Don't be big baby. It was good."

"I called that boy's dad dumb."

Her reply was immediate, "His dad **is** dumb."

Ames smoothly cut in, "Mrs. Tasslewick, many thanks for tea. Many thanks for let Sorch speak to kids. We come back soon."

Ames got a wet kiss on the cheek fur from the normally stern matron. I got a sharp incline of the head, indicating the direction the exit.

I made Ames scout the hallway for any adolescent ambushes. The kids apparently valued their recess time far more than petty revenge. We gathered our guard on the way out, and the three of us sought the safety of the streets.

The spear wielding orc looked around. Whatever he saw or didn't see was apparently enough for him to declare his job over. He wandered off without another word.

Ames nudged my ribs with an elbow. "So, still dreading the return to colder climates?"

I replied, "Let's get the hells out of here before that kid's dad finds me."

Chapter 7

"It's freezing and I hate you!"

I said, "Stop stealing Will's lines."

I did sympathize with my mate. Despite having a natural fur coat, Ames had no chance of being as warm as I was on this trip into the mountains. My Minor Polymorph spell was able to emulate traits from the Red Bark Beetle, specifically its incredible resistance to cold. My day consisted of getting cold for half an hour, casting Minor Polymorph, traveling in perfect comfort for well over an hour, cooling down again, and then breaking for lunch huddled around my magic pot. After lunch, I started the same cycle over again.

Having been successful in the exploration of water and earth based issues for two different guilds, Ames and I had been sent on a mission to the mountain plateau not too far from the Arcane University. Master Gideon, bundled up to a degree that only a were-wolf could realistically achieve, Teleported us to the highest point on the mountain that still retained any features whatsoever. The problem was: Everything above that elevation was so flat and white, so completely devoid of landmarks, that Teleporting there was impossible.

Gideon bid us a safe journey, and then bedded down so that he could Teleport back to the Arcane University after some rest and preparation. The were-wolf saved us an entire day's trek, easily. But even with this arcane aid, Ames and I were taking quite a long time reaching the flat mountain top. The good news was that the mountainside had a fairly well defined path; very little true mountain climbing needed to be done. The bad news was that the air became rather thin at this elevation. A hundred paces seemed like a thousand.

Still, we were on track to reach our destination before sunset. Whether or not the two of us would be able to accomplish anything constructive was a different story altogether. Max had saddled us with a difficult diplomatic task, to say the least.

Yetis. A race so reclusive, many folk believed them to be myth. The more seasoned mages of the Arcane University knew that the yetis were quite real, of course.

I thought back to what I had learned about the school's interaction with this race of ancient snow people. Before the Arcane Syphons started work on the school, the elves sought special permission from these stealthy mountain hunters to begin construction. They knew that their students would be living in the shadow of the yetis' traditional homeland, and preferred not to disrespect the reclusive but powerful creatures. After that first meeting, contact had been spotty at best. In more recent times, only the most informal and chance communications with the yetis took place.

Until now. For the first time in over 70 years, the Headmaster received an official communication from the yeti tribe situated on the nameless plateau above the school. The message said, simply: 'Mend what you have broken, or we will be forced to act.'

Ames and I were called into the Headmaster's office. It had been some time since I saw Max that agitated. He said that we were the perfect candidates to-

"Sorch. Sorch!"

Ames' strained voice snapped my attention back to the present. My mate's eyes were a little bit wild.

I murmured, "Sorry."

The were-cat grit their teeth. "You can't do that. You can't have one of your episodes right now. We aren't safe here."

"I know. I'm sorry."

That cold feline nose pressed against my cheek. "It's okay. Just concentrate. We'll take a break just before we get to the top."

True to my word, I maintained my concentration for the next hour or so. There was only one hard climb that required the gear. The rest of the time was spent slogging up a steep, icy, miserable incline. My second and last Minor Polymorph of the day expired, and I was soon far colder than Ames. But well before the sun would disappear for the day, we made it to the mostly flat top of the mountain.

A small indentation in the mountainside seemed like a good place to warm up and prepare for our diplomatic encounter. It was only a couple of paces deep and a couple of paces tall and wide, but that simply meant less space to heat. I set down my cooking pot, touched it, and said the word: "Blaze." The two of us huddled together under a blanket as the pot started to radiate heat. Towards the end of its hour long cycle we would likely make some tea, but for the moment, we would just enjoy the warmth.

I must have drifted off, and Ames was apparently happy to let me sleep. My mate had suspicions that my 'episodes' were the product of unhealthy sleep patterns. As a result, Ames would come up with any excuse to allow me to take a nap. The journals that I was sharing with Benno showed that the extra sleep was having no impact. But I didn't tell the feline that. I loved a good nap.

By the time I was being shaken awake, our tiny cave was tolerably warm.

"Tea?" asked Ames.

I nodded, and moved to fill the pot from my waterskin. But I nearly dropped it when a voice from outside the indentation said, "When you are done with your tea, please let us know. We would like you to come with us. We shall wait."

Neither Ames nor I had heard anything prior to that voice. If we needed proof that yetis were masters of stealth within their element, we now had that proof.

Ames called out, "We can come with you now, if you like?"

There was a brief pause. Then that same, very calm voice answered, "We have discussed this, and it is our consensus that small things should be allowed to absorb and consume as much heat as possible before coming out into the cold. Partake of your tea, little ones. We shall wait."

I shook my head, hardly believing that this conversation was taking place. I made a black pekoe tea with lots of sugar, just something to give

Ames and myself caffeine and energy. We drank it down quickly, cooled down the pot, and then packed our blankets and gear for travel.

I was the first to poke my head out of our little hidey hole. Sure enough, three massive, shaggy white creatures were crouched on the path outside of our shelter. Each carried what looked like a crystalline spear. The tallest of the three, easily my height and half that again, also carried what looked like a dead goat. I guess their hunt had gone well.

The leader, or at least the one who was speaking for the group, looked down at us with those pupilless red-brown eyes. She said, "We are glad that you have made the journey. This gathering of yetis could be considered a patrol, or a small hunting unit. We serve as both. We shall escort you to our tribal leader. You will call the tribal leader 'Divine' unless you have a reason not to do so, in which case we will ask you to explain that reason."

Their manner of speech was making my head swim a little bit. Or maybe it was the rust colored eyes, which seemed damned near hypnotic. I said, "Ummm, yes, we will follow you. And we'll call your leader Divine."

"We are pleased."

The trek was a cold one. We spent the better part of an hour walking through the shallow snow. The wind was biting, bitterly cold. If it weren't for the two big yeti bodies in front of us serving as a windbreak, it would have been far worse.

Finally, we arrived at our destination. Despite the plateau being flat, I for one would not have seen the village until I was almost right on top of it. That was because the buildings were made of virtually clear ice. I had no idea how they kept the snow from sticking to the structures and marring the wonderful illusion. Even Ames, a native of the region, was stunned by the achievement. The tribe members were white inside a sea of white. The fur of polar bears and winter rabbits made up the majority of the yetis' carpeting and bedding. There was likely some measure of illusionary magic at work as well. The combined effect of all this: The yetis wouldn't be found unless they **wished** to be found.

As our escort led the two of us into the populated area of the plateau, I saw one of the massive yetis simply disappear into the ground. I whipped my head around just in time to see something that I found comfortingly familiar: A dugout. The truth was, not everything that the yetis used was white or perfectly camouflaged. They just chose to hide the more visible objects underground. I caught a glimpse of some kind of distillery and a cooking surface before the white trapdoor was maneuvered back into place.

We walked through their town of ice and fur until we reached what could only be described as their 'palace'. It was twice the size of any other structure, with extra rooms and beds (all lined in white fur of course) as well as a large reception hall with yeti-sized chairs all in a circle. In one of those yeti-sized chairs was a yeti.

As we walked inside, I noticed that the floor was very firm; some kind of white slate or shale that I had never seen before. Then I felt a wave of heat wash over my frozen green skin. I gasped in relief. Even Ames looked happy with the climate change.

Our escort stopped in the foyer. The speaking yeti said, "We must process the bounty of the hunt. Divine is just over there, in the meeting chamber. Can you see her little ones? She is the only yeti seated in the room to your West."

I knew that it might just be their manner of conversation, but I couldn't help but feel like we were being treated like idiot children. I must have had 'that look' on my face, because a were-cat paw was swiftly clamped over my mouth before I could voice my sarcastic reply.

Ames said, "We do see Divine, and we would like to thank you for being a courteous and capable escort."

The three gave us a shallow bow, and then loped back out into the cold.

Once unmuzzled, I whispered harshly to Ames, "And they went away. Can you see that little one? There are three yetis. One, two, three. And they are walking."

The feline waited patiently until I got that out of my system. "Are you done now?"

I grunted and nodded.

We walked into the next room, passing through a large archway in the transparent wall. There was some kind of crystal or clear glass brazier on the floor directly in the center of the ring of chairs. It was quite compact, standing just a few inches off of the ground. But it radiated wonderful waves of warmth.

The seated yeti said, "Greetings. My name is Divine. I would like to extend our hospitality to the two of you. How that hospitality will take form is threefold: Firstly, we have raised the temperature within the palace so as to provide for your immediate physical comfort. Secondly, when the remainder of our hunting and gathering parties have returned to this town, we will offer you sustenance in the form of multiple types of foods as well as fresh water. Thirdly, I personally would like to extend an invitation to the both of you, an invitation to rest in any of the chairs that you see before you. If your preference is the chair that I am currently occupying, please inform me and I shall relocate."

It suddenly dawned on me that we might be here forever.

Ames and I thanked our hostess, and chose the two oversized seats directly across from her so that conversation would be easier. Our legs dangled off the ground. I suppose we **did** look like children to them, to be fair.

Ames took the lead once again, saying, "I am Ames, and this is my companion and mate, Sorch. We thank you for your hospitality. Your use of the warming device, in particular, is both welcome and considerate."

"Ah, yes, that is a heating brazier. Please maintain half a pace in distance, as the flame burns clear and is almost impossible to see if one is distracted."

I raised my brows. "Wood alcohol? That explains the stills."

Divine's huge head tilted. She said, "You are more intelligent than the average small one. I will attempt to modify my interaction to allow for more complex concepts."

I sighed with relief. I said, "That would be greatly appreciated. We're here on behalf of the Arcane University. Headmaster Max received a note from your people that might be described as 'alarming'. We would like to address your concerns."

The yeti's deep, red-brown eyes regarded me in silence for a few moments. Then Divine said, "I am pleased that the missive conveyed a sense of alarm, little one. Alarm is the proper sentiment to convey, and the proper attitude to have, for the events currently happening around us. Should it escalate into a show of force, it would be to everyone's misfortune. Though, I would estimate, particularly to the misfortune of those who are smaller and less able to care for themselves in such a harsh environment."

Ames glanced over at me. Neither of us had ever been threatened so politely.

Divine decided that a different tack needed to be taken. She said, "I believe I have a story that correctly illustrates the current situation, if you will allow me some latitude so that I might draw an interesting and informative parallel?"

Ames said, "Uhhh. Sure, go for it."

"This is a tale of my uncle. His name was Clever. Many years in the past, Uncle Clever found a vein of emerald in a location that we now refer to as the 'old city'. Emerald is useful for crafting tools, for making magic, and for the rare occasion that we find ourselves bartering. Our people started to mine the stone. As years passed, our mining delved deeper into the earth. This eventually roused creatures that we call 'the demons in stone'. These stone demons were not our enemies, but our activities were disturbing them. We dispatched those demons that attacked us, but my uncle called into question the entire process. Though the emerald was valuable, the unknown factors were mounting. We had not researched all of the dangers that we were encountering. We were likely to encroach upon the territory of more creatures with whom we had no quarrel. So we paused our progress to assess the impact that we were having. Uncle Clever took all of the input that the wisest of our people had to offer. And then he shut down the mine. His reasoning was that if the cost would be making enemies and potentially bringing about our own destruction because we were unwilling or unable to research the consequences, then that cost was too high."

I commented, "Your Uncle Clever sounds like a great man. Is he still around these parts?"

"Yes. You are sitting on him."

I nearly jumped out of my chair in alarm. Instead I half stood and glanced down at the fluffy lining of the giant seat. Yeti fur.

Divine said, "Nothing goes to waste here. He would have considered it a great honor."

I nodded, and then slowly settled my weight back down onto Uncle Clever.

The yeti leader said, "Sorch. Ames."

"Yes?"

"You have delved too deep."

My mate asked, "Divine, may I ask: Is this in reference to a specific act, or just a general trend amongst the 'little people'?"

Divine nodded approval at the were-cat's question. "It is a specific act, I am sure. The issue is that said specific act has not yet been discovered. The world of Panos needs you to examine all of the potential causes for the recent and dramatic changes in the environment around us."

I returned the nod. "We are."

Divine seemed surprised by my reply. She asked, "Are you?"

I launched into a story of my own. With Ames' help, I illustrated not only our own recent adventures that delved into these mysteries, but the efforts of the major guilds and governments.

At the end of our tales, Divine murmured, "Well it seems that even in the height of summer, there are times when the bright eye blinks."

I had no idea what that meant. "I'm sorry?"

Louder, the yeti said, "It is a saying. It means that sometimes even the most intractable of beings can find some measure of compromise."

Ames leapt on that opening, saying, "Our crops are dying. Cities are flooding. There are incidents of violence as a result, both mundane and arcane. We want to solve this crisis as well."

Divine said, "I am pleased to hear that efforts are already being made to correct these issues. Allow me to express the specific incidents that we have witnessed. You can add our experiences to those that the smaller folk have reported, and perhaps come to a more informed conclusion and take action."

The yeti held up a large, fuzzy finger, as in if telling us to wait a moment. With her other hand, she directed five white digits towards the clear brazier in the center of our chair circle. Then the big creature murmured an incantation that I never heard before. Suddenly the fire was visible, flickering.

But it was more than that. As Divine spoke, the flames formed images. They kept pace with the details of her tale, providing visual cues that included faces, numbers, and what could only be described as artistic impressions of her story.

"In the last five years, our tribe has not grown. And yet, we are using over twenty percent more fuel. We are having to send out nearly double the number of hunters and scavengers to deal with the sudden scarcity of food and relative lack of natural growth near the mountain. In short, we cannot sustain this pace or lifestyle for much longer."

The yeti's pupilless eyes turned from the fire to regard each of us in turn. She said, "We believe that air elementals and ice quasi-elementals are to blame, in whole or in part, for the harsh cold that we are experiencing."

Looking back into the fire so as to shift the scene to that of yetis searching the mountainside, the tribal leader said, "There is some evidence of this elemental activity, but only in the aftermath. We only know that, after reviewing our own behaviours, we cannot account for this sudden hostility. In other words, we did not provoke it, nor did any natural phenomenon that we can detect. Our priests, our mages, and our rangers have all made attempts to divine a local cause. But all signs point towards a more global issue."

The illusion in the fire shifted from a beautiful if vague depiction of Panos, to a large number of yetis with overstuffed packs on their backs. Divine said, "We are in the process of finding a new home. Even if the cause of these issues were immediately found and reversed, the local wildlife and flora would not recover in time for us to utilize them as resources. But this issue will eventually follow us, of that we are certain. So we would like to stop this elemental aggression. Though we do not know where we shall be when, or if, that happens."

The image in the fire flickered and died.

I was saying it even before I could consider the implications. I was saying it before Ames could stop me, before I could stop me.

"We have a new location for your people."

The look that Ames gave me was disbelief. Perhaps panic as well. Almost certainly with a hint of exasperation mixed in there somewhere.

By contrast, Divine simply tilted her head. "Have you, little one?"

With the same level of compulsion as I experienced at the undersea altar, I started speaking and couldn't stop. I was relating something that didn't seem like my own idea. I wasn't even certain that I was using my own voice.

"There's an area around two miles from the Arcane University. It is heavily wooded along the outskirts, but clear towards the center. The southern exposure is backed up to a cliff face. We have no claim to it. Nobody does. I believe it would be ideal for your people."

Ames said, "Divine, we have not discussed this with anyone, perhaps yo-"

But the yeti silenced the were-cat with a question as cold and as pointed as an icicle.

"Who are you right now?"

I found myself replying, "It doesn't matter."

Divine insisted, "This mortal is not your priest. You have no claim here. Who are you?"

"Someone that I cannot be. Someone who under no circumstances should be talking to you."

The yeti insisted, "Then why? I must know if I am to trust your words."

My mouth was moving again, and I had no idea why. Someone used my voice to say, "Because the rules were bent. And they cannot be mended until they are first broken."

Divine offered two words, phrased as a question, "The Bargain?"

"The Bargain."

Ames hissed, "Whoever you are, why are you using Sorch?"

'My' reply was immediate, fierce, "He was **mine** before he was ever yours, creature."

And just like that, the compulsion was gone. I slumped in my ridiculously oversized chair.

After the long silence that followed, Divine said, "I believe... we should take our meal together now."

And that's exactly what we did. A yeti that we hadn't met yet dropped off a wrapped animal skin, still steaming. The fare wasn't fancy, but it was warm and packed with the kind of fatty nutrition required in this climate. Rabbit meat, roasted pine nuts, and a warm salad of crispy yellow beans that I had never seen before.

After the meal, the other two were kind enough not to ask me questions that I could provide no answer to. Instead, we discussed the outstanding issues. When Ames asked if the tribe would consider working with the Arcane University to discover the source of these disturbances, encamping in the valley near University grounds, Divine said she would talk to her people.

The yeti said, "I do not distrust the source of this suggestion. Nor do I trust it. The priests and shamans will determine the veracity and viability of what has been proposed. But assuming this is the path forward, you would be surprised at how quickly and easily we can relocate. Objects, even those as heavy as the stones we use for our flooring and those as delicate as the distilleries we use for our fuel, can be transported downhill rapidly, and in bulk. It is possible. And more importantly, it is possible in the short term. Once we are situated, it would be our solemn duty to aid in your efforts."

Ames looked as relieved as I felt.

Divine tilted her head again, which seemed to be a catchall expression of consideration, surprise, and amusement. She said, "I am quite encouraged that you little ones have been taking this situation so seriously. If our records are accurate, and I have no reason to believe that they are inaccurate, then this may be one of the most satisfactory responses to one of our inquiries or requests in the last four hundred years."

I didn't really know what to say to that. So I went with, "Great!"

The yeti seemed disappointed with my brevity. Nonetheless, she said, "Darkness is upon us. Little ones should not descend in the darkness, no matter how keen your racially enhanced sight may be. The darkness brings bitter cold, which is a danger that shouldn't be underestimated. Stay the night, we will see you off at dawn."

Our rest was comfortable, if brief. At the crack of dawn, our escort was ready to see us off. They seemed to be confused when we told them that we were heading to the point where the plateau became a sheer cliff face. It wasn't a very long journey, compared to what we had been through the day before. When we verified that this was the concave facing of the plateau, we thanked our escorts. They bowed slightly, as a unit, and then departed without a word.

Ames peered down at the insanely long drop. "You're sure about this? I have the ring as a backup if something goes wrong."

I assured my mate, "I've done it before."

The cat considered, "You might be about to become the fastest moving orc in the history of Panos. I'm not sure if I would set the record for were-cats, however."

I said, "You would be surprised at how were-cats can be transported downhill rapidly, and in bulk. It is possible. And more importantly, it is possible in the short term!"

The feline stared at me. "So this is the game we're playing now. We're taking yeti quotes out of context."

"We are."

Ames smiled at me. Toothily. Sweetly. Dangerously. "In bulk you said? Are you calling me fat?"

"N-no dear. That is to say-"

But it was too late. The were-cat had already shoved me over the edge of the cliff.

It took a couple of thrilling, terrifying seconds for my mate to catch up to me as we fell down the mountainside. Ames was facing straight down, like a diver that was planning their entry for the water below. I was far less graceful, cutting through the air like a plummeting elk.

With a margin of safety in mind, I cast the Soft Fall spell on Ames. Any drain that I would have felt was overcome by the pounding of blood in my ears. Absurdly, I felt my Amulet of Enhanced Enchanting attune to the spell, as it was the first enchantment that I had cast that morning. The cat suddenly started to drift like a feather, and disappeared into the air above me.

As the trees below grew larger in my vision, I invoked my second Soft Fall spell. My downward momentum was arrested suddenly, efficiently, and not painfully thank all the gods.

My mate and I drifted towards the forest below, mentally preparing for the long hike ahead of us. I was also preparing for the report I would have to make when we got back to the Arcane University. Frankly, I wasn't sure how Max was going to react when he was told that my body had been used by a voice that wasn't my own. In a way I wanted to keep it from Max, and from Benno, and from anyone else who might worry or overreact. But the fate of Panos might be at stake. Now wasn't the time to withhold.

I heard Ames call from far above, "Try to find a level spot, I'll follow you in."

I wasn't going to be too picky. Like everything else in my life at that moment, I was just hoping for a soft landing.

Chapter 8

It was breakfast time at 'The Spastic Vole', and I had no idea where my son had gotten off to.

In my defense, it would have been difficult to pick a two headed giant out of this crowd, never mind an orc. The restaurant was packed to the brim. Oddly, time of day wasn't the primary factor for when the Vole would be crowded. Certainly we saw a surge of folks at dinner time, but we were far more populated whenever a caravan arrived. The flood of drivers and guards was likely due to several weeks on the road with the same preserved food and no… intimate companionship.

In this case, the crowd was from multiple sources. The left side of the room was filled with rowdy caravaneers filling their bellies with ale. The restaurant, where Ames and I were currently seated, was host to those brave souls who just finished their night shifts in Ice House. So it was perfectly reasonable, given the chaos, that my son wandered off unnoticed in this bar and brothel.

Luckily, we owned a high percentage of the place, so Benno couldn't get into too much trouble. He sometimes took shifts in the kitchen, and with the rush of drinkers and diners, it was quite possible that the head chef drafted him for a while. My son's Invisible Servants could wash dishes, mop floors, and provide a much needed break for the overtaxed staff.

Ames saw me looking around again. The feline said, "He's fine. He also knows the charter better than you do at this point. I need your head right here." My mate tapped the small pile of documents that represented our next contract with the Adventurer's Guild. I grumbled, but went back to reading.

The date on the charter was late fall, 2720. That meant finals at the Arcane University were over, which was why Benno was able to join us once again. Reports from his professors were very positive. He was clearly the top student in his age bracket, and arguably the best young mage in the entire Arcane University other than Leeson. But my boy caught the adventuring bug, and he was very likely to test out next year in favor of a life on the road. I had objections to that plan, but I kept them to myself. Mostly.

When Toby and Tara reached out to us about a Guild charter taking place in Ice House itself, we jumped on the opportunity. Not just because the entire family was available, but because the minotaurs had some explaining to do. Ames was put in charge, as the were-cat had the most free time leading up to the event. A gathering was called, and I was supposed to have read through the mission details well before now. But there was an enchantment that I was trying to perfect, using that lovely stone boat that Celestial created for me a couple of years ago. The last attempt might have taken. I would know in a few weeks.

I shook my head to clear it, wanting to concentrate on the pages in front of me. I mostly succeeded. I had at least skimmed through the text by the time our big friends walked through the door. We stood as the minotaurs made their way through the crowd. Ames and I both received big, smothering hugs from our friends before being allowed to sit again. We already requested a pair of large, reinforced chairs for two of the Vole's most popular investors.

Ames asked, "Who's watching the little one?"

Toby rumbled, "My wayward wererat apprentice was late to training. Again. He's got babysitting duty until further notice."

I blinked a couple of times at this news. I was all for breaking racial molds but I had to ask, "A wererat paladin? How is that working out?"

My bovine friend snorted. "He's amazingly devout. Just a bit scattered. And somewhat small of course, but there's something to be said for speed over sheer physical presence. His blade and buckler work is something to witness. But that lad is a story for another time, I think. We should order food and discuss more important matters."

Ames poked me in the ribs, pointedly. "Such as." the feline prompted.

"Oh right. Such as Sorch's Salt Company."

Tara's eyes brightened at the mention of her favorite side project. "Oh, you'll be happy to know that we've done very well in our first half year.

We're easily paying back our share of the loans for the new road."

Toby jumped into the fray, his voice just as eager as his wife's. "We've broken into several new markets. The Southern Tribes of course, but also United Diben, Tatertown, and were going to have the stock to service our friends in Royal Moffit soon enough."

Before we could get a word in edgewise, Tara was speaking again. "We've negotiated a discounted rate with the Transportation Guild as part of our recently signed de-icing contracts covering areas around the colder Circles of Transport."

"And the advertising has been-"

Before Toby could launch into whatever enthusiastic progress had been on the advertising front, I shouted over him, "Why didn't you tell us about this company?!"

Toby and Tara looked at each other, clearly confused.

The cleric asked Toby, "Did you send out the first investor report?"

The paladin shook his head. He said, "I thought we were going to combine it with the inception documents. Did we send those out?"

There was a moment of silence as the copper dropped.

Toby cleared his throat. As contritely as the minotaur's silky smooth bass voice allowed, our friend murmured, "Ames, Sorch. We apologise sincerely for the mix up. Yourselves, Rick, and Will should have been kept up to date in a much more efficient manner. All five of us are equal owners in the company, and of course your input is important to us."

Tara's voice was low and somber, "It was likely my fault. With the baby and all, I didn't keep the records and missives as organized as I should have. From the bottom of my heart, I apologise."

Seeing how their expressions fell, Ames immediately let our friends off the hook. We didn't want a shower of minotaur tears before our meal. The were-cat said, "Don't worry about it. It sounds like you're doing an excellent job managing things. Nothing for minotaurs to weep over, we trust you both implicitly. Just make sure to get word to Will and Rick?

With their business taking off like it is, they're going to be relying on your management skills for this salt thing."

The minotaurs promised to get a tidy summary together for everyone, and arrange a get together in Limt. Shortly after, our sugar and honey rolls arrived, and breakfast orders were taken. I ordered Benno's favorite in his absence, scrambled eggs with sharp cheddar. I was confident that the lad would show up when food was at stake.

As we waited for our food, the four of us went over the mission that the Guild laid out. An abandoned section of the eastern caves had been the source of recent disturbances. The first reported victim of these incidents was a surveyor from the local snake farming company. The halfling told his boss that he was going to see if this location was suitable for their expansion plans. He was never heard from again. His disappearance was reported, but the guard thought that he might have simply left town. The next week a couple of shady humans, who would normally have nothing to do with the law, wandered into City Hall. They looked stunned, and efforts had to be made to pry their story from numb lips. Apparently, two of their companions wandered too close to the mouth of the very same cave. They said 'huge red hands' reached out from the shadows and abducted their friends. There was some kind of surge of heat, then sizzling, and then terrified screams.

The city guard shut down the two paths leading to these caverns and kept watch. They reported 'strange and dire' sounds coming from that direction, though there were no further sightings of anything. That was just a few days ago.

The four of us agreed on preparations and a general plan of action, to be executed this afternoon. Soon after, our food and drink arrived.

I glanced around, a little irritated now. "Where is that kid? His eggs are going to get cold."

Ames mentioned, casually, "I think they wanted him up on stage."

Tara and Toby both chuckled, but continued to eat. Neither of them seemed to think anything was odd about that.

My reaction was different.

"WHAT?!"

People from nearby tables glanced over at the crazy, overly loud orc that just knocked over his chair in the process of standing up so quickly. I would have done the same, if that orc wasn't me.

I brushed aside the heavy wool curtains that separated the dining room from the stage area. I wasn't entirely sure what my plan was, but I'd be damned if my son was going to be lewd in front of a bunch of strangers. Maybe I would storm up there and put a stop to things before they went too far.

Sadly, they had already gone too far.

There are some things that a father hopes to never see. I can attest that one of those things is catching an eyeful of your orcish son. Particularly when he was pole dancing for a cheering audience in all his naked glory. And quite clearly, demonstrably, enjoying it.

I quickly turned on my heel and proceeded back through the dividing curtains. With mechanical precision, I righted my chair and sat back down. My mind must have shut down for a while, because the next thing that I remember, Ames was waving a fuzzy paw in front of my eyes.

"Sorch. Come back to us Sorch. Breathe."

I reached out with a shaking hand to grasp my mug of cider. Half of it was gone in one pull.

Ames' expression was somewhere between concerned, smug, and amused. "I guess he never told you that he danced. This is far from the first time."

I saw motion out of the corner of my eye. It was Tara and Toby. Both nodding.

I know I didn't make much sense when I said, "So all of you... he's been up there and... why didn't you stop him?"

The other three glanced at each other. It was Tara who spoke up, "He's a grown man Sorch. I've been up there, and Ames of course. Although unlike your mate, my performance stops when the music does."

I looked to Ames, jaw working silently.

The were-cat rolled their eyes. "No, he doesn't take clients backstage." Then a pause. "At least I don't think he has. If he has I'm going to tan his hide."

I felt a little bit relieved that Ames was drawing the line somewhere.

Until the feline finished the thought, "The house gets a cut when the dancers bed clients, and I haven't seen a copper from him."

I looked around the table for some modicum of support. Toby was smiling silently. I would get no sympathy from him.

Everyone else went back to eating, apparently thinking that there was nothing more to discuss. After my fatherly meltdown, I realized that I didn't have a leg to stand on. Not only was Benno his own man, but he wasn't doing anything that Ames hadn't done. And I 'approved' of the were-cat's activities, or at least accepted them. The only question left was why Benno omitted the pole dancing from any of our conversations; and frankly my recent display probably answered that question well enough.

Suddenly Toby started laughing. Tara asked him why.

"I just thought of a horrible joke involving Benno's eggs getting cold."

Everyone else started giggling. I ordered another drink.

As we finished our meals, I contemplated all of the parenting advice that I picked up over the last couple of years. I knew that it was important to set a good example for my son, and to let him know that I would do things differently. Then again, Benno would also be using Ames as an example of acceptable behaviour, and clearly the two of us held differing opinions on this particular matter. It was a moral quandary. After some somber meditation, I believe that I came up with the best course of action:

I would forget what I saw and never, ever speak of it again.

We used the next few hours to make preparations. According to the letter of the law, we needed to seek the mayor's permission to enter an area of the caves that had been deemed off limits. We also wanted to make sure that the Order of the Snow was aware of our activities. Should something go wrong, it was important that the matter wasn't simply dropped, particularly when the safety of Ice House's citizens might be at stake. Benno, Toby, and Ames went off to do those things.

Tara and I went to the main offices of Serpentine Services, the snake farming company that lost one of their scouts. The human in charge granted us an audience immediately. He said that Sam was always cautious and well prepared. He was a family man, and not prone to stupid risks. The human shared the halfling's preliminary maps and reports, filed just a day before he disappeared.

Tara thanked the man, and then we made our way through the East Gate, entering the caves in the eastern mountains bordering Ice House. Unlike the West Gate, which was a series of caverns filled with corporate merchants and seedy rogues, the East Gate seemed almost boring. Everything was well signed and organized. I suppose when a city's food production was at stake, the government was bound to get involved. The merchants here were primarily dealing in mushrooms, tubers, mosses, cave fish, and snake meat. A far cry from the gemstones, poisons, and exotic weaponry found in the western caves.

With that in mind, I was still impressed by the sheer scope of operations. Even in the early afternoon, the East Gate saw tremendous foot traffic. Business owners, families, government officials, and tourists were welcome to wander the main and side caverns in search of ingredients for tonight's dinner, or perhaps that perfect little snakeskin purse. It was a fairly peaceful place for people of all races to get their daily shopping done.

Which made it far more alarming, of course, that three people were murdered just a couple hundred paces down a little side passage.

We regrouped at the temporary barricade that had been set up by the city watch. At our arrival, Toby handed over the signed declaration from the mayor.

He said, "There you go gentlemen. The mayor, in cooperation with the Adventurer's Guild, has given us permission to examine these passages, eliminate any threat, and claim bounty on any coin or goods that are not clearly identifiable as items reported stolen in the last year. The Order of the Snow thanks you for your understanding and continued service."

As if to lend extra weight to his words, every link of chainmail and every square inch of the paladin's buckler seemed to shine, even in the dim torchlight. Now I remembered why we usually let Toby do the talking.

The older human guard reviewed the papers briefly, but seemed inclined to take the minotaur at his word either way. "O' course, sir paladin. Might I say, good ta see ya out an' about again sir. You'll find th' site just round the bend, then 30 paces on. Happy 'unting, sir."

The three watchmen stood up straight and snapped a smart salute to Toby as he passed. I wasn't surprised. My friend commanded this level of respect even before his world-saving exploits, and his renown in Ice House had only grown over the years.

The rest of us earned a couple of respectful nods in passing. The cloak of Toby's esteem even covered his were-cat and orc friends, it seemed.

A Light cantrip on Toby's shield and another on Tara's belt buckle gave us a clear view of the passageway. The gray stone floor had been worn smooth by centuries of trickling water. According to the halfling surveyor's initial research, this area used to serve as drainage for the rest of the cave system. The fact that it dried up somewhat over the past twenty years was one of the primary reasons that the snake meat company was considering making a bid on the larger cave beyond. It all made sense.

But nothing prepared us for the rapid internal climate change we were experiencing. Within ten paces, the air went from cool and slightly damp to warm and bone dry. By the time we reached the mouth of the large cavern in question, I felt like I was baking in the summer sun on the coast of Eastern Hook. Unless there had been a surge of magma just below this area, the heat was completely out of place.

Then again, so was the wall of skulls.

I think it's safe to say that none of us were prepared for what we saw when we turned to enter the large cavern that was the target of our investigation. A barrier made mostly of skulls stretched across the center of the far side of the chamber. It was impossible to see what was being used as the cement holding the macabre wall together, at least from this range. But the variety of skulls that were on horrific display was just staggering. Everything from the tiniest rat head all the way up to the craniums of some sort of giants had been used as macabre construction material. The majority of them were burnt or bleached, but a few stood out as being more 'fresh'. The fresh ones seemed to be humanoid in size and shape. The smell of rotting and charred flesh was hair curling.

We slowly made our way towards the bone barrier. Our Light cantrips were casting massive shadows over the far wall as the eight pace wide, two pace high structure blocked our vision. Tara and Toby took up positions at either side of the wall, and then quickly turned the corner with shields raised.

"All clear."

The rest of us followed our minotaur companions. The wall hadn't been sheltering anyone or anything at that moment. It simply hid a massive fracture in the earth. Rough, overly large steps of stone had been created within an unnatural looking fissure in the cave floor. Heat emanated from the crack, and with it a faint red glow and the scent of sulphur.

Benno asked, "Did we just find a portal to one of the hells?"

I said, with some certainty, "No. The demons are much deeper."

Behind me, I heard Ames say the word, "Ceramic."

We turned to see what the feline was talking about. Sharp claws ran over the surface of the bone wall, focusing on the material holding it all together. The were-cat stated, "This is ceramic. Clay was caked all around and then baked in place, in order to hold all of these skulls. Something incredibly hot and somewhat portable made this."

Grimly, I turned away from the wall to look down at the primitive stairway, built with something the size of minotaurs in mind rather than puny orcs. I said, "We need to go down there."

Tara nodded slowly. "When the reports mentioned the surges of heat, I prayed for the blessing of Elemental Resistance. But I can only cover two people."

Toby said, without hesitation, "Yourself and Ames."

The cleric and rogue protested, but Toby was having none of it.

"Love, if you fall, our ability to recover from wounds is severely hampered. And Ames... you're in the front line and covered in fur. Be serious, of course you need it more than the rest of us."

The feline grit their teeth as if biting back a retort, but couldn't argue with the big paladin's wisdom.

Tara sighed, but acquiesced. "I'll apply the blessing when we get a hint of something up ahead."

The five of us made our way down the steps. Tara and Toby could accomplish this standing, while the rest of us had to use hands, legs, and butts as in if we were three years old and using stairs for the first time.

The cavern below was twisted, radiant. There was certainly enough headroom for everyone. Whatever force or effort was used to make this passageway, one could not call it 'subtle'. It was easily four paces wide and three high at all times, with sections that seemed to simply melt away into little alcoves and pits. Places where the wall was more pitted and deformed were the greatest sources of heat. Something was behind these walls; within them. Something with an affinity for fire.

Ames said, "There's movement up ahead. I'm hearing it above a very slight background noise."

Tara sounded irritated, voice significantly raised as if having to speak over something, "Slight? It's damn near deafening."

Toby was nodding, eyes squinted to slits as if he might start crying at any time. He said, "Like screaming bone sliding over moaning rock. I can't hear myself think."

Ames glanced over at the rest of the family. The were-cat admitted, "It's not nearly so loud for me."

I said, "Let's move. No need to expose ourselves for longer than necessary."

We pushed deeper into the twisted furnace of tunnels, our minotaurs looking less and less happy with each minute that passed. They didn't need to tell us that we were spiraling down; the declines were unsubtle at times, causing our smaller party members to slide somewhat as we descended.

Benno stopped us as we were about to round the next bend. He said, "Something is cooking. Do you smell that?"

Ames confirmed it, "Weapons ready."

The were-cat drew their well polished hand crossbow and Tara took up her notched cudgel. Then I watched the process that comforted me the most. Toby rolled his massive shoulders, then craned his beefy neck to one side until it made a faint popping sound. Then the Axe of McGrondle was unslung from my large friend's back. Knowing that the impeccably well armed and armored minotaur was on our side was always a huge morale boost.

Tara touched Ames' shoulder and started murmuring her prayer. There was no visible aura, but clearly some sort of sensation went through the feline: My mate's fur started to puff out and stand on end. The same happened for Tara upon the self-application of the blessing, though with her drastically shortened fur it was harder to see. Thusly prepared, we rounded the corner with bad intentions.

What I saw wasn't even close to one of the scenarios that I had imagined.

Instead of crazed cultists, demonic servitors, or fire elementals, there were giants. But not the giants that one might read about in lore. They were mutated, deformed. Perhaps cursed. These creatures were red skinned, looking like they were covered in a series of large infected blisters. Each giant sported a single eye in the center of their heads. Their hands and feet sported a seemingly random number of digits between three and six.

And they were cooking one of their own.

It wasn't even as dignified or formal as a stew pot. The four remaining creatures had simply dug into a wall to expose whatever was causing this intense heat, and then wedged their former-companion into the crack. Parts were torn from the unfortunate (but tender) creature as his brethren became peckish. Evidence of the cannibalistic feasting was strewn all over the cavern floor.

"Cyclopes." said Benno. Apparently his studies had paid off. It didn't seem like any of the rest of us knew what we were facing.

Ames asked, "Suggestions?"

"Uhhh, they look like fire cyclopes so... don't use fire?"

Then again, maybe education was overrated.

I didn't have time to ponder the merits of my son's University education. The four deformed giants charged at our front line. Two of them held massive bone clubs, while the other two preferred bare fists. I wasn't sure that their choice of weapon really mattered. At Toby's height plus half again, they could do severe damage or even crush us with any solid blow. As the mutants closed, an additional wave of oppressive heat flooded the area. Breathing was difficult now, the air so hot as to be painful.

Ames fired the hand crossbow, and caught the unarmed lead giant in the left shoulder. It wasn't a telling wound, but it did manage to stagger the giants' charge somewhat, allowing us to adjust our tactics. Ames let the crossbow dangle from its strap, instead drawing that somewhat battered short sword for the inevitable melee.

I felt the touch of Benno's fingertips on my wrist. We had our own language for situations like this, one only possible because of the near-instantaneous nature of his psychic communication. A series of short and what would otherwise be nonsensical sounds traveled between our minds. And with that I knew his targets, and communicated my ability to support him. In unison, our palms were held out and we were chanting.

Tara and Ames shifted over to face the unarmed fire cyclopes. With the Elemental Resistance blessing, they wouldn't be scalded by the touch of the giants, and could get in close without suffering burns. Toby forced one of the two club wielding creatures to face him. The last fire cyclops came around wide, attempting to charge the two pesky orcs making strange noises.

My Force Bolt struck a fraction of a second before Benno's. With such a large target coming right at me, I could hardly miss the creature's knee. While still absorbing that impact, Benno's own Force Bolt struck the cyclops' opposite ankle. There was a faint cracking sound before we were nearly deafened by the creature's pained bellow. It fell gracelessly, one ankle twisting at an unnatural angle as our coordinated attack took it down.

Within our front line, Ames was faring best. I had never seen the feline be quite so aggressively mobile. Rather than dance about and poke at the swinging fists of their opponent, my mate sought to land far more solid blows. After a nimble dodge to the left that was partnered with a painful slash across the giant's knuckles, the were-cat dove forward. Coming up from their acrobatic roll, Ames stabbed upward, short sword piercing the thigh muscles of the cyclops. It attempted to sit on the cat, but the feline was already moving to the outside, leaving a gruesome open wound along the back of the giant's leg.

Tara wasn't faring as well. She seemed distracted. The cyclops' fist battered against her large shield, leaving the minotaur bruised and winded. But the aggression was met with equal force. As tears of rage coursed down the cleric's cheeks, she smashed at the larger creature's wrist and forearm, bashing away like a crazed carpenter. The result was that both of them had numb arms with painful welts and bruises.

Toby was also wearing a wet mask of rage, but his encounter was far more surgical. The giant bone club met the Axe of McGrondle and came to a swift stop. Deep grooves quickly accumulated in the dry white femur. The fire cyclops screamed in frustration and surged forward, flailing at Toby's axe and buckler. The only actual damage done was by proximity: That oppressive heat was scalding the minotaur's flesh and shriveling his golden brown fur.

The downed cyclops chose me as the target for his rage, scrambling forward on hands and knees with alarming strength and fortitude. This was good news for Benno, who was able to move to the far right where the cyclops-roast was cooking away. He now had full view of the battlefield and starting casting an involved spell to help our friends. I on the other hand only had time to summon my Invisible Shield before the creature thrust that club at me, extending its arm fully to try to catch me with the very tip. It impacted my shield and caused me to tumble backwards. That was fine. Backwards seemed like a good direction when faced with over a ton of screaming, slavering fire cyclops crawling towards you like some kind of night terror.

I was able to glance over and see that Ames was still picking apart the seated cyclops with efficiency. An outsider might think that the half dozen slashes and shallow stabs driven into the flailing creature was some kind of feline cruelty; playing with one's food as it were. But Ames was calculating every swift lunge and retaliatory riposte. The cat would kill the giant when it was overwhelmed by pain and blood loss, and not take any stupid risks in the meantime.

As I continued to backpedal quickly, I heard a pained cry from our cleric. In her fervor, the minotaur left herself open and took a blow to her weapon arm. The priest's armor was precious little protection. Tara's cudgel clattered to the ground, the fingers of her broken arm unable to grasp it any longer. She turned, profile hidden defensively behind that broad tower shield.

The next cry that echoed through the chamber was far more monstrous. Benno learned from many of the best combat mages on Panos, and that included Will. While I sometimes mocked the size of my son's travel spellbook, easily twice as heavy as mine despite my knowledge of advanced rituals, I couldn't fault his spell selection. A portal opened above Toby's foe, and a rain of crushing, freezing hailstones smashed into the face and shoulders of the fire cyclops. It was as in if the mutant had been struck by acid, clubs, and daggers all at the same time. Toby quickly took advantage of the creature's pain, and planted the Axe of McGrondle deep into its breastbone. The cyclops' giant heart deflated, and it fell lifelessly to the cave floor.

I heard Ames cry, "Help Tara!" as I backed out of the chamber. I was forced into the tunnel that led us here, due to the relentless pursuit of the giant that Benno and I knocked over. As the scrabbling creature continued to chase me down, its bulk blocking re-entry to the larger cavern, I added a personal request to my mate's instructions, "And then help me!"

When the fire cyclops dropped its club, I felt that I had caught a break. It was probably succumbing to its pain, I thought. Instead, the cyclops braced against the walls and pulled itself up. My heart sank when I saw it supporting its own massive bulk on that twisted ankle. There was no single spell that I would be able to get off to kill the beast.

I ran.

Letting my Invisible Shield dissipate, I shamelessly turned tail and bolted up the twisty passageway. I swore that I felt the ground shaking as the beast behind me half limped, half ran after the tiny orc that had caused it so much pain. Without the Light spells, the caves were illuminated only by that dim, ominous red glow. My arms and legs were pumping furiously. Only the fire cyclops' wrenched ankle allowed me to stay a step ahead of it, as it was unable to corner as tightly as I could, despite having a size and speed advantage.

But my heart sank when I remembered what was up ahead. Stairs. Ridiculously large stairs. I wouldn't make it up two of the steps before being crushed under the burning weight of the cyclops.

I made a desperate but logical decision. After making a tight right turn that would have taken me into the final hallway leading up to the stairs, I took a sudden left while I was still out of sight. I knew that the passage which I chose was a shallow dead end, but at least it would give me one last chance. I put my back to the wall and started blind-casting, hoping that my target would enter my line of sight before the incantation was done, but not soon enough to crush me before I finished.

My timing was good. The guts just started to melt in my hand as the fire cyclops rounded the corner, glanced first towards the stairs, and then turned left to spot me. My Acid Bolts rained in on the creature's neck and chest, opening up fresh, sizzling wounds that made the giant bellow. It slipped and fell from the pain. But as I expected, it lived. I reached into my component pouch and started my next incantation, knowing that it would be too late unless the creature fell or blacked out.

I saw a blur of reddish-white high in my vision, and I briefly thought that it was that fabled white light that you were supposed to walk towards when you died. It took me a moment to register Ames, in mid flight due to the Ring of Leaping. The cat's short sword sunk deep into the junction of the fire cyclops' neck and skull, destroying its medulla oblongata. It collapsed, quite dead. With its lifeforce extinguished, so was the fire cyclops' supernatural heat radiation. In an instant, I'd been saved.

It all happened so fast that I didn't have time to abort my spell. I was probably too shocked to stop myself even if I had an extra split second. The Spider's Web shot from my quivering green hands, gluing Ames to the fallen giant. I felt the drain on my intellect particularly keenly, as it was aided by my panic, relief, and embarrassment.

My mate looked less than impressed.

"Sorry, sorry."

I used my dagger to free the were-cat's sword paw, and then the two of us cut the feline loose. We ran back down the passage to check on our friends. After Ames dispatched their foe it was three members of our party up against a single battered giant. An almost certain victory, but it was best to be sure.

We arrived to see Toby preparing to perform the Laying of Hands on Tara. Benno was keeping watch over the chamber's exit on the far side of the room. My son looked anxious. Our reemergence seemed to relieve some of that anxiety, but he still cast the occasional worried glance towards the minotaurs.

I soon discovered why. They were snapping at each other, something completely uncharacteristic for the couple.

"Hold still damn it, do you want to screw this up?"

"If you're that incompetent, you can always hack it off with your axe and try again."

It was Ames, covered in webbing, dirt, and cyclops blood, who straightened them out. The were-cat said, "Both of you, get your heads on right. Whatever personal issues you may have can wait until we're out of danger."

Toby grit his teeth, then bent his will to the task. As the paladin's hands glowed, Tara's twisted arm crackled and straightened. The cleric's squinted, teary eyes widening at the sensation. As soon as the healing took hold, Tara wiped her eyes. She gripped Toby's forearm and started to murmur her more powerful healing prayer. The bigger minotaur's burns faded, and he gasped with relief.

It was Toby who responded to Ames' concerns. "I'm sorry everyone. It's this damn noise, just buzzing at the base of my skull. It's driving me mad!" The minotaur's volume was far too loud, as in if he was screaming over some kind of deafening background noise.

And Tara was doing the exact same thing. "It's affecting me as well. We should finish here as quickly as possible!"

The rest of us had no idea what they were talking about.

It took Benno walking over and touching Tara's hand to figure out what was happening. When she briefly relayed the sound to my son's mind through their psychic link, the younger orc staggered back as if he had been struck in the forehead.

Benno said, "Wow. They're hearing and feeling this... thing. A resonance. It's through their connection to the earth. And it's painful. Maybe we should go."

But Toby overruled that suggestion, saying, "Let's find the cause if we can, and eliminate it. If it becomes too much, we'll let you know."

There was only one other exit to the chamber. It was smaller and tighter than the way in. The largest of the fire cyclopes must have barely been able to squeeze through. Toby led the way, followed by Ames. The rest of us waited to be waived in. When the signal came, it was almost hesitant.

After entering the next chamber, I understood why my mate wasn't giving us an enthusiastic go-ahead. The scene in front of us was brutal, bizzare.

Clearly this was some kind of quickly constructed temple and treasure room. Crudely scrawled depictions of a nebulous being trapped inside of a circle adorned every wall. One of the more defined drawings gave me the impression of a blocky looking chick within a strangely round egg. Coins, packs, and even a few weapons were scattered around the room without any apparent rhyme or reason. But it wasn't the inanimate objects that drew our attention just then.

A blistered crimson cyclops sat cross-legged on a makeshift altar in the center of the small chamber. There was nothing but glowing red rubble on the far side of the room, this creature having sealed the deeper passages upon hearing telltale signs of the imminent demise of his companions.

I say 'hearing' because the condition of this creature made seeing the encounter impossible. The large central eye of the cyclops was gone, replaced by an otherwise unremarkable looking boulder. The replacement looked intentional, almost surgical. Other presumably self inflicted wounds covered the giant's body, focused mainly on his chest, neck, and scalp. The creature was already talking, but it was difficult to say if we were its intended audience, or if the cyclops had enough sanity left to consider its audience at all.

The fire cyclops rocked back and forth on their rump and thighs as it spoke, "Embrace the Hum. No pain with Hum. No worry with Hum. It take bad things out, then put in rock. It wash bad thought out, then put in plan. Hum will cleanse whole world."

Tears streamed down Toby's cheeks, likely from fighting against 'the Hum' himself. The minotaur asked, "Why did you come here? Kill those people? Harvest all of those skulls?"

The crazed giant turned its massive head towards Toby's voice. The cyclops said, "Their skulls no echo. They no hear sacred Hum. Took skulls from them, try make them hear. And now they do. Now everyone do. The Hum shakes us all. The Hum takes us all. Praise the Hum."

Tara hissed through gritted teeth, "It's getting worse."

"Not worse. Better. More. Soon you worship Hum in self forever. It tell you what next. It just tell me what next. All praise."

We readied weapons and spells as the insane creature got to their feet on the large flat stone. The cyclops put its arms out wide, as if delivering a benediction. Then it simply allowed itself to fall backwards from the 'altar'. The sheer weight of the boulder in its eye socket shattered the giant's skull upon impact with the cave floor.

The creature's insane action shook me to the core. The expressions on the faces of my friends and family told me that they were similarly horrified. The red glow within the walls flared as our silence dominated the cavern. Then there was a faint tremor. A chill swept through me, despite the intense heat all around me.

It was Ames who took charge, snapping us out of our horror. "Two minutes. Grab everything you can, we need evidence and then we need to get the hells out of here."

I grabbed one of the intact packs and swept chains, rings, and loose coins into it. Benno did the same, and in the process found a journal and signet ring that could possibly explain some things. Tara and Toby collected weapons that might be used to identify some of the dead. Ames went through the 'holy relics' which were mostly macabre trophies. The feline took the only salvageable thing that might serve as a clue: An old cavalry sabre that seemed to have been cared for lovingly.

The next tremor was far stronger than the last. Both minotaurs cried out, as in if the shaking was physically painful to them. Tara said, "It's deafening!" She was once again shouting over the non-existent sound.

I made the call, "That's it, out. Everyone out!"

The minotaurs didn't need to be told twice. They charged out into the larger chamber without looking back. We quickly followed in their footsteps, doing our best to stay within the radius of the Light spells that they carried. The next tremor caused a small rockfall even before we cleared the corpse-strewn room, which still smelled like slow-cooked giant.

Once again I was charging up these twisty red tunnels, and I wasn't enjoying it any more the second time around. I took up the rear, since I already knew the way and wanted to make sure that my family was safe. The walls seemed to be pulsing like the arteries of a titanic stone entity. I felt my flesh starting to scald, but I knew that it was only three more sharp turns until we were at those ridiculous stairs. So I grit my teeth and ran.

We were just coming up to the point where I 'ambushed' the crippled cyclops when the wall to our right simply gave out. In my mind, everything seemed to be moving in slow motion. Ames was beyond the fall, and I was behind it with plenty of room to get around to my left. But that left Benno right in the middle. I watched as a sea of hot stone engulfed my son.

A father's mind and body work incredibly quickly when his child is in danger. As I charged towards the rockfall, I was already calling for the one person who could help:

"TOBY!"

I grabbed fist sized stones and started hurling them away, ignoring the way that they burned my hands. Metal crawling with living runes flashed just over my shoulder, and the Axe of McGrondle obliterated the largest stone. I was briefly worried that Toby may have just hacked off my son's arm, but I continued my frantic digging. Another well placed blow caused the pile of stones to shift, uncovering my son's unconscious, scalded face and one shoulder.

That was all Toby needed. He threw me the axe and grabbed my son's torso, not bothering to be delicate given the situation. Benno's broken body found itself rested on the minotaur's broad shoulders. Then Toby charged forwards like a maniac, mounting those giant stairs incredibly quickly for a man his size. Tara was waiting for me, massive hand already extended. She grabbed the shaft of the Axe of McGrondle and used it as a lever. I was propelled, practically thrown up the first few steps. Ames was waiting to pull me up the last one, and Tara scrambled past to reach her husband and my fallen son.

I lay on the ground, the skin of my hands cooked and peeling, my hair smoking. But I only had eyes for the scene unfolding three paces away.

Toby ignored his own burnt arms and smoking fur, instead touching Benno's twisted arm and murmuring a prayer to Aro-Remset. The god of fair battle answered his servant, pushing the bone of the open fracture back under skin and muscle and stemming some of the bleeding. Then the glory of Melflavin was invoked, Tara touching my son's chest where it had gone slightly concave due to the broken ribs. His torso took on a more normal shape, but I strained to see if my son's chest was moving at all. Finally Tara invoked the last of her healing on the young orc's legs, stemming the bleeding from a foot that was crushed nearly flat.

I didn't even notice that Ames has been quickly wrapping my bleeding hands in clean bandages. They were still clenched tightly around the shaft of the Axe of McGrondle, which was now bound to me with long strips of cotton. In the back of my mind I knew that they were leathery, inflexible, useless for spellcasting. But all I could do was squint with dust and smoke stained eyes to see if my boy's chest was moving.

"Ow."

It was weak, almost so faint that I thought I had imagined it. But Benno followed up his quaint declaration with a miserable little moan. I heard Ames let out a held breath, and saw Tara and Toby collapse in relieved exhaustion.

My were-cat called over, "The Hum?"

Tara answered, "Gone, as soon as we climbed the stairs."

The feline rose with a growl. "Still. We don't know if the instability is restricted to those infernal caves. Let's inform the guards, they can take whatever action they feel is required. And we can get Benno to your temple."

Tara added, "And you boys are both in miserable shape."

Toby snorted, clearly about to deny the severity of his injuries. But when the big minotaur looked at me, he just blinked and stared for a moment. Then the paladin bellowed with laughter upon seeing his axe lashed to my hands with bandages.

Ames said to Tara, dryly, "I think yours is broken."

Tara sighed and watched her wounded husband roll around in mirth. "There's a training exercise for young warriors that involves... nevermind. Let's get them to the temple."

I'm not certain that the guards would have let me past without Toby and Tara present. An angry, singed orc with a battleaxe strapped to his hands was not exactly the standard fare, even in Ice House. Properly escorted, the five of us limped into the Temple of the Order of the Snow.

I recalled the first time that Toby told me about this religious collective. He had said that the Order of the Snow was a unified temple combining the clerics, the paladins, and the militant faithful of several different gods. But what he didn't mention is that it was less of a temple and more of an enclosed courtyard. There was plenty of room for prayers, training, teaching, whatever a group of paladins and priests might need to tend to their flocks and prepare future generations of the clergy.

This wasn't my first time within these walls, but something always surprised me. Today, that surprise was the person tending to the open infirmary. Her name was Tajuff, and she was a stern looking half orc matron. The gray haired, light green skinned cleric wore her holy symbol of Kenvunk proudly.

She looked us over, and then said, "Boy in dis bed. Idiot with axe in next bed. Rest of you, sit on floor."

The rapidity with which Toby obeyed the cleric's orders made me think that he knew her well, and chose not to mess with the matron. Once Benno was deposited and I had been made comfortable, Toby and Tara sat heavily in the aisle between the cots. Ames preferred to stand and pace.

As Tajuff was the dedicated medic, she was well prepared. The half orc immediately treated Benno with a healing prayer that was more powerful than anything we had access to. The sound of my boy's happy sigh nearly caused me to weep with relief.

Suddenly Tajuff's face was directly in mine. She asked, in Orcish, "Why you sitting up?"

For some reason I felt guilty, even though there was a good explanation. I replied in my native tongue, "I have my backpack on and another strapped to that, but can't get them off until these bandages are cut away."

The matron snorted. Nevertheless, she took my wrists lightly in her hands and murmured another healing prayer. A sudden warmth and numbness washed through my hands. I felts the bandages unstick from my flesh as cracked skin became whole and muscles tormented by fire were soothed and repaired.

Tajuff gestured to Ames, the closest person with a pointy thing. "You, cut him loose, yes?" she said in Common, more of a command than a request.

My mate nodded. Without thinking, Ames drew the sabre that we rescued from the 'relic' pile in the cyclopes' cave. As soon as the slightly curved blade cleared its sheath, it burst into flames. This startled Ames just as much as it did the rest of us.

Tajuff clarified, dryly, "Maybe not wit' dat."

As the wide eyed were-cat sheathed the firebrand sabre, our cleric continued making the rounds. Ames used my trusty dagger to cut me free of the Axe of McGrondle. Each of the wounded received another minor healing spell to promote the rejuvenation of our burned skin. Tara and Ames, protected by the minotaur's Elemental Resistance prayer, escaped with only a bit of a tan. Tara did accept a little healing for her battered and bruised arms.

While the half orc went over to assess the long term injuries of Benno, the rest of us sorted through everything that we grabbed prior to our retreat, so as to avoid any other unexpected surprises. Anything that had a name or a signet on it was set aside, to provide authorities and the Guild with a list of victims that fell to the crazed giants. A fair portion of the loose currency was earmarked as a donation to the Order of the Snow for their aid and healing.

The journal and matching signet ring, sadly, had no real name attached to them. Simply the initials 'X.Q.Z.', which nobody recognised. There was no mention of snow in the journal at all, mainly nameless woodlands were referenced. However, there was one hint. The last entry was about a mysterious forest fire that had broken out, which apparently raged for days. The date was last year. With some research, we would be able to figure out just how far this journal had come, and possibly a reason why the fire cyclopes set X.Q.Z.'s forest ablaze.

Tajuff stomped over as we were finishing our sorting. She said, "Boy sleep now. His arm broke. Many toes broke. Need more healing later. Probably two week rest. Keep him away from axe and fire sword."

I said, "Don't worry, I plan to."

The half orc nodded curtly, and then headed off to find someone to relieve her, having channeled all of the divine power that she could for the evening.

Ames asked, quietly, "What do you mean by that?"

"I mean that's Benno's last adventure. He's seen how stupidly dangerous it all is. He has his grand tales to tell his friends. Enough is enough."

Tara and Toby rose quickly. The big paladin said, "Why don't the two of us go make these donations and our tithes."

Tara didn't wait for us to reply, "Okay, we'll just go do that then."

And they were gone before the fighting could start.

Ames politely waited until our friends were out of earshot before saying, "He's a grown man, love. It's not our decision."

I practically snarled, "You're damned right it's our decision. Do you think Max will risk losing our services? Does the Guild really want to put one of the few psychics on Panos in the line of fire? If we insist, they'll take that as enough of an excuse."

The were-cat remained calm. "Sorch, if he wants to walk that road, he can always go it alone. Without Guild support. Without University support. Just out there on his own. Is that what you want?"

I balled up my freshly healed fingers into fists, relishing in the ache. Letting the pain take some of the damned rationality away. "If I forbid him, do you really think he'll go against my wishes? He never has in the past."

Ames begged, "Don't put him in that position hon. He has to make his own life decisions."

I growled, "I want him **safe**! Why in the hells do we do this if not to make a better future for him? So that he doesn't have to wade through the same muck as we do? So that he can deal with the stuff and things that really matter."

My mate suggested, softly, "Like the safety of Panos?"

My arm swiped through the air, as in if banishing that idea. I said, "Someone else can deal with the safety of Panos. We've done our part. Haven't we given enough?"

Ames' tone was firm, "I want you to sleep on this before you have any conversation with him. I'm not going to stop you. But I'm not going to help you either."

I clenched my jaw, silent for a while. The next words that came out didn't really sound like me. Whoever said them was crying. "I just want him to be safe."

The white furred feline embraced me, right in the middle of the infirmary floor. "I know. I know."

Toby and Tara returned a couple of minutes later. The big paladin said, "Got us some space for the night in the old squire's tower. They're still rebuilding the top floors, but we can take the beds on the second floor. Minotaur sized, of course."

Ames asked Toby, "What about the sword? Something as distinctive as a firebrand weapon would surely have been reported missing."

The minotaur shrugged and replied, "We're going to send all of the identifying materials to the Inspector General. We'll include a description of the sabre. If anyone has made a claim on it, he'll get back to us. But until then, you're the caretaker."

After stowing our own gear, we packed away all of the personal effects into one of the spare backpacks that we had grabbed. Toby made one of his apprentices run the contents down to the Inspector General's office for analysis. Then Tara picked up the snoozing Benno, and we made our way to the courtyard's Northwest tower.

As my son slumbered and we prepared for some much needed rest ourselves, the four of us discussed what we learned. We knew that the source of this issue was deep within the earth. 'The Hum' or whatever it was had been resonating somehow. This caused heat, and quakes, and disruption. And in this case, the insanity of creatures that possessed an affinity for the earth. Minotaurs were not entirely immune to this effect.

Ames and I related our recent experiences and put forward a theory: Whatever this power was, it had been forcing the creatures that are usually hidden deep in the earth to move up and away from the source of the disruption. This accounted for at least some of the issues that were being reported all over Panos. Similarly, this power was having ill effects on elementals of all sorts, including the air and ice quasi-elementals that were driving the yetis from their home.

Toby looked to Tara after hearing our theory. The stub-horned minotaur considered for a while. She said, "You're on to something. But not all the pieces are there."

I sighed, but couldn't disagree with her. Even as we all laid down for the night, I had a nagging feeling that this puzzle was far from solved.

Chapter 9

Back at the Arcane University, my son was being a pain in the ass.

Despite being in agony, despite having to hold on to both of his parents to have any mobility whatsoever, Benno was insisting that he couldn't miss certain classes. I pointed out that he couldn't actually cast spells in his condition, which seemed to make him even more upset. Ames had to promise to get Gideon to visit him so that he would have advanced theory work to study.

After making sure that Benno got back to his room, and giving Titan instructions for proper dosage on his herbal painkillers, Ames and I proceeded to the North Wing for a meeting with Max.

The group was back in the Headmaster's dining area, as squeezing two huge minotaurs into Max's office seemed like a bad idea. Ames and I were the last to arrive.

The old codger gave the two of us a scowl and said, "Finally. Sit, we have much to discuss."

After pacing around while we settled ourselves, Max pushed aside one of the padded redwood chairs, preferring to lean over the dinner table with braced arms. It was likely that his back was acting up again.

"Well, as usual, you've found new and impressive ways to screw up what should have been a simple mission."

We all groaned. It was going to be one of those meetings.

Max slid a scrap of parchment across the table to Ames, "750 gold has been deposited into each of your accounts. I have early reports made by the constable to the local Guild presence. At least some of the personal items that you recovered were from missing persons cases. So in that minimal way, you were successful."

I glanced over. It was a short list of names. I was glad that those families would at least have some closure.

Max was quick to quash any good feelings, "However, as you yourselves point out, we have only wispy threads to pull at, insofar as the overall climate mystery is concerned. I have yetis camping in my backyard and farmers waving pitchforks in my general direction. And before you could go in and get confirmation as to the source, you had a cave system collapse on you. **Again**."

My mate pointed out, "The last time we had a cave collapse on us it was a Culinary Guild mission. Unless you plan to pay for the teleportation fees, you have no right to moan about it."

The Headmaster sighed. He said, "And we have another mission that needs to be completed before the school year starts up again. Sadly, our star student carelessly stumbled into a pile of rocks. So much for family adventuring. I think we're starting to see the pedigree of this particular bloodline."

Ames' voice carried a note of warning, "Max."

Tara added, "Stop."

But the Headmaster continued unabated, "I suppose I shouldn't be shocked that the junior greenskin screwed up. Like father like son after a-"

I almost made it. I was already halfway over the granite table when Tara's fingertips caught my shoulder. She barely managed to restrain my forward momentum, causing my right hook to miss Max's jaw by a scant inch. Ames' and Tara's sudden grip on my ankles prevented a second lunge for Max's throat.

The Headmaster staggered away from the table until his back impacted the wall that separated our room from the kitchen. He cracked the wood of the shutters that covered the kitchen's serving hatch. His face, unsurprisingly, was a mask of shock and alarm.

Throughout all of this, Toby sat stoically in his seat, muscular arms folded across his chest. His helpful suggestion was, "Let him go, let's see what happens."

Fathers understand.

It was up to Tara to bring order to proceedings again. First the cleric scolded me for resorting to violence instead of using my words. Then she roundly lambasted Max for mocking Benno's condition, particularly when his parents were in the room. At the end of it all, I was emotionally contained, and Max seemed to be ashamed.

After a brief period of silence, something unexpected happened. It might have been one of the signs of the apocalypse.

Max said, "I'm sorry."

Even Toby raised his eyebrows at that.

The Headmaster continued, "Sorch, your son is hurt and I spoke carelessly. I misread the situation and I underestimated the parental bond. Please accept my apology."

I didn't trust myself to speak at that moment. I grunted and gave Max a guarded nod.

With everyone calmed down, the Headmaster continued.

"At any rate, we have a temporary replacement who you have worked with before. He has agreed to step up while Benno is on the mend."

A young man stepped out of the short hallway leading to the kitchen. He was more pale than usual, so I assumed he witnessed my little attempted scuffle from his hiding spot. I felt a slight rush of shame. Had I known that my 'little brother' was watching, I might have actually managed to restrain myself rather than fly off the handle. For his sake.

Leeson must have been around 20 years old by now, and he had grown. The lad hadn't gotten much taller, but to say that the once-scrawny kid 'bulked up' was an understatement. Leeson possessed the physique of a boxer: Lean, powerful, but not to the point of sacrificing speed. He had the same raven black hair, and his training hadn't quelled the kindness in those intelligent brown eyes. But my friend and former student was a man now.

This unexpected appearance was enough to make Toby stir from his seat. He laughed and walked over to give the human a big bearhug. As everyone was greeting Leeson like the old friend that he was, I thought back to the last time I saw him. It was less than a year ago as I recalled. I seemed to remember it was a rather exciting affair. Ah yes. Gideon needed help assessing his student's chosen speciality. It was seasons ago, but I distinctly recall saying:

"Melee magic."

I had said the words in much the same way one might say 'dry toast'. I recognised it as a food, but had no appetite for it.

Master Gideon snorted at me. "Get off your high horse, Sorch. Flaming swords, magical shields, Ebon Chains? Given your own repertoire you can hardly look down on Leeson for wanting to get in there and mix it up."

I shot back, "Gee mister were-wolf, I wonder if you might be biased at all?"

Throughout my playful banter with Gideon, Leeson remained silent. Apprehensive. It was clear that my approval mattered to him. And I understood why: Apparently his parents reacted badly to the announcement of his chosen mystical specialty. They didn't see it as particularly helpful for when his time came to take over the family interests.

Leeson trusted and respected my opinion. I let him off the hook.

Turning to the young human, I said, "If you're passionate about this, I know you're going to be a success. In the last year, I've watched you transform. It hasn't been unimpressive. So you're taking this all the way then? Finals topic, possible post graduate studies?"

The young nobleman nodded eagerly. "Whichever route I go, I know this is going to be my passion."

I turned back to Gideon, "Sounds like the kid's mind is made up, why did you make me come all this way?"

The were-wolf smiled toothily. "I thought you might like a little sparring practice."

And so I found myself in the Testing Chamber. It was a fancy name for a dead-end cave at the far side of the Arcane University's West Wing. This was where they sent advanced students who were trying out dangerous new spells, or conjurors trying to open portals to dangerous quasi-elemental planes. Or a trio of combat mages looking to start a friendly little brawl.

Gideon reminded us, "The iron lockbox by the entryway has a couple of emergency healing potions, should anyone get carried away. Try to pull your punches though."

I knew that I was a distant third in this contest. 'Distant' being the key word: Most of my spells were focused on striking from a distance or making distance to work with. Even though Master Gideon gave me some hints as to how I should prepare before I came to visit, my repertoire matched up badly against these two; a mystical brawler and a focused, well rounded combat magus. Still, I had some tricks up my sleeve.

I palmed a cloudy crystal from my pouch as the human and were-wolf shook out their arms and cracked their knuckles. I started casting exactly as Leeson said "Go."

When the cloudy crystal slipped from my grasp and into the ether, there was a duo of groans. The Fog spell was simple, but effective. It filled the chamber with a thick mist, reducing visibility to just a few paces. This was an environment that I was used to, having grown up in a damp seaside area. More importantly, it gave me the time and space that I needed to be more cagey.

I knew the two spells that were being cast, although neither were in my repertoire. Rick and Will used to cast Mirror Image on a regular basis, so when I heard the arcane words being snarled out, I knew we were about to see multiple phantom were-wolves. And I recalled a certain elven magus incanting the Enlarge spell to reverse the shrinking effect on my minotaur friends. So I expected to see a giant Leeson in the near future.

As we circled in the uncertain Fog, I went over my options. I had Silence ready, which would give me a chance against Leeson but would be suicidal against Gideon. Alternatively, Ebon Chains of Binding could catch someone in a moment of weakness, but I wouldn't use it against either of my opponents unless I was at the peak of my power.

I heard a yelp of surprise, followed by a snarl. That was my cue to conjure my Shield before cautiously stalking forward. I wouldn't summon my Flaming Sword until the Fog lifted. It would glow like a torch in this misty environment and give away my position.

I saw an impressive display when I was close enough to peer through the Fog at my friends. Leeson, now standing head and shoulders above his were-wolf opponent thanks to the Enlarge spell, had 'popped' two of Gideon's Mirror Images at the cost of a nasty little gash across his ribcage. The two were locked together now, muscles straining as they fought over possession of Leeson's elven staff. I took the opportunity to take out Rock and throw it through the last Image, which was comically grasping at the air.

Knowing that I was planning mischief from the flank, Master Gideon ceded control of the staff, instead using its leverage to roll away from the big human and disappear into the Fog. Calculating that my cover was not long for this world, I took out a burnt stick and started to summon a Flaming Sword, choosing a khopesh to give me a little extra edge against that straight staff. At the same time, my human friend cast a spell that I had never seen before. Later I would discover it was called Aldus' Armor. It made the melee mage's robes as tough as leather, while still being as light as cotton.

After our first clash, I knew I was in over my head. As much as I practiced with this spell, my swordsmanship was weak in comparison to Leeson's obvious prowess with the staff. He parried every attempt to curve a strike around his defenses. The hammering return blows numbed my Shield arm and caused me to stumble backwards under my former student's relentless assault. There was no doubt in my mind: I had taken an unfair fight.

Of course, not only was Leeson Enlarged, but his elven staff was permanently enhanced by the Ironwood spell. A mage could only use the Permanence ritual a handful of times in their lives, assuming they ever mastered it at all. It extended their power outside their body, and overuse would cause their soul to slip away. But given his vocation, Leeson committed to enchanting his gift from the mages of Arbitros. The Ironwood enchantment meant that the human's staff was as light as wood in his hands, but as durable as iron. It stuck with the force and mass of a metal weapon as well. Damned unfair if you were on the receiving end, like I was at the time.

With little fanfare, Leeson deftly disarmed me. My Flaming Sword boiled away to nothingness as soon as it left my hand. Just as I was about to give up, I heard Gideon chanting from not so far away. Leeson and I both knew that particular spell. As my Fog finally dissipated, the human started chanting, meeting my gaze as he did so. I knew this spell as well, having seen Leeson use it to deadly ends. He was daring me to interrupt his rather fast spell and face the might of his melee presence… or let him go. But if I let him go, I knew that I had to do something about the were-wolf. After Leeson Blinked, I would be the only one in range for Master Gideon's spell.

With a frustrated growl, I turned and charged towards the were-wolf, bellowing in an attempt to distract my friend and mentor. The were-wolf did the calculations, and must have decided that I would reach him a split second before his Ebon Chains of Binding could complete. He aborted the spell and opened both meaty paws to face my charge. Rather than trying to stop my forward momentum, Gideon redirected it. I was hurled over the were-wolf's hip. I must have sailed for three paces before meeting the ground with a bruising thump and roll.

I decided that having a little rest on the ground wasn't such a bad idea. It allowed me to watch as Leeson approached his Master and started to circle. I wasn't quite done meddling, however. My next spell would require no material components, no gestures of any sort. Moving nothing but my lips, I performed all of the mental gymnastics required to cast the Dispel Enchantment spell on Leeson's Enlarge. The human looked genuinely surprised as he shrunk back down to proper size. The betrayed look that he shot me was answered only by my tired smirk.

The next minute was breathtaking. One would think the wounded human would have no chance against a were-wolf, even if that were-wolf was a slightly battered magus. One would be wrong. Although not reaching the sheer speed of Ames, the balanced prowess of Bruce, or the might of Toby, my young friend was holding his own. He had sufficient training to allow his Aldus' Armor spell to absorb some of the more glancing rakes of Gideon's claws. Soon the punishing counters started to wear on the Master's wrists and forearms. Leeson was winding, but Gideon was slowly being picked apart by that whirring, relentless staff-work.

A calculated blow to the back of the were-wolf's left heel put Gideon on his rump. Immediately both paws went up in the air, indicating surrender. Leeson doubled over in exhaustion, panting hard.

This was my chance.

I scrambled to my feet and charged towards the seemingly distracted and winded human. He would have interrupted my Ebon Chains of Binding, but that didn't mean that grappling was out of the question. I just needed to close the final two paces and-

In a display of practiced reflex, Leeson lashed out with the butt of his weapon. The Ironwood staff impacted with my jaw perfectly. It pushed the bone back into a sensitive spot that boxers called 'the button'. Push the button hard enough, and you knock your opponent out. Orcs were not immune to this effect.

The next thing I knew, Leeson's concerned face was hovering a couple of inches away from my own. He was calling my name, trying to bring me back.

"Sorch. Sorch?"

I was back in Max's dining room. Leeson had greeted everyone else before walking over to me and looking into my somewhat distant eyes. My lack of immediate reaction clearly confused the young human, who was now caught somewhere in between an uncertain hug and an awkward handshake.

I solved this issue by embracing my friend warmly. "Good to have you on board." I said. And I meant it.

With his chin on my shoulder, the young mage was able to ask, very softly, "Where were you just then?" Benno had a big mouth, and told Leeson what signs to watch for.

I murmured back, "Our sparring session with Gideon."

He laughed softly and whispered, "Oh I remember that. I got lucky. That was before I mastered the Haste spell, and developed that silly new Shield."

My young friend was being modest. His new spell was far from silly. 'Leeson's Living Layer' or just 'Layer' for short, was heralded as a tool that would reinvent melee magic. Much like Tara's Divine Hammer, the Layer moved independently of the caster's arms. It was larger than a buckler, smaller than a tower shield. The existence of this new spell meant that a defensive shield could be cast and then forgotten, leaving both of the mage's hands free for other things. The built in animation and intelligence also meant that there was a chance that the Layer would defend the caster against dangers that they personally didn't even know existed.

In Gideon's latest update, the were-wolf mentioned that Leeson had become a 'true terror' in combat. That sounded good news for our little adventuring party.

As I let my young friend go, Max mentioned, "Toby is in charge for this one. I need that ample bovine elegance and charm on full display. This is a sticky situation." The archmage gestured at the big paladin, who explained the scenario.

Toby cleared his throat, and then said, "Let's all take our seats again, this won't be brief, unfortunately."

We all sat back down, making sure that Tara and Toby got the largest chairs once again. Even Max pulled out one of the padded wooden chairs. Briefly I wondered if I had tweaked his back when I forced him to retreat earlier. There was no guilt associated with the thought.

The paladin began to explain the mission.

"If you recall, the Adventurer's Guild and Arcane University had several teams in the field a couple of years back, attempting to deal with the portals that had been opened to the Plane of Negative Energy. There were some setbacks and tragic losses until a friendly mercenary company, known as the Company of Glass, volunteered to help. Several of our people were saved, and the bodies of several more recovered for proper burial, because of these brave men and women."

Toby gave Max a nod. The image wall flickered, and an illusion came into being. "This is the Glasson Desert, which is also where the headquarters of the Company of Glass happens to be. It's not a very hospitable place. But to them, it's home."

We all stared at the large dunes surrounding a featureless plain of sand. I for one would find a better home.

Toby continued, "Our friends are calling in their marker. Supply and weapons caravans, key to the company's continued operations and the survival of their members and families, have been getting ambushed. The chaos witches of the Glasson Desert are responsible. We know this, because they have all but declared war on the Company of Glass. Negotiations with the witches have broken down."

The scene flickered, only to be replaced by a face half shrouded in a red cowl. "This is their leader. Her name isn't known. We do know that her control of chaos magic is one of the primary weapons being used in these caravan ambushes. She claims that these attacks are 'in retaliation for the fire elementals'. Which means this might tie into our other problems. That is why it's us making the trip and not someone else."

After a moment, the wall was just a wall once more. The big paladin said, "Losses on both sides seem pointless. As the mercenary company has no idea what the witches are talking about as far as elementals go, they need neutral representatives from the Guild to broker a peace. That's us. Questions?"

Leeson hesitantly raised a hand. The young man said, "Begging your pardon Toby, but if all we're doing is negotiations, why isn't this a group of politicians?"

The minotaur pointed out, "That's one of the reasons you're a good choice for this, lad. As well as myself and Ames, who have had a lot of experience in recent years with shaking hands and saying nice things. Negotiation needs to happen, but this is a dangerous place. And if talks break down, the chaos witches have already resorted to violence with the Company of Glass, who's to say they wouldn't turn on the negotiators? So we need to be ready for anything."

I added, "Our preparations should be broad. Combat is important, but so is research and communication."

Leeson nodded. The young human said, "Of course Sorch. I shall try to keep a balance of spells for the mission and not overly focus on melee magic. I won't let you down."

Echoes of my son saying those exact same words rolled through my mind. Now I was worried that my 'little brother' might get hurt too. I banished the thought from my mind, reminding myself that Leeson was actually a far more seasoned adventurer than my Benno.

I forced myself to smile, and then said, "I know you won't."

Toby waited to see if there were any more questions, and then stated, "This is a hazard pay situation. The Adventurer's Guild is offering 1,500 gold pieces each. They figure that they owe the Company of Glass at least that much for services in times of need. Assuming everyone is alright with this, get your hot weather gear packed and we'll meet at the Circle of Transport in two hours."

I told Ames that I would meet them back at the guest room shortly. I walked with Leeson so that I could talk quietly to the lad as he headed back towards his room to get ready.

"Is Jess okay with all of this? This one seems a bit hairy."

Leeson swallowed visibly. He admitted, "We've been fighting, Sorch. About stupid things. Well stupid to me I guess, **not** stupid to her. Da- I mean, Master Gideon says that she gets like this sometimes. Something about were-wolf blood. I just need some time away. I need to think."

I squeezed my young friend's shoulder. "At some point you might want to discuss a wedding, kid. Assuming that this fighting is a temporary thing. I mean you've been together for years now."

Leeson asked, "Haven't you and Ames been together for longer than that?"

"Um. Yeah I guess we have. You're right, none of my business."

The young human started to say, "What I mean is Sorch, why aren't the two of you m-"

I spoke over him, "Yup, yup. None of my business. I'll see you at the Circle in a while."

As I headed back upstairs towards the guest quarters, I pondered the answer to the question that I didn't allow Leeson to ask. The truth was: Ames had never asked, and I had never offered. Marriage was never a consideration in our lives. But now with Benno grown up and the two of us taking on dangerous missions once again, maybe it was a discussion worth having. Establishing legal heirs and all that. And an outward sign of... something more.

I shook my head to clear it, and then increased the length of my stride. "Get your head in the game Sorch." I muttered to myself. An elf peered at me as I passed him. He caught me half-jogging and talking to myself like a loon. I sighed. This was probably another rumor about 'that crazy orc' being born. Lizard crap!

Chapter 10

The 'garden' in the rear of Omi-Suteth's temple in Glasson was lifeless. Any yet, it was beautiful in its own way. Clergy members and parishioners had made the fine sand in the courtyard surrounding the Circle of Transport into a 'meditation garden'. They would use large sticks and trowels to inscribe fascinating patterns into the ground. Some of the vast spirals and waves extended to the low stone walls that contained the courtyard, spanning nearly a hundred paces. Other patterns were no more than a pace wide, drawn with small sticks or even fingers. In many cases, these tiny displays were no less impressive. I found the setting to be relaxing, almost hypnotic.

In the interest of full disclosure, I have to say: I'm not sure that I would call Glasson a proper city. When we stepped out of the confines of the temple garden, the first word that came to mind was 'outpost'. And a sprawling, disorganized outpost at that. Over a stretch of tens of thousands of paces, there was a myriad of structures: Tent cities, permanent stone buildings, caves carved into rock outcroppings, and bazaars. All of these enclosures combined to form the most unlikely of urban ecosystems. And yet, it all somehow worked. The kind of shelter that one utilized depended on how mobile they had to be and what they could afford. The end result was Glasson. I saw it as a community born from necessity. A place that was balanced between practicality and dreams. A city of survival.

And of heat. I was glad that Leeson took the time to give us some tips as to how we should dress for this trip. He spent a couple of seasons here pursuing spells for his particular speciality.

As a result, none of us wore armor or formal robes. All of that sort of thing was stored in our rather bulky packs for the moment. In fact, we were wearing next to nothing at all. I opted for shorts, a very light shirt, and boots. Leeson opted for mostly the same style, but wore 'harem pants' which was the trend among young people in this area, apparently. Our furred companions went bare-hoofed and bare-pawed, wearing only short breaches and a chest wrapping in Tara's case. If anything we were overdressed. It wasn't uncommon to see both men and women of all races walking around in nothing but a loincloth. If that.

Certain folks, however, went a different route. They shielded their skin from the sun with full body wrapping. As I understood it, this was far more wise if you were planning to spend a significant amount of time in the sun, as it would burn the skin rather quickly through constant exposure. Luckily we had a specific, and local, destination. We wouldn't be out in the afternoon sun for long. Our meeting with the head of the Company of Glass was in half an hour, and we had already been assured that casual dress was both expected and encouraged.

The headquarters of the Company of Glass was on the North side of the more dense part of the city. They owned a couple of stone buildings that were about two thousand paces from the Temple of Omi-Suteth. Even conserving our energy, the group was on time. The crossbow wielding perimeter guards reviewed our paperwork and then waved us through. Neither of them looked very happy.

We walked up to the larger of the two buildings and knocked on the door. There was no reply.

I asked, "Maybe it's the other one, Toby?"

The big minotaur peered around. "They said the big building. Maybe we're a bit early."

Then we heard the rattling of chains and the 'thump' of a wooden board being dropped to the ground. The heavy sandalwood door swung open, revealing a tired looking, middle aged half elf. He was wearing an eyepatch and towel.

"Crap. I thought you were... nevermind. It's been hectic, I was just trying to brush the dust out of my hair. Please, come in, have a seat at the big table. Close and bar the door behind you. I'll be right out."

After the man scurried off, we all had a chuckle. Ames rumbled, amused, "He did say 'dress casual'."

We stepped inside of the large stone structure. As requested, the door was barred and the security chain attached. Security was, in fact, a theme around here. Each of the small windows was barred. Every chest and drawer bore a lock. Even the legs of the 'big table' were chained to the floor, though who would be able to make off with the massive thing was beyond me.

The three smaller members of our party sat, while the minotaurs leaned against the wall. There were no chairs sturdy enough or large enough for them. Luckily, we didn't have to wait very long for our host to return. I noticed that the half elf opted to wear almost exactly what I had picked out. He did not sit down.

After adjusting the covering over his right eye, the man said, "I'm sorry to keep you waiting. I'm alone here right now, my lieutenants are out dealing with other matters. Primarily finding replacement food and water supplies so our people don't waste away. I'm Kev Turnbull, head of the Company of Glass."

Toby pushed off of the wall so that he was standing properly when introductions were made. "Toby McGoldberg, paladin of the Order of the Snow. These are my companions and friends, Leeson, Sorch, and Ames. And this is my mate, Tara."

Kev ran a hand through his freshly brushed and slightly damp hair. "You have... really, you have no idea how glad we are to have you here. I mean. Things are a mess. I've only been running the company for a year, but I've served for five. And I've never seen things this bad."

We traded glances amongst the group before looking to Toby.

If we weren't going to get a pep talk, the minotaur decided that perhaps our host could use one. He said, "Not to worry Mister Turnbull. After what your people did for the Guild, it is our pleasure to repay the favor. Your bravery and sacrifice saved not only dozens of our people, but potentially thousands of innocents as well."

The half elf offered a grateful little half smile. He said, "Nice of you to say. I wish we were in that sort of shape right now. I've been told that I can't blame myself, but who else is there?"

Ames said, "I think it only fair that we hear the whole story from you before jumping to any conclusions."

Toby was nodding as the were-cat spoke. "Ames is correct. From what we heard, circumstances beyond your control are very likely where the blame rests. Could you tell us more about the current situation?"

Kev drew a deep breath, and then let it out in a sharp sigh. "I will. At least let me offer you some water as I do that." The half elf walked over to the open canteen area and started to work the hand pump. He slid a thick glass pitcher under the mouth of the spout.

"The Company of Glass was doing fairly well. I had taken over from my uncle about a year ago, after I lost the eye. I couldn't aim a crossbow for crap anymore, and Uncle Dunny said it was about time anyway. He retired to... gods know where. Somewhere cool and wet I imagine."

As in if on cue, water burbled from the spout and started to fill the pitcher. Tara thoughtfully went out to the canteen to gather six wooden mugs as Kev continued his story.

The half elf said, "Then two seasons back, it all went to the hells. Caravans started to go missing, and we'd find the drivers tied up and the guards either knocked out or worse. As the attacks continued, we were less likely to find survivors. Sometimes we would just find ash. I can't say for sure that one of our people didn't fire the first shot, or slight someone at some point. I wish I could. But as it turned out, however it might have escalated, something bigger was ultimately at work."

There was a pause as water was brought back to the table. Ames took up pouring duty.

Toby asked, "Why do you say that?"

Kev scowled suddenly. The half elf asked, "What the 'first shot' thing or the 'something bigger' thing? Nevermind, I can answer both of those questions. One of the first people found in a pile of ashes was a huge hothead. I'm not making a morbid joke there by the way. The man was a complete... well. I won't speak ill of the dead. But I wouldn't be shocked if he started the violence. As far as something bigger, that was implied with the first threat that got delivered."

The commander dug out a piece of parchment that was in his pocket. He slid it across to Toby.

The minotaur read it aloud. "Your naked aggression will be answered in kind. The fire elementals tell the tale. What you've done will be undone. As will you."

Leeson commented, "Less than friendly, I think. Someone has anger issues."

Kev pointed at the young human and nodded his agreement. "I know, right? That's exactly what I thought. And what are they talking about fire elementals for? None of our mages are going to sit there and summon one of those damned things for half an hour. It's also banned by the company, given how easily it could burn down supplies and wagons by accident."

I asked, "What about weather manipulation?"

The half elf peered at me. "I'll be honest, I have no idea. I never saw such a thing when I was on the line. I somehow doubt it though. Why?"

Toby launched into the rather long and involved tale of our issues with elementals elsewhere on Panos. The news, if anything, made the company commander even more somber.

Kev drained his water, spinning the wooden mug as he set it down on the table. He said, "Crap. This is even more depressing than I thought. If there's one thing we didn't ask for in this gods forsaken place, it's angry fire elementals. And people messing with the weather. Because what we **really** need is more sun, less rain, and bigger sandstorms."

It was Tara's turn to provide some verbal comfort. She gently placed her mug on the table before saying, "We're here to deal with the immediate issues that are facing your company. But please rest assured, the Adventurer's Guild and the Arcane University are committed to discovering the cause of these other issues as well. I would add, most major governments on Panos are providing material and financial support in these endeavors."

I glanced over at Tara, impressed. She could give Toby a run for his money in the realm of flowery speech.

The half elf nodded, slowly. He said, "Good to hear. That's all I have for you. Oh, except for the drop point."

Toby tilted his big head to one side, curiously. "Drop point?"

Kev said, "Yep! Uhhh. Hang on, let me get a map. Finish up your water please, I don't want to get this thing wet."

We quaffed our water as requested, while our host went back to his private chambers to get the map. The five of us had all of the mugs collected and the table wiped down with a dry rag before he got back.

The half elf unrolled a large, fairly detailed map of the area. "Thanks, thanks for that. Right. We're here, see? And a couple dozen miles up to the North-Northeast is a triangle of big rocks. And in the middle is a smaller rock, all hollowed out. That's one of the witches' drop points. They consider it a sacred site. No violence there if they can help it. So yeah, it's where you can drop off messages for them. Not that it did us any good, they've ignored everything. But at least our messengers weren't incinerated."

Toby considered. He said, "We may leave more than a message this time. This is a great starting point, thank you commander. I think we're ready."

Kev gave us a tight smile. He said, "Well, now comes the best part. Hitting the open road. Let me tell you something: As much as I used to bitch and complain about the conditions, and the knucklehead locals, and the terrible food… ha! I was about to say 'I'd give my right eye to have it all back.' But that's kind of the issue, isn't it? Ah well. Go ahead, don't let me keep you. I have a dozen things to do today, all without getting killed."

We all shook the half elf's hand, and then made our way out. The door was immediately barred behind us.

Ames commented as we made our way out of the compound, "Under-confident. Paranoid. Slightly bitter. That's who I want in charge of a bunch of crazy mercenaries."

Toby snorted. "Well he's doing the best he can in the situation that he was thrust into. He may yet grow into the role."

I said, "Sure. Max is overconfident, paranoid, and extremely bitter. And he turned out to be a fairly good Headmaster. Kev just needs to achieve that level of assholeishness and he'll be all set."

Leeson tut-tut'ed me, and Ames smacked the back of my head. I deserved it.

Toby changed the subject, saying, "A couple of dozen miles is not an easy jog, even if we travel at night. We're going to need proper provisioning. We may wish to get the three of you camels. It won't help our overall pace since Tara and I will still have to walk, but-"

Leeson interrupted the big minotaur, "I can Reduce you both."

The two bovines stopped, cringing visibly at the suggestion.

Tara quickly tried to avoid that fate. "No, no Leeson. We would have to rest a number of hours for you to commit the spells to memory, miss the cooler part of the day."

The young man smiled brightly as he said, "Oh I have them ready right now. You did say that I should diversify my list for this journey, and I sometimes use them anyway to counteract my own Enlarge spells when needed."

Toby looked around for help. He saw Ames and myself grinning toothily. Tara's jaw was working, but she was out of excuses.

With a big sigh and a neutral expression, Toby said, "Five camels it is."

Secretly, I was excited. I had ridden horses and giant wolves, but never camels. They were such unusual looking beasts. I was looking forward to getting to know their habits.

Leeson also suggested, "As comfortable and native as our current mode of dress might be, I'd also suggest we pick up the proper desert wrappings. Half naked is fine for the city where you can go inside whenever you like, but we don't know what kind of exposure we'll have out there in the desert."

I nodded and said, "A reasonable precaution. I've taken the liberty of learning Rick's 'Zone of Comfort' spell, so the five of us should be fairly well protected during the worst parts of the day."

Toby looked surprised. He asked, "You did that for Tara and me?"

I didn't reply, I simply waved it off with a hand gesture. Like it was nothing. Still, it earned me a kiss on the forehead from Tara.

Plans made, we set off again. The mid afternoon market wasn't too busy. Leeson gave us all the standard suite of warnings: Beware the pickpockets, haggle or you're going to get cheated, and the like. As it turned out, 'cheated' meant paying a couple of extra silver for something. Years back I would have objected, but these days our time was worth far more than a couple of coins here and there. Our lack of bargaining protocol sorely disappointed Leeson. But we had our deep brown body wrappings in all of the appropriate sizes, we picked up some desert-specific supplies, and the camels were ours for a week. The mount vendor was associated with the Adventurer's Guild. That meant we wouldn't have to leave a ridiculous deposit on the animals; if anything happened to them, the Guild would be charged directly. Toby signed all of the appropriate documents, and we were on our way by the time the bottom of the sun touched the horizon.

The party gathered by the Northeast 'gate', which was just an opening in the wall that bordered the open marketplace. Perhaps 'wall' was somewhat of an exaggeration as well; it was a pile of stones that could be easily hopped over. Either way, Leeson was facing down two stoic looking minotaurs.

"Are you ready?"

Tara set her jaw. There was an irritated tail-flick.

Leeson tried to sound cheery, "I rather enjoy it, you get to see the world from a different perspective!"

The flat answer from our cleric was, "Get on with it."

After the incantation, Tara's stubby horns were at the same height as my shoulder. She wasn't crying, but the small minotaur still looked miserable. Ames squeezed the bovine's shoulder, then offered to help her onto the back of her camel.

Leeson opened his mouth to offer Toby some encouraging words, but quickly snapped it shut when the big minotaur gave him a warning glare. Without fuss, the paladin was Reduced to a size smaller than Leeson, horns included. He mounted his own camel without a word. Then we were on our way, five fools heading into the rapidly cooling dusk air.

Oh. Remember when I mentioned wanting to get to know camels? I take it all back.

Camels are the most miserable creatures on all of Panos. They're ornery. They spit and drool. Their breath smells like festering lizard crap. They don't appreciate anything nice that you do for them, and they don't respect boundaries. Four hours of riding these hells-forsaken beasts, and I was ready to suggest that we turn around and trade them in for horses.

One of the nice things that we did for them, and for ourselves, was facilitate the divine production of water. Tara would be able to fill our waterskins a couple of times a day, which meant that one of the main killers of the desert would be kept at bay. But these damnable beasts would stick their noses in their special feed and water sacks, and the water would be gone in an instant. Then they would look at you, as if thinking, 'That's all, humanoid?' I was starting to wonder what camel meat would taste like.

The landscape wasn't as flat as one would imagine, but it was fairly featureless. We didn't use Light spells, relying mostly on Ames' night vision. Normally Leeson would have been the only one with short range vision issues. But in this place, all of the little tricks that the minotaurs and I would have used to improve our orientation were missing. The crescent moon wasn't throwing much light to start with. But more importantly, there was precious little to give any of us scope. An occasional boulder or cactus simply wasn't enough of a reference in this sea of sand. I couldn't tell if something was a massive boulder fifty paces away or a little rock ten paces away. Luckily, Ames' feline senses coped much better in this environment.

We reached the stone triangle an hour before dawn. A quick patrol of the area helped us to measure the distance between boulders; around forty paces between each rock. And as promised, there was a squat, hollowed out boulder directly in the center.

Ames asked, "Where do you want to set up camp Toby? One of the boulders will provide a little shade, and the tarp will be ample cover for the camels."

The formerly-large minotaur pointed at the stubbier rock in the center. "There."

The feline squinted. "Next to the small rock?"

"No, **on** the rock."

We were all quiet for a moment. Leeson was the one who ventured, "That's going to piss them off Toby."

The paladin sounded almost innocent. "Oh, will it?"

And that was that. We set up camp directly on top of the drop point. Toby called it 'effective negotiating tactics'. Tara muttered something about managing to burn bridges in the middle of a desert. Nevertheless, by the time the sun crested upon the horizon, we had the tarp set up and bedrolls arranged. The rock, though not very tall, did present us with a solid surface. We set up our three light tents in a circle around it, utilizing multiple anchors and spikes to provide equal tension on every facing. Tara and Toby would have to use the cover of the tarp, benefitting from the additional shade that the rock and our tents would provide.

Luckily, the harshest third of day was not going to be an issue. After breakfast, I started the hour long ritual that would allow me to invoke the spell that I learned from Rick. The Zone of Comfort was just as effective in the middle of this arid wasteland as it had been in the frozen heights near Thunderscale Mountain. Even with my orcish endurance, the effort of pacing and chanting in the morning sun was taxing. But the sudden rush of cool air over my sweating body made it all worthwhile. I heard a collective murmur of relief go up when the Zone of Comfort encompassed the tents and the area just outside.

Despite my protests, everyone was telling me that my efforts more than counted as my turn on watch. After a final prod from Ames, I gave in. My reward for a job well done was eight hours of blissful sleep.

I awoke to conversation, laughter, and other general loudness. The heat was back, but it was bearable in the late afternoon. I poked my head out of my thin walled tent to see what in the hells was happening.

Everyone was gathered under the tarp. The minotaurs were tall again. They, or more likely my mate, pilfered my magical cooking pot and started making dinner. It didn't look like anyone was drunk. Briefly I wondered if Ames had shared some of their more potent 'stress relieving' chemicals.

I called over, "What in the hells are you doing?"

Ames snickered at my question. My mate replied, "We're going to have a party tonight!" The answer seemed intentionally loud.

Toby added, "Maybe tomorrow night too. This is such a nice spot. We have supplies for a week after all, and this is a beautiful campsite!" Again, my friends were speaking at quite a high volume.

Then it all fell into place in my mind. They were going to camp on the witches' sacred spot in the most annoying way possible.

I played along, "Great, I'm going to do my morning enhancements, then I'll join you for dinner. Afterwards, I'll prepare my spells. You can set up targets near those big rocks and I'll see if I can hit them with Lightning Bolts."

As I withdrew back into my tent, I heard Leeson say, "Great idea Sorch. I'll prepare a couple of Fireworks spells for tonight!"

Max's Expanded Intelligence provided me with the mental enhancement that I needed for the day. It also flooded my body with an all-encompassing euphoria. I forced myself to take deep breaths as I writhed slowly within my bedroll. I could feel every grain of sand shifting beneath the fabric. Lectures on theoretical magical structures danced through my head. It was exhausting and exhilarating at the same time. Fifteen minutes later, I emerged on the other side of the spell's after-effects. And I was voraciously hungry.

After a dinner of turnips and noodles in a chicken stock broth, something that we celebrated far more boisteriously than the taste called for, we started to prepare for tonight's 'party'. Along with my other spells I did memorize Lightning Bolt, though I hoped that I wouldn't have to waste it on a distant target in a display of careless bravado.

The sun was setting when I reemerged from my tent. The others were clearing a space for the planned 'celebration'.

Leeson said, "We should clear out this garbage. And bury this camel dung. Should we dig a latrine?"

Toby replied, "Why bother digging? We have this perfectly good hollow rock right here."

"Stop."

It was a voice that none of us heard before. Our attention was drawn to the southernmost boulder. A weary looking woman in red robes was peering around the edge of the rock.

"Your acting is awful, but I believe you might be just annoying enough to actually go through with it. What do you want?"

Toby wore a smile, perhaps one that was slightly too smug for a paladin. He said, "Greetings, m'lady. We are representatives of the Adventurer's Guild, on a quest to peacefully parley with the chaos witches of the Glasson Desert. Might you be a representative of that group?"

She spat into the sand. "I might, but not a member that has either the authority or the desire to speak with the likes of you. You speak for the men of glass or whatever they call themselves, yes?"

The minotaur nodded. He rumbled, "We wish to bring an end to this conflict, however it may have started. Is there someone that we can speak to about these things?"

The red robed woman considered. "Yes. As long as it isn't me. Pack your things quickly. I will take you to the Mother of Magma."

Ames murmured to me, "That's a nice title. Why don't we have nice titles?"

I murmured back, "I think it's because we annoy a lot of people on the average day."

We were exceedingly respectful of the area, despite our earlier loudmouthed threats. Everything was cleaned up quickly and efficiently. We earned a little nod of approval from the red robed woman, who told us to mount up and stay close. Tara and Toby were Reduced, and then we climbed aboard the greatest mistake the gods had ever made.

We rode into the cool night, allowing the sun to set and the moon to crest. When the witch invoked a Light spell, Leeson and I quickly followed suit. Being able to see where we were going was a novel change. It seemed that we were headed Southeast now. But frankly, the only change that I saw was a slight uptick in the number of cacti.

Then the texture of the ground changed somewhat. It became more firm under our camels' hooves. A rock face rose in the distance. It wasn't tall enough to be called a cliff, but it did provide a break in the otherwise monotonous terrain. As we approached, the air carried the scent of life, of moss and plants.

We followed the contours of the rock rather than finding a way to get over it. This continued until all six camels were hugging the reddish-brown stone wall. Only when we were nearly on top of a sudden gap in the short and rocky hills did we see the archway. Whether naturally or via arcane and druidic influence, a cavern had been formed that pushed all the way through the cliff face. It was illuminated by a mix of torches and Light spells. The sheltered area was perhaps eighty paces wide and similarly deep before opening back up to the night sky.

An oasis. Sheltered from the harshest of the Glasson Desert's sun and wind, water bubbled up from the ground and pooled. Fronds and grass and palm trees held the soil together. Moss grew up one side of the massive domed shelter, and ivy dominated the opposite wall. The unusually fertile area wasn't being wasted. Potatoes and lettuce grew in the more shaded patches of dirt, as well as an assortment of herbs.

Dotted around the area were yurts of all kinds. Each of the animal skin covered tents had its own character. Someone, presumably the owners, painted each yurt in a unique way. Some of the patterns were simple. Others were rendered in painstaking, breathtaking detail. All of them seemed arcane in nature. The wards and subtle glamours of protection often flowed directly into more artistic, mundane patterns. I knew quite a few of the symbols from my classes that involved summoning and defensive spells. Others were a complete mystery.

Our guide led us over to an area that was home to a couple dozen camels. Briefly I wondered if this was a portal to the netherworld. But our beasts were just as glad to be rid of us as we were to be rid of them. Once untacked, they quickly walked into the pen to join the other evil creatures.

We shouldered our packs before being led to a tall yurt that looked much the same as the others. Our red robed guide opened the front flap and called inside. "Mother. We have guests, are you decent?"

The voice that came back was high and gentle, "Yes. Are they?"

We were looked up and down. Then the woman sighed and admitted, "They seem to be the decent sort."

"Then they may enter. Have them remove their footwear and leave their sandy things in the foyer."

I was glad that we had been prompted. I wouldn't have thought about the amount of desert that we were carrying around with us. Boots, wrappings, and packs were abandoned in the tent's first partition. Soon we were back in our 'native' garb; that is to say, we were wearing next to nothing. The night air was actually a little bit cool now, so I was glad when Toby pushed open the next curtain and led us through to the warmer inner chamber.

If it weren't for our host's attire, I wouldn't have guessed that this place was in the middle of the Northeastern deserts. A simple Light spell at the center of the room provided unwavering, rose-tinted illumination to the entire space. The firm red berber carpet stretched wall to wall. Those walls were dominated by simple pine book shelves, filled with tomes both mundane and arcane. In the center of the room was a ring of low leather couches, presumably filled with fine sand by the way they seemed to melt and hold every indentation.

Lounging on one of those couches was a woman garbed in black silk. She was reading a thin book of some kind, in a language that I didn't know. Her auburn hair was cropped short, but to me that simply enhanced her beauty. Her elegant confidence.

Our hostess glanced up from her reading and said, "Sit please. I'm nearly at a good stopping point."

We arranged ourselves in a semicircle opposite the woman as she finished her paragraph. The slim book was closed and set aside. She said, "I am Louise, the Mother of Magma. And I would speak with… you."

The delicate finger pointed unwaveringly at Leeson. All eyes turned to the young human.

"M-me? Why me?"

The Mother of Magma smiled. "Two reasons. Firstly, I can see that you know the book that I'm reading."

Leeson murmured, "The Tales of Lady Adventurer Camber."

Our hostess chuckled faintly. She affirmed, "The same. Secondly, I can tell that your mouth does not easily form lies."

The young human pointed at Toby as he protested, "He's a paladin of Aro-Remset!"

The Mother of Magma said, "That simply means his lies are true."

This statement seemed to defeat Leeson, who had no idea how to respond.

After peering at the young human for a few moments, the woman asked, "Why are you here?"

Leeson cleared his throat and then said, "We want to stop the violence. We just came from the Company of Glass. The commander guy said that he's not sure how this all started, but he knows he's not responsible for the elementals. He wants a truce."

Louise looked sharply at Toby. "He's telling the truth." It wasn't a question.

The temporarily small minotaur said, "He is."

Turning back to Leeson, the Mother of Magma asked, "Was it possible he was lying? This 'commander-guy' you speak of?"

Leeson shook his head, "I mean, I really doubt it. Anything is possible, but he seemed like a guy in over his head. He wasn't choosing his words carefully. And Toby was there and... well. I believed him."

This seemed to puzzle Louise. "All indications were that the fire elementals went out of control wherever one of their caravans passed. We're not seeing this phenomenon anywhere else. How do you explain this?"

"I don't. I mean, umm, forgive me your ladyship. But we were hoping **you** had some answers."

The Mother of Magma rolled her eyes, perhaps at the 'ladyship' moniker. She said, "I have a son who is your age, you speak a lot like he does."

Leeson blinked. He said, "You're too young, there's no way you have a son my age."

Our hostess' rich laughter filled the yurt's living room.

She turned to me and said, "Your younger brother is more flattering than any paladin."

I didn't ask how she made that connection, nor did I correct her. It was true in every way that mattered. "He's a good kid."

Louise regarded each of us in turn. Then she said, "You may all speak now. One at a time, of course."

We presented the case that the Company of Glass was putting forward. The Mother of Magma listened, but didn't comment. Ames and Tara also spoke about the suspected elemental activity elsewhere in Panos, from what they witnessed over the past few years, to what evidence we had collected in our recent adventures. That held the woman's interest.

After weighing our words, Louise said, "You say that the Company of Glass doesn't have the ability to summon or control fire elementals. That was not what we believed they were doing. **We** normally control the elementals. Someone or something is wresting control from us, making them go wild. We assumed that disruption was coming from your mercenary company. Now that we have been told otherwise, we must seek a different answer."

Leeson followed that information down the logical path. He said, "You didn't burn all of those caravans, did you? It was the uncontrolled elementals."

The Mother of Magma admitted, "We may have burned one or two because of this feud. But not in the numbers that you're speaking of, no. You seem to have a vested interest in these elemental issues. You will help us investigate, yes?"

Toby said, "Of course. If you will call your people off."

"Agreed. And you must get word to this commander-guy of yours. I'll contact my agents in the field and let them know that our efforts shall be redirected. The Company of Glass has their truce until we can discover the cause of all this. Then we shall sit down and speak of our... deeper areas of contention."

The more powerful witches were called in to help with this campaign of information. What interested me was that the men were not called 'warlocks', nor were the orcs called 'hegvena'. There was no distinction between races and genders; every member of their adopted tribe was a 'witch'.

With the help of the chaos magicians, several Max's Messages went out. To Kev, to Max, and to a few chaos witches who had been planning retaliatory strikes against the Company of Glass.

When we finished, the Mother of Magma gave her people new assignments, primarily defensive and investigatory. As they filtered out of the yurt to do their tasks, Louise called out, "Tanya. A word."

The familiar red robed witch who had escorted us in paused. She turned and walked over to Louise for a whispered conversation. It got heated. The whispering grew almost loud enough to hear before the Mother of Magma put an end to it by saying, "You will do this. You know why."

The witch in red allowed her head to drop. She gave the slightest shrug, and then a sullen nod.

Louise turned back to us and said, "My daughter will accompany you for the next few days. She is wise in the ways of the elementals, and can help you find them. If any of my people have anything to report, they will contact her. I assume that you have skins of tin and leather. Don them for this journey."

Tara said, "I'm afraid we cannot until we're normal sized again."

Louise peered at the two minotaurs. "I was wondering. If your height had been a defect of birth, I didn't wish to mention it." The Mother of Magma shrugged. "From this point on, wear your metal suits before you are Reduced. You ride into danger. That much I can attest to. Tanya will be reporting back to me regularly. Do not disappoint us."

Tanya, our apparently unwilling companion, started to walk out of the living room. "Come on then. Get dressed at least, I won't stare at… all of that for the entire journey." She paused and looked directly at Leeson. "Except this one perhaps."

Her mother seemed to agree, "I would **certainly** stare at that one." she called out.

A blushing Leeson hurried into the foyer to put his desert wrap on. The rest of us followed at a more reasonable pace.

Once we were ready to travel, we managed to coax our camels out of the pen, where they had been spitting and fornicating no doubt. Mine simply wandered out when the gate was opened and stood there, staring off into space.

As the other four wrangled their mounts, I had a quiet word with Tanya. I stated, "She wasn't using mental contact, I would have felt it. Nobody in this land knows how close I am to Leeson. So tell me. How long have you been watching us?"

Tanya said, matter of factly, "Since an hour outside of the city. You should be more careful who you buy sand tents from."

I grimaced. It wasn't surprising that we didn't notice a native chaos witch in her own environment. But there was someone who would still take it hard. So I said, "Don't mention that to Ames."

She replied, "I shan't."

To say that Tanya was standoffish over the next day and a half would be a colossal understatement. The red garbed witch took meals alone, didn't engage in idle chatter, and looked far more at the pages of books than at the faces of her companions. When we rested, she wouldn't share my Zone of Comfort. Even when we were riding for the night, Tanya was only interested in getting to the last reported elemental sighting. When we found nothing, she started to lead us to the next potential spot without any expression of hope or disappointment. Conversations were brusque, factual, and all business.

Until Pandemonium was mentioned.

When Leeson started talking about possibly mapping fire elemental movements to the wandering patterns of beasts in Pandemonium, the floodgates opened. Tanya wanted to know everything.

"What did this elven Pandemonium portal look like?"

"What sound do the three legged demon dogs make?"

"Were the Shadows hot or cold?"

"Did you try using a compass in Pandemonium?"

"Did the feathered Prince squawk like a bird?"

Suddenly Tanya was riding knee to knee with Leeson. Ames had to take the lead, so distracted was the chaos witch in her question and answer session with the overwhelmed young man.

But it wasn't a one way knowledge exchange. Tanya's second hand knowledge of Pandemonium was impressive. She was able to explain the way 'kingdoms' are shaped, the relative flow of time in the realms of every major Pandemonium lord, and all of the food sources available on a scale of how bad the side effects were.

One part of their conversation stayed with me in particular. Tanya said, "I have not been to Pandemonium. But I was present when the elders opened their portals. You see, there is a rite of passage before one becomes an elder witch. A ceremony kept amongst our people. Arrangements are in place, understandings going back hundreds of years. But it is still quite dangerous. Someday I will step through. And whether or not I survive, it will be the greatest moment of my life."

Twice during their long conversation, I found myself 'there'. The steady plodding of my damnable camel and the surrounding darkness were perfect catalysts for my episodic flashbacks. I caught myself the first time, in deep remembrance of the rescue mission itself. The second time that I drifted off, it actually felt like I was reliving the 'debriefing' party. Tara nudged me awake before I fell off my camel. The concerned expressions on the faces of both of my minotaur friends told the tale: Either Ames or Benno had warned them about my lapses. Apparently my little secret was no longer a secret to anyone I cared about. I supposed that was a good thing.

When we stopped for the morning, Tanya's attitude towards us completely reversed itself. She offered to cook a warm breakfast in my magic pot, even sharing some of her fresh provisions. The result was a savory potato and carrot stew made with some of the rabbit bullion that I had brought. Sunrise conversation consisted of more extraplanar topics, including my brush with undeath. Afterwards I started my ritual to provide our normal temperate zone. But this time, Tanya's tent had been moved close enough to take advantage of it.

At sunset of our third day with Tanya, she received another report of elemental activity. But this one was different.

"It's close." the red robed witch explained. "An hour to the Northeast, on the tall dunes next to the ruins of the Colosseum. The fire elemental was still there this time. One of the more powerful witches saw it and he had a Message spell at the ready."

The relatively diminutive Toby said, "A fresh lead for once. Let's ride hard and catch this one."

As much as I disliked my mount, I had to admit that a camel could really move if pressed. Once Tanya got her steed into a quick jog, all the rest of the animals kept pace. It was a somewhat jarring ride compared to the horses on Leeson's estate, but comparable to what a frisky, spirited giant wolf could inflict on their rider. At least we all stayed in the saddle.

I called over, "Once we get close enough, how long will it take you to get control of it?"

Tanya shouted back, "A minute. It isn't like your summoning ritual. This elemental is here and free. I need only to perform a fire charm on it. You keep me safe while I do that, and it will be ours. Then we find out where it has been."

We made good time, arriving at the reported spot in perhaps 40 minutes. But disappointment filled our hearts once again. Looking to the top of the dunes there was no fire elemental, only the final shimmers of light cast by the setting sun.

Leeson suggested, "Let's go up and have a closer look. There should be some recent signs right? A glassy trail maybe?"

I nodded at the same time that Tanya did. I was the one who spoke up first, "They burn quite hot, there may be some kind of indication as to where it went."

But as it turned out, the top of the dunes was as far as we needed to go.

Looking down the North side of the dune revealed our quarry. It glowed a bright orange-red in the early night air. The fire elemental was a living bonfire with arms and legs, slowly trekking towards the nearby ruins. If it noticed us in any fashion, it certainly wasn't reacting violently. Had the thing been humanoid, I would have said it was taking a leisurely stroll.

Or perhaps it was just after some tourism. The ancient Colosseum was one of the mysteries of the Glasson Desert. It was briefly mentioned in texts from around the time of the First Great War as a place of honorable battle, of art, and of culture. But any modern examination of the sections left standing gave no hints as to who built it, who owned and ran it, and what sort of events were held in it. Over time, the massive stone arena couldn't resist being retaken by the desert. Presumably it was once a much taller structure, but only three stories of the pillars, walls, and stone seating remained above the shifting sands.

Tanya murmured, "I can do it from a short way down if the elemental keeps going at that pace. If it turns on us, distract it."

Tara said, "I think my summoned hammer will give it something to play with, should the need arise."

We dismounted from our camels, who frankly seemed nonplussed by the raw display of elemental power happening right in front of them. We took the time to set out some food for the beasts on just the other side of the dune, so that they would be kept busy and sheltered from any fiery battle that might ensue. Then the six of us half-stepped, half-slid down the next dozen paces worth of sand dune. I heard the words of a spell being uttered.

But it wasn't Tanya uttering them.

The red garbed witch dove flat, sliding down the dune a little bit in the process. We all quickly followed suit, trusting the native mage's instincts. On our bellies in the sand, we watched the scene unfold before us.

The sound of spellcasting seemed to be coming from the South entrance to the Colosseum. It went on for nearly a minute before the meandering fire elemental suddenly flared, as if dry tinder had been poured into its belly. Quickly, the creature walked across the sand towards the ruined structure, casting a large globe of heat and light in a radius around it.

When the elemental neared the Colosseum, its natural illumination betrayed the two figures waiting for it. The first was a spear carrying human, wearing only a tattered loincloth. The second was a robed elf that looked far too young to have those grey streaks in his long blond hair. Both of them possessed tanned skin that looked stretched, almost leathery from so much exposure to the heat and the sun. The elf turned and walked inside of the ancient structure. Human and fire elemental followed at his heels.

Ames whispered, "What in the infinite hells just happened?"

Tanya's voice was shaking. Whether from anger or fear was undetermined. "He took it. He took control of one of our elementals. Those men are not from these parts. They do not belong here."

Toby murmured, "We're about to lose what little light we have left. Enlarge us and let's get down there while we still know that the way is clear."

Soon the minotaurs were back to their full, impressive size. It meant that we would need to rest again if we wanted to ride camels, but the potential danger of the situation meant that being at full strength outweighed mobility concerns. Leeson reported that he had only one minor spell left, another Enlarge. The rest of his complement of spells were more powerful and involved, which meant he was relying on me and Tanya for spells that required faster casting times.

Preparing for the worst, we left our heavy wrappings just outside of the archway. From what I recalled, I knew that the southern Colosseum entrance would have towered above us a thousand years ago. Now, Toby's horns were only a half pace from scraping against the curved stone. Quickly and quietly, Ames and Tanya led the way.

We followed Ames's paw gestures, splitting up so that three of us were secreted behind each of the massive pillars at the mouth of the tunnel's exit. From there we could observe the puzzling activities happening at the center of the Colosseum.

It was a cult. That was the only word that came to mind. The dozens of gathered entities were of every race and stature, and yet they had many things in common. They were unwashed, burnt by the sun, and emaciated. Each and every set of eyes was crazed, filled with pain or with hatred. I remember reading an ancient text. It said that the power of hope is only overpowered by the iron chains of hopelessness. I hoped that ancient philosopher was wrong.

The elven mage who captured and controlled the fire elemental was leading it into the center of the arena. The ranks of cultists closed around them. There was no chanting, no invocation, no prayers. Just a low moan, or droning. Each of the dozens of gathered unfortunates took up the exact same note. The eerie resonance sent a shiver up my spine. It sounded like...

"The Hum."

That was Tara's pained whisper. I glanced over at the opposite pillar, and saw Toby gritting his teeth. Whatever was happening, it produced a very real effect, and my friends were feeling it. I was about to ask if we should do something, when there was a cacophonous rending sound.

All eyes were drawn towards the fire elemental. It was hovering several paces off the ground, 'screaming' in crackling bursts. Then reality seemed to fracture. The elemental was rended into bits. What cinders remained seemed to be enveloped in purple-gray motes and banished from this reality.

For a pregnant moment, there was only darkness and silence.

Then the earth opened.

The entire center of the Colosseum drained of sand, as if a plug had been pulled in a giant bathtub. The cultists stepped back quickly, retreating to the perimeter of the arena before they fell victim to the results of their ritual. The earth started to tremor.

Leeson finished his first spell. He was now easily as tall as Toby after Enlarging himself. The giant human frantically waved us over, wanting to cast another spell of preparation before we were discovered. We quickly gathered around.

I remember when the elven wolf rider, Yarith, cast her Haste spell on me. My heart leaped, my pulse surged. Leeson's rendition of the spell had the same potent kick. We were all twitching, hyperactive. The human was already flowing into his third spell. But the rest of us were out of time.

Two of the cultists who were backing away from the devastation saw our little huddle. They cried out and pointed. One reacted with anger, pulling a cudgel from her hip. The other reacted with fear, climbing up into the stadium's stone seating and putting as much distance between us and themself as possible.

As the alarm went up, that pattern continued. Several of the cultists fled the arena, while a minority took up arms and started to approach our position. We were fine allowing the cowardly ones to leave. No matter how disturbed they were, slaughtering noncombatants wasn't what we signed up for.

The ones brave or foolish enough to confront us moved along the perimeter of the Colosseum floor, avoiding the sinkhole that they had created. The ones in the lead slowed, waiting until they had the strength of superior numbers before confronting us.

I took the opportunity to cast my Light cantrip on a recently fallen piece of masonry situated out in front of us. The illumination extended to the lip of the arena's southern entrance. We could pull back into the darkness of the tunnel if necessary, while leaving our foes exposed in the light.

The minotaurs executed little preparation rituals of their own. Tara summoned her icy blue Divine Warhammer, her prayers to Melflavin answered. Toby, having become one of Aro-Remset's most beloved servants, invoked a blessing that I had heard of, but never seen in person. The paladin bellowed upon finishing his short prayer to the god of fair battle, as Aro-Remset's Divine Strength washed over him. He was surrounded by a rose-tinted aura as his muscles bulged. For a short time, my friend would have the power of a giant rather than a minotaur.

That said, the odds didn't look great. As Toby and Tara lined up between the two pillars, cultists streamed in from both the left and the right, staying wide to avoid the hole that they created in the center of the arena. There must have been over a score of them, mostly unarmored, but nearly all armed.

Fleeing would have been an option if not for the bright glow that we saw in the distance.

The elven cultist was already leading in the next fire elemental at the North entrance of the Colosseum.

"Boost me."

Tanya was eyeing the stands. I hesitated at the thought of sending our new ally in by herself, but I didn't see much of a choice. Someone had to stop the crazed elementalist, and the chaos witch was likely the most qualified. I cupped my gloved hands and lifted when the young woman stepped into the offered boost. She scrambled up to the stone benches. Taking advantage of the Haste spell, Tanya sprinted along the bottom ring of seats. She was halfway to her target in just a few seconds.

Tara's voice was shaky as she requested, "Some help please?"

The minotaurs were backing as the throng of leathery cultists closed in. Big help was coming though. Leeson finished his last spell and stomped into the front lines, flanking Tara between himself and Toby. I knew that even though nobody would see it, the young mage cast Leeson's Living Layer, and a roaming invisible shield would be defending him. Ames, having successfully watched over Leeson's final preparations, appeared next to Toby. I say 'appeared' because under the effects of the Haste spell, it was difficult to track the were-cat's movements. With enhanced speed, the already fast feline was going to be a handful.

Just before the throng crashed into our front line, Toby said, "Tara. Spot for Sorch." Those four simple words defined our entire strategy. I knew my role. While the paladin, combat mage, and rogue held back the tide,

Tara would fight defensively and look for the leaders amongst the cultists. And I would do my best to end them. I was to be the counter-puncher. And ultimately, the group's magical assassin.

Ames waited to unsheath their new blade until the last possible second. I had seen my mate practice this technique in the past, and could attest that the process was blindingly fast even without a Haste spell. The were-cat struck with that initial drawing motion, firebrand sabre roaring to life as a scimitar wielding lizardman got too close. The cultist's blade was beat wide before he received a deep, burning cut that opened him up from breastbone to shoulder. Even as the screaming blue-green creature stumbled back, a heavily muscled human brute swung her broadaxe at Ames' face. Natural awareness and unnatural speed allowed the were-cat to roll to the left. The warrior woman's blade sailed over Ames' head, missing by over a handbreadth. By the time the cultist's axe was back in guard position, the feline was already circling along the curvature of the arena's outside wall.

On the opposite flank, the cultists had never seen anything like Leeson. Hells, I had never seen anything like Leeson. The young human was a hulk. As tall as Toby, as fast as the wind, with an invisible friend that could shield his back. It was a recipe for malice. The melee mage's Ironwood staff flashed in a double arc as he whipped it around in a figure eight motion. The three cultists facing him started to backpedal, nervously. For good reason as it turned out. The giant mage waded in with an overhead strike. The half orc's small buckler wasn't enough to stop the momentum of Leeson's blow. After glancing off of the rounded shield, the staff crushed the humanoid's shoulder. The impact was so brutal that it stole the creature's scream, half of his chest displaced as a result of the downward strike. The human cultist on my friend's left flank thrust his tulwar at the giant mage's kidney. Leeson's invisible floating shield intercepted the blow, much to the cultist's confusion. The counter from the melee mage was immediate and brutal, crushing into the smaller human's neck and jaw, taking the swordsman out of the fight.

Toby was a force of nature. Magically fast, divinely strong, and wielding the legendary Axe of McGrondle, the minotaur was being actively avoided by most of the cultists. The first to stand against him was a barbarian woman with a blood encrusted warhammer. Her first testing blow was knocked aside by Toby's buckler. The second was blocked by the minotaur's axehead, runes crawling hungrily along the surface as it easily absorbed the impact. The paladin's counter was a diagonal chop that separated the woman's head and the upper right part of her torso from the remainder of her body. The rest of the cultists surrounding Toby milled uncertainly just outside of his effective range.

"Mages 10 and 1!"

Tara's warning left me with an impossible decision. Even with my quickest spell, I wouldn't be able to stop both of them. I chose the one ahead and slightly to my right, simply because he was farther away and might feel he was safe enough to try a long, complex, but devastating spell. I held up both hands to cast one of my oldest and most reliable spells. The Force Bolt knocked the cultist sorcerer back, almost causing him to fall into the still-forming hole in the center of the Colosseum floor. He scrambled on all fours, fighting against the tide of sliding sand.

Sadly, that meant the half elven mage was able to finish her spell. A portal opened upon the pillar behind Toby and to his left. The rain of fist-sized hailstones shattered against the paladin's chainmail, bruising and freezing his flesh, sending thin shards of ice through the gaps in the metal and the thin leather lining underneath. Seeing my big friend bleeding and pained, his adversaries quickly crowded in and tried to overwhelm him.

I saw a string of white flashes in the distance. Tanya caught her quarry. Magic Missiles stung the flesh of the elven elementalist. His fire elemental started to slowly wander around the far side of the arena, uncontrolled, as its master focused on this new magical duel.

A nearly hairless wererat tried to get to me through the gap between Tara and Leeson. Just as I was about to draw my dagger, the floating warhammer took matters into its own hands, as it were. It drew itself up high, directly above the stalking cultist. The hammer seemed to hesitate for a moment before swinging and falling with brutal force.

Above the sound of a cracking wererat spine, Tara shouted, "3 o'clock!"

To my right, high in the stadium's stone seating, I saw an emaciated elven archer draw a strange looking arrow back. I palmed the beetle guts from my pouch and started casting. Sadly, I finished my Acid Bolts at the same time that the cultist found his opening and loosed the projectile from his shortbow.

The glass-bulbed arrow impacted with Leeson's wandering invisible shield, but that hardly mattered. It was the conjured cloud of scalding steam that would do the real damage. My young friend screamed, covering his face with one arm as he stumbled backwards out of the cloud. In that moment of weakness, a speartip pierced his robes and poked into the human's hip. He managed to recover, thanks in part to the supernatural speed provided by his Haste spell. Two follow up blows were parried by the blur of a spinning Ironwood staff as the melee mage grimly took up a more defensive stance.

My only satisfaction, as the drain of my orcish curse scraped at the outer edges of my mind, was seeing the aftermath of my own attack. The elf's unarmored chest and belly had been hollowed out by my Acid Bolt spell. There would be no second chance for him.

On the left side, however, the smallest of our front line was proving to be the most devastating. Ames removed the axe maiden's right arm and delivered the coup de grace to the writhing lizardman. There were panicked shouts from the cultists, who couldn't imagine that a counterattack would have been viable given their numbers. But they were wrong. Ames was among them. The were-cat's incredible celerity proved the undoing of an old sickle wielding human, his chest pierced and heart burned out before he could put up any defense. The flash of a firebrand sabre then shattered the skull of the second mage, who was so caught up in continuing her attack against Toby that she ignored the warning and sudden retreat of her front line.

This was good news for Toby. As Ames single handedly pushed back the enemy's entire left flank, two of the minotaur's attackers were forced to pull back and consolidate their ranks, or fall victim to the deadly rogue themselves. Toby got away from the savage group attack with only a couple of slashes to his ankles and his forearm. The surge of Divine Strength allowed the paladin to hold his ground and push back his attackers when they attempted to mob him. Now, with only two foes directly in his face, the Axe of McGrondle could get back to work. Its enchanted blade hacked through the next cultist's scimitar and wrist alike. Fragments of steel and bone fell to the sand below.

The lessening of pressure on the left allowed Tara to shift her attention to the right, and come to the struggling and winded Leeson's aid. A merciless shield bash fractured the nose of the human who had attempted to duck under Leeson's guard. The burned and bleeding mage, now assisted by the cleric, finally managed to stabilize the right flank.

That left me with options. I started to cast my next spell, looking to make an example out of one of the cultists.

The far side of the arena was on fire. I suppose we should have expected nothing less with two desert mages fighting tooth and nail. From here it was hard to tell who was winning. Tanya possessed superior speed and cover, but the elven elementalist's talent was an unknown factor. It was out of our control, for the moment.

The mage that had been knocked down earlier made his way to the far right side of the Colosseum. Perhaps he was looking for an angle to cast his next spell. Perhaps he was attempting to escape. I removed all but one of his options. When the metal links slipped from my fingers and disappeared forever, I knew I had him. An otherworldly rattling accompanied the appearance of pulsing black eldritch chains. The other mage screamed in terror as he was bound to me. The massive drain on my intellect made me feel lightheaded, like after a night of drinking and chewing on ephen leaves. But the mental drain did nothing to inhibit my physical strength. I grabbed the Ebon Chains of Binding and yanked brutally, reeling in the struggling man as his feet slid over the sand, unable to find any purchase. The looks of horror from the cultists battling Leeson and Tara told me that my spell was having the desired effect. It took me no time at all to slide the writhing mage across the sands. He looked up just in time to see my body falling forward, knee leading. I felt that skull buckle under the full weight of my body. There was no need to look down to see the aftermath of my brutal attack against the prone mage. The Ebon Chains disappeared, making the result a certainty.

"It's coming!"

It took us a moment to see what the cultists were shouting about. But then Toby clarified, "Fire elemental incoming."

The next few moments were chaos. All of the cultists who were able to flee scrambled up the walls or ran for the East and West archways. The two of us mobile and healthy enough to move quickly, Ames and myself, bolted up opposite sides of the arena. I had never run flat out under the effects of a Haste spell, but suffice it to say that I feared as much for my own life as anyone that I might have accidentally plowed into. My peripheral vision was just a blur of darkness and the glow of fire as I approached the North side of the stadium.

Then I heard Ames' voice from up ahead and to the left. "Hold, Sorch. It's over."

I skidded to a halt and allowed my eyes to adjust to the light being produced by the residual fires. Tanya was standing, hands held out towards the fire elemental as it made its way down the slope of sand towards the very center of the Colosseum. Her red robes were singed and blackened, and the chaos mage looked shaky on her feet. But she was in far better shape than the elf, who was nothing more than a blackened husk on the ground.

Ames and I stood guard over the chaos witch. None of the remaining cultists seemed to want any trouble however. They disappeared like rats from a sinking ship, making use of every possible egress. After reaching the center of the indentation, the fire elemental seemed to sink into the earth, following the flow of sand that had come before.

Tanya let out a half held breath. She said, "It's going to assess the damage and see what can be done to plug it up. First with glass, then eventually with enough effort and some help, a controlled lava flow. If repair is possible at all."

I asked, "Can you walk?"

She grimaced, but nodded. "Slowly. I twisted an ankle escaping from the worst part of a Fireball."

We each lent the mage a shoulder and helped her to limp back to the rest of the party. Toby performed the Laying of Hands on Leeson, who was still burnt, but seemed to be in much less pain. Tara invoked some initial healing on Toby, and was now helping the paladin to remove his chainmail coat so that the remaining cuts from the ice shards could be treated and bandaged in mundane fashion. Ever the trooper, Toby reached out to our newest ally and invoked the minor healing prayer granted by Aro-Remset, even as he himself was being bandaged. Tanya gasped in relief, the pain of her more severe burns fading, and her twisted ankle mostly mended.

With our healing exhausted, Toby was still bloodied and frozen, Leeson's torso was scalded by steam from collarbone to pelvis, and everyone else was suffering from minor wounds. Save for myself, which was a testament to the skill and tenacity of our melee presence.

"This one's still alive."

We walked, hobbled, and limped over to Ames, who was standing above the one armed axe maiden. The were-cat's firebrand sword had mostly cauterised the grievous wound, though the woman was clearly in bad shape.

She scowled up at us and said, "It still ends. It will all end."

An irrational surge of anger coursed through my body. In that moment I didn't care if she was a prisoner. I didn't care if she was dying. I wanted answers.

I bared my teeth and snarled at the fallen warrior, "Which demon is behind this? Which god would cause this kind of naked devastation?"

The axe maiden laughed, the sound weak but derisive all the same. "Demons? Gods? They are not in control here. You, Stonebreaker, you are not in control here."

Ames hissed, "How do you know his name, wench?"

The dying woman licked the blood from her lips and closed her eyes, "It is part of the Hum. The Hum said the two orcs would meddle. It said that we should drill a great hole all the way from the ocean into the desert. The Hum wishes to wash the world clean."

Leeson murmured, "They were trying to sink it all. Flood the entire valley from Glasson to the Ruins of Poth. That's insane."

The woman's eyes snapped open. "Insane is living by the words of gods and archmages and bishops. Insane is living in a world that is trying to kill you. It all must end. The Hum will end it."

I asked, "If nobody is behind this stupid cult of yours, where do you get the power to do all this?"

With her last breath, the woman spat, "The Hum. That which it breaks, you shall not mend."

Then, silence.

We collected the camels and made camp under the shelter of the southern entryway. The mages sent out the Messages we prepared, while Toby and Leeson chewed on some of Ames' coca leaves to relieve the pain on the inevitable ride back to civilization. Ames and Tara conducted a half-hearted search of the area, but other than a few copper and silver, there was nothing to salvage. We all needed a couple hours of rest. I would mostly top up my intellect enhancements and be ready for the return journey. And of course, despite the pain, Leeson would have to Reduce our large friends for the ride back.

It was Tara who motivated us to get off our butts and mount up. She chided, "Come on lazybones. We can make Omi-Suteth's temple in Glasson just after sun-up. We get our healing, some sleep, and the accolades that go hand in hand with a job well done."

Even Toby was eyeing the cleric after that pep talk.

Tara asked, "What, too cheery?"

Her husband grunted and said, "Just a little bit."

Tara was correct though. We would have to ride at pace if we wanted to avoid making camp again. The cleric rode close to Toby, and Tanya close to Leeson just in case the wounded and coca-dosed men started to fall out of the saddle. The chaos mage was speaking quietly with my young human friend all the while. I thought that she was picking his brain about the other planes again. But upon riding a bit closer, I eavesdropped on a different kind of conversation.

"...she is a very spirited creature. You need to know when to match that spirit, and when to comply."

Leeson asked, "How do I know that, though? Half the time it's noses and kisses, the other half it's snarling and claws."

Tanya advised, "You need to learn the body language. Watch the tail. Stiff and still is angry or upset. Fluid and waggy is happy and playful."

Leeson sighed, "Then she accuses me of looking at her rump all the time."

Tanya laughed softly, "But you can turn that into a positive thing. Just..."

I drifted back out of range. It was a good thing that Leeson was getting some sage advice from another woman where Jess was concerned. The were-wolf lass could be a handful. But it was none of my business, and I had my own were-creature who was a constant source of mystery.

The sun had been up for over an hour and a half, but we were close. We powered through the morning heat until the silhouette of Glasson grew in our vision. A couple of minutes away from the low wall that bordered the open market, Tanya brought her camel to a halt.

The chaos witch said, "This is where we part ways."

I asked, "Did you want to come to the temple and have your ankle looked at? I'm paying."

The red robed woman shook her head. "We have our own holy people. I know a man, not far from here. I shall have shelter from the sun before I journey home."

Leeson offered the other mage a tired smile. He said, "Thanks, for everything."

Tanya's reply was directed at everyone, "You all go take care of your things, both civilized and wild. Do not be disturbed by those whose minds are touched by the sun. We will speak to the men of glass. There will be a peace, and together we will keep this place safe."

Toby said, "Your help was, and continues to be, very much appreciated Tanya. Wish your mother well for us."

The chaos mage nodded curtly. Then she turned her camel and trotted off to the East, towards the rising sun.

The Temple of Omi-Suteth was more than happy to receive us. I remember thinking: *'Of course. Injured adventurers meant more donations, so why wouldn't they?'* Perhaps I was being a bit more cynical than usual given recent interactions with the goddess in question.

Still, the healing was very welcome. Seeing Toby and Leeson resting without pain was worth every copper. Once everyone was tended to, our business in Glasson was done. We were just waiting in the congregational assembly area as one of the acolytes arranged transport back to the Arcane University. Then we could debrief with Max and get some much needed sleep.

We were comparing the temples that hosted Circles of Transport. Leeson favored this garden over the rest, while I of course preferred the rock garden at the Temple of Omi-Suteth in Royal Moffit.

I pointed out, "You haven't even seen all of the transport destinations yet, young man. With this visit, I've seen every single one."

Toby commented, "It's been a busy few years for you, hasn't it Sorch?"

I nodded at my once-again-tall companion, "I must admit, I would have much preferred to see all of these temples as a tourist rather than as a patient."

Ames jokingly pointed out, "We've visited half the temples in Panos, and he still hasn't had the decency to marry me."

My earlier conversation with Leeson replayed in my mind. Well then.

I asked Ames, "Have you ever seen the Orcish marriage ceremony, dear?"

The were-cat shook their head.

I stepped up to my mate, getting dangerously close. "The one doing the proposing asks: Are you willing?"

Suddenly, and uncharacteristically, Ames was nervous. The feline's ears flicked and then flattened a little bit.

After a few moments, there was a quiet but firm reply. "Yes."

There was no length of hair to grab a hold of, so instead I allowed my calloused fingers to grip the flesh and fur at the scruff of Ames' neck. The cat stiffened and snarled. I snarled right back.

Locking eyes with my mate, meaning every word, I intoned: "With these words: You shall be mine."

And with that, I tugged on the were-cat's scruff so that Ames' head was tilted back, and then kissed my mate deeply. The kiss wasn't actually part of the ceremony. But it was certainly fun.

Then I heard Toby's voice.

"Witnessed."

And Tara's.

"Witnessed."

And my 'little brother' chimed in, his voice broken and teary.

"Witnessed."

It wasn't until after my smooth tongue stopped wrestling with Ames' rough feline appendage that an unexpected voice joined in.

The robed cleric who had been passing by said, "Witnessed. And congratulations. I'll file the appropriate papers as part of your already generous donation. May the blessing of Omi-Suteth follow you on this happy day."

Our friends were all smiling and laughing, despite our collective exhaustion.

Ames asked, breathlessly, "Did that really just happen?"

I nodded and said, "I think the Guild is going to merge our bank accounts now."

We agreed to plan a small celebration for our close family and friends, and Leeson insisted that it be held at the Renault family estate.

I said, "I love your parents of course, and I'm flattered that you would offer, but Ames and I don't want to be any trouble. Maybe we should do something small at the University instead."

Leeson said, "There will be steak and cake."

Without hesitation, I said, "Done."

For a moment I wondered if that mysterious power had taken over my voice once again. But then I realized: A sane person doesn't say 'no' to steak and cake.

Chapter 11

"Tell me again."

We all groaned. This would be the third time that the five of us explained the sacrifice and battle at the Colosseum. Max was fixated on the words of the dying axe maiden. Her claim that this power was summoned without the aid or direction of any god or demon had shaken Max to the core.

I said, "They said it was the Hum, Max. The same as the cyclops did. Surely this is code for some kind of demon worship or the power of a god gone mad."

The old mage was pale. He paced slowly at the head of the stone dining room table. "It isn't. At least none of the portents of the elves or reports of any major or minor clergy members back up that version of events. This 'Hum' is something we've never seen before, never heard of. It's not in any document that we can find in the archives. Divination to the gods comes back mute when asked about it. Entities in the outer planes know nothing, or at least they're saying nothing."

The Headmaster seemed half way between frustration and fright. He said, "And all that would be fine if it held no real power. But this, what you described. That's real power."

Leeson said, "Maybe we should focus on the elemental activity? Look in the records for events precipitated by a lot of elemental-"

Max cut him off, saying, "I knew there was a reason we kept you around. Go. Do that, coordinate with Benno and Assistant Donnelly, they're doing similar work already. Maybe we can kill multiple birds with one boulder."

As we stood up, Max said, "Payment is in your accounts. Let my assistant know how long you're staying, I'll arrange for a clerical visit for anyone who still needs it."

I decided to stay for a few days to check in on Benno and spend some family time with him and with Granite. Ames would be in and out, only having the Vole to take care of in the next two weeks. Normally we would get some fishing in, but the R. M. N. 'Taboo' was dry docked for cleaning and refitting. After recent events, a nice peaceful week at the University didn't sound so bad, to be honest.

Which was why I found myself holding my youngest son a couple of days later. Little Granite was doing his damnedest to grab my nose, while his mother laughed at our antics. We were slowly making our way down the hall to Parsnip's quarters, so that the little tyke could get some rest after keeping us entertained all morning long.

Parsnip said, "Have you noticed how much he's grown over the past few months? He'll be toddling around soon enough. Almost as much of a holy terror as his dad. As both of his dads."

I chuckled, dodging a slow poke to the eye from my son. It was easily accomplished with a little head tilt. "You give me too much credit. I may be dangerous, but your husband is genuinely nuts. We aren't even in the same category."

Patricia rolled her eyes. She asked, "How's Benno's recovery coming along?"

I frowned, but kept my voice calm and steady for the baby's sake. "He'll be fine with a few more days of clerical help and rest. And since this is the last time he's going on an adventure, he's going to stay fine from now on."

We walked in silence for a few steps. Then Patricia said, "Does he know that was his last adventure?"

"Not yet."

I glanced down and noticed that little Granite put on an exaggerated frown to match my own. Then the little smartass laughed and tried to capture my nose again.

Parsnip murmured, "You know, you raised Benno well Sorch. He's a strong, independent, talented young man. Which means there's absolutely nothing that you can do to stop him if he decides he wants to be an adventurer. He's going to say, 'Yes Dad, I understand Dad.' And then he's going to go around your back and do it anyway."

I said, "He wouldn't dare."

Parsnip adjusted her robes. "Dear. Not only would he dare, he would plan the outing to such an exacting standard that you would never even know about it."

I sighed heavily. "So I'm just supposed to let him throw himself into harm's way? Let him be as stupid as his father was?"

I felt a delicate hand stroke through my hair as we walked. "You aren't stupid. And I should note: You turned out okay."

"So you're in the same camp as Ames. You think I need to shut up and just be supportive."

Parsnip considered her words carefully for a few moments. Then she said, "I think screaming at the rising tide doesn't stop the ocean. So I think that if you want him to be safe, you need to prepare him, not hobble him."

I would have thrown my hands up in frustration and surrender if the action wouldn't have resulted in a plummeting baby. Instead I just grunted and nodded a little bit. My mind wasn't changed, but I had some new things to consider.

We chatted about meal plans for tonight as we rounded the bend and approached the door to Patricia and Celestial's quarters. Granite's mother gently took the half-snoozing babe from my arms and then slipped inside to lay the child down for his afternoon nap. I waited outside.

With the door cracked open, I heard some very odd stuff. There was the telltale creak of leather under strain, as if someone was working on horse barding in there. Then I heard a muffled squeak and a repetitive swatting sound.

Parsnip hurried back out of her room, blushing furiously. Her face nearly matched that fiery red hair.

I asked, "What in the hells is going on in there?"

The half elven lass closed the door firmly. "Nothing!"

I pressed, "Did you sneak a horse into the University or something? I know you two are into weird stuff but there are health and safety issues to consider."

Patricia grabbed my arm and tugged firmly. When we were walking again, she said, "It's just Ames and Celestial blowing off some steam."

Now my curiosity was piqued. I stopped and glanced over my shoulder, ignoring Parsnip's attempts to urge me onward.

"Maybe they're in trouble and need to be rescued."

The half elf's dry reply was, "I'm sure their release will come soon enough."

I nearly doubled over with laughter. Not wanting to cause a scene in the middle of the hallway, Parsnip linked her arm around mine and tugged firmly. I was encouraged to laugh as we walked.

After recovering from my mirth, I asked, "Is the baby going to be alright in there? We can go back and grab him, put him down in my room."

The mother of my second child shook her head. She said, "He's fine. Granite can sleep through anything."

I teased my blushing friend, "You didn't have to leave on my account. Go back and watch if you like."

That earned me a sharp pinch on the forearm, which produced a yelp that satisfied Parsnip's ego for the moment.

After considering our options, the two of us headed back to my guest quarters so that Patricia could get some rest without having to weather the sounds of recreational abuse. She caught me up on current Arcane University events as we walked.

One of the last things she mentioned was, "Oh, my former roommate has been expelled for attempting to do to another new student what was done to me. What he didn't know is that this particular lizard girl was being scryed because her father was painting a portrait of her from halfway across Panos. Mister hypnosis walked in on their sitting, not knowing that there was a floating Eye in the corner. So as it turns out, he's perverted, immoral, and incredibly unlucky."

I said, "I'm glad he was finally caught with witnesses and proof."

I made a mental note to follow up on my prior lesson if I ever ran into the kid again. It seemed that the first warning didn't take.

As we neared my quarters, I caught Parsnip up on my life as well: The research, the adventures, the unexpected wedding and impending celebrations.

Parsnip asked, "And your visions? The lapses into the past?"

I said, "Oddly, I haven't had one in days. Maybe they were some kind of ineffective portents that were supposed to lead me to the discovery of this doomsday cult. If so, whichever god or goddess engineered the episodes needs to be far more specific next time."

The half elf asked, "The gods have a personal involvement in your life, don't they? Particularly the likes of Omi-Suteth. Is it just your role in trying to overcome the orc curse?"

I considered that question for a few steps before answering, "Mainly. Though I have to say, for someone who doesn't worship a god or demon, I get far too much attention. I don't particularly want them meddling in my affairs, and I really wish they would take care of their own messes. I don't enjoy being used as a mouthpiece, a memory factory, or a research subject."

Patricia joked, "All of these priests and devout worshipers just want the briefest of personal interaction with their deity. And they can't because every time they pray, their god is having tea with you."

"I actually had tea with Koroth."

Patricia sighed. She said, "Of course you did. I should have picked something like fishing. The point being, now we know the real secret to divine interaction: Play hard to get."

I really wanted to ask Parsnip something, but my agreement with Melflavin prevented me from sharing certain things with her. I tried a more roundabout line of questioning.

"Parsnip, do you ever feel like... that is to say, do you ever think that you might be part of some sort of prophecy yourself?"

I felt the half elf's body stiffen. She squeezed my linked arm even more tightly. It took her a moment to relax again. When she did, she managed a reply.

"Let me just say that it wouldn't surprise me in the least, dear. And that as much as I would like to talk about that subject, I cannot."

It seemed like I wasn't the only one bound to silence by Melflavin. I made a mental note to ask Tara if this was a common theme with He Who Wept.

As we walked up to the door of the guest quarters, Patricia decided that a change of subject was in order. She said, "Listen, I'm far enough along now that I can comfortably share the news. Our son is going to have a little brother or sister. And yes, this time I'm certain it's Celestial's."

I let go of my dear friend's arm, only to embrace her in a warm but gently delivered hug. I said, "Gods Patricia, that's great news. I'm happy. For the both of you."

She joked, "It was a tactical decision. We figure that a second one will be entertaining for Granite, and we'll save a fortune in toys and babysitting. That's how this parenting thing works, right?"

I snorted and said, "Given the parents, I think you need to fireproof your apartments."

Parsnip seemed unconcerned, "Oh I'm sure there's a spell for that."

I leaned in to deliver a congratulatory kiss on the cheek. What I did not expect was that my friend would turn her head to intercept that kiss with her lips. It had been a while. I had forgotten the feeling of those soft, tender lips against mine.

The half elf took charge, letting go of my arm to grip my rump in one hand, and the back of my neck in the other. Her ardor was sudden, but certainly not unwelcome. She drew my tongue into her mouth with a gentle suckling, and then teased my flesh with her teeth.

When we finally broke the kiss, both of us were panting heavily. I asked, "What's got you all worked up?"

The sensations of dexterous fingers massaging my behind through the fabric of my robes got me to growl, much to Patricia's satisfaction.

She said, "You mean other than seeing our mates engage in their own entertainment? Freedom."

I tilted my head and asked for clarification, "Freedom?"

"I can't get pregnant twice, Sorch."

I couldn't fault her logic. I allowed myself to be dragged inside of the guest chambers and taken captive. There I was informed that it was my duty to get Parsnip properly tired so that she could engage in a satisfying afternoon nap. I showed her that I take such responsibilities very seriously.

Chapter 12

There was a good reason why one might avoid targeting a sleeping individual with Max's Message: The two dozen words that you get back might be utter nonsense.

I'm fairly certain that my groggy response to being summoned to the Headmaster's office at the crack of dawn was as follows: *'I would but the red spiders are serving dessert and I like the honey coated boots. Can I bring friends?'*

The magical summons was followed up with a far more mundane one. A grumpy looking student who was apprenticing with the Transport Guild knocked on my door. Her gold robes were on backwards and her black hair was puffy on one side and flat on the other.

We stared at each other through the small gap that I created when opening the guest room door. I wondered if this was just a bad dream. The young human looked like she might be wondering the same thing. That continued for a number of seconds, until I prompted the apprentice with my displeased grunt.

The message that she mumbled sounded a lot like the reply I had given Max. Regardless, I understood the bones of the request. The words 'Headmaster' and 'office' and 'immediately' were all contained within her message, although the order of the words were somewhat suspect. I nodded at the unfortunate student, and then shut the door in her face.

Within a couple of minutes, I had sort of fallen into my morning wake up routine. I went to the bathing chambers to wash my stink off, but I forgot to bring a towel. Rather than stomp back to my quarters naked, I shook myself in doglike fashion. Then I just put the old robes back on over my dripping body, before making my surly way to the North Wing.

I remember wondering what in the multiple hells I had done wrong to get called to Max's office before decent people could engage in the comfort of their morning rituals. For a moment I wondered if I was actually enrolled in classes, and I had been called to the Headmaster's office because of something stupid that I did. Maybe the last few years were just a dream. Hells, maybe I was dreaming right now.

The monotone drone of Max's ancient elven assistant was jarring enough to convince me that this was reality.

"You're late. They'll see you now."

I was about to ask what she meant by 'they', but I was already being ignored in favor of the woman's critically important paperwork. I stole more than a couple of cashews from the little jar on the assistant's desk before heading inside.

I really wasn't expecting a crowd.

Crammed into Max's office was the man himself, plus the former owner of the office, plus two psychics.

I observed the chaos as I chewed the sweet, salty nuts that might just have to serve as my breakfast. Hemitath and Assistant Donnelly seemed to be arguing about something, in perhaps the quietest and most civilized disagreement that I ever heard. Benno was scribbling something on a parchment. Max was off to the side touching his crystal ball and seemingly deep in concentration.

It was Benno who noticed me first. "Dad. Why are you wet?"

I blinked at my son's question. I should be the one asking questions here. Still, I couldn't summon the energy or the will to be indignant. So I went for pitiful and said, "I forgot my towel." I may have fired a couple of tiny cashew shards onto the office floor in the process of answering.

Benno's laughter snapped everyone's attention to me for a moment. Hemitath offered a brief, tight smile. Donnelly avoided looking directly at me, instead offering a quick, shy wave before going back to his conversation with the elven archmage.

It was Max who found the time to actually attempt to bring me up to speed. He said, "Ah, Sorch. Late but… at least clean, I suppose. We need a subject matter expert, and sadly, you're all we could find."

I rubbed my eyes with the backs of my hand. I said, "I'm wet. I'm tired. I was having a great dream about… hells I hardly even remember, but it involved dessert. What do you want, Max?"

The old magus gestured to the books and parchments strewn around the room. "I want clarity. I certainly don't want to read all of this from cover to cover. So tell me everything you know about Arcane Syphons."

"I will. But why here?"

Max narrowed his eyes. He asked, "What do you mean?"

I gestured around the tiny office. "There's five of us in here. You're about to be crushed by the books that you've strewn everywhere. If there's research involved I can only imagine you'll want even more books and more parchment an-"

Max cut me off, saying, "Yes, yes. The tribal lad has a point. The dining room is a minute down the hall so let's grab what we can carry and move this little study session to a more spacious venue. I'll send apprentices for the rest."

We relocated to the stone table in the dining room. Tomes quickly covered all available flat surfaces.

I peered at the titles on display and said, "These are all about artifacts and ancient elven magic. I'm afraid what I know about the Arcane Syphons is far more personal and practical."

Hemitath called over, "That's alright, Sorch dear. We need to discuss personal interactions."

I nodded and said, "I'll be glad to. Could you give me some context?"

It was Benno who got around to providing me with an explanation. My son said, "Bill suggested that we explore the sites where elementals have been spotted. Astrally."

I made a mental note that my son was on a first name basis with the other psychic. "Okay."

The younger orc continued, "We were at your most recent sighting, the old arena in the desert. Your pet fire elemental was trying to repair the local damage, but we saw extensive fracturing. And it went down. Way down."

Assistant Donnelly explained, "As we went further down... if you can call anything 'down' in the Astral plane... the gaps started to close up. There were just spiderweb cracks. But we still saw it."

Before I could ask, Benno jumped back in to explain, "There was a glow. A powerful aura at a scale that neither of us had ever seen before. It was emanating from the earth. And it felt just like the energy that was being manipulated when we went after the Voodoo Engine."

Hemitath added, "With all of the Arcane Syphons accounted for, this is disturbing news. So we're discussing ranges."

I turned back to Max, "You're asking if I could somehow put the magical energy into a Syphon here, and translate the energy into producing work up in the Glasson Desert."

Max nodded and said, "That I am."

I replied, "In that case, the answer is 'no'. The arcane workers that the Voodoo Engine made weren't exactly Invisible Servants, but they were close. We tried to direct them to do very distant things. But they got lost or confused after just a few miles. If we had a huge range, we wouldn't have been limited by the ore that was in nearby hillsides. But they were, and forgive me for being blunt, too stupid to find their way across complex terrain, I'm afraid."

Everyone was quiet. It wasn't the answer that they hoped for.

I postulated, "Could the Voodoo Engine have somehow returned? Demonic power or the like. Some kind of mechanism for self repair?"

Hemitath shook her head. "We don't know Sorch. If you could pull up a chair and help with the research, it would be much appreciated."

And that's how my vacation was ruined.

I worked side by side with Benno. We focused on the theory that the Voodoo Engine had somehow returned, while the others were looking for any record of the creation of an Arcane Syphon that wasn't in the Arcane University's possession.

After an hour of reading and making notes, curiosity got the better of me. "Kiddo?"

"Yeah Dad?"

I chose my words with care. "You failed to mention that you were making regular trips to the Astral with Assistant Donnelly."

His reply was smooth. Rehearsed. He said, "Oh, I'm sorry about that. I just considered it part of my studies. I didn't really think too much about it."

If he thought I was just going to drop the subject, he was sorely mistaken.

I said, "That must take up a lot of your spare time."

He laughed a little bit, turning the page of the book that he was scanning through. "It takes up all of my spare time. But it's worth it. I'm learning so much."

I closed the trap by saying, "Your new boyfriend must be devastated that you have no free time for him."

Benno's muscles froze. His eyes were fixed on a single point, not even able to read as his mind raced.

I kept my voice low, but continued pressing. "What was it you said? Older. Smart human. Good job. Kinda shy. Real cuddly."

I reached over and tilted Benno's head up. Soon we were both looking across the table at Assistant Donnelly. The human was deep in conversation with the two older mages, and didn't notice his boyfriend in distress.

Tears appeared in my son's eyes. I quickly closed the old tome before he could cry all over it.

I murmured, "Hey. Hey, it's okay. I'm not mad. I'm just confused. After all of the fuss you made about Rick being too old, I didn't expect this."

Benno snuffled quietly and wiped his eyes on the sleeve of his robes. He half whispered, "I didn't want to l-lie to you so I j-just didn't tell you. I'm sorry. He's shy and wanted to keep it quiet."

I didn't ask about the secrecy. That was their business. Instead I reached out and stroked my boy's hair. I said, firmly, "I don't care about all that. He treats you right?"

Benno nodded.

"And you're having fun?"

This time the nod was quite enthusiastic.

I murmured, "Then assuming his shyness will allow it, invite him to the wedding celebration. Ames will be fine with it. There's room for one more at our table."

I received a sitting bearhug from Benno. That did attract the attention of the others, but nobody commented on our father-son moment.

With the elephant in the room addressed, I was able to work with a clear mind. Half an hour later, it paid off. I remembered something.

"Leeson."

The others looked up at me, waiting for an explanation.

I obliged them, saying, "When we were recovering my belongings from the cultists after my imprisonment, we stumbled upon what was perhaps the largest collection of diagrams and schematics I had ever seen. And they were all about the Voodoo Engine. Currently that collection is in the possession of Leeson."

Benno chimed in, "He was showing some of those to Will a while back."

Max and Hemitath exchanged glances. Then the Headmaster said, "I'm not sure we should involve the boy. He's still recovering from his wounds."

That irritated me, "So is my son, and yet here we are."

Hemitath, ever the peacekeeper, interjected, "Perhaps it's about time that we moved this down to the Artificery. We can enlist the help of some of our young experts and spread out a little bit more."

I glanced around. Apprentices had been dragging in more old books and scrolls every few minutes. We were out of space again.

The pilgrimage to the Artificery involved half a dozen confused students, several Flat Mules, and color coded Light spells to keep things in order.

When our impromptu caravan arrived at Will's doorstep, all he had to say was, "Oh hells."

The Artificery was where the creation of magical items became a reality. As these kinds of enchantments were often long and involved, it was even larger than one of the big lecture halls. There were separate sections for alchemical work, metal forging, woodworking, and the stone shelves and cubes used for 'resting' works in progress safely.

Our invasion was not subtle. Benno brought Will up to speed while Max had Leeson summoned, along with his papers on the intricate details of the Voodoo Engine. Soon everyone was pouring through ancient texts and Arcane Syphon diagrams.

Ultimately, it was the 'fresh eyes' that made the difference. Will's cheery voice drifted through the Artificery. "Hey. What's the Original Engine?"

Hemitath's voice answered the question with another question, "Will, are you reading a book of elven fairy tales?"

The human peered at the title of the document that he was referencing. "The Efficiency of Residual Power Syphoning by Means of the Fergasith Mechanic."

Leeson commented dryly, "Oh of course, that one is a real barn burner."

Hemitath hurried over to Will's workbench. The old elf peered over her former student's shoulder. "What in all creation is this? It isn't possible."

Max asked, "Could you explain for those of us still in the dark? Which is, I believe, all of us?"

The elf said, "The Original Engine is a bedtime story. It's what the elders tell their great grandchildren as they drift off. A fable about the creation of Panos."

My exhausted son asked, wistfully, "Tell it to us, auntie? I could use a good bedtime story."

Hemitath admitted, "I hardly remember any details. I know it was about building Panos from raw chaos. I think it also covered the creation of the moon. And perhaps one or more gods."

Max said, "Time for more subject matter experts."

Soon, elven mages were called in from both Arbitros and Civilia. They wanted to call in colleagues from religious areas of expertise. And they in turn needed to consult their druidic brethren.

By the afternoon, a score of mages and their colleagues were going over texts, debating theories, performing small tests, and the like. Benno and Assistant Donnelly were dragging folks into the Astral plane to test their findings or generate data in some form or another.

Finally, Max walked up to me and said, "We have a theory. Would you care to help us to test it?"

I snorted, "If I said 'no' I'd be contributing to the eventual death of civilization as we know it, wouldn't I?"

Max nodded. "Yes, quite." He paused for a moment, then asked, "Without joining up multiple Syphons as was done in the attempt to destroy Royal Moffit, how far away could you be from the Voodoo Engine for it to absorb a spell's residual energy?"

I said, "I can show you precisely."

And I did. We went out into the hallway and I paced out the exact distance that the smart orcs worked out over the years.

I explained, "Any further than this and it won't register at all. And there's no drop off, no partial registration. It either feeds the Voodoo Engine or it doesn't."

Max didn't look pleased by this news. He disappeared back into the room. I followed, bewildered.

The old mage called over, "Assistant Donnelly. You're the mathematician. Here are the numbers. How large of an Arcane Syphon would it need to be?"

There was silence as Donnelly scribbled on a piece of parchment. He had to dip for more ink several times. When the human got to his final result, his visage paled.

"Massive. The entire core of Panos."

I held up a hand. "Wait. Your theory is that there's a moon-sized Arcane Syphon in the middle of Panos?"

Several of the guest mages were nodding. Several more were shaking their heads.

Seeing no consensus, Max snapped, "We're working on it."

And work on it we did. It took a couple more hours to reach the final conclusion.

Max walked back over to me as I double checked some of my geographical estimates. So far everything seemed to check out.

The old archmage said, with confidence this time, "Our theory is that there's a moon-sized Arcane Syphon in the middle of Panos."

I nodded and said, "I'm starting to believe it."

Max said, "To be specific: The Original Engine may indeed be real, but it would be deep underground where it could access the powers of creation that were once, or may still be, active closer to Panos' core."

I said, "And the closest a mortal could get to it would be the bottom of the Great Trench, in the cove Southeast of the foothills that lay at the southern tip of the main continent."

The old human stared at me, "How in the hells do you know that?"

I gestured around to all of the maps strewn about my area, "What do you think I've been doing for the last few hours Max, plotting my next pleasure cruise? Besides, I'm the smartest orc on Panos."

Max shot back, "Second smartest."

I said, "Yes, well, the smartest orc on Panos is taking a nap."

I pointed down to the far end of the granite table. The exhausted Benno had surrendered to unconsciousness. Leeson joined him. The two convalescent young mages were sitting side by side and shoulder to shoulder, propping each other up in their slumber. Even under the circumstances, I found the sight a little bit endearing.

Max rolled his eyes. He asked, "What's near this Great Trench that we can use as a base of operations?"

I unrolled a small map of the area. My calloused green finger poked at a small dot in the hills on the southern coast. I stated, "Braxen. A small human township in the nearby hills. It's a sleepy little place, but is a popular retirement destination for those who have spent their lives at sea. They have docks, and they aren't unfamiliar with adventuring types. My ship is out of dry dock in about 36 hours. I can take a small crew above the Trench for some initial investigations."

Max turned and announced to the room, "We're done for the moment. Thank you everyone. Please make your final notes, I'll arrange for you all to be transported wherever you need to go. We're closer than ever to solving this thing. I will contact the Adventurer's Guild and start to send runners and resources to the Braxen area so that we can set up a base of operations. Get some rest."

I made sure that both Benno and Leeson got back to their rooms. Then I went back to the guest quarters. I was going to put together a proposal for Max. I set about planning the membership of an elite, rough and ready crew for the initial investigation.

Chapter 13

"How in the hells did we end up with this crew again?"

I was asking this of Assistant Donnelly. At the same time, I hoped my tone implied that I was in no way absolving him of his own uselessness aboard a sailing vessel.

The human looked around to see why I was complaining this time. Rick and Will were arguing over who's turn it was to use 'the big wheel'. Hemitath was trying to teach Dutch how to crawl along the low rigging, and tittering merrily every time the huge snake rolled down the protective netting and back into her arms.

The psychic said, "Well in my case, it's probably punishment for taking Benno on Astral trips without telling the Headmaster."

"Good." I growled. I had already taken the other mage aside and let him know that I approved of his relationship with my son, since Benno seemed happy and healthy. But that didn't excuse getting Benno in trouble with Max. The fact that they came forward about their discovery mitigated any other punishment that they might have received. But that didn't mean that I couldn't be salty about it. Besides, it was my job to give whoever my son was dating a hard time, whether they deserved it or not.

Will called over, "The two of us volunteered. We needed some time away from The Magic Shop, and this sounded like fun!"

Rick said, less enthusiastically, "Yeah. Fun."

Hemitath played dumb as she put Dutch back up on the thick rope, "I thought this was a cruise of some sort. Are we going somewhere in particular?"

I ran fingers through my hair roughly, exasperated with my 'crew'. But instead of expressing further frustration, I announced, "I'm going to get ready."

I managed to avoid stomping as I made my way below deck. Keeping my mind focused on the mission helped. We were about to make one of the deepest magic-assisted dives ever recorded. In the back of my head, I knew why both Hemitath and Assistant Donnelly were along for the ride: They were excellent swimmers with deep sea diving experience. And despite their bickering, Rick and Will had taken the Taboo out before with no issues. The reality of the situation was that whenever you took five mages on an outing, some amount of silliness and absent mindedness was to be expected.

I stripped down to the bare minimum, sporting only breeches and a belt that would support the pouches containing my material components. Knowing how well the Minor Polymorph spell handled cold water, I didn't bother with the grease coating this time around. Besides, should we encounter any sharks, I didn't want to appear as a more tasty treat than I already was.

When I finished stowing my gear, I made my way back above deck. The silliness and bickering had stopped, likely for my benefit. Will was at the wheel, and Hemitath was just handing Dutch over to Rick so that she could get ready. I walked back over to Donnelly as the elven archmage disappeared below deck.

"So you're comfortable serving as a communications medium during all of this?"

The human psychic nodded. He said, "Yes, Benno explained how all of that works. Fascinating. I had never considered the tactical advantage of being able to pass on messages in secrecy, in all environments. Normally we avoid being an 'open conduit' to prevent embarrassing accidental communications. You know, through incidental contact."

I smirked and said, "Nothing like broadcasting your thoughts and feelings to someone who was just handing you a mug of water."

Assistant Donnelly smiled sadly. "Exactly. In my youth I had an incident with one of my friends. Let's just say they had no interest in men, and my thoughts about them were less than pure. It was weird after that."

I tilted my head. I said, "You know... and I hope you don't mind this observation. But your communication skills have improved vastly in the last couple of years. No more meek and shy murmuring, no more looking away when you're speaking. Well, for the most part. You're like a different person."

The human flushed a little bit as he replied, "You can thank your son for that. His confidence and his encouragement rubbed off on me. Not to mention, I never had someone who I interacted with day in and day out. Conversation is a practiced skill, as it turns out. So I made an effort to pry myself away from the archives more often. Benno is the one who told me not to find excuses to avoid people all of the time."

I knew there was a hint of pride in my voice as I said, "Yeah. My kiddo is something else."

A couple of minutes later, Hemitath emerged. Although I will admit that I had some rather racy thoughts about her brother Jarotath in the past, it wasn't until now that I experienced similar thoughts about my former Headmaster. She had chosen a mode of dress similar to my own, with the addition of a silk chest wrapping. For a woman in her 370's, Hemitath was strikingly beautiful. In that moment I understood how the attraction that Shaman had for her went beyond the mental and encompassed the physical.

I traded Bill Donnelly for Hemitath, allowing the human to go get ready himself. The older elf squeezed my hand as we looked over the rail at the vast ocean. She said, "You look nervous."

I wasn't aware of that, and frowned a little bit. "I was really hoping to project confidence."

The elf laughed softly, a somewhat musical sound. "Your jaw sets in a certain tense way when you're nervous. Shaman is the same way."

I snorted and said, "Well I learned just about everything from him, so I'm not surprised we share a 'tell'."

Hemitath murmured, "Nor am I. He calls you 'son' you know. He often asks how 'his boy' is doing when he knows I've run into you."

A swell of pride rose in my chest. I said, "He's the only father I ever knew. I was raised in bits and pieces by the entire tribe, but he was the constant. He was my example."

The smaller elf looked up at me and smiled. She said, "You learned well. Though I think he's still waiting for you to finish learning all this silly magic so that he can teach you the **true** path of Kenvunk's druidic ways."

That made me laugh out loud.

Assistant Donnelly emerged from below deck. We turned to regard him.

I made the obvious observation. "You are a complete mess."

And he was. The human had attempted to create a bandoleer of pouches from shoulder to chest to hip, but it was already sliding down his arm. For modesty's sake, he opted for the same kind of desert pants that Leeson wore recently, but they were slightly too big for his waist and were starting to come off.

Hemitath ended up agreeing with my assessment. She said, "You're going to swim for twenty seconds and lose everything. This is no different from any other dive. How do you normally swim?"

He admitted, "Fully Polymorphed. I don't actually retain any human traits on a deep dive, when I go by myself. This hybrid transformation is a rarity for me. I only learned the Minor Polymorph so that I could learn the full Polymorph spell."

She replied, "Well we may need your spells in addition to your powers, so I'm afraid that's out. Come here, we'll fix you up."

Hemitath whipped Assistant Donnelly into shape, patterning his attire and gear after my own. Minus the Amulet of Enhanced Enchanting of course. Soon he was down to his breeches, and his belt of pouches was secured tightly around his waist.

I said, "Much better." Then I raised my voice and called to Rick and Will, "We're ready when you are!"

Rick, with Dutch coiled lightly around his torso and shoulders, went about preparing the anchor for lowering even as he directed Invisible

Servants to retract the sails. As he worked, the human mentioned, "We're above what we think is the deepest part of the Great Trench. Just South of the cliffs outside of Braxen."

Will tied the wheel down, and then stepped over to the quarterdeck to see us off. "The anchor is only there as a visual guide for you when you return, we're way too deep to touch anything. There will be a drift, but we'll try to keep her just about here. I'll mark the general area with a couple of balls of cork that I'll cast Light spells on, so that you have some orientation. Oh, and the rope ladders and netting will be down this side, but just give a shout if you need to get in from the other side and we'll arrange something."

Once the anchor was deployed, Rick slowly walked over and put a hand on his mate's shoulder. This was apparently an invitation for Dutch to slither from one human to the other, using the arm as a bridge. The snake made her way over to Will's false limb and coiled around it, fascinated for some reason.

Rick said, "We'll be doing some fishing once you're clear. Don't steal our bait on the way back up."

Hemitath, Assistant Donnelly, and myself produced cocoons from our pouches and performed the Minor Polymorph ritual. Soon we were graced with gills, better water vision, and the kind of pressure resistance that would be vital at the depths that we were planning to plunge into. I felt the drain, but having just topped up my intelligence enhancements this morning, it was fairly minor.

We dove over the edge of the wooden railing in relatively graceful fashion. The sensation of breathing water was less disturbing than last time. In half a minute, I was comfortable using my new gills. Hemitath needed about the same amount of time to make the transition. But Bill, having mastered and experienced the effects of full Polymorphs, adapted far more quickly than either of us. We allowed him to lead, making sure that the psychic was within easy reach should we need to communicate via his mind.

The trip was longer, colder, and darker than the last dive that I participated in with my family. We weren't even bothering with Light spells; for the majority of the journey there would be nothing to illuminate other than each other. Our enhanced aquatic vision would suffice.

I admit to losing track of time, but it took at least a quarter of an hour for the three of us to reach the ocean floor. Or should I say, the first ocean floor. The uniform gray of the seabed seemed to simply give way a few dozen paces ahead of us. The Great Trench was like a crack in the world, reaching depths that I had never imagined before. Suddenly I was glad that Rick and Will weren't with us. This kind of vastness might trigger their memories of Pandemonium, and dredge up unpleasant experiences with the absurdities of scale that once tormented them.

We were just passing over the lip of the Trench when Bill's hand grasped my elbow. But he was simply relaying a message from Hemitath on his other side: *"Stop. Something has taken an interest in us."*

I peered through the dark depths, in the direction that Hemitath was pointing. After a few moments of straining, a chill went down my spine. The silhouette was massive. I saw illustrations of hammerhead sharks in scientific texts before, and I once got to see a dead one when I lived above the harbor in Limt. But this creature was easily three times as long and at least twice as massive as that beast. An absolute mammoth of a fish.

And it had two friends.

It was said that in the remote places of Panos, remnants of the old world existed. Creatures that were created before the major races. Creatures that would seem so out of scale with the rest of our world that the sanity of a normal man would be brought into question should they be able to relate the tale. Be it in the deepest depths of the ocean, or at the frigid poles of Panos, or hidden in the dark heart of jungles without any name... encountering one of these remnants was rarely a positive experience.

Hemitath was already casting. We gathered close so that she could sprinkle finely crushed glass over our bodies. She was careful to avoid the gills, thank goodness. Soon we were nearly transparent, as the archmage's Mass Camouflage spell deftly obscured our outlines. It meant that we needed to swim more slowly, and stay very close so that we could feel each other and not drift apart. But that was fine. The giant hammerheads soon lost interest in this strange game of hide and seek, and gave up on their tiny snacks in order to seek out some more meaty prey.

We dove for a while longer. I could see that both Hemitath and Bill were straining now. We had been swimming for over twenty minutes without rest. I did some quick mental calculations. Concerned, I touched Assistant Donnelly's hip and asked him to bring Hemitath into the conversation.

I thought, *"We need to consider time spent in the Astral as well as the return journey. I see a little glow down and to our left. If it isn't too much of a slope, I think we start there."*

The other two agreed. As we swam down, the little sea shelf came into full view. Bioluminescent plants dotted the perimeter of this relatively flat outcropping. Below us, the world continued to slope off into what was a seemingly infinite abyss.

The three of us crouched and huddled close. Assistant Donnelly closed his eyes and started to focus on that other realm, and bringing us into it. Hemitath and I waited quietly. Patiently. Then not so patiently. I was about to ask the psychic if he was okay.

Then Panos disappeared.

But what replaced it wasn't the usual darkness that the Astral plane normally brought with it. Instead there was a strange radiation, a faint background glow. I knew that Bill was to my right and Hemitath to my left. But my perception of them was somehow clouded. Fuzzy.

Although there was no true sensation of up or down, I immediately knew which direction correlated to 'down' in the real world. In that direction, the void of the Astral was replaced by something vast and frightening.

It was Hemitath that gave voice to what we were all thinking.

"The Original Engine."

It was like an overpowering glow at the end of a cavernous tunnel. An impossibly bright square within a fluctuating orb of pure arcane might. Each raw, chaotic lash of power caused tendrils to sweep over the orb's surface until the end of the streamers snapped off. Sparks of red, blue, white, and brown seemed to scatter whenever this happened, the tiny motes drifting off into the Astral infinity.

Bill asked, "Is it shedding elementals?"

"Yes." I answered. I knew this was the case. I didn't know how I knew, however.

Hemitath shivered. The elf asked, "Do you feel that? The waves?"

I certainly did. Waves of arcane pressure seem to wash over us, through us. Undoubtedly, the engine was gathering power through the elemental sacrifices by cultists. Likely more cultists than we were aware of. If every wave represented a sacrifice, there must be dozens, if not hundreds of groups working towards the end of the world.

But we also felt, and eventually saw, faint streams of constant power being fed into this entity at the center of Panos. These light blue umbilical cords intertwined and extended to a point somewhere 'above' us. Hemitath stared at the lines of power as I counted them. We came to the same conclusion, and voiced it at nearly the same time.

"The Arcane Syphons."

I felt a sudden presence. A sense of 'other'. This time it wasn't borrowing my voice, it was borrowing my mind. In a horrific moment of clarity, I saw the past, the present, and the future.

Even at this distance, the Original Engine's power was undeniable. The Syphons were feeding it. They used the schemes of gods and demons, the desires of elf and man and orc. Every time one or more of the Arcane Syphons had done work over the millennia, a fraction of their potential power was fed back to the Original Engine. Like a paladin tithing to their temple, the Arcane Syphons donated a portion of everything that passed through them.

That power had been growing, accumulating. While cities and

universities were being built, while mines were being dug, even when insane demon lords had summoned the armies of the dead, the Original Engine fed. And waited.

But now, the accumulated power of this engine of creation was too much. Or maybe, from its perspective, just enough. It was creating elementals, and with them turmoil and backlash. At some point, the engine of creation lost the ability to distinguish between making life and making death. Now it was simply making. Manifesting.

But the raw elements had to come from somewhere. Right now it was using the earth, air, fire, and water that was close by: The stone and gas, the magma and ocean. In time though, it would cannibalize. The future was one of hunger. As the Original Engine grew, it would demand more from the Arcane Syphons, and from Panos itself. Every township, every city, every race and entity would be consumed. The land, the sea, the trees, even the air itself would be converted. It would use the Arcane Syphons to break down everything into its elemental components. Until there was nothing left.

Tiny magic hands would smash the world.

That feeling of possession passed. The entity left behind the kind of dread that went hand in hand with portents of the apocalypse.

Before I could relate the visions to my companions, a far more immediate threat manifested.

The surface of the arcane sphere surrounding the Original Engine seemed to ripple and quake. That disturbance sent a rolling wave of blackness towards us. It started at an impossible distance. Then the speed of the wave registered in my mind as I finally grasped the immensity of the area that it covered.

Bill murmured, "Anti-magic."

Hemitath's eyes widened. She said, "Out, now! Magic is what's keeping us **breathing**."

The psychic quickly grabbed our shoulders. The landscape shifted.

Sensations of cold and wet briefly overrode the panic that we were all feeling. Hemitath gathered us close and started to cast. I looked down with morbid curiosity at the approaching anti-magic force that threatened to suffocate us and crush us under tons of water. In the real world it was a foaming, pinkish purple bubble that rode up the walls of the abyssal trench at an alarming pace.

The leading air bubbles, dislodged by the pressure of the Original Engine's energetic blast, started to float past my ears. I considered sending some encouraging last words to my friends through the psychic link.

But then, we were elsewhere.

Three mages were laying in the darkness. We were on a wooden floor, hacking and retching large quantities of seawater through mouths and gills alike. The painfully abrupt transition was all that I could focus on for a few seconds.

When I was able to utilize real air again, I drew a breath to compliment Hemitath. It's nearly impossible to Teleport inside of a wooden ship. In fact, to my knowledge, it had never been done before. I only realized that we weren't back on the R. M. N. 'Taboo' when the cinnamon taste in the air filled my mouth and lungs.

In that brief silence between adaptation and realization, I heard a low hissing sound. We all started coughing again, a sound that became weaker by the second. Unconsciousness quickly ensued.

Chapter 14

I awoke from my slumber slowly. The sun of a perfect summer morning warmed me from ears to ankles. I was dressed for the weather of course: Rugged overalls covered my soft cotton undershirt and breeches. I sat up and stretched, flexing my soft green fingers and my adventurously bare toes.

I knew this hillside. The cave that used to belong to the Silverfish was over my right shoulder. But there was no danger, not anymore. Trees provided ample shade, as well as whatever nuts and fruits one might require. The hill sloped gently down to the river, where the broken stone wall awaited me. Water washed gently into a little orcmade tide pool, swirled in a placid circle, and then drained back out through the gap in the retaining wall. It was cool and clean, perfect for drinking.

"Sorch! They're starting to bite, bring your gear."

The sound of that powerful voice brought a grin to my face. My soft hand reached down to grab the fishing tackle, before I splashed through the shallow water and around the bend.

I followed the absent whistling until I spotted my companion. The other orc was a head and a half taller than I was, but I wasn't afraid. He was dressed just like me, but with the addition of a floppy straw hat. His calm demeanor and quiet confidence made me feel safe in his presence.

Kenvunk said, "There's a deep spot around nine paces out. I already got a nibble."

I cast my line, sending the copper lure into the river some distance out. Like my companion, I slowly reeled in the slack before raising my pole again, making the fishing spoon wriggle in the water. It didn't matter if I caught a fish on the first try. We had all day.

After enjoying the sound of Kenvunk's whistling for a few minutes, the huge orc asked me, "How are you feeling this morning, Sorch?"

It was a curious question. I was perfect, as always, of course. "I'm fine, thanks for asking. How are you Kenvunk?"

The god admitted, "I've been a little down as of late. My girlfriend and I are fighting."

I snorted. "What else is new."

Kenvunk shot me a mildly hurt expression.

I murmured, "Sorry. What is it about this time?"

"A stupid bet. Did you ever wish that you could take something back, Sorch? Just erase what happened and start over?"

I had to admit, "No, not really. If I changed something, things could get worse. And maybe I wouldn't ever meet my friends. Maybe I wouldn't have my amazing family. I wouldn't start over. I've lived a brave life."

There was a measure of pride in Kenvunk's voice when he said, "I know you have." Then he paused. When the god continued, he sounded more melancholy. "But in my case, maybe I was a bit too brave. Too sure of myself. Sometimes you have to let someone else be wrong instead of proclaiming that you're right. It isn't the bravest thing to do, but sometimes it's the kindest thing to do."

We both finished reeling in our lures. The two of us re-cast them in unison.

I said, "It isn't all your fault you know. Omi-Suteth isn't blameless here. She cursed us. That changed who we were, who we could be. That changed…"

And suddenly I was angry. Gray clouds started to form in the distance. The light of the perfect summer sun dimmed.

"Shaman. How could you let that happen to him? He loves you. He loves you more than he loves life itself, and yet he's rewarded with Glogur's curse! When are you going to step in? When are you going to tell that bitch enough is enough?"

Kenvunk winced under my verbal assault. He closed his eyes, like he was thinking happy thoughts. Slowly the gray clouds in the distance dissipated. The sun's luminescence was restored.

Then the orc god replied, "I'm sorry Sorch. You don't know how sorry I am. But no amount of divine conflict can reverse the curse of Glogur. It is a mortal issue, and mortals must find a solution. I'm afraid my own ill spoken words contributed to that reality."

I stared into the clear water as I slowly made the copper lure dance and sway in the river's current. I said, "It's just not fair. He helped to save the world, and his mind is taken from him. Rick and Will helped to save the world, and their limbs were taken from them. Everything that happened… it wasn't just the fault of mortals. It couldn't be."

Kenvunk agreed, "No, it couldn't be."

"Then why do we bear the burden?"

The big orc said, "If it were my choice alone, you wouldn't, Sorch. I'm tired of the games and the wagers of the gods. I'm tired of the plotting and underhandedness of the demons. But we don't answer to each other. We answer to a higher power."

I remembered a lecture that I attended once. I recalled, "That's what Lew said. He said that the new gods and the old don't really seem to be in competition. He said that the accord or wager amongst the gods makes no sense unless they had a higher set of rules that they had to abide by. An overseer that limited their power."

Kenvunk said, "Mister Rush is a wise man. I can't say more than that. But Sorch… those rules that you're talking about, that's part of what prevents me from just swooping in and fixing Shaman. Otherwise I would. You know I would. He's like a son to me. One of the most loyal and outstanding druids that I have ever seen on Panos. That was why I spoke through him. That was why I helped you early on."

I snorted, "And yet when you speak through me, you just kind of take over my voice. I didn't have the same choices he did."

Now it was Kenvunk's turn to sound annoyed. "Didn't you Sorch? After you escaped the swamps, you could have learned your magic and attended your University and then stayed out of harm's way. But you didn't, did you? You chose adventure. You chose to meddle with the plans of demons and gods. So yes, I used your voice. You have no idea how much I risked, how close to the edge I wandered. But it had to be you, because you put yourself in the perfect position. It wasn't happenstance. It was design. Your design."

Rebuffed, I concentrated on fishing for a while. So did Kenvunk. It was only after a couple of fruitless casts that one of us spoke again.

"Hey Sorch?"

"Yeah?"

I could hear the tears in Kenvunk's voice, though he didn't allow them to escape his eyes, "Do you... do you think she'll ever come back to me? Do you think we'll be together again?"

I felt a lump in my throat. His pain, his sadness was palpable. I murmured, "Maybe. But fixing something like that doesn't just happen. You need to put in the effort."

Out of the corner of my eye, I saw the big orc nodding a little bit.

I continued, "If you love her... if you really love her, you need to be brave. You have to put aside pride and be the first one to step up. The first to say that you're sorry and that you want to work things out. And make sure she knows how you feel. We orcs, we sometimes want to hold it all inside. But I've learned that you get what you want by expressing things like love and appreciation. You need to do the same."

Kenvunk took a deep breath. When he exhaled, he said, "Okay. Okay."

Suddenly, I felt a tug on my line. Then another, much stronger. I almost stumbled into the water.

Kenvunk set down his own rod. He was quickly at my side, "Oh Sorch, that's a big one! Come on, let's see if we can land it."

Two huge orc hands joined my smaller ones. Together we strained at the fishing pole. It seemed to bend at an impossible angle, but refused to break. The two of us heaved in unison. Then it happened.

The giant rainbow trout was yanked from the water. Kenvunk laughed in delight at such a catch. The force of our tugging sent the heavy fish sailing right at my forehead. There was a wet impact, and then darkness.

"Come on Sorch, wake up. We don't have all day."

That wasn't Kenvunk's voice. I slowly opened my eyes.

I awoke under the curious gaze of Hemitath.

The scantily clad elven archmage said, "Ah there you are. We were worried. You seemed almost feverish and you were mumbling about fish."

After coughing a couple of times, I sat up. I was in a comfortable bed, in a warm and well lit room with wooden walls. "Where are we?"

"Dignity."

I knew that name. Dignity was the traditional personal residence of the Spymaster of Arbitros. I had been here once as part of a celebration. We just rescued Will and Rick and Toby. There was a lot of eating, and drinking, and dancing as I recalled.

I asked, "Hemitath, why in all the hells are we here?"

The elf murmured, "My fault actually. It was instinctive. In my panic and haste, I thought of the first safe place that came to mind. My father was the Spymaster at one time, Sorch. I took you home."

I rolled out of bed. My pouches and belt were hanging from a hook on the wall, still slightly damp. As I wrapped the belt around my waist, I said, "We're alive, so you'll hear no complaints from me. Any spare clothes around? We aren't exactly dressed for a state visit."

From the next room, a familiar voice said, "Not to worry, you won't be making a public appearance. You're among friends."

Hemitath led me out of the guest room. We stepped into the 'debriefing chamber', which was actually a large dining room meant for entertaining dozens of guests.

Our host was sharing a glass of wine with Assistant Donnelly, who looked surprisingly comfortable even in his half-dressed state. The tall, slender elf turned his head as we entered. He was still dressed in his brown work clothes; still wearing a flour coated white apron.

Ashley waved us over, "Welcome back to the land of the living. Come join us for some wine. I was just telling your companion that this is a new halfling red concoction. They add a few fermented persimmons to the grapes. It's lovely."

I knew that my jaw was hanging open a little bit, because I had to make a conscious effort to close it. My expression must have been priceless, because the innkeeper started to laugh.

Ashley said, "Well it wouldn't be much of a cover if it weren't surprising, I suppose."

I padded over on bare feet and sat, heavily. "The Spymaster. The greatest intelligence agent in elven society. Is an innkeeper."

Bill pointed out, "If you think about it, running a popular place in the largest city on the continent is a good way to pick up information."

Ashley said, "I mainly steal recipes, to be honest."

The Spymaster went on to explain that Dignity is fortified against unscheduled intrusion. He apologised for the knockout gas, but assured us that it was a necessary precaution given the sensitivity of his role.

"Hemitath, having been a resident, knew the one room that wasn't shielded from teleportation. We call it the 'arrival chamber'. Sadly, none of you were on the current guest list. Sorch, you slept for a couple of extra hours I'm afraid. I hope the experience wasn't too unpleasant."

I drained my glass of the sweet red wine. I weighed my words before finally saying, "The experience was unique. I'll be fine."

Hemitath said, "I've already sent word to Rick and Will, telling them not to worry and that I would need to rest in order to get us all back to the staging area. They've headed back to shore."

Bill added, "Now that you're awake, Hemitath and I will go study."

The elf nodded, "Indeed, we should do that. Is the second guest room also available, Ashley?"

The Spymaster smiled and replied, "My home is your home. Don't worry, Sorch will keep me entertained."

I found myself wondering how I would accomplish that, as my friends sequestered themselves away to memorize spells.

My internal question was answered when Ashley transferred his apron to my shoulders. The elf said, "Come on, you're making lunch."

I half protested as we walked into the adjoining kitchen, "You're an accomplished chef, aren't you? You've won awards, I think."

Ashley shot back, "The Spastic Vole recently won an award from the Culinary Guild, did it not?"

I used flint and steel to fire up the stove, which had already been prepared with kindling, wood, and some coal. "Yeah, but I wasn't in the kitchen. Or if I was, it was in a dishwashing capacity."

"Hush. Cook me lunch."

I checked the larder and the ice box. Comfortable ingredients caught my eye: There was some tree snake cutlets available, as well as green beans and a cob of corn. I put the iron pan on the burner to let it heat up, and then set my selected food items on the counter for prep.

As I sliced the kernels from the cob of corn, I said, "So by now you've heard what's going on. You know what the Arcane University and the Adventurer's Guild are doing. What's the next step for the elven nation?"

The lean elf considered my words with care. Then he said, "I think they hedge their bets. Providing financial support and research assistance is one thing. But they'll have a multi-tiered plan in place in case your efforts fail. Likely, they'll develop a backup plan to try to save Panos, and a second one to try to save the elven race."

I noted, "You say 'they' instead of 'we'. Why?"

"As the Spymaster, I find it useful to divorce myself from the political realm. What the elven nation does is separate from what I need to do in order to secure the safety of Arbitros. That's why the position is secretive. That's why people in my position are never from families of high power within the elven community. The Spymaster works for the common folk, not the affluent. It didn't always used to be that way, but we found that this approach works best."

When the corn was liberated from the cob, I asked, "Where's the butter?"

Ashley dug around in the ice box until he found a slab. I cut a piece off and allowed it to melt in the rapidly heating iron pan.

I said, "I understand a secondary plan to save Panos. But how would the elven nation possibly save the elves if Panos itself is doomed?"

The innkeeper leaned against the counter to watch me work. "Planar portals. They would find the friendliest, most survivable plane and evacuate as many elves as possible before the end. Their hope would be to start over."

I never even considered using a portal to leave Panos entirely, forever. The thought made me slightly queasy. "Wow." was all I could say.

Ashley said, "Wow indeed. But until we reach such a drastic point, you can rely on the support of the elves. They understand that some of the best minds on Panos are working on these problems."

I seasoned the meat with salt, pepper, and parsley. Then I dropped the snake cutlets into the pan. The sizzling was quite satisfying.

While cleaning the vegetables, I noted, "Any time the Arcane University is involved in something, the elven nation tends to have some visibility into it."

Ashley nodded. He said, "For a couple of reasons. They built and financed the University of course, so their performance reflects on the elves. But equally important, the elves see magic as 'their' domain. With that attitude, keeping close tabs on the future of magic is in their interest."

I flipped the snake and let the other side cook. Then I admitted, "That sounds a little creepy."

The tall elf laughed. "Maybe. Let us just say that I've seen a lot more of you over the last few years than you have of me, Sorch."

I sighed a little bit. I couldn't say I was shocked that the elves would keep covert watch over me, but it was yet another thing I couldn't share with Ames. The were-cat would be quite annoyed.

I stirred the meat and veggies as they fried, and then quickly took the pan off of the heat. Ashley had wooden plates at the ready. The food was divided into two portions, and we took the plates and silverware back into the interrogation room.

The elf dug in. After swallowing the first bite, he said, "Oh Sorch this... this is a truly awful effort."

I had to laugh. After trying some myself, I said, "I'll admit that this isn't my best dish. But I can taste the salt, and the butter. And the snake, sort of."

Despite his critical review, Ashley was smiling. "If one of my apprentices made this, I would put them on washing up duty and have them ponder their premeditated assault upon good taste."

I snorted, "Shall we scrap it and have some jerky instead?"

The elf shook his head, "No. It's perfectly edible. We try not to waste food in either of my kitchens. But maybe..."

I finished the thought for him, "More wine?"

Ashley nodded enthusiastically. "Yes, more wine would help."

And that's how I single handedly got the Spymaster of Arbitros drunk.

Chapter 15

"I have it."

Hemitath's voice was confident as she touched the crystal ball, summoning up a vision of the small hillside town of Braxen.

I looked at the image in the crystal ball. After careful examination, I said, "Yeah, that's it. Looks like we'll be just outside of town. In theory, our base camp should be set up by now and not very far away."

We were gathered in the Spymaster's private study, making use of one of the mystical items that he 'acquired' over the years. Ashley said his goodbyes earlier, then excused himself so that he could sleep off the midday drinking. He had to be recovered in time for the dinner service at the Drowsy Dragon back in Royal Moffit. My orcish constitution served me well; I had only ended up with a pleasant tipsy feeling.

The image within the crystal flickered and died when the archmage stepped away. With the exact position in her mind, Hemitath told Bill and I to stay close. She rested those delicate, aged elven hands on our shoulders and murmured the incantation that would Teleport us to the correct destination.

And then we were elsewhere.

The hilltop that we appeared upon was overlooking Braxen. Although it was a somewhat sleepy place, it was also immaculate. The distance away from major cities meant that land was cheap here. Which meant that the retired seafarers who populated Braxen, many of them former captains and officers, had to find something else to spend their money on. This manifested in high quality housing, stone work, and provisions. But Braxen wasn't a snobbish place. These former professionals rewarded hard work and loyalty. So they ended up hiring dozens of trusted people to keep the town clean and safe for the sailors and their families. It was the kind of place that I would be happy to move into when I retired from the foolishness that we call 'adventuring'.

We made our way downhill, heading away from town in a southerly direction. This area was lightly wooded. In better times there would have been more trees, but the saplings had a lower survival rate over the past decade, resulting in more old stumps than new growth. We quickly found the main path towards the docks and followed it for a few minutes.

I paused at a fork in the path. Southwest seemed to slope sharply upwards, while Southeast continued the downward trend towards the sea. I asked, "Any idea which direction they chose?"

Hemitath pointed to the left. "This way. I believe they said that there was no benefit to setting up on the cliffside. It's a fantastic view, but we're not here for the scenery."

The elf was correct. A couple more minutes of heading down the Southeastern trail brought us to our destination. Just off of the beaten path was a large ring of tents. In the center of it all, the remains of a foundation to a home that burned to the ground decades ago.

Assistant Donnelly stared at the square of stones. He said, "Ah yes, Will mentioned that this was the only place available that already had a functioning well. No ghosts though. The man who used to own it wasn't here when it happened. Lightning strike is what they suspect, apparently. He simply decided to rebuild closer to town, since there was nothing left here and his fortunes had changed."

Outside of the largest tent was a hanging brass bell. Hemitath decided to make use of it, which alerted everybody in the camp to our arrival. Heads poked out of tents and peered in our direction. It reminded me of those little creatures near Eastern Hook. Perhaps we had stumbled upon a community of meerkat sorcerers.

A significant number of the mages emerged from their makeshift burroughs. They gathered in the large tent to hear our debriefing. It was standing room only. Which was fine, because there was no place to sit.

Before we got started, Rick and Will were kind enough to return our packs and clothes. As we thanked the humans, Dutch slithered up to Hemitath, coiling possessively around her legs.

Once that was sorted, Bill and Hemitath related everything they saw and experienced on our journey. Then it was my turn. To say that some of the faces in the tent were slightly dubious would be an understatement. Particularly the elven faces. Many of them were from Civilia and had only met me the one time. I guess they weren't very impressed.

Regardless of the looks I was getting, I pressed on. I told them everything: The divinely inspired vision about the end of the world, the source of it being Kenvunk, the encounter I had with the god after getting knocked out. No withholding.

It was Rick who came to my rescue. He said, "Everything that Sorch has ever said about prophecy, about visions, about gods. All of it has come true, or we've had to stop it from coming true. If you don't trust his words, we may as well give up right now, because everything we've done so far is based on his intuition and his dream of the end of the world."

I said, quietly, "I'll have to take Rick's word for it. I traded my dream to a demon lord as part of a truce agreement."

The room was silent for a moment.

Will and Leeson broke that silence by launching into their highly scientific analysis of the situation. Our story confirmed one of their theories. They spoke a language that even the northern elves appreciated: Arcane theory. It took the better part of an hour, and the two cited a score of resources ranging from centuries-old tomes to the mystical schematics recovered from our raid against the Cult of Harrington two years ago.

Will's conclusion was stated with somber confidence. He said, "Given the amount of power that the Original Engine has likely gathered over the years, and given our current state of affairs, we are certain that destroying the remaining Arcane Syphons is the only way to stop the Original Engine from eventually tearing Panos apart."

Chaos erupted.

Most of us were simply in disbelief. Not that we thought Leeson and Will were wrong, but it was a difficult course of action to accept. The Arcane Syphons had done an incredible amount of good for Panos. They built the Arcane University, repaired devastation from both natural and unnatural sources, created infrastructure in every major city on Panos, and mined precious resources that would have otherwise taken decades to unearth.

The elven contingent was having a more animated reaction. There was anger, there was infighting. Most of them were quite vocally insisting that we find another way to deal with this crisis. Even Hemitath looked shocked. She was not inclined to stop her colleagues from shouting out their protests.

"Typical human reaction, destroy what you don't understand!"

"This is our legacy, and its fate is not yours to decide."

"We should withdraw from these proceedings immediately."

This went on for over a minute, in which time I recovered from my own state of shock. I stepped to the front of the assembly, putting myself in between the crowd and the two nervous looking humans that had just delivered the news.

Mustering all of the diplomatic skills that I learned over the years, remembering some of the political lessons taught to me by Leeson's parents, I delivered a uniquely orcish message to the crowd.

"SHUT THE HELLS UP!"

The volume of my roar far surpassed that of any human or elf. The room quieted immediately, and all eyes were on me.

I delivered the next hammerblow. "However bad you think things are right now, it's worse than that. What Will and Leeson haven't mentioned, what hasn't been factored into these equations, is the existence of the doomsday cultists. As bad as the passive transference of power from the Arcane Syphons might be, we have large groups of madmen actively trying to bring about the end of the world. They're creating magical and elemental conduits that directly feed the Original

Engine. These fissures that they're trying to open up are just the beginning. The scope of this cult and the damage that they have caused is completely unknown. But the flooding in the Southwestern continent? The yetis having to flee their ancestral home? That is just the tip of a very big iceberg."

It was Hemitath who spoke up, "We may have broken the back of this cult, there's no evidence how widespread their activities might be."

I reminded the former Headmaster, "When we were in the Astral, we felt those waves of power washing over us. That was in addition to the umbilicals coming from the Arcane Syphons. The power wasn't just trickling in, it was surging. This growth is active, Hemitath. It's intentional. The fissures that are being opened up, the elemental disruption... all of it could have gone largely undetected save for the one cult gathering we found in the desert. We have no real idea of the scope of the damage that is being caused around Panos as we speak. But if you think that one setback is going to stop a cult willing to bring about the end of the world, I'm genuinely afraid that they're going to prove you wrong."

The elves went quiet. Their faces now reflected states ranging from somber to horrified.

Will spoke up, noting, "We think that without the Arcane Syphons on the surface of Panos, the cult's sacrifices will have no effect. The umbilicals that they create likely allow the Original Engine to tap into the ley lines and channel its power across the surface of Panos. Without them, the power won't be able to flow in either direction."

Leeson cleared his throat. He said, "Why don't you all discuss matters within your particular groups. We'll be here to answer any questions."

The discussions led to even more discussions. Groups were broken down into smaller groups. Finally, it was decided that the input of governments, clergy, and other guilds would need to be sought out before any decision on Will and Leeson's proposal could be made.

Everyone did agree to two measures. We would start gathering the Arcane Syphons in Limt as the various factions discussed their final decision. And both Rick and Will were taking a leave of absence from the Arcane University. They would sail the R. M. N. Taboo back to Limt, where they could tend to their business and still be ready to load up the Syphons for transport at a moment's notice.

I got dressed for travel and shouldered my pack. One of the senior mages from Arbitros needed some resources from the Arcane University. Despite me advocating the destruction of elven national treasures, she was willing to include me in her Teleportation.

Upon arriving in the reception hall, I hesitated, thinking that there was some mistake. The normally busy hub of arcane activity looked more like a ghost town. I saw all of four people meandering around, and that included a scan of the second tier. The elven magus excused herself and walked towards the North Wing. I headed in the opposite direction.

The guards at the checkpoint apologetically informed me that due to faculty activities, classes were cancelled for the day. They assured me that meals were still being served in the dining area. I thanked them for the update, and then hurried upstairs to my guest room, in order to make sure that my family was alright.

I took the steps two at a time. The lack of any other people in the broad corridors was freaking me out. I found myself running down the final hallway at full speed. Upon arriving at our guest room, my shaking green hand twisted the handle and I burst through the door.

To my relief, I was greeted by the sight of Ames and Benno playing cards. Gambling for coppers, to be more accurate. It looked like Benno had just caught the were-cat in a bluff, and was scooping a small pile of coins towards his own stash.

Breathlessly I asked, "Is everything alright here?"

They both replied at the same time, speaking over one another.

"We're **so** bored Dad."

"Entertain us!"

So I did. I brought my family up to speed on the Original Engine, and the results of our exploration. I went into detail about my encounter with Kenvunk. This caused the card game to be cancelled and the table cleared, so that Benno could make detailed notes of my vision.

One of the last questions that my son asked was, "What did Kenvunk look like?"

I closed my eyes, trying to remember all of the details. I answered, "He looked a lot like me, except taller. Stronger. With a floppy straw hat. But I didn't look like me. My hands were too soft, my skin was perfect. It was strange."

Ames said, "And he mainly asked you for relationship advice."

"Yes. Well, it was an exchange of ideas. Of... you know, of feelings."

My mate and son were also exchanging something: Silent, concerned glances.

I insisted, "I'm not going crazy."

Ames asked Benno, "Do you have enough details? When the people from the asylum come by to collect him, I want to have well documented evidence."

Benno sprinkled some fine sand over the ink, and then set the notes aside. "Yeah, we're fine."

I snorted, then asked a question of my own. "How come you aren't in class, kiddo?"

My son explained, "A lot of the classes are being suspended, since so many of the professors and senior students are needed for research and field work in regards to the Original Engine. The junior students are doing what they can to help out, but a lot of them have been allowed to go home for the entire week. It's a mess."

Ames added, "The Transport Guild tells me that I've had three meetings cancelled from all around Panos. Apparently governments are calling emergency sessions, various Guilds are getting involved. I agree with Benno. It's a mess."

I sighed. "Any good news?"

The were-cat nodded slowly. "Apparently sales of your salt have gone up by 13 percent in the last four weeks."

I stared at my mate.

"What? It's the only good news that I have, take it or leave it."

Benno chimed in, "The cleric who was visiting me said that I'm fully recovered and rehabilitated now. My toes still look a little squashed, but honestly I feel fine."

I was relieved. I said, "That really is good news, kiddo. Maybe we should talk about it. About what happened, you know?"

The younger orc nodded eagerly, "We should, because I think next time I'll be able to avoid something like that with a little bit of luck. There were telltale signs, I just didn't recognise them."

Ames said, "Dear, I think your father is trying to-"

But he continued, with that same infectious enthusiasm that he had for everything that he cared about, "There was this sound, and a definite shift under my feet. If I was a minotaur, I would have known exactly what was happening. I talked to Toby about it, and he says that at least some of that stuff can be learned."

This time I was the one who tried to get a word in edgewise, "That's great son, but I was-"

Benno's eyes got wide, "Oh, and Tara said that she would sit with me at some point and see if we could develop a minotaur variant of the Minor Polymorph spell. I mean, clearly I would be doing the developing, but she would let me see through her mind and stuff."

He stopped when he saw us both looking at him. "What?"

The were-cat said, gently, "Your father wanted to talk to you about something."

Benno looked at me. I could still see that raw excitement in his eyes, the passion. And that was just him **talking** about adventure. Whatever plans that I might have had for ending my son's adventuring career died a quiet death.

"I know they're expensive, but I think we make enough on a mission these days that we should start carrying one or two Minor Healing potions."

Ames' eyes widened in surprise. My mate flashed me a bright, toothy smile of approval.

Benno was nodding when I glanced back at him. "Yeah, I think that's a great idea. We can probably get a discount from the Temple of Melflavin. I'll talk to Tara about it."

I said, "And we can buy some of those metallic flasks that can survive a significant impact. If we're making that kind of investment, we should protect it."

After working out the details and logistics, conversation turned to one of my least favorite topics.

Benno said, "I've recorded all of your recent episodes."

I snorted, "Do we really have to call them 'episodes'? I think the term is unfairly pejorative."

Ames made a couple of 'helpful' suggestions, "Nutty daydreams? Crazy trips?"

Benno was more cooperative, "Events?"

I gestured to the younger orc, "Events. Much better."

"I've recorded all of your recent events, and I think that they're as detailed and accurate as they're going to be. They're ready to share with our friends."

Ames was nodding, "In all seriousness, I read most of them. They're fair representations. And if it helps any, everything that involved me seems to be accurate."

My mate's reassurance was helpful. At least I wasn't fabricating any of these strange flashbacks. I said, "Normally I would suggest Shaman first, but he's not likely to be able to participate without undue frustration. Rick and Will, I suppose? And then Toby and Tara? Followed by my mentors here at the University."

Benno nodded and said, "Done. I'll get this over to the guys right away. Unless you had any more recent epis... events that you wanted to add, Father?"

I cleared my throat and then murmured, "I did have one recently, but it shouldn't be included."

Ames scowled. The were-cat said, "What if it's important?"

Benno jumped on that bandwagon, "We should really include everything if we can."

I shook my head. "Nope. No."

Ames asked, "Why? What's so terrible that you wouldn't share it with our friends?"

I looked at my mate and said, "It was about the first time I showed you the Private Sanctum spell."

"Oh. Oh! Yeah we aren't including that."

Benno looked confused. "Why? Maybe it's key to-"

Ames cut our son off mid sentence. "Sex, kiddo. Lots and lots of sex."

I stood and walked behind Ames, rubbing the were-cat's shoulders. I said, "I'm willing to share every stupid thing I've ever done. But that's off limits."

Benno shook his head. He said, "Fine. I admit, it doesn't seem relevant. There are more poetic, well written accounts of such things in the library."

Ames reached up. I felt claws prickling at my ribs through the fabric of my shirt. "Oh I don't know. I think your father and I can be awfully 'poetic' at times."

I leaned down to deliver a gentle nip at Ames' triangular ear. I loved making it flick like that. "But not under the shroud of a Private Sanctum. That experience is less theatrical."

Benno stood up quickly. He said, "Ew. Okay, I'm leaving. I don't need to know about your lurid midnight performances. You can put that in your own journals." The younger orc gathered his things and beat a hasty retreat, closing the guest room's door behind him.

Ames stood up and turned to face me. The feline said, "Well, we've scarred him for life."

I smirked, fangs showing from one side of my mouth. I teased my mate by saying, "If he wasn't already scarred for life after walking in on us with those sex toys that we borrowed from Parsnip, I think he'll survive this."

The memory brought a hot flush to my kitten's ears, and stole any reply that the feline might have had. I leaned in for a kiss, reassuring Ames that my love was unconditional.

A few minutes of necking was all I could take before coming up with an excuse. I said, "It's chilly in here, I'm going to get under the covers."

Ames asked, "If it's cold, why are you taking off your clothes?"

I added, "Oh by the way, you're cold too."

"If I'm cold, why are you taking off **my** clothes?"

"Shut up and get in bed."

The truth was, I was never cold for long next to Ames. That soft white fur brushing over my entire body tended to warm me up rapidly. Even in the most chaste of circumstances, I found joy in holding the were-cat's body against mine.

But these were not the most chaste of circumstances. The feline's merciless teasing meant that I needed to take control. Not that Ames was complaining. Pinned down and helpless under my full weight was one of the cat's favorite positions.

Within this rare interlude of cancelled meetings, we were left undisturbed for the entire night. Our activities degenerated into slow, drawn out love making interspersed with regenerative naps. Dinner wasn't even a consideration. Sating other hungers would come first.

Chapter 16

I knew it couldn't last.

Ames and I woke up to a gentle rapping at our door. Benno had stopped by. He was wondering if we'd like to join him for breakfast in an hour. With no word from either Max or the Transport Guild, the two of us assumed that we were free. We told him that it was a date, and Ames headed off to bathe while I performed my morning memorizations and enhancements. When the frizzy-furred feline returned, I took a quick bath myself, and then got dressed in some nice warm robes.

But such an idyllic start to the day was never meant to be, of course. Just as Ames and I met up with Benno, we heard the most awful sound imaginable.

The alarm itself wasn't the awful part. Sure it was loud, and the tone was designed to awake and disturb humanoids. But the implication was far worse: We would be standing out in the snow until this fire drill was over. The Circle of Teleportation was shut down during an alarm, and everyone was expected to leave the Arcane University via one of the mundane exits.

I was just pondering which administrative moron might have planned this exercise, when I realized it wasn't an exercise. Guards' voices were ringing out from the direction of the South Wing's entry hallway.

One particularly colorful sentry's voice carried above the rest: "This ain't a drill! Get yer butts out th' door, now. The Apprentice Library's under attack."

I glanced at Ames, who in turn glanced at Benno. My son took a step towards the South Wing guard post. Followed by a second, quicker step. Soon all three of us were sprinting towards the announced danger, much to the chagrin of the guards who were trying to get everyone evacuated safely.

Because of the cancelled classes and reduced staff, we didn't encounter much resistance on our way to the East Wing checkpoint. The reception hall was empty as wiser folk sought out the conventional exits. The guards at the East gate were bandaging a small, huddled figure. It took me a moment to recognise her.

I got there first, and crouched by the bruised, scalded, breathless wererat. "Moria, it's Sorch. What happened?"

The little mage opened one puffy eye. A look of relief and fear washed over her furry face. She half groaned, half whispered, "They came through the floor. Dug in."

Ames crouched on the wererat's other side, as Benno got information from one of the guards. The were-cat stroked Moria's neck gently as bandages were being applied to her ribs.

I pressed for more information, asking, "Elementals? That's what the guards were saying."

"Yes. Small. But powerful. Sorch, students still trapped. In stacks. In a Sanctum."

The young guard applying the bandages said, "We need to move her sir. Now."

Ames gave Moria a quick peck on the cheek, and then helped to lift our little friend so that a plank could be slid under her back. She was quickly and efficiently lashed to it, and then two of the guards took our friend away.

Just as the sound of the general alarm ran its course and faded away, Benno rejoined us, saying, "They have half a dozen men at the Apprentice Library's entrance, holding position until they get backup."

I asked my son, "How combat ready are you?"

"Fairly. I was planning an Astral jaunt this afternoon. You?"

I waggled my hand in an uncertain gesture. "Mixed. You need to handle the fire elementals, I have almost nothing against them."

We both looked at Ames. Despite being unarmored and armed only with their firebrand sabre, the feline said, "Let's go."

I knew the guard who was heading up the small contingent at the entryway of the Apprentice Library. The silver haired man was often on night duties at the South Wing's guard post.

He groaned as we approached. "Now, now, mister Sorch. Yer not going in there."

"I am. And as it turns out, so are you, Steven."

The old guard already looked defeated by my words. And yet he said, "We had instructions to wait fer backup mister Sorch."

It was Benno who stole the very line that I wanted to use. My son said, "Backup has arrived." Then he strode into the Apprentice Library, confidently.

Ames just shrugged and followed.

I patted the older man's arm. "Just give us physical support, Steven. Blunts on the earth elementals. Slice bits off of the water elementals. Let us handle the rest."

After heaving a deep sigh, the sergeant said, "You heard the man. Form up. Keep their backs clean."

I joined my family by the front desk. There was a hint of smoke in the air, but at least there were no signs of an out-of-control blaze. The bowl of flat stones used to host Light cantrips had been knocked over, as had half of the wooden chairs. Books were strewn everywhere. I winced upon seeing the splash of blood upon one of the flipped book return carts. It seemed that at least one student impacted with it, head first.

Ames said, "24 facings in total. Number 1 is clear."

Then the feline proceeded deeper into the library. I was sure that the librarians would not approve of the use of a flaming sword near the stacks. But desperate times, and all that.

We made our way down to the ninth facing before seeing any sign of elementals. Then, while approaching the section involving the magical smithing, we saw what could only be described as a vortex of books. It was an air elemental, but smaller than any that I ever saw before. When we summoned our minor elementals, they were humanoid in size. This one was half that height, almost childlike.

But there was nothing childlike about the destruction that it was causing. Oak shelves rattled. Books were thrown across the chamber with the speed of a sling bullet. The guards behind us loosed an arrow and a crossbow bolt. The latter 'hit' the elemental, and apparently caused it some kind of pain. The vortex moved towards us.

Ames moved to intercept the air elemental before either Benno or I could get a clean line to it. The flaming sabre matched speed with speed, as the creature's makeshift limbs coiled and struck at the were-cat using the captured books as mass. The exchanges were so quick, it was difficult to tell who was winning.

Suddenly, the elemental was ablaze. Ames was no longer cleanly parrying the incoming blows, instead opting to let them slowly slide off the flat of the blade while the were-cat acrobatically dodged aside. The extended contact immolated the tomes, and the resulting heat was just magnified by the concentration of air inside of the elemental. A few seconds later, the creature dissipated, unable to hold itself together as the intense heat tore it apart.

I called out, "Is anyone here?"

"Yes! Is it safe?"

A young human woman poked her head out from around the corner of a large, heavy bookshelf.

I said, "Yes. Hurry, we've cleared the way behind us."

"Wait."

Unexpectedly, Benno walked over to the girl. He asked, "Are you alright?"

"J-just scared. I'll be okay."

My son then proved that he was more clever than I was. He said, "What spells are in your head right now?"

The young lady said, "J-just Light, and Magic Missile. O-oh, and Read Magic."

Benno pointed at the guards who were watching our backs. "Stay with them. When you see them shoot at something, cast your Magic Missile at it. Then head back up to safety."

And so it went with the next two students that we rescued, who had been hiding down on the twelfth facing as the air elemental hunted for them. Benno, once part of an apprentice army himself, pressed them into service. He told them whose lead to follow or what kind of elemental to hit with their spells.

When we faced the miniature water elemental and earth elemental in the fourteenth facing, Benno and I weren't the only ones to give them an arcane greeting. My Force Bolt was paired with a bolt from one of the apprentices, producing cracks in the surface of the pummeled earth elemental. Magic Missiles rained in from both Benno and the first girl that we rescued, sizzling into the fluid surface of the small water elemental. Two of the guards rushed in with warhammers to smash the first creature to bits, while Ames' flaming blade made short work of the other.

Although we lost two of our three student mages when they ran out of combat spells and retreated, we picked up two more before facing the next round of opposition. And so it went as we cleared each level. We were gaining more young spellcasters all the while. Our group was quickly powering through the single or paired elemental forces, thanks to this extra firepower. By the time we reached the bottom of the Apprentice Library, a half dozen students fled to safety, and four of the more advanced students were still marching alongside the guards.

The smoke was far thicker when we made our way past the fungus horticulture section on the twenty-third level of the library. As we looked in on our old stomping grounds, my heart sank. The linen closet was ablaze, feeding on the bedding that we used to hand out to students with nowhere else to sleep. The front stacks had already been burned to cinders. Tables had been smashed, the wood fragments mixed with crumbs of charred cornbread. The only thing that gave me hope was the lack of bodies on the ground. Maybe the kids were still alive.

The floor was cracked, pocked with scorched and dripping holes that plunged deep into the bedrock of the mountain. I was about to ask for suggestions on how we could seal these fissures, when the next wave of elementals manifested from the bowels of the earth. They crawled, and oozed, and floated through the fragmented floor.

I called out, "If anyone is hiding, now is when we make our stand. Spread the word." I added the last, knowing that anyone in a Private Sanctum wouldn't hear us. Someone would have to physically breach the light and sound barrier to pass along the message.

Ames' keen eyes picked out a maelstrom forming from the nearest fissure, and dove towards the small air elemental, leading with the tip of their firebrand sword. Benno touched my shoulder, and we instantly formed a target order thanks to the family's psychic combat shorthand. The rapid flow of chopped syllables flowed into my head, and my brief response signalled agreement with no modification. We turned towards an approaching fire elemental and started casting simultaneously. Before it could reach us we squeezed the small water flasks on our belts, and twin Fans of Frost cut the creature down in a hiss of steam.

The soldiers fanned out around us, intercepting the earth and water elementals as best as they could. They played a defensive game as much as possible, and I couldn't blame them. One overextension would mean bruised skin, broken bones, and potentially having one's head engulfed by water and drowning in the middle of a library.

Our students proved their worth as well. As a vortex of books and shattered wood started to rise above us, it was met by a Flame Jet. As it writhed and started to falter, twin Acid Bolts impacted with the half-sized elemental, burning and essentially poisoning the creature. Unable to incorporate the fire, smoke, and acid into its makeup, the elemental dissipated.

Though we blunted the initial assault, the earth elementals were proving to be an issue. With only a couple of soldiers using warhammers, they simply weren't going down. Stone skin was largely immune to the rest of our attacks. And they seemed happy with a defensive stance. Their stalling simply bought time for the emergence of more pint sized elementals from the depths.

Ames thrust a flaming sabre through the center of the air elemental on our right flank. It boiled away like steam rising from a kettle. But the were-cat was forced to backpedal, unable to do anything about the fire and earth elementals that were approaching. Soon I found myself hip to hip with my mate.

Benno was already casting on our predetermined target, but I had to time my next spell perfectly. The approaching earth elemental took two lumbering steps forward, and was only three paces away when I started my own casting. When the portal opened in the library's ceiling, it rained down a torrent of hail and ice on the elemental's upper body. My Force Bolt caught it in the neck, snapping its frozen and cracked head clean off. The small elemental disintegrated, becoming a pile of lifeless rubble.

The guards were taking a beating. Even through thick armor the earth elementals were able to bludgeon them, bruising flesh and bone. Our apprentices helped where they could, managing to aid one of the warhammer wielding fighters with a series of Force Bolts and Magic Missiles, felling another of the pesky earth elementals.

With Ames on the defense, and out of offensive options myself, I was about to call for a retreat. But then I heard a confident, practiced voice behind us. Powdered silver and copper rained down around us as Max joined the fray. I didn't have any idea what spell this was, but I knew that we had to buy time.

I summoned my Invisible Shield and crouched in front of Ames and Benno. A water elemental that slipped past our warriors slammed into me, like an ocean wave battering against a cliffside. Knocked on my rump, I struggled against the strength of the liquid creature. It was starting to ooze around the perimeter of my shield, one watery limb reaching out to envelop my mouth and nostrils.

I heard Benno's Lightning Bolt go off, but had no idea what the target might have been. The last thing that I heard before the water surrounded my head was a hissing sound as Ames' fiery blade struck something wet.

But we bought all the time that Max needed. Before breathing became an issue, the water seemed to fall from my face, as in if someone had just poured it from a bucket. I watched in wonder as the copper and silver motes still floating in the air seemed to take on a life of their own. I found out some time later that this spell was called 'Gustov's Disjunction'. The archmage's spell seemed to seek out each elemental and simply disassemble it. Pyres of fire became smoke; stacks of stone, sand. Air elementals were turned to fog, and water elementals became harmless puddles.

As our ragtag ensemble stared at the aftermath of the Headmaster's spell, Benno summed up my feelings quite succinctly.

"Wow."

Max said, dryly, "Wow indeed. Sergeant, get your wounded men to the surface. Sorch, get off your butt and look for survivors. Everyone else, secure the perimeter while I re-ward the library."

Dripping wet, but glad to be alive, I did as Max asked. I searched behind the stacks until I found a little area of pure darkness. Not wanting to startle the students within, or more importantly get my face taken off by a dagger, I searched for something that I could throw into the Private Sanctum that would obviously be humanoid in nature. I settled on the swatch of fine cloth that I used to clean the jeweler's loop used in the Read Magic spell. It was soaked anyway, and would need cleaning.

I threw in the balled up cloth and waited. A few seconds later, a pale elven face poked its way out of the darkness. I made a 'come hither' motion with one finger.

Soon four students were surrounding me in various states of relief and fear. The senior student who conjured the Private Sanctum explained that they used all of their offensive magic to take down one of the elementals during the initial invasion. Then they ran to a corner, balled up together, and hid in the confines of the privacy spell. Four people in a single Sanctum must have been claustrophobically crowded, but they managed somehow.

I took the young mages over to one of the guardsmen so that they could be escorted up and out of the Apprentice Library. Then I watched Max performing the warding ceremony. His old hands moved deftly. His voice rose confidently over the sound of crackling flames.

Sigils had been created upon the cracked and pitted library floor. Powdered coal was the primary medium, although I saw flecks of gold mixed into the sandy black lines that criss crossed the devastated area.

Max's chanting went on for over five minutes. I tried to follow the arcane language being used, but it was far more complex than anything I had even read about, nevermind performed. I'm not even certain that I could memorize an incantation that went on so long without any kind of pattern or refrain. The mental fortitude that the Headmaster displayed was impressive.

At the end of the ritual, the coal and gold dust was absorbed into the cracked stone. Max stumbled, only to be caught and supported by Ames.

The Headmaster said, weakly, "Someone will need to seal and Stone Shape this back into a usable floor. And I'll undoubtedly need to re-ward some of the lower levels of the University. But we need a more permanent solution to this elemental problem. And we need to find it rapidly. In the meantime, let's put out the damned fires."

I murmured, "We'll clean up here Max. Go get some rest."

I was surprised when he said, "No. Gideon will assign some of his people to reshape the stone. Once the fires are out, go tell the folks waiting outside that the emergency is over. Then go get some rest, memorize your spells, and put a travel pack together. Just before this foolishness happened, I received another missive from the yetis. They need to meet with you in the afternoon. They're expecting you, and I have no idea why."

Chapter 17

The afternoon sun cast shafts of white light through the snow laden boughs of the ancient pine trees. Every step was met with a satisfying crunch; echoes of the crisp compression that a boot makes when breaking through an impossibly thin layer of ice, just before finding a home in the snow below.

The wilderness South of the Arcane University was an immaculate representation of Panos' natural beauty. For the most part, the only hunters in these parts were wolves and snow leopards. The only lumberjacks were giant white beavers. And if any of these creatures saw a humanoid, they might stop and stare for a while, but after their curiosity was sated they would give you a wide berth.

What was odd was that we weren't the only recent visitors to these parts. Ames said that there were multiple sets of recent tracks. Small footprints, clearly not yetis of any age or stature. This puzzled us, because we were told that there were no cabins or outposts for a dozen miles in any direction. Other than the Arcane University of course, and that was a rather large and unsubtle outpost.

The center of this particular forest was a sheltered clearing. It really was the perfect haven for the yeti tribe. A frozen-over brook provided fresh water with minimal effort. There was plenty of wild game in the surrounding area. And some nearby caves even provided nutritious winter mushrooms, which often grew to the size of melons. I was glad that my divinely inspired voice had been right about this place.

This time, there was no stealthy greeting. A contingent of three tall, shaggy white creatures loped up to us as we walked out of the wooded area.

These weren't the same patrolling yetis as last time. They seemed somewhat smaller, perhaps adolescents. Their pupilless, rust colored eyes regarded us with open curiosity. Still, we were greeted politely. "Hello little ones. Please receive our utmost gratitude for making the journey between your stone fortress and the location of our new home.

We shall escort you to our tribal leader, who is still 'Divine', and shall be referred to as Divine. May we proceed?"

We proceeded.

A combination of magic, divine favor, hard work, and gravity allowed the yeti tribe to relocate in short order. Whatever 'rapid downhill transportation' that the yetis had used, it worked. As we approached the translucent ice walls of their homes, we saw that they contained all of the amenities that had been in place prior to the move. Every white stone tile, every massive chair, every white-furred blanket was either successfully transported or somehow recreated.

Divine had once again turned up the heat for our benefit. Even at this lower altitude and somewhat warmer climate, it was a welcome and considerate gesture. The three of us left our packs in the foyer before proceeding into Divine's living room.

The big yeti stood as we entered. She said, "Greetings to you Sorch, and greetings to you Ames. Would you do me the immeasurable kindness of introducing your young companion to me, so that I and the rest of the tribe might utilise the proper form of address when speaking to or referring to said companion?"

I prodded Benno so that he would step forward. Then I said, "Divine, this is my son Benno. Benno, this is Divine. She will have the pleasure of eating you."

Divine replied, smoothly, "Greetings little one with the name of 'Benno'. I am extending the hospitality of our tribe to you. Please rest assured that your father was attempting to use levity when he referred to your consumption. I rarely eat humanoids of any sort."

Benno cleared his throat, and then said, "Thank you for your hospitality and your kindness, Divine. It is an honor to be here among your people."

The big matriarch gestured to the chairs surrounding the heating brazier. "Your words of kindness are both noted and appreciated, I assure you. Please, avail yourselves to the seats that are free. Assuming that none of you have an objection, I will make use of this seat."

Divine sank back down into her chair. After half-heartedly considering an objection to the yeti's choice of seat, I walked over and hopped up into one of the oversized chairs. Ames and Benno did the same. I think Benno was sitting on Uncle Clever, but I would tell him all about that later.

It was the were-cat who started the diplomacy. "We were pleased to have received your message, and honored to be the ones selected to come meet with you. The exact urgency of your need to meet was not clear, but we set off the moment that we finished preparations for such a journey."

The yeti nodded. She said, "It is a subject that we would not wish to seem objectionable about, at least not in an official missive. And in fact, under normal circumstances, we would not object at all to the visiting tiny creatures, as they have proven themselves to be peaceful and curious beings, worthy of our care and attention."

The three of us traded glances. It was Ames who asked, "Visiting tiny creatures, you say? We had no knowledge of this."

Divine said, "Yes, that was another reason not to go into great detail in the written request for a meeting. We did not wish to... how did they put it? We did not wish to 'tattle on' the little mages. Not in any official manner, you understand. It is our sincerest hope that they not be punished in any way. In fact we need to insist that any record that contains our conversation here today reflect the fact that the tiny mages were welcomed by my people with open arms."

I asked, "Divine, what did these tiny mages look like?"

"Most of them were quite small. Some of them were simply small. One or two of them had horns, and those were not so small. But all of them were garbed in the robes of your Arcane University, and most of them had the good sense and forethought to wear additional protective coverings to shield themselves from the cold."

Ames rubbed their forehead, as if coming down with a sudden headache. "Might I ask: How many different and distinct tiny mages have come to visit you over the last few weeks?"

The yeti replied, "I would estimate two to three score individual little ones have visited us in that timeframe. And again, I feel that I need to stress that we did not object. In fact, most of my people have expressed to me how interesting and refreshing it was to have children of another species visit us. Some of the tiny ones brought little things to trade. They brought copper coins, and they brought a fascinating food that they referred to as 'corn bread'. In the future, we would like more corn bread."

Benno said, "So what you're saying is that some of our students have been sneaking off to come see you. And it has become a common thing."

Divine's red eyes swiveled to regard Benno. There was a moment of silence. Then she came to a decision, "Yes little one, I believe that summary to be accurate."

Ames said, "And for reasons of your own, you would like them to stop."

Divine shook her great head. "There are two inaccuracies with that statement, one they call Ames. The first inaccuracy is that we would 'like' them to stop. This request actually brings us some amount of sadness. And yet we believe that it is in their best interest if the tiny mages stop their visits for the time being. The second inaccuracy is that the reasons for this request are our own. On the contrary, the concern should be mutual between our people. This is why you have been invited to meet with us. If you will allow it, I would like to illustrate the reason we make this request, and ask your opinion on how reasonable we have been in the level of concern that we have expressed."

I was able to follow that sentence, if just barely. I nodded, "Of course Divine, please show us."

Divine gestured towards the brazier and murmured her illusion incantation. Suddenly the clear, alcohol fueled flames were visible. As the matriarch spoke, the image shifted to that of a night sky with a clear horizon.

"I mentioned that we would aid in your investigations. And so, we did. My people are the people of the wind, and the people of the snow. But we are also the people of the night. It is within the confines of the night that we explore and survey. It is within the confines of the night that we dream. And the context of those dreams are reflections of reality."

On the illusionary horizon, an ominous silhouette appeared in the light of the full moon.

"This is why the tiny mages must stay away. Our dreams perceived this threat, and so we were able to request arcane and holy portents. Our portents were able to better define this threat, and so we called for surveillance of the night sky. Our scouts were able to catch glimpses of this threat. These sightings were brief and only as specific as one might expect given the circumstances."

The fire flared briefly, and the silhouette became larger. Slightly more defined.

Benno gasped, "Is that a dragon?"

Divine held up one large hand, "We would not presume to label it, not at this stage. Let it be known however that there have been no draconic sightings in this area for over a century. Whether you feel that one hundred years is too long or too short of a time period is up to you as individuals. I will simply say that each day is a new day, and circumstances change. May I continue?"

Benno said, "Of course Divine, I'm sorry."

"There is no need to apologise for a question, little one. Questions are exactly why we are here. If we already had the answers to this mystery, we could formulate a course of action. Whereas the only course of action that we can recommend is further investigation. Is this, as you say, a dragon? If not, what is it? If so, what is the dragon's intentions? All of these questions and several other factors have led us to expand our investigation to include external resources. Resources such as yourselves, should you feel up to the task and have the availability. And of course, until this danger is fully assessed... please have the children stay away. At least for now, as much as that decision weighs heavy on our hearts."

I asked, "For lack of a better term, may I refer to this figure as 'dragon'?"

Divine considered. Then she said, "You may."

"What can you tell us about this dragon? You've scryed, you've prayed, and you've observed. Do you have any details?"

The yeti said, "Precious few details have been acquired so far. Scrying eyes are evaded or dispelled before they can get to a useful range. The relative distances involved would indicate that this is a very large dragon, if it is indeed of that species. We can give you times and locations in the night sky. We can tell you direction of flight for as long as they remained in view. This is assuming, of course, that all of this is real and not illusion, delusion, or hallucination. All I know is that our shamans said this is one of the signs of the apocalypse. I am no expert on the end-of-times, but I share their concern. We need more information. Do you understand, little ones?"

Ames said, "We do understand, Divine. And I think we may have a friend who can help. Are you familiar with the Church of Melflavin?"

The matriarch bobbed her great head, those pupilless red-brown eyes now fixed on my mate. "A minor god, but one that spans races, having popularity with elves, humans, and even some orcs. A curiosity. Why do you mention this god's church?"

Ames explained, "They have a mastery of optics. Of physical lenses. We took part in the restoration of one of their observatories in the past. They have devices called 'telescopes' that can observe objects in the sky."

Divine caught on quickly, "And this being an area of high elevation and away from civilization, I assume they have one of these observatories in the general vicinity. Would they be willing to point one of these devices at the night sky and report back on what they see?"

The were-cat said, "We'll find out."

Divine stood. The illusion within the fire flickered and died. The three of us half slid, half fell out of our tall chairs.

"You are the most reliable small people that I have ever had the great pleasure of associating with. Rest assured that you leave with both our gratitude and our confidence. Please relate this to the tiny mages: Should they be unable to visit for an extended period of time, some of our mages have expressed interest in visiting them at their Arcane University. I will approve this measure when the time comes."

Benno's eyes went wide. He asked, "You would allow yetis to visit the University?"

Divine tilted her head. She said, "That is what I just stated little one." She then turned to me and asked, "Does your son have short term memory issues?"

I immediately responded, "Yes."

Benno slapped my shoulder, "No ma'am, my memory is fine. I was just surprised."

Ames said, "I'll have Sorch or Benno send a Message spell to keep you up to date. Thank you for your time."

The matriarch said, "You have my thanks and the thanks of my tribe. It is my hope that the combination of our continued efforts leads to a solution that will benefit Panos. I look forward to the next update."

Night fell before the three of us made our way back to the Arcane University. Max was annoyed when we told him that students had been visiting the yetis. We then compounded his frustration by mentioning that some yetis might be asking for a tour of the school in the near future. And more cornbread.

The old archmage said, "Please tell me that you have some good news, or else I'm just going to retire and take up basket weaving."

Ames hesitated before saying, "I'm not certain this qualifies as **good** news. But it is a lead. Yeti portents followed by yeti scouts discovered something flying around in the distance. Something fairly draconic looking."

Max said, dryly, "Yes Ames, when I asked for good news, I meant that you should tell me that there's a gods damned **dragon** flying around in the mountains!"

I scowled. "We could lie to you if you like. It was a kitten shaped creature actually. It was flying around, chasing a big ball of floating yarn."

Benno gripped my shoulder. He said, "I think what Father means is that we have a course of action to follow. This could be a solid lead."

Using our physical connection, Benno thought, *"Please don't poke the bear, Dad."*

Casually, I said aloud, "Yes, of course, that's what I meant."

Max eyed me for a moment, before asking, "What's your plan?"

Ames said, "Melflavin's mountain observatory. It's a rough hike, but with Tara's help we can use real optics to see what this creature is. At least, we don't think it will be able to avoid or knock out physical observation the way that it defeated scrying efforts."

I noted, "We'll need to make it worth her while."

Max said, "The Guild will see to her compensation. And yours for that matter. Can you leave in the morning?"

Benno and I looked to Ames. The were-cat said, "I'll go visit her right now and find out. If she's up to it, we'll be ready."

My son and I ate dinner in near-silence. Perhaps it was the enormity of the political and magical situation. Perhaps there was simply nothing left to say. As we stood to head out of the University dining area, I offered Benno a brief, tired smile. I knew that everything was alright when he smiled back. We said goodnight, and headed back to our respective rooms to get some rest.

An hour later, I felt a familiar creature slide into bed behind me. Fur, still chilled from Ice House's harsh night wind, pressed into the skin of my bare back. Ames put a wet nose to my temple and whispered, "We're on for tomorrow. I already told Benno."

I whispered back, "Not like this, I hope."

That earned me a swat on the flank. I was too tired to retaliate. Sleep swiftly took me once again.

I woke up to the smell of fresh pastry. Tara and Ames were chatting quietly just a couple of paces away from where I lay. I reached out feebly from my bed, as if I could grab one of those frosted breakfast rolls through sheer force of will.

The cleric noticed me and smiled brightly. "Good morning sleepyhead." said Tara, in a mocking sing-song voice.

"Gimmie."

Ames tsk'ed my groggily expressed request. The feline said, "Manners, dear. You may have a pastry when you've woken up and properly greeted our guest. I, in the meantime, will deliver two of these to our son and make sure his green ass is out of bed as well."

The were-cat padded out of the room, and I had to watch as a pair of those beautiful morning treats escaped. I sat up and rubbed my eyes. With as much politeness as I could muster, I said, "Good morning Tara. Could you throw me my clothes please?"

Her perfectly white, perfectly square teeth grinned at me. The minotaur simply said, "No."

I shrugged and got out of bed anyway. Tara laughed, but had the good grace to avert her eyes. I didn't mind either way. After all: We adventured together, she'd seen worse. Once I retrieved my breeches and a thin overshirt, I sat opposite the cleric.

"How's Toby?" I asked, before wolfing down my first glazed roll.

As I ate, Tara said, "He's fine. He's on babysitting duty today, much to his chagrin."

My next question was asked around a greedy mouth full of succulent pastry. "We ready?"

"The Order of the Snow has sent word to Master Aharon up at the Eastern Heights Observatory. He seemed unenthused by our impending visit, but accepted the fact that the sightings might be important. He's willing to stop his celestial studies for a couple of hours tonight in order to help us."

I swallowed, allowing the sugar rush to infuse me. After heaving a happy sigh, I said, "It sounds like we're all set then. It's a hard slog though, Eastern Heights is about twenty miles away through deep snow. We're not likely to get there until after midnight."

The cleric seemed to be hesitating. After a long pause, she replied, "Sorch, once we get there it might not be the easiest time either. You understand how minotaurs experience emotions on a binary scale, right?"

I licked the sugar off of my lips, then nodded. "Of course, happiness and sadness, everything being a shade of those things."

Tara started to shake her head. She said, "That's not the case with Master Aharon. In his older years, he has contracted a rare condition that allows him to experience more of the emotional scale. Minotaurs weren't meant to do that. So he may come off as... less than stable."

I peered at the cleric, and then asked, "Tara, are you telling me that this guy is unspooled?"

Her head-shaking become more rapid. She clarified, "No, no. Not at all. He, um. He isn't dangerous, Sorch. Though he does tend to scare people. There's a reason he chose a remote outpost to live out the rest of his life. I just want you to be prepared, and not frightened by anything you experience. He won't harm us."

I reached out to take Tara's big hand in my smaller one. I said, "Was he a friend?"

I felt her squeeze my hand reassuringly. She said, "Of my father's. I remember him from when I was young, mostly. I've seen him three or four times in my adult life. I'll be okay, I know what to expect."

I rubbed the back of the minotaur's hand with my calloused thumb. "It looks like you're ready for this trip. You're finally starting to get fluffy again."

Tara looked surprised and pleased by my observation. She said, "Thank you. You know, the other minotaurs didn't notice. Or if they did, they avoided talking about it so as not to bring up the disintegration business. But you've always been the observant one."

I gave that big hand a final squeeze before freeing mine so that I could grab another pastry. Prior to taking a bite, I outlined my expectations for the trip. "Many layers, snowshoes, and thick cloaks. And I imagine frequent stops to warm up."

Tara nodded. "I'll be carrying a couple of small bundles of dry wood. Ames can just stick that new sword right in the middle and we'll have a nice hot fire for half an hour."

I honestly hadn't even considered the utility of the firebrand weapon on a trip such as this. That might make things considerably less miserable.

After Benno and I took some time to perform intellect enhancements and memorize an appropriate suite of arcana, we all set off on our long trek.

My prediction of the level of misery proved accurate. Fourteen hours of snowshoeing was never fun or exciting. It can be terrifying in the wrong conditions, but still not exciting as such. But compared to our trip to the Ice Caves years earlier, we were relatively comfortable. We rested five times, basically whenever we found a small cave or relatively sheltered rock where we could make a fire. Tara's minotaur senses were excellent for detecting such things. Twice we used Ames and Tara's firewood and flaming sabre trick. The other three times we huddled around my magic pot and enjoyed tea, coffee, or soup.

At the tail end of our trip, we were exhausted. Light spells on the tips of short wooden rods helped us to pick out the best footing. Even seasoned adventurers didn't have the conditioning to muddle through this kind of environment without some lingering effects. We were all grateful when the incline towards the observatory became a well defined path.

Snowshoes were unstrapped, and we made our way up to the stout, domed building.

All of the expense of the Eastern Heights Observatory went into the optics, it seemed. The walls were primarily built with kiln-fired brick. There were no signs, no engravings on the thick wooden doors. No opulence of any kind. And with no obvious bell or lock on the door, we simply let ourselves in.

I was shocked by the sudden wave of heat that washed over my face. We quickly closed the door behind us and basked in that bone-deep warmth for a few seconds. The foyer was simply a small round brick chamber with hooks drilled into the wall and a coat rack standing by the doorway. It funneled out into a single long hallway, leading East.

Once her lungs were filled with temperate air for the first time in hours, Tara called out, "Master Aharon? It's Tara McGoldberg and some of my friends."

The distant, gruff reply came immediately, "Great. Come straight forward. Stay out of the private rooms."

We exchanged quiet glances, but the greeting was in line with the expectations that Tara set. With the minotaur leading, we delved more deeply into the observatory.

The source of welcoming heat became apparent when we entered the central dome chamber. Copper sconces sprouted from the wall every few feet. Gouts of flame, far more impressive than those coming from the small lighting fixtures at the Arcane University, threw light and heat everywhere. Natural gas torches; there had to be two dozen of them ringing the room.

Once my eyes adjusted to the prominence of flame within the chamber, I was able to pick out some interesting details. Melflavin's holy symbol had been beautifully etched on the dome above us. But that wasn't the only thing above our heads. The entire observation platform was raised above the level of the brick walls. Four iron rods sprouted from gear assemblies, which themselves were attached to hand cranks. They disappeared into the perimeter walls, presumably controlling the rotation of the telescope and surrounding dome. Only Melflavin's people and certain human engineering teams mastered this level of mechanical prowess.

A deep voice from somewhere within the metal scaffolding said, "Just stay out of the way. Don't touch anything. I'll be down shortly."

There was a series of rapid clicks, followed by a grinding sound. Over the course of the next two minutes, the great telescope slowly dipped and swiveled to face the northern skies, and the outer shell of the dome moved with it. When the racket ceased, there was a steady metallic thumping: Hooves meeting an iron grate.

The minotaur that made his way down that final flight of stairs was unlike any I'd ever seen before. His fur was a wild, reddish gray hue. He was tall, and would have left Toby at least two handbreadths in his shadow. But at the same time, he was neither wiry nor muscular. This beast was heavy set, bordering on plump. He didn't bother hiding that well padded belly and chest, likely satisfied with the copious heat in his observatory. He did wear workman's pants, cut off at the knees. They managed to contain the minotaur's ample rump and bulging thighs.

Tara greeted the man, "Master Aharon, hello. Thank you for helping us in this dire time."

Aharon half heartedly held out a hand for shaking. He barely made it through one pump up and down before he was releasing Tara's hand. "Yeah. Well, didn't have much of a bloody choice did I?"

The minotaur astronomer's tone was definitely irritated, bordering on angry. Having been around Toby and Tara so much, the difference was jarring.

Tara sighed a little bit. She said, "No sir, I'm sorry about that."

The old minotaur snorted. "Don't get all weepy on me girl. I know whose fault this bull crap is, and it ain't you. Relax."

Aharon eyed the rest of us for a moment. Then he said, "Benno, Ames, and Sorch, right?"

Benno's eyes widened, "You've heard of us, sir?"

The old minotaur rolled his eyes. "Hells no, boy. It was in the Message. Young orc, cat, big-deal orc. Or so I'm told." He paused and then said, "You look like crap."

Ames growled, dryly, "You're not looking so great yourself, tenderloin."

Tara looked like she wanted to curl up and die. Even I thought that Ames had gone a bit far with that remark.

But surprisingly, the old bull bellowed with laughter. "You. You're the one I like. Come on kitty cat, I'm going to show you how to work a **real** man's tool." He clarified the statement by gesturing up to the telescope. As Aharon stomped back up the stairs, he shouted over his shoulder, "Pay attention while I show the were-cat how to make the minor adjustments. Then set up your bedrolls in the Northwest corner, out of the way. Rest until it's your turn at the eyepiece. Could be a long night."

Tara murmured to Benno and I, "I'm sorry about all that."

I shrugged and murmured, "He's not so different from some of the old sailors I know, dear. It's fine. Just a bit of a culture shock when you're used to… well, you and Toby."

Aharon set the focus of the lenses to the correct general distance. He showed us how to use the crank to make fine left-to-right adjustments of the telescope's facing. We could also pull a lever to switch to up-and-down adjustments using the same hand crank. It took Ames a little bit of practice, but eventually, the feline's technique met with Aharon's approval.

The big minotaur descended, and then brushed past us. He said, "I'm going to sleep for a while. Don't break anything. Shout if you spot your flying shadow." And with that, the old minotaur went into his private chambers and slammed the door.

We decided on two hours shifts at the eyepiece. Ames started, then Tara, followed by Benno, then myself. Which meant that I was sound asleep in the corner of the observatory when I was woken by Benno's sharp, clear cry.

"Dragon!"

I was up in a heartbeat. It was a parental reaction. When your child shouts like that, no matter how old or how capable they may be, you leap to their defense.

Tara ran to knock on Master Aharon's door as Ames and I hurried up the metal steps. I watched Benno's right hand crank ever so slowly, so that he was tracking along with the motion of his target.

I whispered in his ear, "You got 'em, boy?"

He murmured, "Yes."

I said, "Show your old man."

Benno slipped to the side a fraction, while maintaining his slow tracking. I bent to put my eye to the viewing lens.

I only took a quick look. Frankly, I didn't need more than that. No matter how distant the creature was, it seemed terrifyingly close. I saw the ease with which the draconic creature kept itself aloft. I witnessed the soulless gaze that scanned the horizon and the ground. Perhaps most frightening, I saw the seemingly perfect coat of gray metallic scales rippling over the creature's chest and belly. Not a single scar. Like it had never been injured. Like it couldn't be injured.

Everyone took a turn at the viewpiece before Aharon managed to rouse himself and make his way over to the telescope.

"Alright, out of the way. Let's see what this nonsense is all about."

Upon getting his turn at the lens, the minotaur snorted derisively. I thought for a moment that the old man was going to tell us that it was just a flying lizard, no bigger than the size of Lizzy. But with each moment of observation, Master Aharon's shoulders dropped a fraction. With every subtle adjustment of the lens, the huge minotaur's hand shook more violently.

He stood suddenly, and with a tight, hoarse voice, he commanded, "Keep tracking it boy." Given the circumstances, I could forgive Aharon's reference to my son. Benno quickly bent to his task, using those nimble fingers to keep the dragon in view.

Aharon half staggered over to his writing podium. His big hand shook as he wrote his observations, saying them loud for our benefit.

"Subject is between fifty and fifty-five paces in length. Mass is equivalent to a sperm whale. Cruising speed of forty miles in an hour. Peak speed unknown. Subject thought to be a dragon. Sub species - Unidentified. Closest matching from lore… Stasis Dragon. Witnessed by four other observers. Let the record reflect that the documenter is sober and arguably sane."

With that, the quill slipped from the minotaur's grasp. He stood, staring at what he just wrote. It was clear that the bull man was petrified.

Tara walked over and reached up to grasp Master Aharon's thick shoulders. She massaged and squeezed them, saying the old minotaur's name over and over again until he made some kind of response. After half a minute, Aharon made a request, his voice trembling with fear.

"Young Benno, describe to me what you see."

My son kept up the gentle tracking as he spoke, "It looks like a dragon from the books of lore. A giant flying lizard. It might be a trick of the light, but the scales look gray. The wings they… they don't seem to beat as frequently as they should. That kind of flight seems impossible."

The old minotaur agreed, "Yes. Yes, go on."

"Its neck can crane around in just about any direction. The tail is long and powerful, almost acting like an air rudder. And th-"

Suddenly Benno jumped, as if shocked. He quickly put his eye back to the eyepiece as he said, "Holy hells did it… I think it just breathed chunks of ice, or boulders! Some kind of solid stream, onto something below it."

Aharon choked on his words the first time, and had to try again. He managed to say, "Untime. The icy rock of untime."

Benno murmured the word, like he was tasting it on his lips, "Untime."

Tara squeezed the Master's shoulders, hard. "Aharon. What is that thing?"

He brushed Tara's hands from his shoulders, and then turned to face us all. "What you kids have there is the Stasis Dragon. It is a creature of legend. A fairy tale. A myth."

Ames said, "I think you had better tell us the fairy tale, Master Aharon. I don't think any of us have heard it."

The old minotaur laughed, bitterly. "Because it's so ridiculous as to be stupid. Elves used to tell it to their babies. When the world of Panos was created by the gods, they used a powerful artifact. What you have identified as your 'Original Engine'. But what if they created something that was a mistake? Something that they need to remove entirely, something whose presence needed to cease and not be able to interact with anything else, or decay, or be found several millennia later? What if they needed to erase something from the world?"

We all glanced to the North, instinctively. Benno's normally steady hand was shivering as he manipulated the crank to keep his quarry in sight.

Master Aharon said, "The Stasis Dragon was supposedly how they accomplished that. It could remove something, or someone, from the flow of time. Make it unreachable, irrecoverable. Instantly dead, instantly isolated, instantly… nothing. The shell of what it once was, doomed to sink like a stone through sand and water. It would be absorbed back into the core of Panos, and never be seen again."

I heard enough. I said, "Please get all of your notes together. We'll need a copy for our return. I'm going to let Max know what we're up against."

I went back to the corner where our furs and blankets were laid out. I sat for a minute, composing my thoughts, before taking out a strand of copper wire and murmuring the incantation.

I sent my Message to Max: 'Foe is Stasis Dragon. Elves know lore. Bringing details home. May be counter-probe from Original Engine. Heading home shortly.'

It took a few moments for Max to formulate a sane reply at this hour of the morning. Then he responded with: 'All deliberating parties will be told about new urgency. Going to press for final decision by time the group returns. Sending Aharon help.'

I mounted the steps again, and let everyone know Max's reply. "Master Aharon, you can expect some company in a few hours. Likely one of our archmages with a couple of journeymen from the Transport Guild. We need them to help you track this and send reports back to us. And, well. You'll want the company I imagine."

The shaking minotaur nodded quickly, not particularly wanting to be alone after what he just witnessed.

To everyone else, I simply said, "Let's pack up. It's mostly a downhill trip. Benno, do you remember our trick?"

My son groaned. Which meant he remembered.

"Get a Message to Divine, then we go."

As Benno sent warning to the yetis, we made sure that Master Aharon was going to be alright on his own for now. He pulled himself together quickly, and assured us that he would be able to keep watch on his own for a while. Once the four of us were packed and properly dressed, we said our goodbyes to the old minotaur. Then the party made its way down the winding observatory path in the crisp early morning air. We donned snowshoes and walked until the sun crested over the eastern mountains.

After our first rest period, I said, "Okay, get the netting out. Once the two of you secure Benno and I, you can get on the net in front of us and hold on. Use the Light rods to help us steer as needed."

The younger mage said, "This is an awful idea. I was barely able to control it when I was alone."

I reminded Benno, "More weight distribution means more stability. Stop being a baby."

I had a plan. It was a plan that Benno and I needed to practice several times before getting right. This revolutionary form of transport was inspired by Rick. My human friend once told me that you should never use a Flat Mule on the snow. 'It tends to shoot off wildly whenever it hits a snowy slope, out of the caster's control.' were Rick's exact words.

Sure. But what if the caster was lashed to the Flat Mule? What if they constantly bent their will towards controlling the slide? As Benno and I soon discovered, the result was quite spectacular. After several disastrous results, my son and I mastered the dangerous technique.

We summoned our Flat Mules. Tara and Ames wrapped us and all of our possessions in ropes and netting, before climbing into the nest of restraints. Ames was with me, Tara with Benno. Were-cat and minotaur wielded rods that they could dig into the snow as needed to help with turning and slowing down.

I called over to my son, "Okay, forward. Let's go."

Soon, we were sliding. Very, very fast.

There was some terrified shouting. This was nothing like wolf riding. The sense of control was entirely in the caster's mind. Gravity was only meaningful as a component of speed. The caster had to use snow banks and hills as a kind of natural guiding force. Fight against it and you would lose control. Use it to your advantage and the result was better control over speed and direction.

When Benno and I were once again used to this form of locomotion, the screams of fear turned into breathless laughter. We even started to race on the more level stretches of our downhill journey. Benno quickly realised that the extra weight that Tara provided was a boon going downhill, but made cornering more difficult. Still, my son 'won' more often than I.

In minutes, we slid the same distance that took us an hour the day before. We would be back at the Arcane University within two hours at this rate.

That was assuming we didn't plummet off the side of a cliff. But science had been good to us today, and this new form of travel was the result of dedicated experimentation. Besides. I had a feeling that Panos wasn't quite through with me just yet.

Chapter 18

"It was perfectly safe." I lied.

We were sitting on desks and chairs in Master Gideon's classroom, waiting for the were-wolf to join us and provide an update. Max was still rubbing his eyes. He wasn't speaking to me directly at this point, and selected Tara as the most reasonable one among us. Relatively so. The cleric was wearing a big smile, exhilarated from the high speed trip back to the Arcane University.

Max asked the minotaur, "Was it perfectly safe?"

Tara shook her head. "Absolutely not. I thought we were all going to die!" But even as she said this, she was grinning like a child.

Benno chimed in with, "We had multiple Soft Fall spells ready. If we went off a cliff."

Ames rumbled, "I had my ring."

"Perfectly safe." I insisted.

The Headmaster said, "You know what? You adventuring fools do whatever you like. But I swear if I find students conducting Flat Mule races down mountainsides, I'll see to it that all of you... what?"

Max stopped his rant as he saw us all exchanging guilty glances.

It was Tara who came clean. "Some of the students who still hadn't gone home may have, possibly, seen us sliding the final distance into the courtyard."

Benno coughed, then said, "It's possible that, in our excitement, exact instructions for sliding a Flat Mule through the snow might have been passed on."

Max nearly tore out a clump of his wispy white hair. He said, "So we have students hellbent on hanging out with yetis, other students potentially trying to break their necks by racing Flat Mules against each other, and a legendary dragon searching for something nearby and belching clouds of untime everywhere. Does that sum things up?"

Our murmured affirmations of his statements were a bit more subdued now.

"I have some good news."

We all turned to see Master Gideon stride into the room. The big werewolf said, "The elves were the last holdouts, and they have finally made their decision. The Transport Guild has already started to relocate the Arcane Syphons from the storage outpost to the staging area in Limt. Will and Rick will take Sorch's ship and get them loaded up as soon as possible. They'll head around the southern peninsula, and then back up towards the Great Trench and eventually Braxen. Our plans could move forward within a single day."

Relief washed over everyone present. It was the first piece of good news we had heard in a while.

Max said, "Alright. Let's get the rest of the students out of here, as well as the staff and all non-combatant teachers. All classes are hereby suspended. We're going to need everyone who can sling a combat spell down in Braxen, to help our psychics to overload the Arcane Syphons in the Astral. Just in case a simple command won't do the job."

Gideon said, "With that in mind, Hemitath has arranged for our friends in Arbitros to play host to anyone who can't go home for one reason or another. For a lot of the staff, the University **is** home. But I don't think anyone will object to a few days of cultural exchange with the elves. Several of our elven allies will be joining us at the Braxen site, via Sorch's village and then wolfback."

That morning was spent helping the guards execute the mass exodus. Most of the staff was well prepared for their forced vacation. The majority of them opted to go to Arbitros. Some of the students protested that they could still be helpful, but we were hearing none of it. With the aid of the Transport Guild, we got them gathered into as few groups as possible based on their final destinations. Then they were teleported to their home cities, with the remainder going to the southern elves for safe keeping.

As we were helping to shepherd one of the last groups onto the Circle of Transport, Ames suddenly froze. The were-cat's eyes went distant for a few seconds.

Then my mate turned to me and said, "That was Divine. She says the dragon has turned. It's coming this way. I told her that we were evacuating the non-combatants and to get her people under cover."

I looked over my shoulder, trying to see past the throng of people. "Max? Max!" I called.

But when I spotted Max, he was standing very still, much as Ames had been moments ago. When he snapped out of it, he turned to me and said, grimly, "That was our people at the observatory. We have ten minutes at most. It suddenly turned and picked up speed."

I suggested, "Let the guards finish the evacuation. We'll make sure nobody is left outside the South exit, then sneak around to see if we can get eyes on the dragon."

Max looked like he was about to protest, but realized that we needed to know where it was if at all possible. We couldn't rely on more Messages from the observatory. First of all they only had a limited number of them memorised. Secondly, once the dragon dipped low to the ground, they would lose sight of it.

"Fine. But don't engage the damned thing. If it spots you, run. Get to cover."

Ames grabbed Tara's arm. "The next group is Ice House. Get your husband, tell the Order of the Snow. Meet us in Braxen as soon as you can get there."

Tara started to say something, but then snapped her jaw shut. The cleric probably wanted to argue, but knew that Ames already chose the right course of action. Time was of the essence. After briefly embracing the were-cat, the minotaur made her way through the crowd to join the next outgoing group.

We hurried towards the South Wing. I noticed that Benno was tagging along. Without using his psychic abilities, my son read my mind. He said dryly, "No. Don't even bother."

I scowled. "Fine. Stay behind us."

Ames corrected me by saying, "**Both** of you stay 5 paces behind me. Damned orcs."

There was a skeleton crew at the southern guard post, and they allowed us through without so much as a word. We made our way to the emergency exit and rushed out into the snow.

Ames took a sharp right, hugging the southern wall of the Arcane University and heading West. Benno and I kept our eyes open for any stray students, but the snow drifts and paths were all clear. Once I was satisfied that only my family was daft enough to be outside during a possible dragon attack, I turned my eyes skyward.

It took us several minutes to reach the Southwest corner of the University. There wasn't a hint of activity. There was no sound of wingbeats, no great shadow imposing itself on the ground. I was starting to think that this Stasis Dragon turned again and found itself a new destination.

But once Ames made the corner, the were-cat made a sharp gesture, paw facing downward. Benno and I fell to our bellies in the snow. The white feline crouched, head and eyes tracking something high and distant. Only when the subject of Ames' attention was due West did Benno and I get to share the cat's terrifying experience.

I recalled that Master Aharon equated the size of this creature with that of a sperm whale. But it wasn't a fair comparison. Whales don't have giant teeth and claws. They don't drift eerily through the sky with an occasional, almost absent flap of their wings. You don't see a sperm whale from 300 paces away and immediately want to double that distance. It's the difference between impressive and oppressive; between humbling and horrific.

The Stasis Dragon was circling low in the western sky, searching for something. I scanned the horizon until I spotted the only thing out in that direction. I was reaching out for Benno even as his fingers found my wrist.

My son thought, *"What is that place?"*

I explained, *"That would be The Outpost. It's where the Arcane Engines are stored when not in use. They used to be stored inside the University itself before they were stolen a number of years ago in a plot against Royal Moffit."*

Benno started to think, *"What does it want to-"*

Just then, the Stasis Dragon dropped from the sky like a rock.

The dragon plummeted towards The Outpost with wings furled until it was right above the flat two story structure. Then it splayed those relatively small gray wings to arrest its fall, defying gravity itself before lashing out. Claws broke stone. That long, whiplike tail thrashed at the top of the building. Once the structural integrity of The Outpost was compromised, the Stasis Dragon simply landed on the roof, and allowed its weight to completely collapse the structure.

We watched in terrified silence as the mythical beast scratched around in the rubble, searching for the Arcane Syphons that had already been spirited off to Limt. Soon there was nothing left but rising dust and fallen rubble.

The dissatisfied screech that pierced the sky sent a chill up my spine. The Stasis Dragon coiled itself before launching that immense bulk back into the sky. Three lazy wingbeats later, and it was gliding towards the Arcane University. The trajectory didn't take the creature nearer to us. Instead the dragon flew towards the Northwest corner of the University: The clocktower.

The three of us scrambled forward so that we could all peek around the corner. The mythical beast seemed to hover uncertainly in front of the pale yellow clock face for a few moments. Then it took decisive action. It inhaled, gray scaled chest puffing out for a couple of moments. Then the

Stasis Dragon unleashed what looked like a torrent of steam and crystal boulders. Everything that the dragon's breath touched was enveloped in a kind of shadowed glass. Soon the entire clock tower was encompassed.

We watched in horror as the Northwest tower seemed to disconnect itself from reality. It started to sink through the ground, as if earth and stone were meaningless barriers to its new, inevitable progression. Soon the entire clock tower slipped under the surface of Panos, taking with it the cocoon of icy untime. All that was left was ragged walls that used to be attached to something, and a gap where the clock tower once was, now existing only in our memories.

Seeming satisfied, the Stasis dragon circled back to the West, sweeping over the ruins of The Outpost once more. After two slow circuits of the area, the massive beast pointed its great neck and maw South. It seemed to put a little bit of effort into its wingbeats, gaining speed all the while. Soon it moved higher in order to clear the tall mountains, disappearing into the frigid clouds above.

The three of us rushed back inside to report what had happened. The guard post outside of the South Wing was now abandoned, the gate opened wide. We found those guards and many more taking up defensive positions around the Circle of Transport. Max was with them, receiving a report from the Captain of the Guard. We caught the tail end of the conversation.

"...no stations are able to communicate on the clairaudient gateway. We can't read auras from anklets. It's a mess, sir."

I said something that would bring clarity to the situation, "Max, the clock tower is gone. It's been removed from time."

Reactions to this news were varied. The Captain simply didn't look like he quite believed it. Max clearly believed it, by the way his jaw dropped open.

But the most curious and poignant reaction came from Master Gideon, who had just padded over to join us. He uttered a single, strangled word: "No." Then the big were-wolf, a man who never seemed to be phased by anything, fell to his knees as if struck through the heart. The sound he made was somewhere between a lupine howl and the keen of a dog in great pain. We were all taken aback.

Max hurried to the were-wolf's side, apparently the only one who knew what in the hells was going on. "Gideon. Gideon, I'll see what I can do. It doesn't end here, I swear it. I'll get into it as soon as this crisis is over. It does **not** end here." His ancient hands gripped the lupine's shoulders.

The inconsolable were-wolf rocked back and forth on his knees, eyes fixed on the stone floor, paws clenched tightly at his sides.

Max looked to Benno, and said, "Go find his daughter, boy. She should be clearing out some things in the Artificery. Bring her, quickly."

My son rushed off to find Jess.

The Headmaster then told me, "We need to revert back to the old system, which means we need Assistant Donnelly. Magical Crafting annex, hurry. Tell him what's happening, and then bring him to me."

Ames stayed behind, trying to help soothe Gideon. I rushed towards the West Wing, passing a number of confused guards and cursing mages on the way. As it turned out, I didn't need to go all the way to the Magical Crafting annex. Bill Donnelly met me halfway.

The older psychic looked relieved to see me, "Sorch, what in the blazes is happening?"

I grabbed him by the shoulder and tugged. "Come on, I'll tell you on the way."

Assistant Donnelly became more pale with every detail that I was able to provide. I pushed him to the edge of his stamina, as we ran back towards the center of the University. He arrived quickly, but sweaty and panting.

Max wasn't about to give him time to recover either. He said, "Assistant Donnelly, we need to reestablish the old system. Master Gideon won't be able to help you. Can you do it?"

Bill opted for a non verbal response as he caught his breath, nodding his head vigorously. He went over to the greeting area adjacent to the teleportation circle. The older psychic entered the New Students booth and started to rifle through the paperwork within.

I looked down at my friend and mentor. The were-wolf wasn't even rocking back and forth anymore, he was just staring at a fixed point on the ground, motionless. It wasn't until Jess sprinted over that Gideon registered anything whatsoever.

The younger were-wolf was upset as well, tears streaking her fuzzy cheeks. But she reached down and took one of Gideon's arms in both of hers. She rumbled, "Dad. Dad, come on. We need to get out of the way right now."

Slowly, Master Gideon rose. He allowed himself to be led off by his daughter, seeming completely devoid of his own will.

I shook my head. "Max, what in the hells was that about?"

The old mage looked... guilty? But also angry. He kept his voice low, the reply intended for my ears only, "I can't say, and don't ask me again. It is a private matter."

Donnelly shouted over, "I think I have it, all of the codes and sigils that I need. I'll need to coordinate with the Guild bank, they keep separate records and everything has to be lined up."

Max answered, "I'll have someone called in. We need you here to read auras, make sure that there are no imposters coming or going."

Benno arrived on the tail end of the Headmaster's statement. He was panting hard. Jess had easily outpaced him once she learned that her father was in distress.

Ames asked, "What about us?"

Max heaved a frustrated sigh. He said, "Get to the Southern Tribes circle. Without a ready ship, that's going to be the fastest way to get to Braxen. You can likely meet up with others who are on their way as well. Be quick. You're racing a dragon."

Chapter 19

The scene outside of the Southern Tribes' Circle of Transportation was chaos. It was like someone tried to route a multicultural military parade through town without the proper authority. Locals were keeping their distance as Arcane University mages, elven wolf riders, human soldiers, and confused orcish guards milled about in the middle of the street.

Hemitath and Shaman were present, but clearly at their wits' ends. We pushed through the crowd towards them. Shaman caught sight of us and decided to dump this whole mess in our laps by loudly announcing:

"Here come Sorch of Engine and Great Cat of North. They tell what going on."

There was an awed silence from the surrounding crowd of orcish citizens. This seemed to manifest as confusion amongst the assembled 'army'. Nevertheless, we were ushered forward to stand in the back of the straw cart that Shaman had been using as an improvised stage.

Now surrounded by dozens of warriors, mages, and clerics... not to mention around a thousand tribal orcs... everyone was looking to us for a sane explanation to this insanity.

Benno nudged me. My son said, "Speak in Common, I'll translate."

I looked to Ames for a rescue. The feline was the one who spent the last two years learning to be more political after all. The were-cat just smirked at me.

I drew in a deep breath before launching into an explanation.

"People of Panos, brothers and sisters of this tribe and all tribes. We seek to repair a great flaw that has manifested in our world. The flaw has resulted in the rise of the ocean, the death of our crops, the spread of the deserts, and less fish in the sea. Some of this was caused by the gods, but some of it was because of the Voodoo Engine and the Arcane Syphons used by the other races."

I paused as Benno finished translating that for the hundreds of orcs that didn't have a great grasp of the Common tongue just yet. Shaman was nodding his approval, silently adding his weight to my message.

When my son caught up, I continued. "Just as the Voodoo Engine was sacrificed, so must we sacrifice all of the Arcane Syphons. Their time has passed. In this new world, the hands of orcs will join the hands of humans and elves, of minotaurs and were-wolves, of lizardmen and were-cats, of every race who understands cooperation and honor. And our joined hands will build things that will overshadow anything constructed by magical artifacts."

The general reception of my message by the surrounding troops was somber. But Benno's translation had a much larger impact. The surrounding orc population raised swords and spears, frying pans and fists. There was a roar of approval.

I summed up what was to come, "We ride West to face a great dragon, and who knows what else. Should the battle spill over the hills and into the swamp, be alert. Be ready. Keep the young and the old safe. And remember that we fight for more than our village. For more than our race or our country. We fight for Panos."

That got 'em.

The orcs howled. My fellow mages cheered. Elves raised their bows. Even the hardened human soldiers beat swords against shields in approval.

But the most unexpected thing that happened was two arms being wrapped around me. Orc arms. Shaman's arms.

I couldn't recall the last time that Shaman hugged me, if ever. Between two orcs, it was something reserved for mates, for blood relatives.

The Chief, my friend, the closest thing I ever had to a father, whispered to me. "Proud of you. Go. Be careful."

Tears in my eyes, I hopped down from my perch. My speech had the intended effect. The locals were being helpful now. The Jeywafa tribe didn't have very many horses or mules, but those few that were available were harnessed to carts and wagons. Makeshift troop transports were created. Supplies were offered.

I wiped my eyes with the sleeve of my robe so that I could see what was going on. Ames was deep in conversation with Professor Sevritz. Benno was translating something for the soldiers from the University. Which meant that nobody was there to warn me that I was about be to assaulted.

Huge paws found my shoulders from behind and applied considerable weight. I was bowled over. I rolled awkwardly onto my back, having to bridge my spine up against a full backpack. I must have looked like a misshapen turtle.

There was a massive white wolf staring down at me, jaw hanging open in amusement.

In the saddle on Laoghaire's back, an already-Reduced Toby was also staring. He said, "Well? Are you running for mayor, or are you coming along?"

Laoghaire crouched as Toby offered a hand. With their help, I mounted up behind my friend.

Another familiar voice caught my attention, "Hemitath is going to Teleport a handful of the most heavily armored soldiers directly to Braxen. The mages and druids will speed up the horse drawn wagons. Where's the rest of your family, Sorch?"

I turned my head left so that I could properly see the speaker: Jarotath. The golden-blond haired elf no longer sat on the Council of Arbitros, but he was still quite the inspiring sight. Astride the mighty Zaira, the warrior was dressed for battle. He wore a stylized leather cap, glimmering arcanite platemail, and a sword belt that carried his signature silver longsword.

I pointed out where my mate and son were. Within minutes, Ames was astride Uistean, seated behind the Reduced Tara. The powerful Zaira carried both Benno and Jarotath.

Jarotath said, "All of the wolves are doubled up with riders, so it's going to be slower going today. But don't worry. We'll outpace some glorified flying lizard."

The elf's confidence and bravado were inspiring. But I realised that he was likely correct. I didn't see any of the usual druidic wolf riders. They were probably busy enhancing the horses so that our cart based transports would arrive in Braxen reasonably quickly. But I did spot Yarith astride Teagan, who was loping over to join us. The elven mage's Haste spell would assure our pack's swift arrival. Not to mention that the wolves didn't need to take the path of least resistance. They would go directly through the hills and adapt to the terrain as needed.

It's easy to pretend to be nonchalant about wolfriding. When you're swapping tales with other adventurers, you don't make a big deal about such things. You look and sound much tougher if you casually mention that you rode a giant wolf to the tavern so you wouldn't be late.

But there's nothing 'everyday' about riding a giant wolf. It's thrilling, and it's terrifying, every single time. Feeling half a ton of muscle and fang and claw surging below you as the landscape whizzes past is nothing you can acclimate to. One mistake could mean that you're being peeled off of a tree trunk and talked about in the past tense. Luckily, these great beasts were not known for their mistakes.

Despite our breathtaking mode of transport, I learned one comforting thing on the journey to Braxen: I wasn't the only one to carry on one sided conversations with my wolf. Toby, in the front position and crouched over Laoghaire's shoulders, could often be heard chatting the lupine up. I listened quietly as the minotaur told his mount about his daughter toddling around, and his wererat apprentice driving him insane, and the new responsibilities and powers that Aro-Remset granted him. Laoghaire took it all in stride of course.

Towards the end of our journey, the wolves were getting playful. Fallen logs became balancing beams. Hilltops became launching platforms. Even Laoghaire, without a doubt the most relaxed of the giant wolves, became competitive. He charged up one particularly steep hillside, only to leap over a ten pace gap in an attempt to reach the next hill without having to go down and around. I very nearly cast Soft Fall on the flying lupine. Instead, Toby and I held on for dear life and were forced to trust our mount's judgment. The landing was 'firm', but we survived. Laoghaire looked over his shoulder briefly, either surprised that he pulled that off or fishing for praise at how well he had accomplished the jump.

Luckily, we arrived at the outskirts of Braxen before our mounts managed to kill us. The giant wolves skidded to a halt at the center of our little tent town, and waited patiently for us to draw enough water from the well to slake their powerful thirst.

As the wolves drank their fill, Yarith said, "We made good time. I suggest that you rest and prepare. As I understand it, the ship with the Syphons will arrive in a couple of hours."

Jarotath agreed on this course of action. "Hemitath is supposed to be warning the townsfolk and offering martial protection as needed. Everyone will be meeting back here to organise. We can take these boys and girls hunting in the meantime."

Just before our lupine friends loped off, Yarith made sure that Toby and Tara were Enlarged again, much to their relief. The two minotaurs grabbed Ames and went to get the lay of the land. Benno and I entered one of the empty tents. As the two of us waited for word of the R. M. N. Taboo's arrival, we rested and prepared our full allotment of spells, focusing on a mix of combat and utility magic.

Benno finished before me, and was outside keeping watch. I heard him speaking to someone in murmured tones, but kept my curiosity in check as I finished the memorization of my final spell. Only when I was confident in my repertoire did I poke my head out of the tent.

My son was stroking the mane of a charcoal gray destrier. The horse was easily 17 hands tall, and muscled enough to almost ignore the partial chain barding that it wore. Astride the warhorse was a man that I never saw before. His hair color almost matched the horse's fur, as did his shaggy beard and thick mustache. The old warrior wore leathers, and had a jeweled cutlass hanging at his hip. Although he and my son seemed to be getting along, I still wanted to perform my due diligence.

I stepped out of the tent fully and said, "Greetings, stranger. I see you've met my son. Were you waiting for me? Do you have business here?"

The old human nodded slowly. "Yep. Yer elven lass sent me from town. Wanted ta let ya know that you got some creatures and cultists and things comin' from the East. My people spotted 'em some 7 miles out, but they don't look ta be stoppin'. That was an hour an' change ago."

I blinked at the phrase 'Yer elven lass'. "I'm sorry, do you mean Yarith the wolf rider, or Hemitath the archmage?"

That question resulted in a pair of raised, bushy eyebrows. The man asked, "Ya have a second elven lass stashed 'round here son? Must be the luckiest orc on Panos, you. Hemitath was her name. She and her guards are gonna help secure the town. Some number of mages are apparently arrivin' by cart, and she plans ta split them between Braxen and the southern coast. My boys are warnin' yer people all along the path ta shore."

I offered a hand, and it was grasped by one just as calloused and beat up as mine.

I said, "Thank you. What's your name, sir?"

After a brief but firm shake, the old human withdrew his hand. "Not a sir anymore. Was a sir when I was captain of the 'Burglar's Prize'. Now I'm just Renver. Renver DeWalt."

I smiled, "Many thanks then, Renver."

Benno asked, "Where are you and Alice off to now?" I assumed Alice was the name of the man's warhorse.

"Gonna stake out th' South of town. The boys got some nasty traps ta set up, but they gotta be watched just in case someone innocent bumbles by."

We said our goodbyes and Benno stepped away from the destrier. Renver made a clicking sound with his tongue, and Alice trotted out towards the main path, before turning North and taking off at a gallop.

Benno said, grimly, "Dragon coming from the North. A cultist army from the East. Probably elementals from gods know where."

I said, "Your job is to stay safe."

Benno started to object, but I cut him off.

"The only two psychics that can pull this off are you and your boyfriend. He's currently holding the Arcane University together with spit and baling twine. Without him, anyone could potentially use the Circle of Transport. Including doomsday cultists. He may have something figured out in the next couple of hours, but I wouldn't count on it. That means there's one person who can get to the Astral and set the Arcane Syphons to overload, assuming that works at all. You."

I poked my son in the chest, to punctuate the point.

He gently batted away my hand. The younger orc looked like he was trying to formulate a retort, but then his shoulders slumped and he sighed.

Benno said, "And what exactly happens if I can't get them to feed back on themselves?"

I shrugged, "We'll have a literal boatload of mages with you. You can take them in and they'll start blasting the Syphons. You know, the old fashioned way."

"Didn't the old fashioned way nearly get us both killed?"

I squeezed my son's shoulder. I didn't really have anything comforting to say, so I went with honesty. "Yup!"

He peered at me through narrowed eyes. "Great pep talk, Dad."

A new voice said, "The old fashioned way shouldn't be required. In this close proximity, all of the Arcane Syphons should be linked. You issue the command from the Astral to one, and all of them should blow."

I turned and walked over to my 'little brother'. Leeson received a bearhug so tight that even the muscled human had to let out a grunt. He returned the gesture as well as he could under the circumstances.

After letting him go, I said, "Good to see you. How did you get here?"

Leeson said, "Max just teleported the final group in. I'm here to escort Benno down to the shore to help Rick and Will as soon as they arrive."

My son said, "Oh come on, now I need a bodyguard?"

Leeson offered Benno a smile. "A babysitter, I think Max said."

Benno said, "Fine. It might not be such a bad thing. We've got cultists coming in from the East."

The young human nodded. He said, "One of the riders from town caught up to us. We'll all be ready."

A sudden, chilling thought came to mind. I asked, "What's to stop the Original Engine from sending water elementals after Will and Rick?"

Leeson said, soothingly, "Even with the magnified power from all of the Syphons being in the same place, having them at the bottom of the ocean is next to useless. The Original Engine, and by extension the cultists, want the Arcane Syphons in a place where they can actually absorb magic. They'll try to capture them, not sink them. That will require humanoid hands and some way to get them back to shore."

Benno said, "But once we sink the Syphons, they won't be so restrained."

Leeson nodded his agreement. "The cultists won't be pleased either, even if they win it will take a lot of work to recover those sunken Syphons. Here's the good news: Max will be performing Gustov's Disjunction just before we dive. That should give us an elemental-clear window so that we can overload the closest Arcane Syphon and start the chain reaction."

I wasn't privy to this part of the plan. I asked, "Wouldn't sinking them in shallower water mute much of the explosion? Why over the Trench?"

Benno said, "The Great Trench gives the Original Engine direct access to the surface world. From your description, the whole thing isn't open to ridiculous depths, just the portion South of us. So the explosions can seal that part off. Two lizards, one rock."

"You'll have someone who can Teleport you out if it belches one of those anti-magic waves at you?"

My son said, "Even better. Hierophant Petrinoth and some of the most senior druids of Del-Nekbenth will be diving with us. As dolphins. When they transform, they **really** transform. They assure us that if things go wrong, they can get us safely back to the surface in short order."

I still had reservations about the plan, but all of them revolved around the fact that it was my son down there and not someone else. So I simply grunted and nodded.

Benno asked, softly, "How's Jess and Master Gideon?"

Leeson frowned. He looked down at the ground and absently kicked at the dirt. The young man said, "Jess is upset, of course. I don't have the full details but... nobody was in the clock tower when the Stasis Dragon attacked. I know that much. Whatever mechanism was running the security and identification stuff at the Arcane University was housed there. For some reason, Gideon was devastated by the loss. Jess could only say that it was a family thing, and she would explain later. Right now, Gideon is nearly comatose. He's just sitting in his room, staring straight ahead."

Benno looked to me. He asked, "Dad, do you know what that's all about?"

I shook my head. I said, "No. I'm sorry guys, I can't shed any light on that. I just hope Gideon is alright."

Leeson was about to say something, but our companions chose that moment to come back from their snooping around. Leeson was given a warm greeting by Tara, Toby, and Ames.

When asked what they saw, Toby's reply was firm, "We have to move. This place is a death trap."

Ames was nodding agreement. The feline said, "Refill your waterskins from the well, but then let's get out of here. The hills to the East naturally funnel into this area. It has a path leading right to it from the North and South. We could easily get surrounded and not even know it."

Benno asked, "What's preferable?"

Toby pointed a big finger off to the East. "The other fork on the path. The one that leads up to the big bluff overlooking the ocean."

Tara said, "The bluff area is perfect, assuming our mages have a few Soft Fall spells and flight or transport types of magic?"

Benno, Leeson and I were all nodding.

Ames stuck a fuzzy thumb in the air. "Perfect. Between those and my ring, we can get 6 people off of a cliff side if needed?"

The three of us consulted briefly before I answered, "Yes, I can Levitate and then we have four Soft Fall spells among us. With your ring, that covers the six of us."

Toby rubbed his meaty hands together. "That's excellent. We'll have high ground, an escape tactic that non-mages can't duplicate, and as much tree coverage as we need."

Benno said, "And as soon as the Taboo arrives, I can dive off and Soft Fall down to them."

We grabbed some dry food from the tent and water from the well. Then the six of us set off to the North, backtracking until we found the fork in the forested path. We started our southwesterly uphill climb, knowing that danger was approaching from the West, but prepared to face it head on.

A few minutes into our upwards trek, Ames held up a paw. The were-cat said, "Smoke. North, Northwest-ish?"

We needed to get to a relatively clear spot in order to visually confirm the findings of my feline's nose. Sure enough, there was a small billow of smoke to our Northwest, just outside of Braxen. Tara's guess was, "Mages. Fire elementals. Or perhaps just arson."

Benno had a different theory, "It might be the traps that Renver mentioned as well."

Toby shrugged his big shoulders. He said, "Either way, we're probably about to be in the thick of it if the town has met opposition."

We drew our weapons and prepared spell components, knowing that the enemy was close now. Soon, there were immediate signs of that proximity. A careless snap that signified a branch being broken. An unidentifiable shout from the West, far too far inland to be one of our people. The doomsday cultists had arrived, and it was likely that they pulled out all the stops.

Ames suddenly paused and pressed right up against a tree. The feline took a quick second glance around the trunk, then exposed just their crossbow arm. A quick 'twang' was followed by an angry, pained bellow. Immediately, the were-cat started to reload. "About ten mixed regulars. Thirty paces and closing fast." was the feline's assessment.

Tara and Toby crouched, using the rise of the hill as cover more than the trees themselves, given their width exceeded that of the trees surrounding us. Leeson crouched with them and started to cast a preparatory spell.

I was too focused on my own magic to listen to whichever incantation the young human had chosen. Benno and I selected our own trees as cover. Both of us spotted the half elven archer, jogging towards us far too boldly. The man looked emaciated, crazed. I exposed only as much of myself as required to start casting my first spell at him. The appearance of my head and hands prompted a rushed shot from the half elf that embedded an arrow in the roots of my tree. Benno responded by sliding halfway out of cover to start his own spell. Soon the unwise archer was airborne from the brutal impact of my Force Bolt. My son's Magic Missiles rained in on the screaming cultist. If he wasn't dead before he landed, the impact of neck and spine on the trunk of a stout spruce tree finished the job.

The rest of the enemies approached just as quickly, but as a group and with more regard for their own lives. Three of the cultists were wearing either scale or chain armor and held shields in addition to their longswords. One of them was bleeding from the arm, having intercepted the were-cat's first shot. Ames' next crossbow bolt was deflected by one of these lead warriors. With no time to reload, my mate went to the firebrand sword and spun out of cover.

That was the cue for Toby to rise and stride forward, standing hip to shoulder with the were-cat. Tara joined them, derisively smashing a sling bullet out of the air with her large shield before planting her hooved feet. Finally Leeson stepped up to guard the opposite flank from Ames. Neither of his enhancement spells had a visible effect, so I assumed he prepared himself with Aldus' Armor and Leeson's Living Layer. It was a formidable front line.

I took a moment to assess the battlefield as my friends blunted the cultists' initial charge. "Eight!" I shouted out, indicating how many living enemies I saw. In addition to the three well armed and armored foes that Toby, Tara, and Leeson were engaged with, a lightly armored woman with a whip and an unarmored man with a wickedly studded tetsubo squared up to Ames. The source of that sling bullet was, unfortunately, one of two dark green skinned orcs in the far treeline. I didn't like killing my own kind, but in this case I would make two exceptions. They were already slotting the next smooth stones into their slings for another try. Finally, a black robed elf was just catching up to his 'friends', taking cover behind a broad evergreen while he regained his breath.

Benno's shout of "Eight!" confirmed my own sightings. Now that we were on the same page and our rather busy friends were aware, the two of us went to work.

I baited the first sling bullet by stepping out from behind cover, and then immediately ducking back behind the tree. Polished stone met bark with a satisfying crack. What I didn't realise is that one of the two orcs held their shot, so when I stepped back out into the open I caught a glancing blow to the right shoulder. It stung, bruised, but there was no permanent damage. Cursing my own tactical stupidity, I turned to face the far left flank and palmed the slimy guts that I would need from my pouch. Benno also stepped out and started casting, though I couldn't see what he had grabbed from his own stash of material components. My son's eyes were focused far downfield.

The center line was a standoff. The cultist warriors seemed happy with a stalemate, counting on their missile slinging allies to turn the tide. Toby made as much use of his buckler as he did the Axe of McGrondle, just trying to make space and create an opening. Tara seemed content to trade bruising weapon-to-shield blows with her warrior, as her superior strength would numb the human's arm far before she tired. Leeson, on the other hand, seemed to be befuddling his foe. Not only were some of the cultist's blows being blocked by a floating invisible shield, but the melee mage was landing bruising low blows. The tip of his Ironwood staff would frequently catch the warrior's armored shin or the toe of his boot, detracting from his mobility.

Ames was in full flight mode. The feline had only been caught by the whip once, but it sliced open the rogue's leather armor and bruised the ribs beneath the impact zone. From that point on, Ames used the relatively slow and lumbering blows of the man with the studded club as cover. Every roar and swing was met with a nimble roll or a little backwards hop. Every evasive action left the whip mistress blocked by her comrade. It wasn't a sustainable strategy, but the cat delayed them long enough for me to finish my spell.

Twin Acid Bolts sailed into the big tetsubo wielding maniac. I scored hits on his left side, causing the barbaric man to scream in pain. The acid left his ribcage exposed to the air, clean white bone sandwiching shrivelled flesh. Ames took the opportunity to strike low. The cut itself was just a flesh wound on the bellowing man's ankle, but the firebrand sabre set his pants leg on fire. He howled and rolled off to the side, trying to put the blaze out.

Meanwhile, Benno landed the longest Web spell that I had ever seen. It had to be right at the limit of his range. Nevertheless, the sticky strands entangled both orcish slingers, giving us a temporary reprieve as they struggled to draw daggers from their belts and cut themselves free.

Just when we thought our situation was improving, the ground started to vibrate. That was when I realised that the black robed elf wasn't catching his breath. He was channeling. His earth elemental broke from the far tree line and started to stomp towards the left flank. It was a bad matchup for Ames.

I shouted, "Nine, Toby!"

Toby turned the distraction into advantage. He feigned a turn towards the elemental, and the armored warrior lunged in with his longsword. The Axe of McGrondle found the weapon in mid thrust, shattering the tip and allowing momentum to bite into the enemy's hip. The screaming and distraction allowed the paladin to withdraw and hustle over to support Ames' flank by meeting the elemental head on. This left Tara and Leeson in a two on three situation. But between the sliced hip of the center warrior and broken toes on Leeson's opponent, two of the enemy fighters already had mobility issues. The young melee mage alternated long staff thrusts between his original opponent and the one hobbled by Toby. Tara stopped trading shield blows with her foe, playing a more passive and cagey role, shifting right a bit so that the wounded and abandoned warrior would think twice about making a wild lunge towards Leeson.

I reached into my component pouch, and my gloved fingers found the smooth bit of rock that I required. I knew that the orcs were almost free, and I needed to buy some time. Concentrating on the mid-point between us and the far treeline, I murmured an incantation that I hadn't used in a number of months.

I wasn't paying attention to what Benno was doing, with my monitoring of the greater tactical situation. Then I saw a bright flash out of the corner of my right eye. My son conjured a Flaming Sword and stepped up to help Leeson. By the way his left arm was bent in front of him, I could only assume that an Invisible Shield had also been cast at some point. I wanted to shout at him for being stupid, but I was mid-incantation. Besides, it's probably what I would have done myself three years ago.

The cloudy crystal that I had palmed slipped into the ether. Even considering my earlier minor spells, I felt the mental drain as a mere irritation. This was simple magic, if effective. A billowing cloud of Fog appeared between our melee front and the far treeline. The slingers, who I assumed would free themselves shortly, would have no way of picking out targets through this soup. The elven mage also wouldn't be able to control his elemental by sight. He would need to get inside of its head, leaving his own physical body vulnerable.

As my gaze scanned back towards Ames, I noted a secondary threat. There was more smoke from the South, closer to the shore. The were-cat was a bit too preoccupied with the whip wielding warrior to take notice. But I was keenly aware that we needed to make the cliffside sooner rather than later, or risk being cut off by multiple wildfires.

But at the moment, fire was the were-cat's ally. While the unarmored brute was tearing off his pants to avoid being immolated, Ames took another slashing blow from the whip, but this time it was intentional. The leather weapon snapped as it cut through the feline's armor and wrapped around Ames' left bicep. The were-cat snarled and locked arm against torso, trapping the whip for a split second. The firebrand sabre lashed out and severed the whip to a uselessly short length. This caused the cultist to grimace, her main weapon destroyed. The woman drew a jagged looking scimitar instead.

Only myself and Ames had been in the group who faced off against Koroth's bishop and Duke Harrington all those years ago. The two of us had seen Toby pick apart an earth elemental using the Axe of McGrondle, in between our own violent efforts. I'm proud to say that my friend hadn't lost a step in the intervening seasons. If anything, the paladin advanced his technique into a genuine art form. Toby spun to avoid a heavy handed strike from the stone creature. His axe blade, runes writhing excitedly along the bloody surface, bit deeply into the elemental's left leg. It staggered back. One more strike like that and the earth elemental would be helplessly maimed.

"Eight!"

The cry was, surprisingly, from Benno. He used Leeson's distracting staff blows to rush the toe-crushed human from the side. His conjured long blade took the warrior by surprise, sinking into his lower back and through the kidney. Leeson put the man out of his misery with a skull crushing coup de grace.

The cultists' front line crumbled. As the hip-hobbled swordsman attempted to stumble forward and attack the two mages in melee range, Tara deftly dislocated his jaw with a backhanded swing of her cudgel. My son and 'little brother' were on the next fallen foe in a flash. Soon there was a cry of "Seven!"

Followed by Toby's low, calm declaration of "Six." He removed one of the hobbled earth elemental's arms at the shoulder, and was able to move in close enough to sever that thick head at the neck.

Ames added to the count, just not verbally. The speed of the were-cat wasn't something that the leather clad warrior woman could handle. The blur of Ames' flaming blade chopped off her wrist. Before she could finish voicing an agonised scream, the were-cat added a detached head to the unfortunate cultist's list of injuries.

While the final longsword wielding warrior was being overwhelmed, I spotted the burned barbarian staggering to his feet, now pantsless. As he turned to run I was already in motion. It wasn't the cleanest of tackles, but I held onto his wounded ankle and twisted until he fell down again. That was enough time for Toby to make his way over and finish what I started. Messily.

Wiping the blood out of my eyes, I peered around the battlefield. The Fog spell was starting to dissipate, but I didn't see anyone remaining at the treeline. "Three fled?" I called out, uncertain.

My companions surveyed the area before agreeing with my assessment. The mage, upon losing his elemental, wisely beat a retreat. There was no sign of the enemy orcs other than a couple of dropped sling bullets, left behind in their haste to get away.

As Tara called upon Melflavin to heal Ames, Toby called upon Aro-Remset to heal his wife's bruised arms and ribs.

I said, "There are multiple forest fires all around us. I don't think anyone has time to put them out right now. We need to make the clearing on the cliffside."

Ames took the lead. All of us were nose-blind and red-eyed from the low levels of smoke in the air. But the were-cat still had the best eyes in the group under just about any conditions. Tara took the rear, more likely than any of us to be able to detect any sort of elemental disturbance.

The trees thinned as we approached the cliffside clearing. Suddenly dirt and twigs gave way to brown sand, gravel, and stone. The exposed cliff face ceded all of its vegetation to the erosion of wind over the millennia. For the moment we stayed inland, using the last few trees as cover as we awaited word of the R. M. N. Taboo's arrival.

We hunkered down to catch our breath and sip some water. The sky had at least four rising columns of thick black smoke, ranging from the shore all the way back to Braxen. I silently hoped that our people were faring better than the enemy. I also felt a pang of guilt for bringing the conflict to the doors of a bunch of retired sailors and merchants. Hemitath would do everything in her power to defend them, of that much I was certain.

"No more spells."

I was snapped out of my reverie. Ames spoke the words quietly, but with an unusual harshness. The feline was offering my son that wicked little hand crossbow and a pouch of bolts.

Benno snarled, "I'm fine. Don't henpeck me."

The were-cat noted, "You're one major spell away from having to enhance again, and we don't have that kind of time."

Knowing that Ames was an expert in gauging the limits of both Benno and myself, I laid down the law. "Son, save it for the Astral. There's no curse there and the Arcane Syphons will need to be set off if a simple command doesn't work."

The younger orc looked like he was about to object again, but saw five sets of stern eyes staring at him.

Toby summed it up best, saying, "You **are** the mission now, kiddo."

Reluctantly, Benno took Ames' crossbow and started to load it up. The two bantered back and forth while the rest of us kept watch.

The feline said, "Remember your lessons."

My son said, "I do, don't worry."

"I do worry, because you're a lousy student."

"Hey I was hitting your silly targets after a while, wasn't I?"

"Barely. Go ahead, take a test shot."

"You have the trigger so sensitive on this thing that it practically goes off by itse-"

There was a twang followed by a scream.

I had one of those parental moments, thinking that my beloved son somehow managed to shoot himself with my mate's crossbow. The truth was far stranger. Whether by instinct or accident, Benno's test shot had sailed all the way across the clearing and into the copse of trees opposite us. Where he hit something.

Benno made the call, uncertainly:

"One?"

And then there was chaos.

The thing that burst from the trees was the size of six horses placed end to end. Glossy black serpentine scales covered its belly and sides. But the top of the creature was adorned with red and white feathers. From my scholarly studies, I knew that its eyes would be a luminescent yellow-green. But I also knew enough not to check.

I shouted, "Basilisk, don't look it in the eyes, 'ware the spit!"

But my warning came too late for Tara, who met that draining, hypnotic gaze for a long moment. The minotaur screamed in pain and fell to her knees, as her right arm and right leg went limp. It looked like the basilisk's paralysis was only partial, but without even engaging, it had already swung the odds.

This monster of the earth was joined by a creature of the sky. The massive air elemental swept up rocks, branches, and copious amounts of leaves in its vortex. One tree was stripped bare as the elemental entered the clearing, as if demonstrating the disturbing ease of its power. Fifteen paces behind the elemental was the same damnable elf from before, hiding in deep cover as he channeled his control.

The unfortunate orc that Benno had hit in the shoulder moved up to the edge of the forest before yanking out the slim bolt with a pained yelp. His friend took cover behind the next tree over, and started to load up his sling so that he could line up a shot.

Tara tucked in behind her shield and started to murmur a prayer to Melflavin. Toby stepped in front of her, tears of rage in his eyes. The paladin stalked towards the basilisk, looking for all the world to be a bull with bad intentions.

The first sling bullet was once again fired my way. This time I was in motion however, and the rounded stone whizzed past my head. I was sprinting around the perimeter of the clearing. As unintuitive as it may have seemed, I was heading **towards** our foes at the far end of the clearing. I needed an angle on the mage who was channeling if we were to have any chance of beating the elemental. The second bullet, fired from the sling of the wounded orc, rolled to a stop in front of me. I glanced off to my left, trying to see why his shot went so far awry.

A small crossbow bolt was embedded in the tree trunk that the wounded orc was using as cover. Benno calmly reloaded and fired at the same target. The close call must have panicked the other orc and forced an early release.

Ames faced an impossible task: One small white were-cat against a massive vortex of wind and debris. The feline tried the same trick that we used in the Apprentice Library. When the air elemental was close enough, my mate thrust the flaming sabre deep into the funnel of wind, attempting to ignite the debris inside. Instead, Ames received a powerful shock that threw the feline back five full paces. The were-cat managed a backwards roll and landed in a crouch, every strand of fur standing on end from the excess static electricity.

Leeson was finishing a spell that I assumed was preparatory. I was incorrect. When my young friend finished the Blink incantation he appeared on the other side of the clearing, in between two very startled orc cultists. The sound of hastily drawn short swords and pained yelping ensued.

Toby barely managed to raise his buckler in time to catch the wad of acidic phlegm that the basilisk launched his way. The excess spattered onto his armor and started to erode holes in the chain and leather before finally losing its potency. The triple-scythe claw attack missed high as the minotaur ducked and charged in. He landed a solid chop to the beast's forearm before the backswing sent the paladin tumbling away, like a toy soldier propelled by the boot of a frustrated child.

Tara, still immobile, finished her prayer. Her icy Divine Warhammer rose up from behind the prone minotaur, like a vengeful spirit. As Toby recovered from his tumble, the ethereal looking weapon proved just how solid it really was. A concussive blow landed on the earth serpent's long neck, freezing a patch of scales and causing it to shriek and recoil. The basilisk snapped at the handle of the spiritual weapon and managed to fling it away. But the Divine Warhammer approached once again, an inexorable force that needed to be dealt with.

With Leeson doing more than just holding his own against the two orc cultists, I was free to advance. Soon I found my quarry. Taking the amber wand from my pouch, I pointed it at the helplessly distracted mage before rubbing the swatch of fur against it. Soon the conduit to the quasi-elemental planes formed, and my Lightning Bolt coursed into the elven cultist. I felt Glogur's curse bite deeply into my psyche, my mind starting to unravel with the rapid use of combat spells. But the enemy mage, completely unaware of my assault, was electrocuted. His heart had been caught between beats, doomed never to make the effort again.

As I tried to recover from the drain, I turned to see what impact, if any, my elimination of the elf made. The air elemental was playing a far less cagey game now. Rather than gathering its static electricity and using it defensively, it lashed out at Ames from a distance. Charged branches and stones were hurled from the vortex. My were-cat deftly rolled and dodged, clearly straining with the effort... anyone would be after having their muscles jolted time and again.

Benno realized that there was a target in front of him, one literally as big as the broad side of a barn. My son reloaded and fired as quickly as he could, pumping bolt after bolt into the distracted basilisk's ribs. He might not have been doing that much damage, but the bolts were causing the creature some pain, and thus distraction.

As the giant basilisk started to shamble towards my son's position, Toby and the Divine Warhammer converged on it from either side. The Axe of McGrondle crashed into the creature's rib cage, sending a spray of acidic green blood into the air. The icy floating hammer struck the basilisk's shoulder, albeit somewhat ineffectually. After loosing an eardrum-pounding shriek of pain, the beast swiped at the Divine Warhammer, catching the weapon in its claws and pinning it helplessly to the ground. A sudden, fierce lash of the creature's tail tore Toby's buckler right from his arm, snapping the leather straps, sending the paladin staggering backwards from the impact.

A quick glance at Leeson gave me the impression that he had the situation well in hand. One of the orcs had been felled, and the other was simply being outclassed by the speed and power of my young friend's staff work. I chose my next target.

I darted in, far closer to the melee than I was comfortable with, to be frank. Squeezing a small waterskin, I feathered my fingers towards the basilisk's rump and completed the brief incantation. My Fan of Frost washed over the base of the creature's tail, cracking scales and shattering feathers. The overgrown lizard stopped its advance towards my son. Apparently a much closer orc now had its attention.

Ames was watching a log. To be specific, a heavy log trapped within the air elemental's churning winds. It orbited slowly within the creature's vortex, or at least far more slowly than the smaller pieces of debris. After dodging a stone the size of a melon, the were-cat leapt. Ames rode the log up towards the center of the elemental, where a tight ball of twigs and leaves fluttered, like a massive heart. The rogue timed their stab perfectly, igniting the sheaf of detritus. The air elemental became a fire elemental. Very briefly.

But Ames wasn't done yet. Using the force of the explosion and the Ring of Leaping, the were-cat soared through the air towards the basilisk. There was nothing between my mate and the giant reptile's skull other than a few meters of empty air.

Which meant that there was no way to dodge the wad of viscous spittle that the basilisk sent hurtling towards the airborne feline.

I helplessly watched the aftermath of my mate's brief flight. Twin screams met my ears. The first was the were-cat's agonised cry as the acid started to sear through fur and flesh. The second was the death knell of a basilisk, as a flaming sabre sunk through its feathers and into the creature's brainpan.

Toby dropped his axe and dove to catch the writhing Ames, who fell off of the basilisk's skull soon after the Ring of Leaping had provided sure footing, ever so briefly. The big minotaur managed to lessen my mate's impact with the ground, avoiding further injury.

Leeson's voice rang out to assure us that he dispatched the final orc cultist, and we could properly deal with the aftermath, "Zero. Clear."

Benno rushed over to Ames and Toby. Even as the paladin prepared the Laying of Hands, my son was upending a full sized waterskin on the were-cat's face, washing away as much of the foul spittle as possible.

Much as I wanted to help, I knew that there was nothing I could do for my mate that wasn't already being done. Schooling my emotions, I instead ran to our other impaired friend. I said, "Tara, where does it hurt?"

The cleric had a bewildered look on her face. "Nowhere. I- I can't feel my right arm or leg. I know that they're attached, but they..."

She trailed off, just staring at her useless limbs in something akin to disbelief.

I took a deep breath, and then let it out in a relieved sigh. "If it doesn't hurt, it's just temporary paralysis. I've read about the effects of the basilisk's stare. The sensation before your extremities start to turn to stone is supposed to be excruciating."

Tara peered at me. She said, "You need to work on your bedside manner, Sorch."

I glanced over my shoulder. "Sorry, I'm a bit distra-"

She cut me off, "Go to your cat. I'm fine here."

Leeson made his way over to us. He was limping slightly, bleeding from an upper leg wound. He also had the start of an impressive black eye, looking vaguely pommel-shaped. He said, "Go, I'll stay with Tara."

I didn't need to be told a third time. I retrieved my mate's sabre on the way over, pulling it from the overgrown lizard's sizzling skull just as the feathers surrounding the wound burst into flame. When I got over there, Benno was dabbing at the were-cat's damp face with a cloth that he had fished out of his pack. Toby's glowing hands were just withdrawing, as the final bit of Aro-Remset's healing was channeled into Ames.

I asked, softly, "How are you feeling?"

Ames responded, just as softly, "Blind."

Toby was quick to point out, "We treated the acidic venom right away. There's a good chance that the effects are temporary."

The were-cat said, "It's my own damn fault. Bit off more than I could chew that time."

I carefully slid the cat's sabre into its sheath, extinguishing the flame. "Actually, you killed it. I would call that a pretty good chewing, love."

Toby rose. His eyes were elsewhere as he said, "Ames, you're going to require further care. We need to get you out of here."

Seeing the big man's distraction, it was my turn to say, "Go. She's got temporary paralysis from the basilisk, she'll need to be evacuated too."

The paladin hurried over to speak with Tara, as we completed our swap of convalescent mates.

Benno put away his cloth as he said, "I can summon a Flat Mule. We can take them back down towards the town. Most of the fires are East, Southeast, and West." Then the younger orc's green, hazel-flecked eyes became distant. "It's Max."

I waited quietly as my son took the Headmaster's Message. My gloved hands stroked Ames' neck, eliciting a weak, rumbled purr from the feline.

Benno said, "The ship is a few minutes out. They're going to start seeding the seabed along the Trench with the ten Arcane Syphons. I told him that we needed to get Ames and Tara to safety. Dad, I don't know what to do. I need to get on that ship, but I can't just abandon you all."

I replied, "If you told Max, then help is on the way. Sit tight for a few minutes while the Taboo gets into range."

My son looked bewildered. He said, "There's fighting everywhere. There's fires. Cultists. Elementals. How can you be sure that Max is sending help?"

It was Ames who answered, "Kiddo, either we're holding our own and we'll get help. Or we're getting creamed and we're all dead anyway. Either way, you have a ship to catch."

I voiced my agreement, "It's true. Don't worry, we'll be fine. We'll just sit here and enjoy the view."

Ames snarled at my obvious prodding, "I hate you so much right now."

"I know."

Our banter was interrupted by a shout from Tara, "Wings on the horizon!"

Benno and I looked out to sea. The younger orc's keen eyes spotted the danger before my more 'seasoned' perception caught up. I followed the line of his pointing finger until I too saw that distant, deadly butterfly.

At that moment, the silhouette of the Stasis Dragon was remote. Tiny. But the speed with which it cruised over the ocean left no doubt in my mind that the creature of legend could be upon us within minutes.

Benno said, "I don't understand. It's heading in the opposite direction of the Taboo. And it's circling."

My reply was grim, "That's because it isn't looking for the Taboo, son. It's looking for the only two people on Panos with a history of destroying Arcane Syphons."

My son's head whipped around. He stared at me in shock as realization set in.

I continued to watch the Stasis Dragon slowly spiral closer. There would be no outrunning it. Benno reached out to squeeze my left forearm tightly. Ames was already doing the same with my opposite hand. We were all thinking the same thing: If it had to end, at least we would be with family.

I murmured, mostly to myself, "Come on then, you son of a bitch. We're right here."

Chapter 20

Unexpectedly, a different son of a bitch arrived.

Laoghaire bounded out of the woods behind us. Smelling blood and ichor, the giant white wolf started snarling at the deceased basilisk. I had to walk over and lay a hand on the big lupine's shoulder before he would calm down.

"He's dead, my friend."

Laoghaire snorted. He turned his rump to the creature and swiped his hind paws on the ground a couple of times, 'burying' the basilisk once and for all.

That made me chuckle, despite our dire situation. "You're alone?" I asked.

That great head nodded once.

Benno called out, "I see the Taboo! It's coming around the tip of the peninsula. It should be below us in a few minutes."

I said, "We need a plan."

But Toby already had one. He asked Leeson, "Can you Reduce Tara?"

Benno already saw where the paladin's thoughts were headed. My son helped Ames up. The two of them walked over to join me next to the giant wolf. Ames used Laoghaire as support so that the were-cat could remain standing while Leeson answered.

"I can Reduce Tara, Ames can ride in front, and we can lash them both to Laoghaire's saddle."

Tara snorted and asked, "Don't we get a say in this?"

Leeson, Toby, and I all said, "No." at the same time.

Benno likely would have joined us, but he was touching the white wolf's shoulder. He reported, "Laoghaire says that Braxen has been held, so far. Hemitath has rallied the mages that arrived by wagon. The ex-sailors have pitched in on the defense. He says they've set up an infirmary. He made it up here without getting too close to fire, so the path back is clear."

I said, "Leeson, Benno. After Tara is Reduced, help her and Ames into the saddle and get them both secured, please."

While my son and 'little brother' did as they were asked, I dragged Toby further away. We huddled together by the cliff's edge, speaking in the faintest of whispers.

I murmured, "I have a plan."

Toby said, tiredly, "I know the plan, my friend. The Stasis Dragon is hunting you. If our mates are to escape and your son is to play his role, we need to be more convincing targets than they are."

I nodded. "And we can't run, because-"

My friend cut me off, "Because if Benno is the easier target, it turns on him. So we fight the legendary dragon, which is apparently impervious to mortal forces."

I murmured, "Yes. About that..."

I proceeded to lay out my plan for Toby. The minotaur labeled it as 'insane' more than once. But upon hearing the whole thing, he agreed that it was our best chance.

Toby glanced over to where our mates had been secured, and our friends and family waited. He said, "You have to tell them yourself."

I asked, "Why?"

The paladin reminded me, softly, "Because I can't lie, Sorch."

I nodded to my friend, slowly. We walked back over to the rest of the group.

I said, "As we speak, the Syphons are being sunk all along the rim of the trench. We can destroy them and attempt to seal the hole in Panos at the same time. But with the Stasis Dragon closing in, we need to buy time for Benno to get down to the Taboo. And it has to be soon, as Max is likely about to Fly out there himself and clear the area of elementals."

Benno said, "I can Soft Fall from here and glide out to the ship."

I said, "That's the plan. In fact, we're all splitting up. While Benno glides, the four of you will head back to town. That way any reports will have our party heading North, not out to sea. Meanwhile, Toby and I will lead the Stasis Dragon on a merry chase."

Leeson said, "Are you insane? You can't outrun that thing!"

I shook my head. "No, but it isn't faster than gravity. Once we have its attention, we'll jump. And we have the Axe of McGrondle. We can use our own Levitation and Soft Fall, and then some well timed Fog. We should be able to get down to the sea caves and carve out a passage that the Stasis Dragon can't get into. Then we dig in. With luck, that will buy Benno enough time to do his Astral tricks."

My son was silent. He walked back to the cliff's edge, peering out at the sea, perhaps trying to catch a glimpse of the Taboo. There were some general grumbles from the others, but they didn't have a better plan. Leeson took a metallic potion bottle from his pouch. He quaffed the potion of Minor Healing so that he wouldn't be slowing the group down with his limping.

Toby was already taking off his backpack. I followed suit. "We need to travel light for this. I hope Laoghaire won't mind." We added our packs to the white wolf's already significant load. In typical relaxed fashion, Laoghaire had no objection to being used as a pack mule.

Ames tried to play the pity card, "You're going to leave a poor, blind kitten out in these woods at the mercy of a big bad wolf?"

It took every ounce of self control that I had to remain composed. I wanted to say 'No'. I wanted to cry. Instead I turned the trussed-up were-cat's head so that I could plant a fierce kiss on Ames' muzzle. When it was over, I simply said, "Yup."

Toby took the opportunity to share a kiss with his wife as well, though it was more chaste. Then he said, "Get them to Braxen safely, Leeson."

The young mage raised a hand in farewell, and then trotted alongside Laoghaire. The four disappeared into the woods.

Benno was still looking out to sea. I thought he was watching the approach of the dragon, or the progress of the Taboo. It was only when he turned to face me that I saw the real story.

My son stared at me, his face a mask of pain and tears dripping from his green cheeks. He had been hiding his reaction from the rest of the group. He knew.

"You can't outrun it."

It wasn't a question, it was a statement. My voice broke as I said, "The smartest orc on all of Panos."

There was a mighty crack as Toby drove the Axe of McGrondle into the rock. Then he took another couple of steps and let fly again, the artifact weapon biting deeply into the cliff with every blow.

Benno walked up to me, fists clenched helplessly at his sides. "You're not a distraction."

"No, son."

"You're bait."

"Yeah."

The axe fell again, a cracked line being drawn in a broad semicircle along the cliff's edge. When Toby was satisfied, he started his next project: Cutting a vaguely square boulder from the solid rock.

My son's shoulders were shaking now. Even with all of that intelligence, with all of that reasoning, he could only come to one conclusion. "It's not fair!"

I embraced my boy, allowing my own tears to fall freely now. He opened up his mind to me and in a few seconds I was able to share how much I loved and treasured every moment that I had with him. Benno shared his love for me, and his wish that we could trade places. Then I shared an image of Granite, and the sensation of holding him for the first time.

In that instant my son knew that for Toby and I, there was no choice. This was about our mates and our children. It wasn't a sacrifice. It's just what fathers do.

Toby created his boulder. It was so heavy the big minotaur could barely roll it out of the hole that he had made. Then he called over, "It's coming. Fast."

I kissed my son's forehead, even as I was reaching into one of my pouches. Using the Gloves of Secrecy, I took Rock into a pocket dimension. Then I rolled the silk gloves off of my gnarled hands and slid them onto Benno's smoother fingers. "If you run out of spells in the Astral, you know what to do. Come on."

I escorted Benno over to the cliff's edge, off to the side where Toby had started to make his incision in the rock. The minotaur dropped his axe briefly to give my son a powerful bearhug, which the young orc returned fiercely. Then Toby let Benno go, and went back toward the center of the area that he prepared.

We peered over the side. The R. M. N. Taboo started to make her close pass. I saw a speck far below us, just starting to pass over the water: Headmaster Max under the effects of his Fly spell. I squeezed Benno's shoulder, and simply said, "Go."

After a final teary glance back at me, the younger orc allowed himself to make the leap. His Soft Fall spell arrested most of gravity's hold. Using his robes and cloak, my son started to guide his downward drift towards where the Taboo would be when he reached sea level. He needed enough time to land on the ship, cast Minor Polymorph while Max performed Gustov's Disjunction, and get underwater.

That was fine. Our plan involved all the time in the world.

I wiped my eyes with the sleeve of my robes, then took up position behind Toby. We were visible, exposed. Easy prey for a dragon. And I was about to announce my intention to stay right where I was.

Taking out a small block of clay, I flattened it to resemble the ground. As the Stasis Dragon loomed closer, cutting through the sky with incredible speed, I started my Stone Shape incantation. The drain on my already taxed mind was intense, but I knew that I had enough intelligence left for one big spell before I reverted to my more base, primitive self. Once the sensation of loss passed, I prodded the flat clay until the ground shifted beneath me. Soon my feet were sinking into the earth, then my legs. When I was knee deep in rock, I formed the clay until the stone surrounding me was an incredibly tight fit. I was one with the cliff, tethered by the earth itself.

The scaled gray creature that drifted towards us was the size of a church. The physical reality of it seemed impossible. Those wings shouldn't support that whale-like bulk. As it closed to within a hundred paces, an aura of terror, of otherworldly wrongness washed over me. Every instinct in my body told me to run, so it was a good thing that I couldn't. And Toby's faith in Aro-Remset wouldn't allow him to succumb to a pedestrian instinct such as fear. He was calmly murmuring a prayer.

At thirty paces, the creature arrested its forward momentum and hovered. It regarded us with soulless gray eyes, before starting to crane its neck down and to the right. Towards my falling son.

Toby decided to get its attention.

Prayer finished, Aro-Remset's Divine Strength filled my big friend. The rose-tinted aura was barely visible in the daylight, but I had no doubt that it was working. The minotaur easily picked up the boulder that he could barely move just moments before. With a powerful bellow, Toby hurled the massive chunk of earth towards the indecisive dragon.

Toby's boulder smashed into the Stasis Dragon with the force of a siege engine. The creature shrieked, sounding for all the world like a leviathan speared by a giant harpoon. It wasn't used to this strange sensation. It hadn't experienced pain in centuries. My ears were ringing in the aftermath of the legendary dragon's cry. I would have checked for blood if my hands hadn't been reaching into a pouch to grasp the component that I would need next.

The powerful assault was enough to make up the Stasis Dragon's mind. Even as I started casting, unable to hear my own incantation, the creature flapped its relatively small wings and took up a position just above us. Still Toby didn't pick up his axe. He rolled his neck and cracked his knuckles, as if planning to wrestle with this fifty ton behemoth.

The link of steel melted away, joining the thousands of other sacrifices I had made to magic. Sacrifices that included the remainder of my enhanced intellect. I was left with no viable magic. No more tricks. Nothing clever to think of or to say. My mind was locked on a single, simple thought: Protect my boy.

The Ebon Chains of Binding produced a ghostly metallic rattling that was so loud and jarring, it managed to cut through the ringing in my ears. The pulsing black chains surrounded me and stretched up into the heavens. They wrapped around the Stasis Dragon, entangling its torso and fouling the base of its wings. Still the creature didn't fall from the sky, due to its odd relationship with gravity.

An odd relationship that Toby planned to take full advantage of.

Powerful minotaur arms, enhanced by the strength of Aro-Remset's own divinity, wrapped around the taut eldritch links. The Stasis Dragon started to struggle, but its own freakish buoyancy worked against it. Those fouled wings, already weak relative to the size of the beast, weren't able to produce enough lift. I added my own strength to the effort, reeling in the slack and permanently closing the gap every time Toby yanked the dragon closer.

The Stasis Dragon was trapped. It had never been trapped before. Gone were all ideas of melee prowess. Gone was its timeless invulnerability and composure. It started to thrash in the air, helplessly swatting at the taut chains with claws that could rend stone. But as Gideon taught me not so long ago, the Ebon Chains of Binding only disappear when the duration runs out or when one of the bound targets dies. I guess the creature hadn't studied advanced hexes.

Toby shifted his weight, edging closer to the Axe of McGrondle so that he would have it on hand when the time came. The Stasis Dragon was only a dozen paces away. Ten.

The great dragon finally realized how it could overcome this predicament. It would solve this puzzle the way that it had solved so many puzzles over the millennia.

I saw the creature's neck crane back. It started to inhale with such force that twigs and pebbles were lifted off the ground. That was our cue. I screamed, "Now Toby!"

My friend let go of the chains and rolled, deftly grabbing his weapon in the process. He found his hooves swiftly, and with a wordless cry the paladin swung the Axe of McGrondle one last time.

You see, minotaurs know stone. They can detect the slightest downward pitch in a cave deep underground. They know when an earthquake is happening a hundred miles away. And they know exactly how much force is required to destabilize the edge of a cliff.

The Axe of McGrondle bit into the stone, driven on by Toby's corded muscles and the Divine Strength of his god. It finished the job that my friend started earlier. The crack that Toby had created became a rift. Tons of stone separated from the rest of the cliff. We started to slide just as the Stasis Dragon unleashed its ultimate weapon.

A solid stream of untime poured from the open maw of the dragon. It enveloped the chains that bound us together. It enveloped Toby and the Axe of McGrondle. It enveloped me... and most importantly, everything attached to me.

The frigid stone of untime spiraled up the Ebon Chains of Binding, forming a thick harness around the Stasis Dragon's wings and midsection. As it crept over my body, the icy fingers of the Stasis Dragon's breath found me irrevocably bound to solid rock, thanks to my Stone Shape spell. It sought the edges of the stone that held me, and discovered them due to Toby's last efforts. Tons of detached cliff face were encompassed by the dragon's breath weapon.

It is an odd feeling, transitioning from 'is' to 'is not'. Untime snatches. It kidnaps. There's no pain involved. However there's a feeling of separation; a gap between mind and body that quickly becomes a rift. Soon I had no affinity for the physical world. It was finally done with me.

The Ebon Chains of Binding disappeared, because one of the bound targets had died. But the rocky shell of untime that surrounded those bonds remained. The harness was eternal now. And it was forever attached to twenty tons of falling stone.

The Stasis Dragon screamed in fury as for the first time in its existence, gravity had its way. The massive ball of rocky untime that used to be the cliff's edge plunged into the ocean. Struggle as it might, the great beast had no way to slip from its entangling yoke. A thrashing tail was the last thing that was visible, and then the ocean took the Stasis Dragon forever. As Master Aharon said, it was doomed to sink like a stone through sand and water. It would be absorbed back into the core of Panos, never to be seen again.

My soul stood next to Toby's as we watched the Original Engine's living weapon sink into the churning waters below. Time was meaningless as the two of us were able to peer through the ocean's depths like it was so much glass. Perhaps minutes, perhaps hours passed. Eventually we watched as the Great Trench was rocked with arcane explosions. I felt a surge of relief and of pride. Benno had done it. After the druids escorted the diving party back, we looked down upon the R. M. N. Taboo. My son and Rick and Will celebrated their victory together, and wept over their losses together.

It was over.

But why were we still here?

A delicate hand found my shoulder. I turned and saw a young elven woman with hair the color of straw. She wore a sad smile.

It was Toby who greeted her. "Omi-Suteth." Then the minotaur turned to me and said, "I'll leave you two to talk. Take your time. Let me know when you're ready." And with that, the minotaur paced to the far side of what cliff still remained.

Omi-Suteth murmured, "Here we are again, Sorch Stonemender."

"Well. You told me to be open to new opportunity."

That comment drew a genuine laugh from the goddess. "Even here, at the end of your time, you offer your joy to others. It would be rude of me to withhold the glad tidings that will undoubtedly lift your spirits."

I gestured towards the ground, and the two of us sat down, legs dangling over the cliff's freshly cut edge.

Comfortably seated, Omi-Suteth said, "The Curse is lifted, Sorch. Glogur's legacy is over."

If I had a heart, it would have been caught in my throat. Did that mean... "Shaman?"

"Is fine now. Anyone, living or dead, who was impacted by the orcish legacy is now free of its burdens."

I squinted at the goddess, "Living or dead? What does that mean?"

She explained, "It means that the cumulative loss of intelligence that was in some cases passed on from parents to children will be erased as well. Every orc and half orc alive today will be restored to what their intelligence would have been if the Curse of Glogur had never existed at all."

I caught on to what she was hinting at. "No more intelligence enhancements."

Omi-Suteth nodded. She said, "For many if not most of your 'smart orcs', it won't be required. Certainly not for your son, I can tell you that much."

Relief spread through my soul at the goddess' words. I said, "Thank you. And all this is a reward for saving Panos? For giving my life? Or was it a function of the Original Engine itself?"

The young elf lass hesitated, then looked away.

I reached out with my smooth, green fingers and gently tilted Omi-Suteth's head back in my direction. I whispered, "It's okay. I won't be mad."

She took my hand in her smaller, more delicate elven fingers and squeezed gently. Then the goddess admitted, "Not because of any of those things. Sorch, I loved Kenvunk very much. And then we got into a stupid fight. In my anger, I told him that his orcs would never accomplish anything great without my blessing. And in his anger, he made a bet with me that I was wrong, that an orc could change the course of Panos without my magical aid. I took that bet."

I murmured, "And Glogur was just..."

"A catalyst. Or an excuse. If I was right, the orcs would be forever cursed. But if he was right..."

She trailed off. I gave her some time to gather her thoughts.

After a few deep breaths, Omi-Suteth said, "If Kenvunk was right, I would give up my position as the goddess of magic. Which I just have."

My eyes widened, or would have if I really had eyes. "You're no longer a goddess?" I asked.

The straw-haired elf laughed softly. She said, "I'm still a goddess, but Vinara will take on all of my aspects and powers on Panos. I will have no worshippers, or at least gain no benefit from having them. I will withdraw from the game of the gods. Word is spreading through my former clergy as we speak."

I murmured, "I'm sorry, Omi-Suteth."

She shook her head, almost eager in rejecting my pity. "No, no Sorch. Don't you see? Now I can be with him. My obligation to Panos is fulfilled. Now our stupid game has been played, and we can have happiness. If Kenvunk will have me."

My reply was immediate, "He will. He's been asking for your forgiveness, for your love. He pines over you like a heartbroken teenager."

Omi-Suteth smiled. She absently kicked her legs out over the cliff's edge, looking for all the world to be just another happy elven girl. She said, "Truly, you have earned your new name."

"Stonemender? Because I helped close the rift in The Great Trench?"

The goddess glanced back towards me. "Because you, against all odds, took two hearts of stone and made them beat again."

I smiled and said, "That's poetic."

Omi-Suteth shrugged. "I've been known to dabble."

After a few seconds of silence, I glanced over my shoulder at Toby. He was waiting with infinite patience. I said, "Well. I guess we should be going now."

The goddess tilted her head, "No, you need to finish your notes. It's the least I can do."

There, in my lap, was my journal. In my hand, a quill that I knew would never run out of ink.

I remembered my life, all the way back to when I was in the swamps of my homeland. That was in the journal. And my awakening, and my adventures, they were in the journal. I remembered the last few years, and my new family, and the wonderful people who I would be leaving behind, but in a better world.

I admitted, "I'm not sure what else to write."

Omi-Suteth laughed softly. "But Sorch. You've been writing for hours. You just need to record what's happening right now. And what's about to happen. And the wolf."

Then it all became clear. The flashbacks. I had been reliving the past as I searched for all of the important moments that I needed to write down. That might not have happened the first time around. I wasn't sure anymore.

But I did as the goddess suggested. I wrote down everything that happened after the dragon. Then I wrote about what was about to happen. And I wrote about the wolf.

When I set the eldritch quill down, it dissipated.

Just then, I swear that I heard Shaman's voice in my head. He was asking me, 'Is it wonderful?'

"Yeah."

I felt a big hand on my shoulder. "Sorch. Who are you talking to?"

I looked up. The goddess was gone. Instead, Toby was smiling down at me.

I stood and looked at my dear friend. He was glowing now, and behind him was a doorway. Through that doorway was everything.

The minotaur made a compelling suggestion.

"Come on. Let's find the next adventure."

I set the finished journal on the ground, at the cliffside where everything had ended, and everything had begun. Then I followed my friend into the light.

After we left, a single white wolf padded onto the cliffside. Laoghaire looked around, then snorted. After quite a bit of sniffing, he padded over to find a curiosity. It smelled like a friend. The giant wolf gently took the journal into his great maw, and then bounded away.

Chapter 21

I found myself standing out in the snow, watching my extended family through the window of Ames' two story home in Ice House.

I wasn't trying to be creepy or anything, honest! Ames and Benno already had guests though, and any sudden knocking at the door would have ruined the moment. Patricia, Celestial, their new baby Sarah, and the toddling Granite were all visiting. The were-cat's place was big enough, and since the events of a few months back it became a sort of gathering point for all of us. A kind of haven.

It looked like the guests were getting ready for bed. I totally understood taking an early night. Parenthood looked really hard! Mother, father, and baby girl went to the downstairs guest room to retire. Ames took the toddler into the second guest room, the one Benno normally used when he stayed over. There was a warm little cot for Granite, and the toddler loved all of the attention that he got from both Ames as well as his big brother. Benno took the time to help Ames tuck Granite in for the night. He was such a well behaved kid, nothing like I was at that age, if the tales that I've heard were true.

The orc and the were-cat watched the tired half orc boy drift off to sleep. I could tell that they were sharing a mutual feeling of peace, and in that moment I was happy for the both of them.

But I was also freezing my butt off. So after I felt that Granite drifted off, I stepped over to the front door and gently rapped on the oak portal with the tip of my staff.

A few moments later the door opened. Ames' face lit up upon seeing my cloaked, snow-dusted form.

"Leeson! Come in, come in. We weren't expecting you."

I stepped inside to enjoy the benefits of a roaring fire and the company of two of my favorite people in all of Panos. After I shucked my cloak, I used my Ironwood staff to prop it up in the corner of the room next to the doorway. That way I wouldn't forget it.

The white were-cat locked the front door. That accomplished, Ames embraced me warmly and asked, "Are you staying the night?"

Before I could answer, Benno chimed in, "Throw him out, we have a one human limit in this household."

I shared a little smile with Benno, who was next in line for hugs of course. After I let him go, I answered the original question, "I can stay the night, but I need to be off early. I have to get back to Jess and Gideon in the morning, we're having a fancy breakfast at my parents' place. I'm actually on a mission tonight."

The feline and orc exchanged a quick glance. Ames said, "The kids are in bed. We can gear up for a little night jaunt. Who's the target?"

I blinked owlishly. "Oh! No, no, nothing like that. You're the mission. Or, um, the target I guess. But in a good way. Can we sit down?"

We all made ourselves comfortable around the kitchen table. I noticed that there were still some snacks left over from when they were entertaining earlier in the evening: Snake puff rolls from the Spastic Vole. Wordlessly, Benno nudged the plate over to me. I devoured three of the delectable treats before getting on with 'business'.

I took off my pack and gently removed a slightly beat up tome. I said, "I recently transcribed everything to a new library. Well I mean, I say 'recently', but it took months and months and was a complete pain in the rump."

Benno chuckled. Ames had an eyeroll ready for me, however. "Yes, you poor thing. Your hand may have even cramped a few times in the process. Does it still hurt? Shall I fetch a cleric for you?"

I put on my best pout, then I said, "Is that any way to treat a guest bearing gifts?"

Ames perked up. The feline said, "Oh, we like gifts! Sarcasm retracted."

I slid the book across the table to Ames. "This is my first travel spellbook. It has some interesting tidbits about the early career of a young human mage, but that's not what's going to interest you. Have a look at the red bookmark."

The were-cat gently opened the old spellbook and started to read. Benno was perched over the feline's shoulder, reading along. I knew that they had realised what they were reading when the orc swallowed hard, and Ames sniffled once.

I explained, "That is Sorch's entire history up until a few weeks before you met him, Ames. I couldn't tell you, or anyone else about it, because I was under the effects of a Bonding Curse. Mom and Dad saw the whole thing because they stole my spellbook one night while I was sleeping. But other than them, nobody has seen this. The curse was meant to keep his secrets out of the public eye and control the spread of his new intelligence enhancement spell. But with him gone, the Bonding Curse has dissipated. And I thought you should have this."

Now the tears were really starting to flow, and I found myself joining in. Everyone was careful not to get the pages of the spellbook damp, of course.

I ate another snake puff roll to get the lump out of my throat. Then, after I took a deep breath, I said, "I know that you probably don't need any of the spells in there Benno, but I can't think of a better caretaker of your dad's history than yourself. Everything I need is in the new library, so this is yours now."

Benno reached out with shaking hands to pick up my old spellbook. He closed the tome, taking care not to disturb the bookmark. He cradled it tenderly in his arms, as if it were a child. Without a word, the orc took the book back to his guest room, where he could study it by candlelight as his little brother slumbered beside him.

When the guest room door closed, Ames rumbled, "Awful nice of you, Leeson."

I smiled, perhaps a bit sadly, "I owed him that, and a lot more. How's he holding up?"

"Better now. You know how the lifting of the orcish curse left him a bit dazed. Too smart for his own good really, second guessing every decision. Coming up with ways that maybe would have changed the outcome of things. But he's accepted the past and grown into his new brain, finally. They say he's on course to be one of the youngest archmages in the last century."

I nodded and said, "I believe it. There's nobody at the Arcane University more driven than your son."

The were-cat snatched a snake puff roll with one claw and deftly devoured it. Ames said, "Shaman making a full recovery helped immensely. Hemitath is happy, Benno can still go to 'auntie and uncle' when he has something that he doesn't want to discuss with me. Which is natural."

I mentioned, "You know that Rick and Will want to fund a marble statue of Sorch? It would sit right in the middle of their shop floor."

That made Ames laugh. The feline said, "Oh gods, he would hate that. I approve though."

I had to ask, "How's Tara?"

The were-cat was somber once again. "No better, no worse. Preoccupied with little Janet. The rest of the Order of the Snow is helping out as much as possible. And I have the girls over as often as I can. Everyone misses Toby of course... oh hey. If you want to talk about tributes, the elves of Arbitros have already started interweaving a series of trees that will supposedly bear Toby's likeness perfectly. It will take years for them to grow of course. But I think he would have enjoyed that."

I nodded and said, "Well if there's anything that I can do, please let me know."

Then the were-cat was staring at me, intently.

I sat back in my chair, a little nervous now. "W-what?"

"You mean that?"

I murmured, "Of course, Ames."

Then I was being dragged upstairs.

I quickly found myself in the third guestroom, across the hall from Ames' bedroom. The bed was neatly made up, the closet open and empty. On the simple wooden desk were two leather bound journals, looking oddly identical.

I slowly made my way over to the desk. After a visual examination, I said, "Okay, well. These look like the same maker. But this one has... teeth marks in it?"

Ames said, dryly, "It wasn't me. After the battle at the cliffside, after you delivered Tara and I to the clerics in town, you went off to help the mages hold the northern part of town, remember?"

I said, "Yes, I recall that. And after that we had to set a couple of back-fires to stop the advancing flames before they got too close to the town."

The were-cat nodded. "Exactly. So you weren't around when Laoghaire strolled into the middle of Braxen, walked right into the infirmary, and dropped that journal in my lap."

I had to laugh a little bit at the mental image. "Did the healers panic?"

Ames affirmed, "They lost it. Once one of them described what was going on... mind you I was blind at the time. But once they explained that there was a massive white wolf just sitting there staring at me, I got them to calm down."

I ran my fingertips over the indented tooth marks in the journal. "What is it?" I asked.

The feline pointed at both tomes. "That one is a clone of that one. Sorch's journal was sitting safe in his backpack, attached to Laoghaire's saddle. But this new journal appeared out of gods-know-where. And was delivered to me via giant wolf."

"So other than the dental indentations, they're the same?"

Ames sighed and said, "No. The toothy one has a final chapter in it, apparently written by Sorch's spirit. As some kind of reward from that bitch Omi-Suteth. And if it's real and not some sort of sick hoax-"

I cut the were-cat off. "It's real."

I had no idea why I said that, or how I knew that. But despite all logic, despite not having read the contents, I already knew that this book contained Sorch's final thoughts.

Ames didn't question. After nodding slowly, the cat said, "If it's real then there's a problem."

I opened the 'new' journal and started to leaf through the final pages. I asked, "What's the problem?"

"There's a blank chapter at the end entitled, 'Final Notes From a Friend'."

I froze in place. I just flipped to the very end, and was observing exactly what Ames had described.

The feline rumbled, softly, "Not final notes from my mate or my son. From a friend. I don't think it was intended for Benno or myself. Leeson, you knew his entire history. You helped me save him when there was nobody else I could turn to. You lived with him at the University. I think the last chapter might be meant for you."

I stared at the mostly blank page in silence.

Ames murmured, "I might be wrong. There were other friends, but he trusted you in a different way. Do you think I'm wrong?"

"No."

I felt a paw on my shoulder. The were-cat said, "There's ink and a quill in the drawer. I'll be just across the hall if you need me." I heard Ames pad away, shut first my door, and then shut the door to the master bedroom.

I took out the inkwell and the beat up quill before pulling out that sturdy, orc-worthy pine chair and taking a seat. Before I set pen to paper, I read every word of Sorch's final journal entry. It made me unspeakably happy to know that he and Toby were in a wonderful place now.

With Sorch's final thoughts, words, and visions fresh in my mind, I started to write.

Well. First thing's first.

My name is Leeson Renault, and I was a friend of Sorch Stonebender. I've been entrusted by his mate Ames and his son Benno to write these final notes. I am of sound body and mind, and I hope that I can do my dear late friend justice with these words.

I can already see how future sages will see Sorch, and they're going to be right: He was a great hero who sacrificed himself for the good of Panos. And the exact same can be said about Toby McGoldberg, who is survived by his wife Tara and his daughter Janet. To any historians reading this: Sorch and Toby were nothing short of legendary. The pair of them absolutely deserve their esteemed place in history.

But I don't think that's what I'm here to talk about.

I think I'm here to talk about my friend, my mentor. My 'big brother'.

Sorch came from a life of near slavery. His job was to feed the Voodoo Engine the same spell, over and over again. And he very easily could have gone on doing that for the rest of his life. He wasn't the first orc to live as an abused indentured servant, though I'm proud to say that because of his efforts, he was one of the last.

So the question is, what caused Sorch to deviate from the path that had been chosen for him? Why would he risk his life, indeed his very sanity, for a couple of humans that he never met before?

It was because when he saw Rick Bright and Will Flemming fighting for their lives, something inside of him was inspired. He saw two mages, on the road and trying to make their own way in this world. It was a dream that he never thought possible. Up until that point, that life was beyond his grasp. And he'd be damned if he saw that dream taken away from someone else, right before his eyes.

He didn't know at the time that Rick and Will would give him a gift that would change not just his life, but the course of Panos' future. All he knew was that people were in trouble, and he had the ability to change that. So he did. Is there any more fitting definition of the word 'hero'?

I don't think Sorch would ever call himself that, by the way. When others called him a hero, he would change the subject. He just saw himself as a guy who was there to get the job done. Sometimes that job was survival. Sometimes that job was to help one of the guilds that he proudly served. Sometimes that job was to protect his friends and his family. And sometimes that job was to discover knowledge, to learn it and to share it with others.

But there was a reason that he was able to save Royal Moffit, and destroy the Voodoo Engine, and eventually save the world and restore magic for all orc-kind. The reason why Sorch was successful is encompassed by his mantra. Sorch lived by four simple words, and he spread the spirit of those words with every action that he ever took:

Live a braver life.

That was his final message to us all, and the one that he would want everyone to remember. Live a braver life so that the next guy has a chance. Live a braver life so that your family will have a better world to live in. Live a braver life, because someone has to stand up.

Sorch was living proof that no matter what your station or means, no matter how humble your beginnings, living a braver life is the gateway to a better world.

Because the bravery of one will inspire dozens more to bravery, and so on, until stalwart souls will stand against the darkness, at all costs. This is not only how you save a world from darkness, but how you build a world worth saving in the first place.

I miss my friend, Sorch Stonebender. I miss his easy, sharp wit. I miss his fiercely protective streak. I miss his incredible arcane mind. Most of all, I miss the love and respect that he had for anyone who would count him as a brother.

But he wouldn't want us to be sad for him. He would tell us that the last few years of his life were filled with so much joy and love, that he wouldn't change a thing.

Goodbye big brother. I'll see you on the other side.

A Back Cover Scribbling

This is Ames. For the record: None of this is my idea.

Stuffed inside the back of this journal is a ragtag collection of stories and articles. You may notice that the pages have deep indentations. Those are the tooth marks of a crazy wolf.

Several times over the years, Laoghaire has just shown up at my door. He wouldn't shut the hells up until I let him upstairs, and he would then proceed to whine at me until I added his pages to the back of Sorch's journal. He then eats me out of house and home, and I have the pleasure of shipping his fuzzy ass back to Arbitros.

Why are they important? Don't ask me. I'm sure that in Laoghaire's addled little brain, all of this makes sense.

Who lets a giant wolf onto a Circle of Transport unattended anyway? I need to talk to those idiot elves.

Laoghaire's 'Tails' - #1 - The Second Moon

Excerpt from 'The Divine Fiat' by Lew Rush - Ice House Religious Press

It is said that there is a second moon circling Panos; a moon that nobody sees. The clergy of Melflavin, using their wonderful lenses and other scientific toys, says that they have enough physical evidence to prove that a second celestial body orbits around us.

Why, then, do we never see this second orb in the sky? Apparently it is located directly behind the first moon at all times. Over time their orbits have somehow become locked to one another in perfect harmony. And for some reason the second moon, presumably smaller than the first, is not crashing into the larger one. Perhaps it is too distant, or perhaps other celestial influences are simply stronger than any attraction between the two moons.

And now perhaps an even bigger 'why': Why am I talking about moons in a text about religion?

Yvaroline the Banished.

Yvaroline the Banished was the old orcish god destruction. Mentions of this god within the orc community are rare, because his name was to be stricken from all records. Effectively, Yvaroline was erased from orcish history. However elven records from prior to the First Great War do shed some light on this particular subject.

It is said that Yvaroline originally agreed to the accord of the gods. But the resulting detente was so boring to the orc, he actively sought out ways to torment the other gods. Yvaroline started to ignore Panos itself, drawing power directly from the heavens and the underworld. He corrupted demons and even certain angels, enticing them to ignore the great game and worship him directly. After amassing a great army, Yvaroline start attacking the strongholds of the gods themselves.

Yvaroline ultimately failed in his attempts at deicide (the act of murdering a god), and thus earned the second part of his name. He was banished to a place where none could see him. It is said that he is tethered to a great mountain in the sky, tormented by both fire and ice on a daily basis. The other orcish gods forbade their people from even speaking his name. It came to pass that the symbol of Yvaroline the Banished evoked an unnatural, irrational rage in others. These measures have been effective in suppressing any active worship of Yvaroline on the face of Panos.

So where is the final resting place of Yvaroline? Where is this great mountain in the sky?

Well nobody knows for certain. However, it is said that there is a second moon circling Panos; a moon that nobody sees...

Isn't it lovely when a story comes full circle?

Laoghaire's 'Tails' - #2 - Avatars of the Gods

Excerpt from 'The Divine Fiat' by Lew Rush - Ice House Religious Press

Most accounts of direct contact with the divine take place within the mind. A worshiper or clergy member will pray to their god or goddess (or demon or demoness), and in exceedingly rare cases, they will be granted an audience. This audience takes place in some kind of ideal mental realm, where the direction and context of the divine interaction is heavily steered by the petitioner's own mind. Those who have received multiple divine interactions claim that it gets 'easier' each time. With a more relaxed mental state, the mortal's interaction with their god becomes casual, almost matter-of-fact.

However, in exceedingly rare cases, a god, goddess, demon, or demoness is forced to seek out someone upon the mortal realm who does not necessarily have the means or desire to execute a mental petition. One must imagine that these visitations are strictly controlled by whatever agreements and wagers that the pantheon has in place. Historical and religious texts certainly aren't littered with stories of direct visitation from the gods.

The staggering power of divinity cannot be allowed to simply float around on the surface of Panos. So, at least according to the rare recorded tales of such visitations, the god wraps some kind of physical form around themselves. This might be a created shell, or it might involve the possession of a loyal follower.

The physical embodiment of a god walking the face of panos is called an 'avatar'. Avatars are simultaneously the consciousness of a divine entity, as well as a high priest serving in their name. They can, presumably within the limitations set forth in certain celestial accords, act as a conduit of power similar to the prayers granted to the archbishops of various faiths.

Some uses of an avatar are incredibly subtle, consisting of using a mortal tongue to speak their words, and then withdrawing. Other avatars are quite unsubtle, announcing themselves loudly and living amongst their people for weeks or seasons at a time.

A mortal falsifying such a divine visitation is universally censured. Every major religious organization condemns the faking of an avatar's visit. The result of being caught impersonating the manifestation of a god is, historically speaking, quite horrific and most often fatal.

Those are the rules of mortals of course. It is quite unclear how the pantheon determines the 'legitimate' use of an avatar on the face of Panos. One might think that this falls into the realm of that mysterious overseer that I have theorized about. But as I have no direct evidence to support such a claim, I will simply join the reader in contemplating this mystery.

Laoghaire's 'Tails' - #3 - Master and Apprentice

Excerpt from 'Out of the Rathole' by Wendell Hines - Second Burrough Press

The longsword was nearly bigger than I was, but years of practice allowed me to wield it like no other wererat had before. The buckler was heavy upon my forearm, but intense endurance training allowed me to fight through the burning strain that would have forced lesser men to quit. The freezing rain falling from a black sky in solid sheets would have been an excuse for others. But not for me. I would burn it away with the grace of Aro-Remset, with the intensity of my convictions, and with my anger.

With me, anger was never in short supply.

I spun in the mud, the grip of my hind claws allowing me to deliver yet another punishing backslash to the abused training dummy. At the end of my rotation, I lifted my armored knee sharply. My reward was a satisfying 'crack' when it impacted with my opponent's wooden shin. A real foe wouldn't be walking away from that.

I ignored the raindrops cascading down my whiskers. There were four more attack sequences in this kata, and I would finish them before I even contemplated a rest. After going back to the starting point, I launched myself into the next series of moves. Thrust into feint. Parry and roll right. Slash high, followed by a shield bash to the gut.

I heard the telltale sound of leather straps snapping even before I felt the buckler hanging loosely from my forearm. I came to a halt in front of the old training dummy. For a moment, all I could do was stare down at my damaged shield. My entire body started to shake, and sadly the cold rain had nothing to do with it.

"You gods damned, pus soaked, worthless piece of rusty scrap!"

Before my words could even echo back at me in the empty training courtyard, I heard a sharp reply.

"Wendell!"

Immediately, I regretted my outburst. I had heard the one voice on Panos that could make me feel genuine shame in situations like this.

I raised my head towards the silhouette standing under the nearby covered walkway. I couldn't see her clearly with the rain and other liquid in my eyes. But I already knew that it was Lady Tara, my dead master's wife, and my last friend within the Order of the Snow.

When I had control over my voice again, I called over, "I apologise m'lady, there is no excuse for that."

"Get over here." was her reply.

I joined the minotaur on the sheltered pathway. I knew before I wiped my eyes that she would look sad. Probably because I was a huge disappointment.

Even when Toby was still alive, I could be described as a screw up. I was the smallest trainee among the new paladins, of course. But that was the least of my problems. I would argue with trainers. My relationship with Aro-Remset was… 'turbulent', to put it kindly. And I couldn't seem to put my anger behind me, even when things were going well. I was shocked when Toby chose me as his apprentice. Honestly, I never knew what he saw in me.

At least I could do my best to be respectful to his widow. So I waited quietly in front of the tall cleric, jaw clenched tightly to prevent me from saying anything stupid. She must have considered me a truly pathetic creature: Standing there in ill-fitting chainmail, shield busted, barefoot and muddy, eyes downcast in shame. And of course, dripping like a drowned rat.

I felt the minotaur's big hand on my shoulder. Then she said the four words that always calmed my mind and soul.

"What would Toby do?"

I let out a held breath. 'What would Toby do?' had been our mantra since the big man passed on. Tara said it when she was feeling lost, and looking into the eyes of their baby daughter Janet. I said it when I was right on the edge and needed something, anything to drag me back onto the path of righteousness. We said it to each other in our moments of weakness.

After a few moments of contemplation, I murmured, "He would get out of the rain, set the buckler aside for later repair, and regain his strength."

Wordlessly, I allowed Tara to lead me into the Temple and steer me over towards the old squire's tower. Since other people were around, I made a conscious effort to keep my whiplike tail from dragging. In the entry foyer, we found a spot next to the fireplace. We weren't alone. Candidates, apprentices, and squires used the old tower as a place of solitude and restoration. Even the bravest of paladins needed a place where it was okay to be weak for a while.

Tara's big fingers deftly tugged at the leather straps and chain hooks that were holding me together. With her help, I created a pile of armor and clothing on the raised hearth stone. The minotaur murmured, "I'll find a towel. If you aren't too tired, take human form. It will be easier to dry."

She was right as always. I crouched and closed my eyes. Knowing that others around the room were resting, I intentionally slowed down the transformation. There was no need to send sounds of cracking bone and melting flesh throughout the foyer. Slowly, my gray fur withdrew, leaving only tanned brown skin. My leathery tail fused into my lower spine and disappeared. Pointed rat ears slid down the sides of my skull, managing to round themselves out some before coming to a rest. My jaw popped quietly and the muzzle receded as my face took on more human aspects. Short cropped black hair adorned my head. Curlier patches of dark fuzz graced my short, muscular body. This coat of 'fur' was perhaps a bit thicker than what a typical human might have, but still within the realm of normality.

By the time I was done, Tara was waiting behind me with a worn tan towel. She dried my hair briskly, before handing me the thirsty cloth so that I could finish recovering from my losing battle with the elements. When I completed the drying process, I wrapped the towel around my waist and sat in one of the padded chairs.

The big cleric took the larger chair right next to mine. She murmured, "Are you alright now, Wendell?"

I couldn't lie. "No, ma'am."

She combed my damp human hair with those big fingers. She said, "Tell me why."

"Because I'm angry all the time and I have no impulse control."

The cleric of Melflavin snorted softly. "What else is new, dear?"

As much as I appreciated her attempts to soothe me, the floodgates had been opened. I pressed on, saying, "Toby was the only one to give me a chance. None of them believed my devotion. My passion. Now he's gone and they all hate me. They look at me and they're thinking what a rotten deal they got, losing Toby and gaining me."

Tara's big hand shifted from the top of my head down to my shoulder. She gave it a squeeze, and then said, "Not all of them. Some of the masters tell me that your sword work is exceptional. They have no students that move with your speed and confidence. 'The Dervish', that's what some of them call you."

I said, glumly, "I think that just means they want to banish me to the desert and never see me again."

"The eastern forests, actually."

I looked up at the minotaur, sharply. Her expression was somber, neutral. She wasn't joking.

"Well that's great. I'll just pack my things and those old, shriveled, ugly gods damned moro- mmph!"

I was cut off when Tara covered my mouth with her meaty hand. She leaned down and whispered, "Do you know how hard I had to fight to keep you in this Order?"

Tears of frustration rolled down my human cheeks, only to be soaked up by the cleric's furry digits. I sniffled and nodded.

"This is your future Wendell. No, the Order isn't pleased with you. But there are extenuating circumstances, and the masters know it. It is up to you whether or not you can serve Aro-Remset to the best of your ability at this new post. If so, I'm sure you'll thrive. If not, my door is always open. We'll figure something out. Okay?"

The minotaur slid her hand away so that I could answer. I swallowed and said, "Yeah. Okay. Thank you for fighting for me, Lady Tara. Not many have. It is appreciated, I swear it."

We sat in silence for a little while. The roaring fire warmed me to the core. I took the opportunity to slowly transition back to my wererat form, sprouting whiskers, tail, fur, and claws. I was bone dry now.

After flexing my jaw a couple of times, I asked, "So the forest, you say?"

"That's where you can find your new master. I don't know his name. He apparently lives in a wilderness outpost West of Ice House and South of the elf lands. So in the forested area bordering the tundra."

I sighed softly. "I've been exiled."

Tara couldn't argue the point. She said, "Janet and I will visit as often as we can, dear. Caravans pass through on the way to Civilia, so I'm certain there are salt contracts to be had all around that area. But you need to promise me something."

"Anything."

"You need to learn self control with your new master. Anger is not a useless tool. Indeed, I see others expressing it and I'm somewhat envious... it looks like it could be quite a release."

I had to smirk just a little bit. I said, "It's quite a release, yeah."

The cleric continued, "And yet, it is holding you back. So keep an open mind and allow your new master to teach you the benefits of being calm."

I murmured, "Yes ma'am."

Under Tara's instruction, I replaced my buckler from the stores. That night I packed everything that I owned for the journey ahead. It wasn't much. Tara asked if I would let Janet cuddle up with me tonight, as it might be some time before the little girl saw her favorite babysitter again. I knew all of that was for my benefit rather than the child's, but I accepted the minotaur's kindness anyway. With the little one held protectively in my arms, I slept and did not dream.

The next morning I found myself walking out of Ice House's North gate. I was due to join a small caravan company that normally ventures towards the western reaches before turning North towards the elf lands. My armor felt particularly heavy in the frigid pre-dawn air.

Briefly, I contemplated turning around and walking down the road. There were half a dozen mercenary companies who could use a good sword, and didn't much care what kind of body the sword arm was attached to. Aro-Remset would appreciate the battle, even if I wasn't destined to be one of his chosen.

I restrained the impulse and squeezed my eyes shut. There were answers in the darkness, if one knew how to look for them. I fought against the anger and the uncertainty. I boiled down my decision to a single question, and found myself asking it aloud:

"What would Toby do?"

Then, I listened. In the brief silence that followed, I felt that I had my answer.

Straightening my shoulders, I trekked towards the waiting caravan. Deep down, I knew that if Toby was here today, he would make the journey into the West. I would not allow him to make it alone.

End of Book 3

If you enjoyed *'Another Stupid Apocalypse'*, please consider **leaving a positive review on Amazon and Goodreads**. The more five star reviews that we get, the more people we can reach. And the more people we can reach, the more Panos books I'll be able to write.

To **join the fan club** and mailing list, and to get your **FREE** copy of *'Another Stupid Spell'*, please sign up at the top of Bill Ricardi's fan site - http://billricardi.com

If you would like to **go the extra mile** to support the author, please consider:

Sponsoring my Patreon at https://www.patreon.com/billricardi

Or buying the audiobooks at https://www.audible.com/author/Bill-Ricardi/B0047O87T6

Bibliography

'Another Stupid Spell' - Book 1 of Another Stupid Trilogy

Sorch is an orc mage in a world where orcs are cursed with stupidity every time they cast a spell. While foraging for food one fateful night, our hero happens upon two human mages who are in big trouble. He saves their lives, and in return they give him an amulet that will make his life easier. Unbeknownst to the humans, their gift grants Sorch the power to break the cycle of intelligence drain and physical abuse. With the help of his friend and mentor, Shaman, Sorch becomes a real mage.

Sorch leaves his swamp and embarks on a series of incredibly exciting and dangerous adventures. During his travels he encounters horrible injury, magical treasures, love, snow, university admissions tests, a plot against the Kingdom, and then of course he saves the world. Or does he?

Get *'Another Stupid Spell'* for FREE at: http://billricardi.com/

'Another Stupid Demon' - Book 2 of Another Stupid Trilogy

Sorch is a former orc mage, and the prisoner of a demon worshiping cult that is trying to steal his nightmares. One jailbreak later and Sorch is unleashed upon the world once again. But this time, he's not so sure that he wants to go back to a life of magic and adventure. Being the smartest orc on all of Panos wasn't all fun and games.

With the help of a new friend, Sorch rediscovers his purpose in life. He embarks on a quest to save his friends, who were trapped on another plane of existence. During his travels he encounters more horrible injury, more magical treasures, casual love, university midterms, a plot against Panos, and then of course he saves the world. Or does he?

'Another Stupid Apocalypse' - Book 3 of Another Stupid Trilogy

After destroying the possessed Voodoo Engine that threatened to enslave his tribe and start the next Great War, Sorch took some much needed time away from the peril of adventure. In the two years that followed, Sorch finished his arcane education and learned to be a real father to his recently discovered son, Benno. But the world wasn't done with Sorch and his family just yet. Drought, flooding, and deadly creatures driven up from the depths of the earth itself threatened to destroy cities and towns all over the world. It would take the two smartest orcs on Panos, and all of their brave friends, to discover the forces that threatened to tear the planet apart.

In a race against time, Sorch is forced to lead his family into unparalleled danger. During his travels he encounters even more horrible injury, even more magical treasures, yetis, the power of fatherhood, frightening school children, an ancient threat to all of Panos, and then of course he saves the world. Or does he?

'A Princess of Last Resort' - Book 1 of The Blackstaff Siblings

16 years after Sorch saved Panos, a new threat arises, and the next generation of heroes must answer the call. After escaping an invasion force in the northern elflands, young Sarah and her half brother Granite find themselves far from home. Neither she nor her brother were prepared for the harsh elements, or for a mercenary army's dogged pursuit.

Now the clever young mage and her fiercely loyal brother not only have to survive, but they also need to find new allies that can help answer the questions that haunt them: Are their parents still alive? Why can nobody reach the elven royal family? Was the firestorm a natural event, or something far more sinister? Finally, who are these invaders, and what do they want with the Blackstaff siblings?

'Rhythm' - Book 1 of The Ihy Saga

'Rhythm' follows Lucas Andrews, known as 'Lucky' to his friends. Lucas is a young man who managed to become legally emancipated from his abusive parents. On paper he lives with the family of his deceased best friend, but in reality they can't afford to keep him. Instead, Lucas lives in an old station wagon parked in the Massachusetts woodlands. He endures constant bullying at school. He's able to muddle through the pain, work in a record store in order to earn food money, and quietly finish school as a straight B student.

On the morning of his 17th birthday, Lucky gets the offer of a lifetime. He's invited to become a Host if he willingly shares his body with Ihy's son, Izadore. After weighing all the pros and cons, Lucas accepts the god's offer and is merged with 'Izy'. This fateful decision puts Lucas on a dangerous path. Being a Host also means being hunted. Will Lucas and Izadore be able to hone the power of their new partnership in time? Or will they be overrun by forces who will do anything, including murder, in order to maintain the religious status-quo?

'Cadence' - Book 2 of The Ihy Saga

Lucas Andrews is on the run. As a Host, he willingly shares his body with the spirit of Izadore, one of Ihy's 72 sons and daughters from Ancient Egypt. Hunted by religious extremists, their music-inspired powers spiralling out of control, the pair flees to New York City in order to pursue the only course of action that they've been given: Find one of the legendary Muses of Apollo.

But the big city offers big problems and precious few solutions. Just as Lucas and Izadore start to find personal and financial success, they're plunged into metaphysical chaos and mortal danger. Will they be able to find the right help and training in time? Or will the nebulous Void or their dogged pursuers catch up to the pair and silence them forever?

Made in United States
Orlando, FL
06 April 2023